D1681270

Dinah Faire

Also by Virginia Coffman

MARSANNE

HYDE PLACE

THE HOUSE AT SANDALWOOD

THE DARK PALAZZO

MISTRESS DEVON

VERONIQUE

FIRE DAWN

THE GAYNOR WOMEN

Dinah Faire

a novel by
VIRGINIA COFFMAN

ARBOR HOUSE
New York

Copyright © 1979 by Virginia Coffman

All rights reserved, including the right of reproduction in whole or in part in any form. Published in the United States of America by Arbor House Publishing Company and in Canada by Clarke, Irwin & Company, Ltd.

Library of Congress Catalog Card Number: 78-73863

ISBN: 0-87795-218-3

Manufactured in the United States of America

For Donnie Coffman Micciche and Johnny Micciche, with all my love and thanks for their unfailing help and good advice

Part One

Chapter One

FROM the train window he saw the girl first. There could be no mistake about that. She was the only woman under forty near the tiny New Mexico station.

She seemed more attractive than he remembered her, which didn't make things any easier. He was not a man who normally resisted temptation, and he looked her over with interest.

She was tall and rangy for a female. Some men would mind that but he didn't. He was tall and lean himself, and making the most of it, he always dressed to suggest tall elegance—it threw these western suckers off the track when they plunked themselves down to face him in a poker game.

Nick Corrigan had found there was something of the "lamb to be shorn" about a young man who dressed like a New York actor and gazed over his poker hand at the cattlemen and sheepmen of Arizona and New Mexico with great, limpid dark eyes while he lost the first pot and still joked about it. Much encouraged, his opponents would then gather for the kill and by some miracle the shorn lamb's luck would change along about halfway through the evening.

"The dude just begs to be taken," was the remark he had overheard a hundred times, beginning with the Buffalo Exposition of 1901 when he was a lanky beginner with a reserve of nervous charm, going on through the years to Chicago, New York, Fort Worth, Denver and St. Louis. This fall it would be San Francisco, one of his favorite cities. There, as a twenty-nine-year-old veteran of his profession, he would exercise his talents at the 1915 Panama-Pacific Exposition, celebrating the completion of the Panama Canal.

If poker games were elusive, he was always successful at the weight-guessing machines. Delighted young ladies paid to be "guesses" and weighed at every fair he attended. He had a light touch which traveled over their bodies without upsetting parents or husbands but which satisfied the ladies, whether he guessed right—as he often did—or not.

The ease, the charm and general air of romantic mystery that surrounded him, thanks to Irish and gypsy parents, should have carried him further in another profession. He was a born actor. But he liked what he did—fleecing the suckers fairly by his skill and his bluffs—and he had no wish to venture into another field just yet. . . .

As he gazed through the window a dust cloud rolled along the ground beside the slow-moving train and when it cleared three horsemen swung off their sweating mounts, descending exuberantly on Dinah Faire, the girl on the station platform, showering her with outsized presents and wishing her a happy trip. Behind this hullabaloo several Indians, probably Navajos, Nick thought, were talking with Dinah's mother, Ellen Gaynor Faire. Ellen's husband had been half Navajo, a U.S. marshal, and it was clear to the watcher on the train that Ellen herself was on excellent terms with these hard-faced, blanket-wrapped men.

Observing her, Nick Corrigan was impressed by her comradeship with the stoic tribal leaders, although it was difficult for him to admit admiration for the two women. They were Gaynors, after all.

Nick Corrigan liked most things in life. A powerful exception was the Gaynor family, those lordly neighbors of the Corrigans in southeastern Virginia. And yet, here he was in godforsaken New Mexico, pressed into escorting Ellen Gaynor Faire's daughter back to Virginia for a visit with her arrogant cousins. There wouldn't even be the fun of winning her Gaynor money as he would have delighted in doing if she had been a man. And as for romancing Dinah Faire to while away the nights on the train, you didn't seduce down-home folks, even if they were Gaynors. He was enough of a Virginian to share that scruple, in spite of hints from his family.

Nick saw several American flags waved vigorously along the right-of-way and this surprised him. Obviously the flags had nothing to do with Dinah and her mother, nor in all likelihood, with the war in Europe. The largest passenger liner in the world, the British RMS *Lusitania*, had been torpedoed four months ago by a German U-boat with appalling loss of life, but tragic as it was, it seemed to have little effect on the western United States. In these parts, all Nick heard about was the daring Mexican bandit, Pancho Villa, and his exploits in the Mexican civil war that threatened U.S. border towns. Nick decided the flags were being waved as a warning to Pancho Villa, not to the Germans whose threat was far away.

The train slowed but before moving through the Pullman to the steps, Nick watched Dinah and her mother with their enthusiastic friends that now included several women in sunbonnets. He remembered the Gaynor women from their visits to Virginia. Ellen, a slender, handsome fifty, seldom changed—even her light hair still looked like corn silk—but he noted for the first time that her daughter, Dinah, had a lovely, questing expression about her high-planed face. Nick's long, sensitive fingers ached to trace those elegant facial bones. The Gaynor blue eyes, of course, were light and far-seeing, but Dinah Faire's expression was freer, less fettered by her background than her mother's, and he found it tempting.

In some ways he wished she had turned out homely and awkward. Her beauty only made the Corrigan's long-smoldering bitterness harder to keep in mind. His aunt Amabel Corrigan, who did the laundry at Gaynor House —and whose letters always reached him somehow—had written on the Gaynors' behalf, asking him to escort Dinah back to Virginia for a visit. He suspected his aunt had her own motives.

Nick had been returning home by way of the southwest anyway, and the idea of doing a favor for the high and mighty Gaynors intrigued him, though he resented Aunt Amabel's gross suggestion when it was spelled out in one of her grease-stained, badly written notes:

> It'd be right funny if you was to add her to those other females that take such a fancy to you. Imagine you havin' to make an honest woman out of one of those Gaynor folks!

Considering the girl's looks, it was a tantalizing prospect, but he'd rather not have it presented to him so badly . . .

Worst of all, on the rest of the way home he would have to curtail his professional activities. Dinah Faire's light blue eyes looked as though they wouldn't miss much. Which meant that if he wanted to show off and give the girl a picture of a prosperous Corrigan, he was in serious trouble. Paying double bills all the way home would be impossible without ready cash from a few games. . . .

The puffing black engine stopped with a suddenness that hurled the cars against each other. Knocked into the window, Nick Corrigan managed to recover his balance and hoped the women outside hadn't seen him make a fool of himself. He threw his coat around his shoulders, tucking the threadbare velvet collar partly out of sight and wishing suddenly that he had bought a new wardrobe with his Denver winnings instead of throwing them away on fancy restaurants and fancier women. He damn well didn't want any pity from the rich Gaynors!

He straightened to his full height and went down the aisle, watched by other passengers. Apparently he was the only person in this Pullman car who had any business in Lariat, New Mexico. . . .

Lariat might be small but there seemed little doubt that the Faires were its first citizens. Ellen Gaynor Faire was the editor of the Lariat *Tribune,* a weekly newspaper that frequently battled the Goliaths of Santa Fe and Albuquerque. Her husband, Jem Faire, had died four years ago, defending a Navajo sheepman against two miners on a shooting spree.

Dinah Faire appreciated the enthusiasm of Lariat's well-wishers but was relieved when her mother said, "The train is in, dear," and she could escape the alcoholic fumes around her. She looked up and saw the Pullman car whose number matched the one on her long streamer of tickets. Her excitement reached its highest pitch. She had dreamed for a long time about faraway places . . . after reading about atrocities against the conquered Belgians, she had even thought about joining the Red Cross in France. But her mother, like most of her western readers, was dead set against anything to do with the foreign war. The next best way to satisfy her urge was to visit the Gaynor relatives in her mother's native Virginia. There would be lots of excitement there, things being done—Belgian and French relief organizations, collecting and knitting and partying for the allied cause and stimulating contact with people entirely different from her parents' often illiterate friends in this desert country. Home was a warm place to return to, yet there must be more of the world than what she had seen at home and during two very brief visits to Gaynor House in Virginia.

But wanderlust also meant leaving her mother for three or four months and this was the part that worried her. Ellen looked straight-backed and unconquerable, like great-grandmother Varina Gaynor, but she was only one woman battling endlessly in her newspaper for the rights of individuals against the honey-tongued, ruthless powers of the new West. . . .

Suddenly anxious and depressed as the moment of separation came, Dinah hugged her mother so tightly that Ellen gasped for air, then kissed the girl on both cheeks. Looking over Dinah's shoulder, Ellen whispered, "Don't laugh, for heaven's sake!"

Dinah looked around at the Pullman steps as a young man jumped lightly to the ground. Seeing at once what her mother was referring to, she had to suck in her cheeks to keep from smiling. Who on earth had advised him to wear an elegant overcoat with a velvet trim? He looked as if he had just stepped out on a New York stage. And no hat, in all this dusty heat. Good lord! With his height, his great shock of black hair and that olive complexion, he had to be Nick Corrigan.

Dinah was still staring as her mother consoled her, "He's quite good-looking, in his odd way."

"But imagine going clear back East with him. Like spending your life in a third-rate theater . . . I'm sorry. I shouldn't have said that."

"You certainly shouldn't have," Ellen said. "You must be very polite to him. We owe it to his family. They're such close neighbors back home, always invited to Gaynor House at Christmas, things like that. And it was Amabel Corrigan's idea for Nick to help you on your trip. So you mustn't hurt his feelings, whatever you do."

Dinah watched the young Irishman striding toward

them. "I wonder if his feelings are as tender as you give him credit for. He's been about. You can tell. Women are always attracted to men like that." As her mother glanced at her quickly, Dinah backtracked, "Some women."

"Hush. Here he—well, hello, Nick. It's good to see one of the home folks. My! How you've grown!" Ellen held out her hand and Nick took it, bowing his head with an old-fashioned gallantry.

Watching him, Dinah thought, "He does it very well." She wondered if he could possibly mean it. Thinking back to old wrongs, she had never quite understood why the Corrigans and the Gaynors remained on reasonably good terms. Since the Irish family had been the loser in a land deal that went back to 1886, she assumed they felt there was more to be obtained by friendship than enmity with a family as powerful as the Gaynors. . . .

She had a chance to judge Nick Corrigan's sincerity more closely when he turned to her and said, "Here's someone else who's grown. The last time I saw you, Dinah, you were just about so high. It was a Christmas eve."

"Nineteen-ten," she said. "I was a very skinny fifteen years old."

"I remember. Only five years ago. I can't believe the change in you. That is—I mean—"

Both women were smiling.

Though he apologized with a great deal of charm, Dinah noted that he didn't like to be laughed at. He would have to get over that if he meant to deal with westerners, she thought.

Ellen saved the awkward moment by pointing out the Pullman porter at the steps gesturing to them. "Train's leaving in one minute, sir. You and the young lady better board right away."

Ellen hurried the young pair to the train where Dinah turned to hug her once more. Ellen assured her, "I'll be fine. You mustn't worry about me. Now, give my love to sister Shelley and her poor husband. Tell Marsh we're counting on his full recovery. Kiss little Neily for me, and give my best to the Wychfields." After a tiny pause she added quickly, "And the Corrigans, of course."

"I'm afraid they're signaling to us," Nick put in and boosted Dinah up the steps without further discussion. They were followed by the porter, leaving Ellen on the rocky siding.

"She looks so alone," Dinah murmured.

"Alone?" Nick's smile made her glance back again to see the townspeople surround Ellen until she was completely hidden among her friends.

By the time Dinah reached her seat, occupying the one facing forward, the train had chugged past the little one-story adobe station and she could only press her fingers flat against the window in the hope that Ellen would see her last affectionate signal. The train moved out onto the desert again. Cactus and mesquite dotted the landscape in all directions, with jagged mountains far to the north. The porter shoved the smaller of her suitcases under the seat opposite her. The other case had been put in his charge at the end of the car, across from the little toilet compartment.

By the time Nick came through the car, and after a second's hesitation sat down facing her, she began to get over the thought of her mother's loneliness. Ellen would always manage well. She was often solitary by choice. Dinah told herself wryly, I'll probably be the lonely one, not mama. She looked across at her companion, and remarked in a casual tone, "It's a lot less dusty than traveling by buckboard. Or walking. We don't have many autos in Lariat."

"A strange country, but it has its own beauty," he said, watching her with an amused glint in his eyes.

At first he made her nervous and she avoided his glance, looking around at the other passengers. A young, harrassed-looking woman was dividing one orange among three grabby children. Two salesmen of middle age rode alone and silently, taking down their sample cases now and then to sort the merchandise. An elderly, well-dressed woman at the far end of the car read a *Ladies' Home Journal.*

The car was becoming warmer now in the heat of the afternoon and Dinah began to wish she hadn't insisted on wearing her new fall tunic dress—ordered from New York—with its fashionable full skirt over a georgette blouse with a high ruffled collar. She prided herself on resisting the absurdly tight harem styles recently popular, but now even her tunic felt tight. Surreptitiously she wiped perspiration off the bridge of her nose before she unpinned her wide-brimmed hat with its georgette hatband.

Finally she returned her attention to Nick Corrigan, who appeared to be asleep. At least his eyes and his mouth were closed and his long legs were stretched clear out under her seat. He had made a few adjustments in his own dress that she envied in this heat. Like a practical Lariat man, he had loosened his collar and taken off his tie. With his throat bare he looked younger than his twenty-nine years. She stared at the smooth olive-fleshed column of his neck, feeling a sensuous shiver at the sight, and revised her first opinion of him. With his lean, hard frame, she guessed that he could be a tough customer if provoked. . . .

A door opened behind her at the end of the car and amid the rattle of wheels over the tracks she heard the conductor ask one of the traveling salesmen, "You got on at Mesa Blanca, sir? Ticket, please."

Dinah got out her long streamer of tickets and had it ready as the stocky conductor reached her seat, calling in a mechanical voice, "You got on at Lariat, ma'am? Tickets, please."

He examined the whole sheaf of tickets, each perforated and representing one segment of the journey across the country. He looked up over his glasses at her, tore off the bottom ticket and said, "You've got this gentleman's seat, ma'am."

She glanced at Nick Corrigan. He was grinning and she was sure he had been watching her from under his lashes. Obviously he had known she was in his seat all the time.

The conductor explained officiously, "Your ticket is for the upper berth. That means the gentleman rides facing forward. You ride facing the rear."

"Oh." She got up in a hurry, collecting her purse and hat while the conductor stood sternly by. Nick yawned and stretched and said in a lazy voice, "I always ride facing back. I like to see where I've been."

At this the conductor gave up and went out of the car, leaving Dinah standing and waiting for Nick to rise. He waved her back to her seat. She laughed, sat down again and thanked him as she dropped everything in a heap beside her.

This time he unfolded his long legs, got up and miraculously found hooks for all her possessions. "Now unfasten the neck of your dress, or whatever that is, and be comfortable," he said.

She suspected he enjoyed being so much wiser and superior at this moment and wondered if it had something to do with his upbringing in the shadow of two great Virginia families. Actually, she considered his suggestion about her dress was pretty fresh, as her Lariat beaux might have said.

She settled back, deciding she would only spite herself by suffering, and untied the ribbon laced through the neck of her blouse. She felt better right away and would have thanked him but his eyes were closed—or semi-closed?—again. It made her a little nervous. There were times in the next half hour when she was sure he slouched there, not sleeping at all, but studying the view he had of her throat and the upper swell of her breasts . . . just as she had been affected by the look of him some minutes earlier. She knew she should cover herself with a handkerchief or her hand but wouldn't give him the satisfaction of letting him know he bothered her. She began to enjoy the excitement of guessing whether or not he was watching her.

She finally dozed off and awoke to the sound of a window curtain snapping up.

"Damn!" It was Nick's voice as he reached for the curtain over her head.

The space between their seats was suddenly ablaze with light and she closed her eyes quickly. "Where's the fire?"

He pulled the curtain down again. "Just your western sunset. Pretty dazzling, too. Sorry. I didn't mean to wake you up." He looked down at her. "You know, you look rather pretty when you sleep."

She laughed, as he had intended her to.

"That's better. Feel like dinner?"

"Starved."

She asked him to give her a minute to make herself presentable and went down the car past interested stares to the toilet compartment. She wore little makeup, conforming to the custom of her small town, but was proud of the Paris perfume sent her every Christmas by her glamorous aunt Shelley Sholto Wychfield, who owned the one fashionable dress salon in Gaynorville. To fight the drying desert climate, Dinah had begun very early to use a light cream on her face and was careful always to wear sombreros or wide-brimmed hats when she went outdoors.

On this late summer afternoon she combed out her sandy-gold hair, put it back up, powdered her nose and colored her lips with enough rouge to give them a "natural" look. After a severe examination of the result, she rubbed just a drop of face cream into both cheeks to highlight her cheekbones. As she went to all this trouble, her mind kept flashing images of Nick Corrigan's wide, sensuous mouth. She stood there swaying as the train clattered around a curve, wondering what it would feel like to have her own mouth crushed hard by those lips. . . .

"Dinah, you are the limit!" she scolded herself mentally, snapping shut her compact. "It's an ugly mouth. Nobody would admire it but somebody looking for—"

What?

She blanked out her mind and unlocked the door. As she started back to her seat she heard the end of Nick Corrigan's conversation with the traveling salesman in the next seat.

"Beginner's luck, I reckon, sir. If it had been a real game, you'd never have let it happen. I'm right sorry about that." Nick was really overdoing the southern innocent.

The salesman, however, waved away Nick's apology with an expansive gesture. "Makes me no mind, boy. Ain't the first time somebody forgot to stand on seventeen and went bust. You just take your little lady into dinner and have a good old Texas-fried steak on me, that's all."

"I'll do just that, sir. I always heard the West was mighty hospitable."

"And so it is, boy. So it is."

Dinah retreated quietly and when Nick returned to his seat she came up the aisle. "I hope I haven't been too long."

He had the nerve to assure her with a straight face, "Missed you every minute. But I can see it was worth it."

Chapter Two

NICK had a chilling second or two when he saw the girl —or, as it was turning out, the young woman—standing there in the aisle only a couple of yards behind him. But she probably hadn't understood the blabbermouth salesman's reference to their brief blackjack hand. It was pure luck that the salesman had been shuffling a deck of cards, trying to lay out a solitaire hand. It was just as well that Dinah hadn't been around to witness the episode. A certain amount of acting was involved and he wanted her to think well of him.

Dinah seemed open and friendly but he guessed that if she knew how it affected him, she wouldn't be offering so much temptation with her easy freedom of movement, her half-naked look earlier in the heat of the afternoon, or that face which badly needed kissing. She was slender, somewhat lacking in softness and curves, but he couldn't forget that white bosom of hers. Imagine making love to one of the porcelain Gaynor women! His childhood had been haunted by those cool ladies who hired aunt Amabel to do their laundry as an act of kindness and who charitably invited the white-trash Corrigans up to Gaynor House on special occasions like Christmas Eve....

He looked Dinah over, wondered whether her self-assurance could be overcome within the week they would be traveling together. He suspected that in spite of her inviting smile she was still a virgin and whatever the satisfaction, not to say pleasure, he might enjoy in taking her, he didn't usually seduce virgins. Still, she was a provocative challenge. . . .

He took her arm and led her through the train to the diner, careful not to overprotect when they were knocked from side to side making their way between the cars.

At the table, with glasses sparkling in the sunset and a clean, starched cloth and napkins at hand, he observed small details about her manners, her way of doing little things like picking up a fork. He wished Amabel's little girl Katie could study this woman. Manners might help Katie erase that stain of illegitimacy which reinforced the low esteem in which the Corrigans were held by the people of Tudor County. As he watched this young woman he was fascinated by her and resented her at the same time. No matter what the priests said, God was unfair to give so much to her and so little to Katie and Amabel, and his dead mother and father. When Dinah looked across the table at him, happily choosing from the menu, he gave her his best smile and wondered if she had the remotest idea of his ambivalent feelings.

True to her western upbringing, she ordered steak fried to the consistency of shoe leather while Nick ordered chicken stew. She looked around for wine, asked for a "red vino" without leaving it to him, and he had to remind her that with the talk hot and heavy about prohibition in some states, she might be out of luck. But the waiter showed up with a net-covered jug and, while Nick was mentally figuring up the cost of it all, filled both their glasses.

She got Nick talking about San Francisco restaurants and admitted she wanted to go there someday. "I wish I had seen the Tower of Jewels at the exposition," she confided.

"And the Palace of Fine Arts. I wish I could see the Golden Gate at sunset—" She circled the wine glass with her fingers. "I want to see everything in the world before I die." She raised the glass, studying his face through it. "You were at the Buffalo Exposition when President McKinley was assassinated, Aunt Shelley says. What were you doing there? You must have been awfully young."

"An aging fifteen. I had a job that involved . . . weights and measures." He changed the subject. "Not very good wine, is it? More like vinegar."

"Really? The kind we get is always like this. To us, it's rather festive. Don't you people drink wine?"

He ignored the "you people." "Just don't give it to my uncle Timby. He's aunt Amabel's brother and he'll drink anything." He shrugged, treating it lightly. "Timby would drink the gasoline from his car. If he had a car."

"I know a man like that. At the newspaper office he'd drink the coal oil right out of the stove if he didn't need the heat in winter." They laughed together and she added, "He's the best printer in the southwest, though."

"I can't say as much for Timby. If it hadn't been for him, we'd still have all the land along East Creek—" He saw she was clearly surprised and immediately wished he hadn't brought bumbling old uncle Timby into the conversation. He grinned, trying to soften the truth, or a part of it. "You wouldn't believe it but pa—he was Sean Corrigan, died in Cuba in '98—he and Timby and their parents had some of the most prosperous fields in Tudor County. Then your grandmother, Maggilee Gaynor, married her second husband, Captain Bill Sholto . . ."

"He's aunt Shelley's father," Dinah put in with interest. "I like him but I suspect he might have been a bad lot when he was young."

"He was. He claimed that Gaynor land had been stolen after the War Between the States. While they were fighting about it in court, the Gaynor dress shop caught fire and

Captain Sholto said Timby caused it. So the Corrigans lost all that land they'd been working for twenty years. It was that or send Timby to jail. Blackmail, in plain words."

He hadn't told it so well. She was skeptical and she was no fool. She finished her wine and asked him with that disconcertingly direct look, "Well, was Timby guilty? Did he set fire to the salon?"

"My father said it was an accident. Timby was doing a little shooting. Too much to drink, I reckon. He aimed at a candle in the window of the shop and the whole building caught fire. Father helped to save both your grandmother and Miss Shelley, who was a baby then. You'd think they'd take that into account. But to the day she died, Maggilee let Sholto take everything we had. Of course, we're all friends now. It was a long time ago."

He might have known she'd never understand. Worse, she kept going straight to the point. He wished she would beat around the bush for a change but she asked, "How on earth did you remain friends with the folks at Gaynor House? Why don't you hate them? Why are you doing this favor for me now?"

He couldn't very well say, "Because Aunt Amabel needs a job and because once in the worst time of my life I had to wear made-over clothes that the Wychfield boys in my school, and even the girls, had worn.... Because doing a favor for the Gaynor women is something I used to dream about when I had to wear those hand-me-downs." He looked at the fine linen of his shirt cuff. Worn, but of good quality. When he first went out on his own, he made it a point never to settle for cheap materials. He remembered all too well how it felt to wear clothes that were no longer good enough for the Gaynor houseboys....

He grinned. "Maybe I wanted to escort you because I remembered Dinah Faire at the Christmas Eve party in 1908."

"Nineteen-ten. And you thought I was a bean-pole."

Luckily, at that minute they passed a tiny hamlet on a spur line and Dinah said, "Oh, look! Billy the Kid spent the night there only a few months before he died."

After that it was easy to keep the conversation away from the Corrigans while they finished dinner. He paid, adding a show-off tip, and they went back to their car. The berths had been made up and a double line of heavy, dark curtains billowed along both sides of the aisle.

Dinah grimaced. "We seem to have spent too long in the diner."

"I hope you aren't sorry."

"Don't be silly, but we should have brought along that jug of wine. Then we could talk and get drunk and it wouldn't matter when we went to sleep." She caught herself, regretting her flippant act. "I didn't mean that the way it sounded."

He was tempted to press her, but followed her lead and ignored the implication. "If there's an observation platform, we can go out and count the mesquite."

"New Mexico *is* beautiful at night. All the stars. But there isn't one on this run, so we'll have to stand in the aisle talking. Or go to bed . . . to our berths, I mean."

He let her hasty addition pass and opened the curtain behind them. The entire space between the two seats had been converted into the lower berth. "If you don't mind rumpling up your bed, we can sit here and talk a while and, if you insist, dangle our feet in the aisle."

It was so ridiculous that she laughed, which was fine with him so long as she agreed. He very much wanted to find out more about her, to know Dinah the way he had always wanted to know what it was like to be one of the Gaynors.

Unfortunately the conductor went by in pursuit of the latest passenger arrival, and she shook her head. "I'll climb up to bed. The upper berth is mine, you know. He made that clear."

"Don't be silly. I'm sleeping up there. I'm very fond of high altitudes."

That struck them both as funny and they laughed until the elderly lady stuck her head out between the curtains at the end of the car and commanded them to stop their raucous behavior. Decent people wanted to sleep and so forth.

"She's right," Dinah said. "Good night," and in spite of his whispered protests she rang for the porter, climbed the ladder he provided and then leaned over her berth, her long hair tickling his face.

"You've been awfully good company. Thanks so much."

He wondered afterward what she would have done if he'd kissed her when her face was so handy. . . .

He was surprisingly nice, Dinah thought, and had no reason to change her mind for the next twenty-four hours. He wasn't the least bit forward, which made him a much more exciting man. Traveling in the greatest intimacy like this, she could see that they would certainly have few secrets by the time they reached Chicago.

Before lunch the following day, on Dinah's suggestion, they whiled away the time playing draw poker with a pack of cards borrowed from their salesman neighbor. Dinah could see that she had caught Nick by surprise with her skill.

"Papa taught me. He used to come in after two or three days on the trail chasing down some no-goods. He'd be too tired to sleep. He'd get the big galvanized tub filled up and take a bath out on the back porch. Then he'd come in and play cards with me. After that he could go to bed with mama. They loved each other's bodies as much as their souls. It was beautiful . . . Two cards?"

He blinked, and she knew she had startled him by her outspokenness. She was amused to see that he had gotten his poker hand confused and repeated, "Are you drawing two cards?"

"Er—yes. Hit me."

He wasn't a bad player, she thought, if only he would concentrate, but he kept glancing at her or at her hands while she dealt, as if he couldn't believe what he saw. No doubt he had some qualm about women gambling. To change the subject when she won that pot—two dollars and twelve cents—she asked him with her startling frankness if his parents had been happy together.

"Well, they yelled a lot, but they must have been happy between quarrels. Ma was an Irish gypsy. Grandmother Corrigan sent to the old country for her to marry pa. She laid a frying pan across his head on their wedding night. Or so Timby tells it. Ma died of galloping consumption the same year Maggilee Gaynor Sholto died. Nineteen hundred. Things had been bad everywhere down South that year. Shipyards cutting back with the war over, hardly any work. Pa, of course, died in the Spanish War in 'ninety-eight. Served with Colonel Roosevelt in Cuba."

"You discarded an ace. Did you mean to?"

He managed not to swear out loud but she was certain he was cussing himself as he examined his hand. "Look," she said frankly, "let's quit for a little while. I'm going to the toilet"—she saw she had restored his amusement in her—"or should I say the washroom, and get ready for lunch."

It was times like that and her freedom with him that made her consider how surprisingly suited they were. . . . The night before they arrived in Chicago she recognized just how strongly she wanted him. She was about to ring for the porter when Nick said casually, "I think I know you well enough now to save you another trip up that ladder."

"What's your plan?" she asked with a pretended innocence that was not really her style. "It's my bunk. I'm not changing."

"Certainly not. I've become attached to my lower berth. I know exactly where to lay my watch in that little green net hammock without letting it trickle through."

She waited for his touch, all her senses alive. She caught a glimpse of his eyes as his hands closed around her hips. His long fingers were warm and surprisingly strong. He held her close to him for a long few seconds twisting her body against his in a way that affected her as no man's touch ever had before. She was shaken with her desire for him as his hands moved over her flanks and hips, boosting her up into the upper berth. With a terrific pretense of calm she tried to avoid looking at his face as he lifted her.

She had read the excitement in his dark eyes and would remember it, reliving his touch all night as she lay on her hard, narrow shelf, hugging her bare shoulders, trying to make up her mind whether any deeper physical relationship was possible between them. She had been reared to believe that sexual enjoyment was possible only after marriage. But in spite of the familiarity that had developed between them, she was afraid that he wanted her only for a casual fling. He had no way of knowing she might well be a perfect wife for him . . . well, somehow she would have to show him—

Stop it, she told herself, and thought of all the illustrious members of her mother's families—the Gaynors and the Wychfields—whom she was going to visit in Virginia. Once the Corrigans had also been accepted as eligible if pushy neighbors who had made the most of farmlands gotten from the Freedman's Bureau in 1866. But then in 1886 with the return of their fertile fields to the pre-war owner, Gaynor House, the Corrigans had gone downhill. Shelley Wychfield, Dinah's young aunt, might have arranged with her laundress Amabel Corrigan to have Nick bring Dinah safely to Gaynor House like a good servant, but that was as close as the Gaynors would like to see the present-day Corrigans.

"Sorry, aunt Shelley," Dinah thought, "you may have to accept Nick Corrigan a lot closer than you think." . . . But what a ridiculous idea . . . as if anything like marriage could come of a week's relationship, no matter how intimate she and Nick felt, and how well they got to know each other.

Ridiculous . . . all the same, Dinah decided to work on the idea. Something to pass the time . . .

Chapter Three

THREE days later Dinah's young aunt Shelley Wychfield was leaving her dress salon in Gaynorville with the day's mail, to return, somewhat troubled, to the white three-story Gaynor House on Virginia's Ooscanoto River. She had to discuss her half sister Ellen's letter with someone, even Marsh, with whom she no longer had anything in common except their ten-year-old son, Neily. Things were desperate when she had no one to gossip with but her bookish, invalid husband.

Shelley was the only one in Tudor County who didn't consider her life an unusually lucky one. She was born to beauty, money and position, unlike her half sister Ellen Gaynor Faire, whose arrival in the last days of the War Between the States at a time of defeat was ignored by her father and dreaded by her beautiful, self-willed young mother, Maggilee. Shelley, born twenty years later to Maggilee and a second husband, Bill Sholto, had been an adored child. Now at thirty she was often called the most beautiful woman in Tudor County with a handsome husband who was once the most sought-after man in the whole area.

"Much they know!" she had been heard to remark since her husband's fall from a horse two years ago. Home was so cold, so unloving and lacking in attractions that she preferred to spend most of her year on the road as a kind of superior traveling saleslady, buying new sample fashions or peddling her own creations. Occasionally in some distant city she combined business with pleasure. Her overnight lovers were almost always highly respectable family men, as anxious to forget her afterward as she was to forget them. . . .

She drove around the gravel drive to the east porch of Gaynor House, honked and stepped down from the high Model-T while the former stableboy got in and chugged off to the new garage.

Shelley looked around as she crossed the porch between the modest wooden pillars. No sign of Marsh's mother, thank heaven! Loud, bossy Daisy Wychfield often descended on them these days, supposedly to cheer up her son who had never fully recovered from his fall and still walked with a bad limp. To Shelley's ever-growing frustration, Marsh now seemed more interested in his precious books than in such basic matters as keeping his wife satisfied in bed. In her frustration she had often called him impotent —until she came to believe it. Certainly, he did nothing to disprove it.

Quite different that Nick Corrigan, she had no doubt. Heaven knew his family became plain trash after the death of the old folks, and Nick, who was nothing but a gambler, had to support his aunt Amabel and Amabel's drunkard brother Timby . . . Amabel, who earned seventy-five cents a week ironing Shelley's linen, was a born chatterbox and it was easy to pry out of her anything Shelley wanted to know.

Shelley was uneasy over a nagging suspicion that had come to her today when she read the note from Ellen. Was it possible Nick might actually enjoy his trip with Dinah?

"Hardly what I had in mind when Amabel suggested it," she thought ruefully. Dinah was all legs and arms like a colt when she visited Gaynor House four years ago. What would Nick Corrigan see in her? Shelley hadn't reckoned on those four years. All she had thought about was the excuse it would give her to invite Nick to Gaynor House. They could meet socially with no raised eyebrows from their aristocratic neighbors.

It was a far cry from the unforgettable summer evening two years before when she had enticed young Nick Corrigan to make love to her in Gaynor woods behind the Corrigan farm. It was a curious experience. She had always had the notion that Nick hated her, even during their passionate coupling. Perhaps it was due to his memories of their youth when Shelley and her school friends derided the Irish gypsy with his straight unkempt black hair and hand-me-down clothes.

On that night, lying in the sweet-scented grass, she had done her best to make him forget those schoolgirl pranks. Obviously she hadn't succeeded or he would have made an effort to repeat those minutes with her. Instead, he seemed coolly amused by her when they did meet, always in the company of others.

But even if he despised her now, what a lover he had been on that single occasion! At least she had the memory of that . . .

Shelley told herself she had no intention of committing adultery with him again, despite her husband's "impotence." Just to flirt with and be in the presence of a sensuous man like Nick Corrigan would be a pleasure, and such pleasures were few and far between. She remembered her last buying trip to New York in February. She had gone to a fellow buyer's room where they drank the champagne she loved and one thing led to another—eventually, to bed.

He had been a piledriving fellow with no finesse; he had satisfied her for the moment. The next encounter occurred in her own bed in a Baltimore hotel where she was showing her spring line for 1915. What the devil did that fellow do for a living? Oh, yes. He was a member of a traveling stock company at the local theater. . . .

Nothing since. Not like Nick Corrigan. None of them were like Nick. Was Dinah Faire old enough to divert a man like Nick . . . ?

Shelley smiled at Edward Hone, butler of Gaynor House since before she was born, and went directly up to her husband's room. After his accident he had been given the sunny corner bedroom overlooking the Ooscanoto River, a twin of the room occupied until her death in 1908 by that ruthless matriarch Varina Dunmore Gaynor, Ellen's grandmother.

On the stairs she met her son Neily coming down one step at a time and putting his full weight on the delicate banister as he threw himself forward in some boyish game. He looked up, his thin, wistful face so like his delicate father's brightening as he saw her.

"Mama! Are you going to have supper with us?" He would have thrown himself into her arms but he knew better than to demonstrate his love until she gave him permission.

Touched, she held out her arms. "Yes, yes, let me hug my big boy."

"Will you stay home all night? Will you? Honest?"

"Honest, honey." It was nice to be wanted, even if only by one's son. He turned his head away when she kissed him because this was the established behavior, but his cheek bloomed under her caress. "Now you run along to cook and see what we have for supper and I'll go up and say hello to daddy."

Reluctantly he went his way, scuffing across the carpet on the lower floor and looking up once just before he disappeared into the kitchen quarters. She lingered long enough to wave over the banister before entering her husband's room.

He was still the handsomest man she knew, with his fair

hair and pale blue eyes and the faint smile that disguised the rigidity of a pale, set mouth. But it wasn't her imagination that saw contempt in those eyes every time they studied her. It was infuriating when the grounds for contempt should be all on her side. . . .

He looked up from a long brief from his partner, Barney Kent, who had handled most of their legal work since Marsh's accident. "Yes, my dear?"

It wasn't very encouraging. "I have a letter from Ellen. I thought we ought to discuss it. She seems to have found Nick Corrigan rather attractive."

"Some women, of course, would. Though it is surprising to find Ellen Gaynor taken in."

It annoyed her when he used his pompous college manner on her but she ignored that now. "It seems sister Ellen did, at any rate. I reckon she's worried that Dinah might be seduced. As if a man like that would bother with poor Dinah. She always put me in mind of that leggy colt pa bought me from Ironwood when I was Neily's age."

He turned the long sheets of the legal brief which were handwritten in the beautiful penmanship of Barney Kent's mother, Persis Warrender Kent. The thought of Persis always annoyed Shelley, though they were social friends. A good-looking widow of nearly fifty, Persis still had flowing, wavy, dark hair. Dyed, of course. One more indication of why she worked in her son's office. Obviously she was on the prowl for a new husband and Shelley resented such women. They only made things harder.

"I remember the colt," Marsh said, thinking back. "You and your father and I rode up to the county seat and back that summer. How lovely you were . . . all that red-gold hair loose and streaming in the wind. However, I think you're wrong about Dinah. She showed every sign four years ago of turning into a stunning creature."

"And your wife?" She couldn't help it. She knew this was a demand for his compliment but it was so upsetting suddenly to find all her men praising the looks of her long-legged, harum-scarum girl niece.

He set the brief down on the little chess table beside his elbow. "Shelley-Ann, what are you trying to say to me?"

"Don't call me Shelley-Ann!" she cried, seizing on the least of all his offenses. He knew she disliked the childish name she'd been christened with. When she saw that her tone had made him withdraw from her again she crushed Ellen's letter, throwing it down as she knelt by his chair in one more effort to win back the old adoring Marsh who had spoiled her the way her father Bill Sholto still spoiled her. "Honey, what is it between us? For god's sake, tell me!"

He looked at her. Was it pity in his cool eyes or the polite indifference he normally showed? Just when she thought he was going to avoid answering, he said evenly, "I know about that buyer in New York. Only five months after my accident."

Her hands fell away from him as if they didn't belong to her. Panic made her speak rapidly. "Who told you that . . . it was a stupid lie—"

"Barney Kent told me. His mother was staying at the same hotel. She *saw* you with the man. . . . she knew you stayed all night."

A woman started the gossip, naturally. That hateful Persis Kent with her dyed hair! Shelley saw no way out but the truth. "Marsh, I was so lonely for you and our married life. And you didn't seem to want me—"

"I was *sick*, my dear."

She didn't give up. "He meant nothing to me, not a thing—"

"And that makes it right?"

She swallowed, trying to calm her panic. Her world had been so secure until recently . . . she could always cajole people, especially men, since her earliest memories. This couldn't be happening. . . . She pleaded, "Marsh, haven't you any weaknesses at all? Don't you ever forgive?"

He said nothing. Worse, he picked up the brief again.

She said finally, "It wasn't the buyer's fault. Please don't blame him. I was the one."

He didn't even turn to her. "Of course. I knew that."

She put her hand out on the floor, bracing herself to get up off her knees, and found Ellen's crumpled letter. And into her thoughts came a picture of Nick Corrigan's wide, dark eyes with their warm stare, heavy lids. She looked up, saw ice in her husband to chill the image of Nick. . . .

She stood up, thankful to have recovered her voice without tears. "Let's hope that Corrigan gambler doesn't try to take advantage of your precious Dinah."

He sat up stiffly, a flash of anger in his face. "This is what comes of your meddling. The child should never have been trusted to his care."

"The child? I thought you said she was a young woman now. *A stunning creature.*"

The contempt was back but directed at Nick as well as at Shelley. "Corrigan isn't going to seduce Dinah Faire, if that's what you're afraid of. It would be a sorry day for him and his ragtag relations if they ever tried by any means to step into this family."

"Well"—she'd have the last word—"I'm glad to see *something* brings you to life, even if it's only my niece."

But he'd hurt her enough to make her ache for revenge against this marble man she had married, a revenge that involved exciting Nick Corrigan. Where did he usually stay while he was in New York? She must find out the exact day he and Dinah were due to arrive in that city. . . . "And I'll be there. If I can't bring him back to my bed, I'm not the woman I thought I was."

Coming East with her father and mother to visit "the folks at Gaynor House," Dinah had always stayed in Chicago at a familiar family hotel. Ellen hadn't liked it too much but she respected Jem Faire's determination never to use any money beyond his own salary. After his death four years ago Ellen and Dinah had returned home to Virginia, hoping to put a barrier between themselves and the empty house without the man they'd adored. Because Jem wouldn't have approved, Ellen refused to stay at the celebrated Palmer House. But four years had passed and this time Ellen wrote for reservations at the great hotel which she knew would delight her daughter.

Nick Corrigan had a sinking feeling when he heard about the hotel. He didn't object to delivering Dinah there. In fact, he was beginning to find the minutes away from her a total loss. But obviously she expected him to take a room at the Palmer House too and that took a bit of doing, financially. It didn't prevent him from entering the elegant hostelry with Dinah, presenting her with emphasis upon her name—which meant little to busy, industrious Chicago—and registering for himself as well in "a single room . . . inside or outside, it doesn't matter. It's only for the night. . . ."

"Very good, sir. A large, outside corner room on the sixth floor. The young lady is on the seventh. A very fine, large corner room above yours."

Nick groaned privately at the idea of paying for "a large, outside corner room" for himself but he signed the register. Appearances were everything in his business and he certainly didn't want the house detective developing an interest in his friends or his source of income. If Dinah hadn't been along, he could have utilized that large room to good advantage for a poker session. The script seldom failed: Innocent young Southerner with money—the expensive room—is persuaded to give a poker party for those new friends he met in the lobby or dining room. Of course, he knows little about poker but they won't mind. They'll take that into consideration. After all, they're only killing time in fun. . . . And in the end the "innocent young Southerner" usually profited. . . .

He went up with Dinah to her seventh-floor room. She

said, after the bellman had gone, "It's big enough for a whole family! And look at that bathroom! I could spend hours in that tub. At home I bathe in a galvanized tin tub."

He found damn near everything about her endearing ... certainly it was hard to feel the old resentment against her as one of the Gaynors. Her candor was especially refreshing ... well, he took the opportunity now to explain that his "weights and measures" position required him to meet several gentlemen that afternoon, even though he'd rather show her Chicago, he told her, meaning it. "Anyway, I want to take you to dinner if you haven't anything else planned."

"I'd love to. Where?"

"One of my favorites is a German hofbrau but since the *Lusitania*'s sinking, I doubt it will be very popular. We'll think of something," he promised her. "Maybe we can be stylish and have dinner in this elegant room. Or mine."

She grinned. "Mine. Sounds more proper. Don't worry about me today. I've got museums and that Marshall Field store and the lakeshore. And I could go see a film. Mr. Griffith's *Birth of a Nation* is on. They say it's very exciting and all about your South."

"Not my South. But I'll say one thing. At least Griffith is a Southerner." Nick felt a pinch of disappointment at the ease with which she could get along without him. While she was taking off her flat-crowned hat, swinging it by the wide brim, he moved behind her and looked into the mirror of the heavy bureau. He slipped aside a strand of her hair, asking lightly, "Have I done the gentlemanly thing so far?"

She shivered at his touch. "Yes, indeed. Why mention it now? Were you planning to become the Foul Ravager of Innocence after we leave Chicago?"

"Good god! Foul Ravager! Is that the kind of drama you get in Lariat?"

She shrugged. "I'm careful. I respected my parents too much to ruin the body they gave me." She put the tip of her tongue out at his reflection.

"Aren't you *ever* going to ruin that body they—" He saw her laughing and took her shoulders, holding them motionless while he bent his head and touched his lips to the back of her neck, where he let them linger until he felt her answering shudder of delight, then whirled her around and pressed her mouth—closed for once—to his.

She responded immediately, and showed him that she wanted him as much as he wanted her. . . .

He drew her back from the bureau but suddenly she dragged her feet, very much aware that the bed was far too close and used her elbows to free herself. He decided this was no time to antagonize her and let her go.

Breathing quickly she told him, "I was afraid I'd have to use your mother's frying pan."

Which changed his mood. He couldn't, after all, make love when he was laughing. "Do you always laugh men out of making love to you? No wonder your body isn't in a state of ruin."

"Nick, do you think I'm a complete fool?" (Whatever that meant.) "Now, you go along. See you for dinner. . . ."

Shaken, he went down to his own room, looked around and set the stage for business. He put out his silver hair brushes and left his elegant if worn suitcase within view. He washed, changed to his one expensive shirt with no sign of frayed cuffs and put on his white-gold wristwatch whose price fairly screamed the wealth of the owner.

When he was dressed for the part he went down the hall, passing an Irish chambermaid with a smile that livened his day. "She could be a sister of mine," he thought. . . . Or—she could be his mother. Like all those ambitious, driven immigrants who worked their way up in America from these menial jobs. Sometimes like the Corrigans they became the richest independent farmers in Tudor County. Until it was all snatched away from them.

He had clear enough vision to know that his uncle

Timby was largely responsible for their fall to their present circumstances which disgusted Nick every time he came home. But knowing the truth didn't make it any easier to bear. . . .

So it was back to the southern planter's son act and a sharpening of all the theatrical nuances he had used before at the poker table. In the lobby he surveyed the various loungers: hotel guests and people in from State Street waiting for other shoppers while they took in the wonders of the elegant, pillared lobby and its patrons. His experienced eye lingered speculatively over two salesmen with their sample kits. They were both bored. One of them looked fairly prosperous as he flipped a silver dollar, checking it each time for heads or tails on the back of his palm—a good sign for Nick's purposes. The other salesman looked absently at his watch, shook it and made a comment on the slow passage of time.

They were joined by a younger man in loud plaid, a gray slouch cap and a very tight collar. Nick, behind a pillar and appearing to look vague, heard him complain loudly, "Well, hot damn! There's got to be some place we can find a little excitement. Three hours to kill. Whew!"

Nick moved languidly out from behind the pillar, crossed to a divan in full view of the three salesmen and signaled to an ancient bellman. Keeping his normally rather deep voice low, he asked the little man to bring him a pack of cards and casually passed him a twenty-dollar bill. It hurt to do it, but it made the impression he intended.

"Any sort. An assortment, you might say," he added clearly. "And keep the change."

"Yes sir!"

The old man went off at a trot. Nick slouched onto the nearest divan, stretching his legs out as if boredom had overcome him. He was also presenting as much of him as suggested money. His shoes were far from new but they were expensive. A good eye would recognize that fact and the salesman tossing the dollar probably knew quality.

When Nick felt he had their attention he raised a hand and signaled to a young bellman waiting by the head bellman's desk. In a languid but clear voice he asked, "You-all think I could have a tall julep 'bout now? Reckon, I'll be just nothin' but dust if I don't get somethin' to wet my whistle."

"Sorry, sir. If you could just step over to the dining—"

Nick waved him away. "Don't go on, please. I get tired just listenin' to you talkin' like a runaway steam engine. Reckon I'll have to set and dry out 'til time for my train. Here, boy, for your trouble." He winced inwardly as he waved a two-dollar bill and handed it to the boy with a careless gesture.

The plaid-suited man muttered something to his companions. A southern sprig throwing away the old plantation's profits. The old bellman returned with a sealed pack of playing cards on a little silver tray. Nick looked wide-eyed at the tray and then at the bellman who appeared impatient, expecting Nick to pick up the pack so that he could return to his duties. And tips. But Nick was behaving oddly. He fingered the cards, turning the pack over in his hand and giving the salesmen a good look at them.

"Now, what am I doing with these here things? Can't very well play by myself, even in my room upstairs. Not very sociable."

"But sir, you asked for cards."

"Cards. And so I did. But I meant views of your fair city. I've got a long wait for my train. Thought I'd just write me a few cards to my friends down home."

"Sorry, sir. I'll get you some postcards. Give me a minute."

In spite of his impatience the fellow was just too damned obliging. Nick had to reach out fast to stop him with a movement that almost spoiled his careful performance of the languid, out-of-town young heir but it didn't seem to kill the interest of his audience.

"No bother. Reckon I could just go up and lay out a little solitaire."

Relieved, the bellman got out of reach and Nick examined the pack of cards, breaking it open and awkwardly dropping the joker which flipped to within inches of the prosperous salesman's shoe. He and Nick reached for it at the same time. They collided head-on and Nick apologized. "These long waits 'tween trains . . . Never know what to do with myself. Name is Nicholas Corey. Chantal Parish, Lou-siana."

"Glad to know you, sir. George Reed. Denver, Colorado. I'm in hardware. Cutlery."

"Well, sir! Proud to shake your hand," Nick said. "You're pretty far from home. Me? Reckon you'd say I'm in my daddy's business. Rice, sugar and tobacco. Thought I'd amble on to New York and enjoy a bit of high life. Delmonico's, the other restaurants. Some fancy ladies."

"Good town," the plaid-checkered young dandy said. "Where d'you stay there?"

Nick smiled to himself. They wanted to see if he had enough money to be worth plucking. He admitted modestly, "Family kind of has a habit of stayin' at the Astor. Don't get up often enough to know some of the new ones."

The third man put in, "Nothing wrong with the Astor. Little stuffy, maybe. But mighty classy. Yes, sir."

"So here you got a pack of cards and time to kill," the plaid one said.

Would they never make the proposition? Every minute could be a dollar lost. On the other hand, it might be putting off a calamitous run of bad luck. Nick usually calmed down at about this time, figuring the thing was set and from here out everything depended on his skill, at both cards and acting. But this afternoon something else unnerved him—the thought of that young woman upstairs who was rich and used to the best, whose family had been established in Tudor County for over two hundred years.

He had to show her he was her equal . . . otherwise he could never really win her, not permanently . . .

Was *that* what he wanted? He had to be crazy. Imagine bringing Dinah Faire home to live with aunt Amabel and drunken old uncle Timby and that poor little ragamuffin Katie! It didn't bear thinking of. But the reverse was equally impossible. Nothing, not even Dinah, could make him come under to the Gaynors. . . .

"Sure wish I hadn't checked out of my room," the plaid young fellow hinted. "Not that it was big enough for a poker game, even a little one. Just a closet."

"Oh. You gentlemen play poker? I have a corner room. Fairly big."

The prosperous George Reed pocketed his silver dollar and said abruptly, "I know those corner rooms. Plenty of space." He rubbed his hands. A good sign, Nick thought. He certainly wanted to play. Reed went on genially, "How would you feel about a friendly little game, Mr.—er—Corey? Just to pass the time. We're not—I'm not much of a player but—what d'you say, boys? A few hands? Kill a little time?"

"All right with me."

"Count me in, too. Dinty Harmor." The plaid one added an expansive apology. "Not that I'm what you'd call a hot player. But hell! Gotta do something to take up the slack. Nothing doing here in the lobby, that's sure."

Nick was evaluating them . . . Harmor, the young plaid one with the thick neck, would bluff his way on two pair and then all the signs would spill over in his hands and eyes and mouth if he drew a good hand. The prosperous one, George Reed, was a careful, observant player and probably a good one. The third man was the only question mark, until Nick studied him in a good light. Lean-cheeked, skinny and with greedy eyes and lips that didn't quite stretch over his dentures, he suggested caution, especially the way those hands curled up as if feeling the coins now. Not bills. Coins . . .

Reed and the skinny one stopped in the lobby to cash checks. In the elevator the skinny unknown introduced himself tersely as "Abner—Ab for short—Bickerstaff. St. Paul. Farm implements."

They were all very satisfied with Nick's room. While the table and two chairs at the side window were moved further out into the room and Nick rang for more chairs, he noted how Bickerstaff and Harmor took in his silver-backed brushes and his suitcase. Yes. this down-home young reb was what he claimed to be. He could back his play.

When the chairs arrived Harmor said, "How about a bottle to wash down all this dry air? Bourbon all right with you boys?"

Nick was glad the suggestion came from someone else. He drank very little, especially when playing. He was haunted by visions of Timby Corrigan. But when the other players drank it usually gave him an edge. And today he needed as much of an edge as he could get. . . .

"Cut for deal," Bickerstaff said, and cut, showing a six while Reed and Harmor discussed various forms of poker peculiar to their sections of the country.

Nick maintained a suitably bewildered look. He was careful to have tall glasses at every place, as well as dishes for cigar or cigarette smokers. The men sat down, rolling up cuffs or pushing them back. Harmor sported a glistening diamond on the little finger of his right hand. Nick's eye made it out a fake.

The salesmen had set their cases near the hall door. Taciturn, long-drink-of-water Bickerstaff's case of farm implements was enormous. George Reed's case was neat, narrow and unpretentious. Dinty Harmor specialized in ladies' lisle hose and carried it in a case Nick knew to be the careless imitation of an expensive leather bag. He insisted on having it near his knee, half under the table. Nick wondered if Reed and Bickerstaff recognized it as fake.

Not that it matters, Nick thought, remembering how careful he was to keep Dinah Faire from knowing about the real Nick Corrigan, second-rate gambler. But at least, he flattered himself, I know what I am and my linen and jewelry are genuine. Worn, maybe, but genuine . . .

He cut ten high and then saw with a gambler's superstitious uneasiness that George Reed cut queen high and won the deal.

It wasn't difficult to make his act good by losing the first pot. They had agreed on a friendly opener with multiples of quarters—two bits, Reed called it. Nick threw in with a pair of sixes. Reed dropped out in the second raise while Bickerstaff raised twice and was finally called by a loud, crowing Harmor who won on a full house, king high. Bickerstaff lost the pot on triple aces.

Things didn't improve much for Nick, who won the second pot, a small one, and then Reed suggested raising the ante to four bits. When Harmor won the third pot he proposed opening with dollars and their multiples. Nick began to "understand the game a little more" and as he pointed out, "I had a mite a luck this hand." The luck consisted of his outbluffing them all through several raises until even Harmor threw in with a flush and Nick won upwards of fifty dollars with two pair and an ace, a pat hand which his opponents presumed was either a full house or a straight flush.

Nick lost the next pot, throwing in after one raise. The others were still soothed, satisfied by his play which seemed to demonstrate caution and ignorance of bluffs.

By the time the playing got hot and heavy and the pot contained over two hundred dollars, Nick could see a trend to real money. Reed and Harmor had thrown in, so Nick called Bickerstaff, who, he was certain, had either four of a kind or a straight flush. Bickerstaff was no bluffer. As Nick had expected, Bickerstaff's four of a kind took the pot from Nick's full house. Nick felt reasonably comfortable now about his prospects.

Two hands later, sparked by Bickerstaff's riches and Harmor's unexpectedly good hand, they began raising after Harmor's twenty for openers. Nick's nerves tightened but he felt calm even when dealt three spades—king, queen and jack. He discarded two hearts, figuring to drop out on the next round and wait for a better hand. When George Reed dealt him two cards, his calm was so great he thought for a minute they were clubs. A second, harder look showed him he held the king, queen, jack, ten and nine in spades. A straight flush, in fact. He had to force himself not to show surprise.

Harmor had drawn one card and was sweating over the edge of his tight collar. He licked his lips, a habit when he held an exceptional hand. He probably had either four of a kind or a straight flush. It seemed inconceivable that it was king-high to match Nick's, and Nick had never witnessed a game in which two players held a royal and a straight flush during the same hand; so he knew he had Harmor beaten. His objective now was to keep raising the ante to make the pot as high as possible without scaring the others out.

By the time the others were eliminated, the pot was six hundred eighty dollars and Harmor was wiping his face with a big handkerchief. Bickerstaff sullenly studied the pot while George Reed watched the two players with interest and a faint smile.

"Just to weed out the amateurs," Harmor blustered, "I'm going to raise you—" He counted five twenties and threw them across the pile.

Nick was aware of George Reed's quiet eyes and decided not to press. He put out one hundred dollars in a mixture of bills, not daring to think how little this left in his wallet. He called Harmor, who fanned out his cards with a flourish. Like Nick's, it was a straight flush, in diamonds but only ten-high. The pot went to Nick amid table-slapping and a snicker from Bickerstaff, who had lost previously to Harmor.

George Reed saw Nick glance at his wristwatch, an object which intrigued the others. Reed said in his quiet voice, "Late for your train?"

Nick knew quite well there might be hell to pay if he quit now. Reed's question was a reminder. "Not at all, sir. Not at all. Well, gentlemen—" As he drew in his winnings— "you-all want your revenge? I'm beginning to get the hang of this thing, I reckon."

It was Harmor's deal and he almost leaped onto the cards. Nick was careful not to make his small loss on this next hand too obvious, but at least he soothed Bickerstaff, who won. Reed won the next two hands, playing well and consistently. After Nick won a sixty-dollar pot and Harmon finally won two hundred, Nick felt lucky enough to try a bluff with George Reed. Partly it was a challenge, but most of all he was hoping to add to his winnings. It would mean he could pay generously for anything connected with the trip. With some left over. It hurt like knife cuts, just the idea of Dinah knowing how broke he was, he and the Corrigans he supported so inadequately.

Bickerstaff and Dinty Harmor dropped out early. George Reed and Nick both drew three cards. Nick assumed Reed had a pair. Nick's own pair were tens. He drew a three, a jack of clubs and a nine. No help there. But he could read nothing from George Reed's calm face and hands. The challenge grew. It began to overshadow even the money and the purposes for which he needed the money. Was he a better man than George Reed? It seemed to him as he raised the ante and was topped by Reed that years of wondering about himself would be answered in these few minutes. Was Nick Corrigan anything at all in life? Or a cipher? A stupid, untalented fellow who couldn't even keep his family from the edge of poverty?

But if he could win from a man like George Reed, prosperous, intelligent, *somebody* in the world, then in a special way he would build his own self-image.

Nick raised again, studying his cards and trying not to overdo his customary acting. He had a strong notion that George Reed would see through any face he put on. One thing did give him a little tinge of pleasure . . . he caught Reed taking a drink, the first in half an hour. Tired, aching in his calm, Nick raised again—fifty dollars in mixed paper and cartwheels. Harmor whistled. For one terrible minute Nick thought George Reed would call. Reed considered his hand and threw it in. Nick had won.

They all looked down at Reed's discarded hand. Like Nick, he held a pair, but they were queens. Nick had outbluffed him with a pair of tens.

Reed pushed back his chair. "Now, I really do have to catch my train. It cost me a bit but it was a pleasure to get in the game with—" He glanced at Nick, looked away "—with men whose minds work so far ahead."

Harmor took this cryptic remark as a compliment to him and said breezily, "Practice, practice."

Only George Reed shook hands with Nick, murmuring, "I like your style, young fellow. I don't mind losing to a man with style."

A few minutes later they were out in the hall, verbally replaying several hands as they waited for the elevator. Left in his room, Nick felt as exhausted as if he had just gone ten rounds with heavyweight Jack Johnson. His total resources, winnings plus original stake, now reached a satisfactory nine hundred plus dollars, which would go far even in this war-oriented economy of 1915. Nick began to straighten up the room. He was getting rid of the whiskey and the remains of George Reed's wet cigar end when there was a brisk knock at the door. One of them must have forgotten something—unless it was the house detective. He looked around quickly, saw nothing but the debris of the poker party and went to the door.

Dinah Faire stood before him, eyebrows raised.

"I just heard your weights and measures friends going down the hall. My! I had no idea how interesting weights and measures could be. . . . Hands and pots and ante up . . . Very instructive." She squeezed past him into the room and sighed. "What a mess! You should have called the housekeeper to get this cleaned up. Unless, of course, you-all were doing something just a smidgen against the law." She rolled up the white lawn cuffs of her navy-blue silk tunic dress.

"Have you no shame, girl?"

"None. That's why I'm being sent back to my lovely aunt Shelley, I suppose. To become another Shelley Sholto Wychfield."

"God forbid!" He said it so firmly he startled her. He saw at once that she had no notion of his real feelings about the beautiful people at Gaynor House. . . .

Chapter Four

IT was the German hofbrau after all. The European war seemed to have had little effect on its popularity in this midwestern city far from the Atlantic. The place was full and the timbered walls exuded the aroma of spareribs, sauerkraut, dill, sesame, sauerbraten and Yankee frankfurters and Dinah knew she had met a kindred soul when Nick sniffed and said, "Almost as good as ma's potato stew."

"Imagine, a gypsy who likes German food," she teased and when he smiled observed how tired he was. He seemed strained and tense though he tried to hide it. "You look as if you'd been breaking horses or trailing an Apache."

"I feel like it."

All the same he tapped the back of her neck mischievously as they sat down together at a long, cushioned seat against the wall just beneath a ferocious looking boar's head complete with tusks.

When they had ordered dinner and were taking a first long thirsty drink from beer steins, Dinah questioned him again. She knew perfectly well that he had spent the afternoon gambling and that he didn't want her to know. As if it mattered. Whether he needed the money or not, he surely realized she would understand. Her father had been every bit as poor as the Corrigans and he had been illegitimate to boot. At least Nick was not a bastard child... She intended to break down all this false pride of his. It was a stupid barrier.

"Nick, are you poor?"

He was so surprised he forgot the aching tension of the last few hours and burst out laughing. "No. I can honestly say I'm—"

"Rich?"

"Let's say well-to-do at present."

"All right. Then I'll let you pay for my supper."

Abruptly he leaned over and kissed her; then he had the nerve to complain that her lips tasted like beer.

It was a happy dinner. Afterward he insisted on hiring a real honest-to-goodness touring taxicab and showing her the Windy City. They saw it with all its strange white city lights and ominous dark patches in between and later it was mixed up in Dinah's memory with the feel of Nick's arm holding her close, her cheek against his throat, and the crisp, freshly ironed smell of his linen shirt. All that and his humor made it easy to forget the theatricality about him that had caused her at first glance to ridicule him to her mother.

"What's your ambition?" she asked as the taxi turned away from the lakefront and back toward the hotel.

"To be rich enough so the Corrigans need never take charity from—" He looked down at her. "What did you mean by that question?"

"Not what you did, evidently. I meant what is your ambition as far as I'm concerned? To seduce me or marry me?"

She felt him swallow abruptly and smiled, waiting for his noble lie.

After a moment's reflection he said, "Seduce you first, of course. And if that fails—which is highly unlikely—" She poked her elbow in his ribs but undeterred he finished—

"get you safely to Shelley Wychfield and her husband at Gaynor House."

That took the wind out of her sails, and she could only admit silently that he had won this round. She promised herself there would be others. She hoped he won those too . . . providing the decision was hers.

When they reached her room at the hotel, Nick, who had taken her key and thrown open the door, started to follow her inside. She got in his way, saying tenderly, "Good night, Nick. It was a wonderful evening, I'll never forget it."

She realized at once that she had made a mistake. She felt his painful clasp around her elbow but even so she didn't expect that angry look in his eyes, as if somehow she had made fun of him. He stepped inside the room with her, closing the door with a shattering bang. She knew she had been wrong letting him think he might seduce her when she had no intention of going to bed with him unless—until?—they were married . . . All this fine thinking did nothing to diminish the urgent desire she felt for him.

He demanded, "Is it because I'm Nick Corrigan?"

"What on earth has *that* to do with it? I wouldn't let any man do—well—whatever you have in mind. He would think I'm . . . no good."

He stared at her, his expression gradually changing to an unexpected smile that glittered and did little to reassure her. "No good?"

"Quaint, I suppose, but that's what we call it in Lariat." She wriggled her fingers, reminding him that his grip was hurting her. Though he freed her arm, his hand moved upward, slowly enough to make her even more nervous, his fingers caressing the long, pale column of her neck.

"Sweetheart, that's a mighty fast pulse. You really want me to go?"

"I *have* to let you go," she confessed weakly. The touch of his fingers, light, skilled, maddeningly effective, stirred her and she tried to remove his hand without making him angry. "This is going to sound ridiculous to you, but I just can't go to bed with you without being married, or engaged. Or *something* . . ."

"You've been honest with me, straight with everything. So tell me, would you go to bed with me if I was—say—Shelley Wychfield's husband?"

She was bewildered by a question that had nothing whatever to do with them. "I wouldn't care who you were. My parents were very free-minded, but they wouldn't want me to make love with somebody I wasn't married to. Or—"

"Something," he finished for her, and laughed. "Well, so much for all your challenges about letting me seduce you."

"I never said that, I only asked your intentions."

"Purely dishonorable. I haven't the remotest idea of getting married yet. You see, I can be honest too."

It shook her, but she had enough confidence in herself to feel that she still might win in the end. Meanwhile, she felt a great relief that he wasn't angry and she at least hadn't lost him entirely.

He interrupted her thoughts with, "This duty to your parents, it doesn't forbid a good-night kiss between friends, I hope."

Anxious to appease him, not to mention her own hungry need, she said, "Not at all. Mother says we're all kissing cousins in Tudor County, Virginia."

"Good. That gives me a little leeway."

She raised her head expectantly, closing her eyes to enjoy at least a little of what they'd been working toward all evening. As his hands touched her face, framing it between his palms, she raised her arms and linked her fingers around the back of his neck, holding herself tight against him as he kissed her. The warmth and hardness of him excited her to a pitch she'd never experienced before. She thought she might never know its likes again . . . the devil with all her teachings! She wanted him *now*, and he certainly knew it by the reaction of her body to his. She didn't care so long as he loved her, even if only for tonight—

His kiss was unexpectedly violent, and because his hands held her face so she couldn't breathe, she found herself struggling against him, which she hadn't intended to do at all. There was anger, frustration in his heavy lips as they kept her to him. She dug her fingers into his hair and pulled, without result. Just as she tried to kick him in order to take a breath, he freed her mouth. With his head turned to one side, his wiry, black hair more disheveled than ever, his lips lingered over her throat and neck and in spite of her breathless state, she found the last of all caution gone.

When she found herself flung on the stiff hotel counterpane, she thought, "He warned me. It's my own fault," but all regret faded under his hot, pulsing flesh ... and her body received his as if it had waited a lifetime for him, the pain like a sunburst ending in unbelievable ecstasy.

If only he could realize that marriage meant this pleasure might go on forever! Timeless minutes later he had freed her and lay beside her on the bed, staring up at the ceiling with his arms crossed behind his head. She almost giggled to note that he had thrown her silk evening coat over her body and was himself fully dressed, all immaculate black and white as usual except that his hair badly needed combing. It was as if he were trying to make everything look virginal and proper the way it had before. Didn't he know that nothing would ever be the same again? ... Lord, how could she possibly have thought he was ridiculous?

Becoming aware of her gaze, he raised himself on one elbow, searched her face and grinned. "You learn quickly."

"Well, I suppose some things come naturally."

He was startled, but as she noted with pleasure, fully aroused and ready to begin again. He reached for her. This time, she wriggled out from under his hands, laughing, but as she watched him, adoring every exaggerated feature of his gypsy face, she thought he might be violent if pushed too far. His eyes were wide, more Irish than gypsy, but there was a warning darkness deep within them. She wasn't sure how to go on from here, how to let him understand she would not be his mistress, only his wife, but at the moment, in their euphoria, neither wanted to hurt the other.

So there was no more lovemaking that night. Nick seemed to realize how she felt and returned to his own room. But first he tantalized her by slipping away the delicate lace of her camisole and kissing the aureole of her left breast.

After he'd left her, still shivering with pleasure, she got under the covers, trying to keep alive the feel of him with her finger over the place on her breasts his lips had touched. It was a poor substitute. . . .

In the night she woke up, stripped off rumpled clothes and bathed. In the tub she began to worry. What if he would never marry her? Just how strong was her willpower? Could she go on forever without again sharing what they had tonight? Damn him! What right had a Corrigan to be so stubborn, so high and mighty with a woman who was both Gaynor and Dunmore, families that had been the pride of colonial and revolutionary Virginia? Oh, stop that nonsense, she told herself . . .

Besides, contrary to her expectation, the next day Nick made no reference to his easy conquest. She, though, was very much aware of his body when they were close. His touch reminded her, but he didn't try to make love to her again. She even began to wonder if he were only interested in despoiling virgins and promptly forgetting them. . . .

But the next night things began to look up. They took the train for New York, its route east and up over northern New York State, then down the Hudson River to the great city itself.

Whether or not Nick had only enjoyed her body for the moment, or really loved all of her, she at least knew he felt a passion of some kind and he showed it. They stood together now out on the platform of the observation car as the train chugged and swayed past the Chicago railroad yards. Since the evening was windy, they had the platform to themselves. There was a real camaraderie between them, one more point in their favor, as Nick pointed out . . . "I never thought I could have this much fun with a woman," he told her, and meant it.

He was holding her tightly against him so that she had no fear of falling over the rail to the silver tracks running below them. She squeezed him about the ribs. She loved his body, enjoyed touching him, but she rationed her touch, afraid he wasn't a man to be smothered with affection . . . "It's certainly more fun than I've ever had; I'll remember this trip as long as I live."

He looked troubled, and Dinah wondered if she had gone too far, showed too much enthusiasm. She backtracked hurriedly, though she wasn't accustomed to concealing her real emotions. "You've made it a grand time. Just right." And she added brightly, "I suppose, years from now, when somebody says, 'What do you remember about Chicago?' I'll say that's where I had a good time with a terribly attractive man."

"Don't!"

Good! she thought privately. She asked aloud with uncharacteristic innocence, "Why? I hope I didn't offend you. But it *has* been lovely. Why shouldn't I tell you? Mother will be so pleased—"

"What!"

"I mean, to hear that you helped me pass the time so pleasurably." She didn't smile when she said it.

"She's a sensible woman," Nick said, thinking he understood. "My father used to say she treated the Corrigans the same way she treated the Wychfields and the Faires. Besides, she trusted—" He stopped, stared out at the last pale white lights of Chicago's night life. His voice was uneven as he repeated, "She trusted me."

Dinah shook his arm playfully. "It wasn't your fault. I was just as much to blame. Anyway, I'm not sorry."

In the darkness, with the train platform rocking under their feet, she waited uncomfortably for him to echo her feelings. When she had almost given up and was deciding to forget Chicago if she could, he broke the silence with an unexpected question.

"What was your family life like?"

She drew from him a little, only to have him tighten his arms around her. "But you know all about papa's death. After it happened we went back to Virginia for a while four years ago. Papa was in the papers. Even the cities back East—Chicago and New York and Richmond—mentioned him. They said he was a 'hero out of the Old West.' But we lived very simply when I was young. Mama worked on the newspaper. It was tiny but a lot of people in the area read it. And papa encouraged her. He was always very proud of mama. It was such a love match, I used to envy them."

He squeezed her slightly, making her laugh. "So even though your father was half Navajo himself, and poor, I think you said, he was still special."

"He was. And is in our part of the world."

He leaned over the rail watching the tracks separate, come together, separate, become parallel. She wondered why he seemed distracted.

"You know something funny?" he said abruptly. "The Corrigans never were special. Nobody ever did anything in our family except Sean, my father. When he was seventeen and the Gaynor shop was on fire, he tried to save your grandmother, Maggilee, and her baby, your aunt Shelley, and he couldn't even do that right. He fell two stories and nobody could give him much credit for that."

"I'm sorry about your father. Papa always said Sean Corrigan was a brave young man." She touched his free hand on the rail and felt more hopeful when his fingers closed over hers.

"What do you really know about other lives, Dinah? You think poverty is living with someone like your father, a brave, bold throwback to the old West. A big, Spanish adobe house your mother and a Mexican or Indian servant, maybe both, keep clean. You don't have fancy dresses made for you every week like your Aunt Shelley and her Wychfield in-laws; so you call yourself poor. But believe me, sweetheart, poverty is rotten manners and filth in the house and incredible selfishness." He looked at her. "Sometimes, it's brutality. Though that's one thing you needn't ever worry about from me. I hate it!"

She drew a long breath, not quite angry but impatient with his assumptions about her life. "I'm not completely ignorant. I've been in Mexican huts and I've seen women give birth in sandhills full of ants. I've cleaned out Navajo *hogans*. You seem to have me confused with my cousins at Gaynor House. And even there my great-grandmother Varina Dunmore Gaynor used to tell me plenty of stories about the last days of the War Between the States when the whole family made do in old Cousin Jonathan's little house at Gaynor Ferry. Don't think it was easy then, with the Yankees occupying Gaynor House and Wychfield Hall and Fairevale—"

"I've heard all about those days," he said dryly and made her happy by a sudden bright smile. "But we don't have to stay poor, do we?"

This was distinctly hopeful. "No! I made up my mind a long time ago. Why be poor just because our parents were?"

"That's my girl!" He moved his arm and hugged her more closely. "Maybe I'll be the first Corrigan to be rich. I was poor yesterday and rich last night. It just goes to show. What do you think?"

Not so hopeful. He had returned to thinking of his life

in the first person singular. She reversed herself. "Still, being poor doesn't really bother me . . ."

The chill night wind off the lake ruffled them on the little platform but they didn't notice. He was kissing her and then whispering, "You're my girl, all right," but even as he said it she suspected all his doubts hadn't been overcome.

Chapter Five

WHEN the train arrived in Buffalo Dinah mailed a letter to her mother, wishing by some miracle she could talk to Ellen over the telephone. Some celebrated scientists and important people had already made the first calls across the continent along the singing wires to San Francisco, but nobody in Lariat had a telephone except the owner of the biggest saloon in town and his line barely reached the front faro tables.

Dinah explained carefully how it was possible to fall in love with a man she had known casually all her life and "intimately" for a single week. She was afraid Ellen wouldn't understand the permanence of her feelings and she filled many pages of stationery taken from the Chicago hotel describing this aspect of the relationship between herself and Nick Corrigan. She mentioned their comradeship, the fact that the friendship as well as the passion between them was very like the enviable love that had existed between Jem Faire and Ellen Dunmore Gaynor. She did not say that they had gone to bed together. Even her mother wasn't that modern. . . .

Nick didn't ask to see her letter, though she offered to show it to him. He had already written to his own family, mailing the letter from Ohio when the train stopped briefly. From his scowl Dinah suspected he had laid down the law to them, though she didn't know just why he felt he had to take such stern measures with the Corrigans, who had always been polite to Dinah and her family (except Timby when he was drunk). Nick's aunt Amabel, a faded, sickly blonde woman just under fifty, had been almost too friendly, and Dinah remembered mistrusting all that fawning praise. But she made up her mind now to accept Amabel's friendship at face value. She was prepared to like them all. Anything to help make Nick want to marry her.

I'll never be snobbish, she promised herself, wishing she hadn't thought it necessary even to remind herself of it. I'll remember how aunt Shelley used to annoy me with the way she patronized everyone who didn't have quite her Gaynor roots in Virginia."

When Nick started to explain his family and what she had to expect of them, she cut him off with, "For every Aunt Amabel you have, I can match your Corrigans with an Aunt Shelley. Last time mama visited her she called Aunt Shelley 'Lady Bountiful' and she wasn't being complimentary. We're even. We both have terrible relatives. Isn't it nice that you and I are so perfect?"

"It's clear we were made for each other," he laughed.

"Absolutely clear," Dinah said firmly, turning to touch his lips with hers. Then she kissed him bruisingly until they broke away, breathless and laughing.

"I love you. I do love you, you crazy woman!"

On a heat-drenched morning with the air a furnace of fumes and haze, they arrived in New York's enormous and stately Grand Central Station. With the calm of an experienced traveler, Nick got a redcap for their bags and escorted Dinah through the labyrinth to the streets and a taxicab. The automobile chugged over to Fifth Avenue and up that wide thoroughfare toward distant Central Park.

The taxicab reminded Dinah of their lovely night ride to the Chicago hotel. She had never seen so many cars in her life as she had on this journey . . . it was all you could do to find a horse and buggy amid these metal monsters and even horsecars seemed to be absent from all but a few side streets. Remembering Chicago, she associated autos with romance, and soon had only the tenderest thoughts—which got all tangled up with Nick's arm holding her warmly against his body, his chin resting on the crown of her head as she half lay against him. If I can't get him to propose after all this . . .

The taxicab drove around a fountain and up in front of a huge gray building that soared into the hazy sky, with Central Park for a northern neighbor. The doorman had to have been at least a general in some crack regiment on the western front. He gave them the hint of a bow, looking Nick over in a way Dinah didn't like and reserving his polished manners for her. Forgetting her first impression of Nick, she resented this insolence but forgot it when Nick ushered her into the big rotunda where she saw with delight an indoor garden cafe, crowded with well-dressed men and women all chattering at once. It was a little alarming but exciting all the same to see so many men in uniform, and surprisingly, several women as well, wearing the cloth headpieces emblazoned with the red cross to remind the world of blood being shed across the Atlantic in Flanders Field and Picardy. The European War seemed much closer to New York than to Lariat, New Mexico.

She was much impressed when Nick asked for two rooms and received them adjoining—a veritable suite, a new experience for her. Both rooms had fireplaces but the weather was far too muggy for them. Her window opened on a tiny railed space she called her balcony. Looking down to the fountain in the Grand Army Plaza fifteen floors below, she was amused at her own enjoyment of anything dedicated to the Union army which the Gaynors and Faires had fought so bitterly in her own mother's lifetime.

The fountain and plaza were in the process of being beautified by additional ironwork and were fenced off temporarily, but the richness of this open space in a crowded city impressed her.

"Look at all the silk top hats, Nick," she called out. He was obviously pleased at her enthusiasm and joined her at the window.

"Uniforms, too. More than I saw this spring when I was here."

"Those hats! I think our stetsons out west would be much more practical in this sunlight."

Which made him laugh. "I can see all those bankers and lawyers now, riding in their electric broughams or being chauffeured in those touring cars wearing stetsons."

He had his arm around her shoulders, one hand gently squeezing her slim, pale neck between thumb and forefinger. Remembering his sensitivity about gambling, she remarked, "I reckon you have to see your business friends this afternoon?"

He was too casual. "Only for a couple of hours. Would you like to have dinner in the hotel tonight? Awfully swank, but good food."

"I'll test it out long before dinner. I'm going to have a sandwich and a parfait in the rotunda downstairs in the afternoon after I walk over to see the tallest building in the world."

"The Woolworth building? Not alone!"

"Certainly. Why not?"

"Well, because—look here, you act as if you intended to enjoy yourself without me."

With eyebrows raised she gazed at him. He colored slightly, murmured with a fine pretense of indifference, "Not that it's my business, of course. I was only afraid you might get lost wandering around a strange city alone."

Good! His concern had given her an idea. She would appear to lose herself ever so slightly—and by the time she returned to the hotel he would have had ample opportunity to miss her and be worried. Next he would, she hoped, realize that the best way he could assure her permanent place in his life was by marriage. "I'll wash and get ready now. I hope your business contracts bring you luck. See you at—shall we make it seven?"

He didn't like this independence of hers one bit. There might have been moments during the last few days when he feared being tied down, his style of life threatened by a girl who wanted to marry him, but now the shoe seemed on the other foot. Maybe he wanted to be free but he didn't want her to feel so easily free of him . . . "Not that late, I should have my business all done by five, probably before. Let me take you to the Woolworth building."

She freed herself and began to unpack her mother's old portmanteau. "Not for the world. And have you worrying about the clock during your business meeting? I'll just walk over to Broadway and then up or down to the building, as the case may be."

"Up or down? Good god! You don't even know where it is. I'll take you. I'll cancel my meeting and go with you."

But she refused lightly and playfully pushed him toward the open door between their rooms. He didn't like being teased, but he went all the same.

Do him good, she thought with satisfaction and set about changing to her only other suit skirt, topping it with a crisp, fresh white blouse and a wide-brimmed straw hat pinned jauntily through her thick hair.

Chapter Six

DINAH rode down in the elevator, fascinated by the tiny room that moved up and down according to the skilled touch of the operator. Nothing like this in Lariat.

Her spirits were undisturbed by the terrible heat rising from the sidewalk . . . she was used to worse heat back home and ignored this minor unpleasantness. It was less easy to ignore the pushing and shoving of passersby. Nothing about these arrogant city dwellers could compare with the confident, easy-moving grace of the westerners she'd grown up with.

Across the street the big city park sprawled along parallel to her sidewalk, but she had seen plenty of forests once the train headed out of the Southwest. The skyscrapers were more interesting. Five- and six-story buildings were nothing here. She began to count the giant stone mountains that towered more than ten stories. She wouldn't want to live here but still it was rather exciting, like the walls of the Grand Canyon. . . .

Dinah marched along at a good clip, congratulating herself on a shrewd reading of Nick's character. Everything interested her. She soon came to a huge circle where the traffic could hardly make up its mind which way to get around a statue of Columbus which rose in the middle of streaming automobiles, electric cars and horse-drawn carriages and drays.

By the time she returned to thoughts of the world's tallest skyscraper, the Woolworth building was nowhere to be found. While she planned to be "lost," she had no intention of actually getting mislaid in this jungle. She had crossed numerous streets without looking at their names—she almost lost count of the skyscrapers—and somehow by following her nose she had arrived at a very odd sort of area. It was noontime, as her little gold lapel watch told her, but she would have guessed it by the bedlam all about her. She stopped suddenly. A man in cap and overalls ran into her, knocked her breathless and hurried on with a pail of beer under his arm.

She had been headed for the Hudson River with its long line of sheds and piers where many of Europe's passenger liners were waiting out the war. Not a savory neighborhood. She started back, retracing her steps, trying to figure out where she had somehow gotten off 59th Street and onto this lesser thoroughfare with its European-looking population . . . Let's see. I was looking up at that thin building with the cornice, and I crossed to— No, that was the alley when I crossed and that silly electric car hooted at me. She wished she hadn't strayed from 59th Street, but by making a generally easterly progress she began to recognize landmarks like the distant circle around the statue of Columbus and the green of the park. Thank heavens for the safety of Central Park . . .

A slimy-looking little man in a pinstriped suit had been watching her, and now got in her way. He was small but his beringed hands looked hard as he held them up to stop her. "Lost, little girl? Looking for something?"

In ordinary circumstances she would have been amused to be called little by a man who barely stood shoulder high to her. Not now, though. She tried to move around him. "No, sir, excuse me—"

"Not very friendly, are you, blondie?"

She put her hands out, palms first. His fingers snapped around her wrist like handcuffs.

"Now, now, that's not nice, bl—"

He got no further. A bright female drawl startled him into letting go just as Dinah was hauling off to kick him.

"My land! It's young Dinah Faire, isn't it?"

The man hustled away. As for Dinah's rescuer, it was almost too providential that she should be Shelley Wychfield, pert and beautiful in cool green printed voile made in the harem style. Her red-gold hair and expensive, sensuous look made most women feel distinctly inferior, but to Dinah, her mother's young half sister was simply "family." Shelley hurried toward her on fashionable French-heeled pumps.

"What a *coincidence*, honey! You *are* Dinah Faire . . . I knew you were coming South but who'd have thought we'd meet in little old New York, of all places? I'm here for the late winter collections . . ."

She gushed so fast Dinah could hardly get a word in until Shelley had hugged her, murmuring, "You poor lamb! It's plain to see you're not used to Broadway mashers. But surely, you aren't here alone! Not a well-brought-up young lady—are you?"

It was all much too pat, this meeting. Dinah reminded her, "You sent Nick Corrigan to escort me to Virginia. Remember?"

And very likely soon after Nick registered at the hotel, Shelley had learned of it. She must have been checking Nick's favorite hotels all morning. What was between them? Or was it all on Shelley's side? Dinah didn't flatter herself this meeting was arranged out of a desire for her own company. . . .

Shelley said sweetly, "Oh, how cozy! Then Nick is here with you?"

"In the same hotel. Yes." She didn't want aunt Shelley writing to Ellen before she had a chance to explain further her real relationship with Nick Corrigan.

Aunt Shelley, of course, pretended to seem enormously relieved that her niece was in good hands, like any respectable, unmarried, young Virginian lady. She tucked her arm in Dinah's, asked where her tall niece was staying, and insisted she had nothing to do as important as laying down the law to that rogue, Nick Corrigan.

"A dreadful flirt, he's famous for breaking hearts among the poor whites. But I reckon he wouldn't try anything with you, honey. You're not his type, thanks be."

Dinah almost smiled.

By the time they reached the hotel it was clear from aunt Shelley's chatter that her whole trip to New York was now a success because she had met her "dear, funny niece" and was prepared to tolerate Nick Corrigan. Dinah began to suspect that aunt Shelley protested too much. The older woman had never regarded Dinah as anything but a coltish child whose presence was best expressed in silence. Why all this fluttering now?

Shelley was married to Marsh Wychfield, a perfect gentleman, rich and handsome. She had snatched him up against all competition from her "darlin' friends"; yet Dinah couldn't help suspecting that Shelley's friendship now in New York was based purely on an interest in Nick Corrigan. . . . Well, for the first time in her life she meant to fight for a man. . . . If she had been suspicious of aunt Shelley's motives before they reached her hotel room, suspicion became certainty when Shelley, discovering that Nick was off somewhere at a "business meeting," in less than five minutes recalled a "few dull meetings she simply had to attend" in her own business line. "Those awful garment people, so primitive, not a gentleman among them, I swear. But I'll be back this evening, honey, and I insist on taking you to supper at one of those little cafes I know."

"How nice, auntie!"

Shelley wrinkled her nose at the title, and her features stiffened perceptibly when Dinah added, "I don't suppose Nick would care to come along with us. He's so used to New York. But of course you and I can have heaps of fun gossiping about the family."

Shelley smiled. "You just leave that boy to me. I'll make him toe the line. I've known him so long. We went to school together, you know. He's such a naughty boy. 'Bye, honey." Shelley stood on tiptoe and pressed her cheek against her niece's. "My, what a big girl you've become!" She went out quickly.

Dinah stared at the retreating back, her look meant to kill. And meanwhile she realized her not so clever plan to make Nick miss her had failed miserably. She was back at the hotel with nothing to do. After giving it some thought, she went down to the ground floor and into the palm-fringed rotunda which was beginning to look like a tea-dance floor as the diners left and newcomers drifted in, so many of them in army uniforms.

While she ate too delicate little watercress sandwiches and drank unaccustomed tea, she wondered how in the world she could get rid of aunt Shelley tonight. . . .

She still hadn't worked out a plan when she looked up and saw Nick Corrigan moving between the little tables, heading directly toward her. His dark face was in a scowl. She couldn't imagine what had happened unless —had he lost all his winnings in that "business conference" this afternoon? It was difficult dealing with a man when you had to pretend ignorance of the way he earned his money . . .

She looked up, beaming. "Nick, how nice! Is your meeting finished?"

"What meeting?" he demanded, raising his voice over the Lehar waltz being played by the little orchestra.

"But you said you had business meetings all afternoon, what are you doing here at this hour—"

"What am I doing? What am *I* doing?" He pulled out the chair opposite her and sat down. "Do you know where I've been for the past hour and a half?" He didn't wait for her puzzled answer. "Looking for you at the Woolworth building and thinking you must have been kidnapped or murdered or hit by a car, any of a dozen things that would explain why you didn't show up. And all the time you hadn't even left the hotel!"

She could afford to be patient with him, delighted as she was that he'd given up a profitable poker game in order to be with her. Her plan to worry him hadn't succeeded, but even better, he seemed to be worrying on his own.

"I really intended to go to the Woolworth building, Nick. I walked a long way. But then I was stopped and had to come back." She played a shabby little trick here but she was still worried about aunt Shelley's imminent arrival; her influence on males was well known even in the Faire household of Lariat. "She practically pushed me back to the Plaza."

"Who is this *she?* Anybody I know?" This was added lightly. She caught him by surprise. He must have expected a dozen other excuses . . . not this. She could see his body relax and noted her own reaction to the slightest change in his moods.

"Aunt Shelley. She found out we were going to be in New York today and since she had business here for her shop, she must have checked to see if we were at the Plaza and followed me when I went for my walk. I can't think of how else she was able to meet me right in the middle of the sidewalk."

"Shelley Sholto? Any business she had in New York was about—well, never mind." His warm smile broke through his gloom, making her ache to touch him. "Never mind at all. All right, sweetheart, let's not waste the rest of the afternoon. Finish that and we'll do something together for a change. Here, I'll help you." He borrowed her unused fork and dipped into her dessert, a delicate pastry. His other hand closed over hers on the table.

She said nothing, pretended to take the moment easily. But she couldn't help thinking that if life never gave her another moment this one was close to perfect. . . .

Hours later Nick was still recovering from the shock of what this maddening young woman had put him through. Of course, it all turned out to be worry wasted. While he walked up and down before the immense Gothic front of the Woolworth building for an hour in the broiling heat, conjuring up all the evils that could happen to a country girl in New York, she had been enjoying herself elsewhere. And she certainly hadn't cared earlier when he told her about his afternoon meetings. Almost as if she was glad to be on her own. He had never known a female so damned independent.

And now came the distinctly unwelcome news that Shelley Wychfield was prowling around the neighborhood. Knowing Shelley, he wondered whether she had given Dinah a few hints about that old one-night affair of theirs. It was Shelley's way of putting her brand on every male she could. Dinah didn't seem to be jealous, but with her charm and family background, she probably had a dozen admirers, any one of them more eligible than he was. . . . Even now in broad daylight while Dinah looked out her window, spellbound by the view of New York rooftops, Nick considered his own ineligibility as a husband. Since he had never before considered marriage, it hadn't been necessary to dredge up the ugly truth about himself. But it rose starkly to the top of his mind now as he stood behind

Dinah, pointing out various towers, spires and landmarks.

Some husband he'd make! He was the sole support of his aunt Amabel and almost of his uncle Timby as well. Timby might be a periodic drunkard now but it was Timby who had supported the entire family during Nick's childhood. As for aunt Amabel, she had reared him as an orphaned boy. Like her brother Timby, Amabel was a feckless character, but without her and Timby, Nick Corrigan would have been farmed out to be raised little better than an unpaid bondservant in the Virginia farm country at the turn of the century . . . I *could* get some kind of legitimate job, he thought. . . . There must be some way I can make the kind of money I make now at poker . . . Still, he dreaded the alternative, the idea of a prosaic job as a shopkeeper or clerk. Not for Nick Corrigan, damn it. . . .

"You're looking very serious," Dinah was saying.

What a pure blue her eyes were . . . it was going to be hard to hold her. He asked abruptly, "Have you ever been in love with a drygoods clerk?"

She looked so astonished that he had to laugh, lifting his mood.

"Never mind. It might not be painful, after all. But we've got a mighty short time before your precious Aunt Shelley comes around hounding us to take her to dinner. Let's get out, quick."

Dinah teased him, "I think it was the other way around. She was set to take us to dinner."

"Such a sweet creature, full of generous impulses." His sarcasm made her look at him quickly. Under her stare he tried to cover his resentment—and fear—of Shelley's rattling tongue. He shrugged and said, "Anyway, you and I don't really need a chaperone, wouldn't you agree?"

"You're turning down a chance to have dinner with my beautiful aunt?"

"I'll force myself to forego it."

He played Dinah's lighthearted game, still secretly uneasy over what Shelley was up to. The troublemaking bitch ... he'd once taken what she offered and he remembered his motives at that time. Unlike his easy relationships with other women, the Shelley affair had been the culmination of a brooding resentment dating back to when they were both children ... Shelley, the pretty, spoiled little heiress to the Gaynor salon, Gaynor House and lands, versus Nick Corrigan, for whom life's worst moment had been his arrival at the schoolhouse wearing one of Shelley's plain gingham pinafores made over by aunt Amabel into a boy's shirt, for God's sake ... Nothing could ever blot out the horror of those days but the evening he had made love to Shelley, entering that soft, eager flesh of hers, he told himself that, well, in a way he had entered Gaynor House itself as its master ...

It wasn't an argument Dinah would understand, and to his relief she seemed as anxious as he to avoid her aunt. He hurried her into the jacket that matched her dark blue skirt, an outfit far too heavy for this late summer heat, though it didn't seem to bother Dinah. Then, like a good wife fussing over her husband, she smoothed down his thick straight hair and helped him on with his own light and fashionable summer jacket that effectively concealed the fraying collar and cuffs of his linen shirt.

Behind him she hugged his broad shoulders. He turned his head and brushed her cheek with his lips. "Shall we forget supper?"

She laughed, punched him between the shoulder blades. "Certainly not. I'm a decent girl, as you may not have observed. Besides, I'm hungry."

They started off on this high note that lasted all the way to the street floor, until a well-remembered feminine voice called to them from one of the rotunda tables. "Dinah, dear child, there you are! And that's—why, I declare, it's that handsome escort I sent to you."

Shelley was hurrying toward them, dazzling in grass-green silk with a matching turban. She was not alone. Nick recognized her husband's stout, friendly young partner, Barney Kent, another of Nick's old schoolmates but he had never seemed to feel the gulf between the Corrigans and himself, so clearly demonstrated by Marsh Wychfield and Shelley Sholto. Nick shook hands with him and would have offered his hand to Shelley but she was putting her cheek against Dinah's, exclaiming, "What a very big girl you've become! I must stand on my very tiptoes."

"That's because you're so—what the French call—petite," Barney assured her gallantly.

Shelley murmured, "Dear Barney" without looking at him as she turned to Nick.

Her lips were pursed and Dinah was watching him, closely. He ignored the lips, felt for Shelley's small hand and pumped it. Dinah relaxed.

Everyone began to talk at once. Barney seemed to feel an explanation was in order. "Old Shell" decided to come up North to buy things for her little old store so I just tagged along. Had some legal business, luckily. Gave me a chance to protect old Marsh's wife from these Yankee slickers, you know."

"And a sweet protector you've been too, honey." Shelley patted his plump, high-colored cheek. "He's taking us all to dinner, aren't you, Barney?"

"Surely am. I know just the place. Chinese. Each little booth is closed in. Privacy, and all. So you two young ones can flirt to your heart's content and we old folks will be your chaperones, won't we, Shell?"

"We *surely* will," she mimicked Barney, wanting to kill him.

She failed to wedge herself next to Nick in the taxicab —Dinah was in the middle and Barney sat beside the driver while they drove downtown. In the small crowded street that seemed to be all too near the big Tombs prison, they were proudly ushered into Barney's favorite restaurant.

Each curtained booth held only a table, two pairs of chairs facing each other and a buzzer system. Nick lingered behind to see where Dinah was seated and was about to slide in beside her when Shelley chided him playfully.

"No, no. You-all must be very proper. I know my sister Ellen. She'd expect me to be right on my toes. I'll sit by young Dinah."

Dinah smiled sweetly at Nick, who reached under the table and squeezed her hand.

The women were fascinated by the various dishes, trying to decide what the contents could be. When Dinah tried to guess what Oriental oddities she was eating, Nick reached across the table, offering to taste and identify those odd-looking strips that could be mushrooms or birds' nests or some other exotic ingredient. Shelley gave a little scream, protesting, "Oh, what an awful thing! I might have been poisoned! Please, should I eat it?"

Nick pretended not to hear Shelley, he was eating from Dinah's fork; she had put aside her chopsticks early in the meal.

Shelley seemed affected either by the tea or her own thoughts. Her conversation verged closer and closer to a threat, almost verbal blackmail . . . "How nervous Dinah's dashing escort looks, Barney! Do you reckon he has secrets? Are you keeping deep dark secrets from the child, Nick? Let's see. What wickedness could you be up to? I know. Some secret love in your checkered past?"

Barney nudged her playfully across the table. "Shell, your tongue does wag a bit. It's none of our business what old Nick does—I mean did—in his love life."

Nick's mouth tightened until Dinah laughed and said, "How right you are, Barney! We're interested in today, not yesterday."

Nick looked at her and made up his mind. The hell with his money problems! He had supported aunt Amabel and uncle Timby for years. He could certainly support one tall, slim, glorious Gaynor. He cleared his throat and burst out with, "I have to test everything I say and everything Dinah eats because . . . I want this lady very healthy and happy . . . when she marries me."

Dinah's chin came up. "Do you mean it, Nick? Or should we all laugh?"

Dumbfounded at what he had heard in his own voice, Nick could only nod. He leaned across the table, cleared his throat and insisted, "I meant it. Ever since Lariat, as a matter of fact."

It was Shelley who upset the table. She had dropped her chopsticks and now tried to duck down to find them. Barney was confused and hurriedly joined her under the table. "Lose something, Shell?"

By the time their heads reappeared above the table, Barney red-faced and Shelley laughing too loudly, Nick had Dinah's hand tightly in his. He felt as pale as he knew he must look but Dinah was flushed . . . with pleasure, he hoped . . .

It had all been much simpler than he'd expected. It wasn't even necessary for Dinah to say yes. There were things that were understood without being said. He refused to dwell on the other side of the coin. A gambler might not be an ideal husband for Dinah, but there was no law that said he couldn't change. . . .

Dinah glanced at the discomfited Shelley and Barney, then flashed her smile at Nick, who at that moment took an oath never to let it disappear from his life.

Chapter Seven

HAPPY as Dinah was, she worried about her mother. Ellen's blessing *was* necessary, though. She and Nick were going to be married no matter what, but it would be a sad business if she and her mother quarreled. . . .

On the night train down to Virginia, with Shelley and Barney shut away in their respective compartments, Dinah and Nick talked about the future, and she discovered, with hastily concealed surprise, that he was a little worried about her acceptance by his own family. He kept telling Dinah how much they had done for him when he was young, as if she didn't respect him for supporting them! It seemed, though, that he was afraid she wouldn't approve, which fear on his part only made her feel more tenderly toward him . . .

Her mother had always stressed that the Corrigans had been unlucky, that their condition was not their own fault and that they had once been well-to-do respectable farmers. Dinah's father Jem Faire, half-Irish himself, had once been a close friend of the Corrigans when he too lived near Gaynorville. Dinah had very few fears for her own future so long as she was able to marry this marvelous Nick Corrigan, whom she loved increasingly every minute. . . .

The more time Nick and Dinah shared as their train approached Ashby Junction, Tudor County's seat, the more they found in each other to delight them. They argued over nonsense like identifying wild violets and then laughed at their own heated tempers. They were still laughing when the train pulled into Ashby's little wooden station and they discovered how many people had received their letters about their plans.

As they lined up ready to disembark, a man and woman passing from the diner to their Pullman looked out. The porter had opened the door and let down the steps. The man remarked, "Biggest crowd I ever saw at Ashby Station."

"Reckon it must be their local mayor arriving."

Dinah and Nick looked at each other. The waiting crowd was divided into two more or less even groups of people. A dozen, at least. Nick shook his head. "I can't believe it, but I think they're all here to meet us."

"And Shelley and Barney, of course," Dinah put in hopefully.

The porter set down their luggage.

A soft, faded woman dressed in a long-waisted lawn dress that had been turned and remade had to be Nick's aunt Amabel. Also there, and looking choked in a genuine collar and tie, was rugged uncle Timby, reasonably sober, grinning from ear to ear, a big bear of a man. Between grins for his nephew, however, he cast dour looks at the clan from Gaynor House, who ignored him.

Dinah waved to all the Corrigans, but her first attention was for her mother's family. They stood off from the Corrigans, who had poured onto the northbound railroad tracks by now. Shelley's and Marsh's handsome ten-year-old Neily, held in place by Shelley's pink-gloved hand, was shuffling nervously. He had run to meet her, been told, with Shelley's best smile, "Gently, gently, my boy," and was behaving with commendable restraint.

Dinah stepped down into Nick's arms. It seemed to her that all the relatives cheered, but this might have been her imagination. Captain Bill Sholto, rugged, sunburned and almost as good-looking as ever at sixty-seven, was genuinely enthused at the sight of her and she thought Aunt Shelley's husband, Marshall Wychfield, was too. Ever since his injury in the riding accident, he had limped badly and been something of an invalid, but Dinah always found the company of this tawny-haired man with tired, pain-shadowed eyes, quiet and restful. It didn't hurt that he was also the handsomest man she knew.

All of which didn't matter now . . . Nick Corrigan had so much more life. Poor Marsh seemed a little ghostly in spite of his flawless appearance. He greeted his wife with an embarrassing lack of enthusiasm, which her father Captain Bill Sholto counteracted with his exuberance.

Though Nick and Dinah were immediately surrounded by Corrigans, Dinah's relatives came forward to form an outside circle. They were almost too polite to Nick, which made Dinah uncomfortable, especially Shelley, the way she patted his shoulder, standing on her toes in high-heeled pumps and announcing to the world, "Isn't it exciting? He's going to marry our Dinah." While they digested this, she murmured, "Dear Nick, you are a lucky boy," and warmly kissed his cheek.

Dinah didn't know whether Marsh Wychfield even objected, his feelings were so contained. Few people nowadays even looked to him for decisions on the administration of Gaynor properties; Shelley's father, Captain Sholto, handled the Gaynor fields while the dress salon in Gaynorville belonged to Shelley.

Nick and Dinah were separated now as their respective families drew them away. Shelley put her cheek to Dinah's, whispering, "Honey, you're so *pretty*. I must say, I'd never have thought one of *them*, even Nick, could make such a difference."

Nick heard this in spite of Shelley's efforts and winked at Dinah.

Captain Sholto elbowed his way past his daughter's husband and embraced Dinah with a kiss as near as possible to her mouth while Dinah was trying to watch Shelley. The golden head moved among the Corrigans to exchange another few words with the prospective bridegroom. Dinah saw Amabel Corrigan looking Shelley up and down. The difference between the fifty-year-old pale and faded Amabel and the sleek thirty-year-old Shelley was shocking, and the pity was, Amabel knew it.

Marsh Wychfield took Dinah's hand with his usual good manners and then, seeing her friendly look, drew her closer and kissed her gently on the cheek. She was surprised that Nick would pay attention to this little encounter with Marsh as he ignored his uncle Timby's bear hug. It seemed silly to suspect Nick of jealousy. Dinah assured herself that she wasn't the least bit jealous of the attention her aunt Shelley showered on him. He had made it plain in New York that he never regarded Shelley as more than a nuisance . . .

Young Neily was eagerly examining all the luggage and Dinah pitied him. He had everything, yet he looked so very alone, and of his two parents, his father seemed much more concerned about him, aware of him as a person. His mother merely petted him . . .

Meanwhile Captain Sholto sauntered over to Amabel Corrigan—flirting, from the look of Amabel's pink cheeks and flustered air. Amabel's brother Timby scowled and would have interfered but Nick said something to him and shortly had him exchanging opinions with Marsh Wychfield about the weather and the war in Europe.

Nick and Dinah edged over to meet each other. She took his outstretched hands and they kissed, not caring who saw them. She loved his touch, his look and *almost* as much as the excitement of him she loved the sense of a bond between them. Except for her mother and father, she felt that this sort of enjoyment between a man and a woman was all too rare. She felt she was amazingly fortunate and she meant to tell her mother so.

Their moment together was shattered by Neily tugging at them. "Look what mama brought me from New York!" It was an authentic caboose built to scale for Neily's train set, and with it signals and more switch tracks.

Just then Amabel Corrigan reached Dinah. "I'm right proud to hear the news, Miss—I mean Dinah. We been thinking about the house since we got Nick's letter."

"The house?"

"Your room. You know, yours and Nick's. You ought to have pa and ma's room. We been using it for storing a passel of old stuff, and sometimes we hang the wash there when it's bad out." Dinah hugged Amabel, thanking her and resolving in private to work so hard the Corrigans would soon return to the position they had occupied before Gaynor House took back the land the Irish clan had cultivated.

"You are a dear . . . I know we've set you a big job, making up our minds so fast, but you know Nick, so you can imagine how hard it is to resist him . . ."

Amabel returned her embrace, first with hesitation, then enthusiastically. "Don't I know! Ask any girl who knows him. I mean—I didn't mean that like it sounded, Dinah. He's crazy about you. Anybody can see it. Never asked any other girl to marry him, far as I know. But then, you being a Gaynor and all, well . . ."

I'm going to get a lot of this, Dinah thought, and tried to shrug it off. "*I'm* very lucky, Amabel. I know that, I've never met anyone in my life like Nick."

"And we'll get together right soon and plan the wedding and after. About the house and all, if we had a little money, reckon we could just about make a new house out of the old place. Nothing been done to it now for thirty years and more."

It didn't sound too hopeful and now there was this hint about money. Did the Corrigans really think she had money? If Nick hadn't insisted on paying for her food on the trip, she would be practically broke now. She knew that Nick wasn't marrying her for her family's imaginary money, he'd come to know her situation and her mother's too well. But Dinah was pretty sure that Amabel Corrigan still lived in a fantasy world where all the Gaynor House connections were rich as Croesus—

"We're going now, honey," Shelley broke in with a gentle but insistent tap on the shoulder. "Good morning, Amabel. It was so nice seeing you down here. I loved the way you did my new French cuffs, by the way. I wore them in New York. Do you have new irons or something, my dear? Whatever it is, keep it up."

"I'll do that, Miss Shelley. I surely will." Amabel's smile was almost a smirk and Dinah couldn't blame her. Would anything ever get rid of that patronizing air that Shelley, mistress of Gaynor House, managed to show the world? There were only two women Shelley had never been able to patronize—her half sister Ellen and her mother-in-law, loud-voiced, opinionated Daisy Wychfield. Daisy went even further than Shelley. Widowed shortly after her son's birth, she had promptly reverted to her maiden name because everyone knew the Wychfields of Virginia and as she said, "The McCraes were a dime a dozen." It was a logic Shelley understood. She much preferred being Mrs. Marshall Wychfield to Mrs. Marshall McCrae.

The Gaynor House chauffeur had been waiting all this time in a kind of well-bred stupor at the wheel of a big, new touring car, and now the Gaynor House group rushed Dinah toward it. She didn't want to be impolite, she had never seen anyone more polite than her Virginia relatives but she didn't want to be separated so abruptly from Nick, who had turned to answer one of Amabel's questions and swung around again to find Dinah missing.

"My girl! You're stealing my future wife!"

"Help! Nick!" The whole thing *sounded* playful but she knew Nick was annoyed by the obvious effort to separate them, even temporarily... Everyone laughed, but still they were being pushed and pulled further apart as the Corrigans headed for an ancient horse and wagon and the Gaynor group neared the touring car. Dinah was glad for her height, it gave her a chance to look over her aunt's head and wave to Nick, who was ironically blowing a kiss to her.

"Later," he called as she was boosted into the back seat of the big open car and pulled onto Bill Sholto's lap. Everyone else pushed in afterward and found a place. Young Neily wanted to sit beside "Cousin Dinah" but settled for his father's lap. After Shelley had gotten in next to Bill Sholto and an uncomfortable Dinah, the two parties started off along the recently paved road between Ashby Junction and the Gaynor family estate.

"Now," Aunt Shelley said with a deep sigh of relief, "that business is over, thanks be. They get more impossible every day." She put her small hand on Dinah's knee. "Honey, how *are* we going to get you out of this? We must all put on our thinking caps."

Chapter Eight

GAYNOR House, smaller than the other plantation houses on the Ooscanoto River, had been built with two fronts, one looking west on the river and the other east on the road, with parallel parlors, screen doors and many windows.

Dazed at being moved from point to point so rapidly, with no time to become acclimated, Dinah tried to assure herself she and Nick could settle things tonight without the damnable interference of her aunt.

It had been difficult there for a few minutes in the car when Shelley made that shocking remark. Now Dinah paced up and down in her mother's old room on the second floor of Gaynor House, trying to wear down her anger before meeting the family again. She wasn't a bit sorry for her reply to Shelley . . . "Auntie, I hope you won't make any more jokes like that. It might upset the Corrigans if I went to live with them before we settled our wedding plans." She followed it with a laugh but her meaning and a hint of steel were clear. Bill Sholto had said coolly, "Shelley, don't interfere in this. You'll only make things worse." He wasn't on Dinah's and Nick's side but at least he'd put his daughter in her place. For the time being . . .

When aunt Shelley showed Dinah to her mother's old bedroom she had said with sweet venom, "I knew it was a mistake when your dear mama let Nick escort you here. But Amabel was so persuasive, so anxious to please. You know Amabel. She means well but such a useless person! The Corrigans have sunk mighty low. Amabel *was* once a very pretty girl, you know, though simpering and spoiled, mama says. She and Amabel went to school and parties and cotillions together. In fact, mama used to be envious of Amabel's popularity with the boys." Shelley rolled her beautiful hazel eyes. "Now I can only say, honey, how have the mighty fallen!" . . . Oddly enough, Captain Bill Sholto hadn't uttered a word against the Corrigans. Maybe he felt guilty about snatching back that Gaynor land those thirty years ago—land given to the Corrigans by the federal government after the Civil War. If that hadn't happened, maybe the Corrigans would be as high on the social scale as the owners of Gaynor House and their upriver neighbor, Wychfield Hall. Wisely, Sholto remained his charming, noncommittal self.

Dinah only wished aunt Shelley would do the same. . . .

Amabel Corrigan sniffed deeply, her little nose in the air. "Don't you just love it! Rheba Moon's Irish stew, Nick. You've missed it all over the world."

"Not the world, darlin'. Just the U.S."

"I love you in those clothes, Nick. You look right handsome."

He had taken off coat, collar and tie and was wearing his old Donegal sweater with its high rolled neck. The deep shades of green and black were flattering to him and so was the high neck of the sweater; he had spent two weeks' winnings on it years ago. Now he had the distinct feeling that the powerful aroma of cabbage boiling in the kitchen was pouring into his sweater and into his freshly scrubbed skin, into his very soul . . . Thinking about it he asked himself, am I a snob? The idea upset him. He had always disliked the Gaynor-Sholtos and the Wychfields for this very quality; and what had *he* to be snobbish about? But coming in this afternoon, fresh from the wonderful, elusive scent of Dinah, he'd been greeted by this overwhelming cabbage smell. He had always hated boiled cabbage, even as a boy. On the other hand, the last thing in the world he wanted was to hurt the feelings of his relatives, who were, after all, *his* . . . just as he was theirs . . .

He tried to stretch out his legs but there never was enough room in this little parlor. He preferred the big kitchen but he'd be damned if he was going to share that pleasant sunny room with Timby's mulatto mistress Rheba Moon, who seemed to have become mistress of the entire house in the last few months. She wasn't satisfied with old Timby. She had her baleful, hypnotic eyes on Nick as well, as if she had him pegged to succeed Timby in her bed. It made him edgy—her arrogance and the offhand way she treated Amabel . . .

He could hear her and Timby in the kitchen now, one of them had dropped an old pewter plate that was still used to hold the fresh-baked biscuits for each meal. The Corrigans might be poor, Amabel said, but they knew what was proper. Any decent home had spoon bread or hush puppies or just plain beaten biscuits ready to hand at all times. If there was no butter for the delicious doughy biscuits, there were always Amabel's melon or tomato preserves.

Earlier Amabel had told Nick, "Somebody has to watch Rheba. She steals. That's why we never have any salt or cocoa or corn meal. She trades things off to the Finch tenants upstream for gee-gaws and whatall."

It was all so starkly different from those magic days and nights traveling cross-country with Dinah. About the only money the Corrigans saw in a year, besides Amabel's wages from laundering for Shelley Wychfield, was what he brought home. Between them, Timby and Amabel let it all be stolen from them by dribs and drabs and petty theft. And he had the crazy notion of asking Dinah Faire to share this impossible household! . . . He got up and walked around the house, avoiding the kitchen. He'd always had a generally optimistic view of life. Without that he could never have made a living as a gambler, much less have been able to help support two other adults. But when he came back to this old frame farmhouse today after seven months and was almost forcibly separated from Dinah by that arrogant family of hers, he'd been swept by one of his black Irish moods. And, he knew it was, more than just the cabbage . . .

The front screen door, *blackened and ramshackle*, had a big broken place and the screen itself was bent back near the hook that held the door closed. It didn't take a genius to figure out that Timby had come home drunk one night—or day—and finding the screen door latched just rammed through it with his fist or maybe his old skinning knife. That was understandable. Everyone had an uncle Timby of one kind or another. But why had no one done anything about patching the hole? No wonder two blowflies were making a racket in the parlor. He made a mental note to find out how the door should be repaired. He had no mechanical talent whatever.

Then there was the dusty parlor into which a visitor walked directly from the stoop and the porch—the latter muddy in winter and gritty in summer. It didn't make the dark, over-furnished parlor any more inviting. All that Victorian furniture collected by Nick's grandmother with its fancy trim and doodads and dark colors that showed dust five minutes after being cleaned . . . He liked the player-piano, though. Amabel played it when she was in the mood . . . poor Amabel, who had been raised as an equal of the Gaynor and Wychfield and Warrender girls and now had sunk to the level of the poorest tenant farmer, black or white.

If I could only make a killing, he thought . . . *If I could get together a big stake and with any kind of luck at all . . . I spent too much on this last trip. I always do. It's my damned show-off habit . . . How could I have had the gall to ask Dinah to marry me? I must've been crazy drunk . . .*

He hadn't been, though. He knew that. Timby Corrigan presented too awful a model. To Nick all drunks were like his uncle. Besides, anybody knew you needed a clear head for a poker game . . . He looked out at the wagon tracks leading from the once immaculate white fence that separated the road to the Ooscanoto River plantations from what was left of Corrigan land. The big gate had broken on its hinges long ago and still sagged forlornly halfway across the wagon ruts that once had been the dirt road up to the farmhouse veranda. This meant a detour around the gate every time the Corrigans rode in with the mare and the wagon or the buckboard. Worse, it was an eyesore to the infrequent Sunday visitors of the neighborhood, those fine ladies who still called on Amabel once in a while. Nick had heard them gossiping in the Gaynorville Emporium about "that poor Amabel. I do declare, I was real shocked to see how shabby she looked at services last Sunday. I rec'lect when Amabel was the prettiest thing at Bertha-Winn Wychfield's wedding back in '85. You-all rec'lect the way she used to toss those yellow curls?" After overhearing that, Nick had taken his next winnings from a round-trip excursion on the Washington-Old Point Comfort steamer and instructed Amabel to order herself some fancy, specially made church dresses at Shelley Gaynor's dress salon. But six months later when he returned from a trip to Louisiana, he discovered that Timby and Rheba had shamed the money out of Amabel on the grounds that it was needed for the winter hay and grain supplies. Since Nick had already provided this money the previous autumn he was fit to crack his uncle's skull with the nearest ax-handle. He was doubly frustrated having lost everything in New Orleans after winning a sizable stake on the Southern Railway. . . .

Nick heard his name called now from the window of Amabel's bedroom and after once more inhaling the rich sweet smells of an autumn evening in rural Virginia he went back into the house to his aunt's room.

He found her stretched out on the narrow white, hand-hewn bed that had been hers since girlhood. The room was half dark. She had pulled the shade down so far that the last rays of sunset barely illumined the room, which was just as well. The bureau and the closet were cluttered with souvenirs and old clothes Amabel had saved from her happy, popular girlhood. She had kept every ball gown ever worn during those triumphant years from 1884 to 1887 when the family's property loss began to affect their lifestyle. Nick was depressed by this room but he was very fond of his aunt. He kissed her sweating forehead. "Hello, honey. How's my pretty colleen?"

"Go along with you!" But she looked surprisingly pretty at his praise all the same. Her hands pulled him closer. "You did what I wanted you to, didn't you?"

"I always do. But what was this in particular?"

"Now, don't be sly with your old auntie. It was my idea for you to fix it so's she'd want to marry you."

"Amabel—"

"And that's just how it come out. Nick, we can have money and clothes and nice things to eat again. Just like when I was a girl. And people riding up to the house in carriages—"

"Not carriages, this is 1915, honey, and I—"

"You know what I mean, dearie. And she's right sociable. Acts like she means to be friends, and all. not like some I could mention. Why, my hair was ten times prettier'n Shelley's when I was her age. And popular? You wouldn't have any notion how popular I was with the boys 'round Tudor County. Reckon I should of married the Kent boy when he asked me, but what with all them nasty-tongued things his mama had to say to ma and pa—that was after Captain Sholto took our land. Before that I could've had any boy in the county. I even used to dance with Jem Faire before he married Ellen Gaynor—"

"I know, Amabel, but see here, there's something we have to get straightened out. About Dinah and me—"

"Dearie, you needn't tell me the bad part. You wa'nt too rough on her, I hope."

He felt a hot flush rise to his face that he hoped she wouldn't notice in this dim light. "That's what I wanted to talk to you about. Dinah isn't that kind of girl. Anyway, I had no intention of carrying on all the stuff you talked about in that letter you sent to me in Arizona."

Amabel tried to sit up against the old pillow that shed feathers with her every movement, her right hand fumbling beside the bed. When Nick tried to make her comfortable, still scowling angrily, she begged him, "That bag on the floor. Just rest it easy-like on my forehead. There's a dear."

Angry at himself for having upset her and wishing he hadn't even entered the room, Nick fumbled along the faded carpet until he found a hot cotton bag full of a substance that shifted like sand between his fingers. "What the devil is this?"

"Salt, dearie. Hot salt. It helps when I get the migraine."

He was ashamed of his abruptness and set the bag carefully on her forehead. "There. That better?"

She sighed comfortably. "Much. You're a good boy, Nick. Like your father. Sean was always right kind when I needed him." She sat up suddenly, dropping the salt bag. He groped around on the floor again and found it, but she pushed it away. "What's going to happen to you, dearie ... I gave my word to your ma on her deathbed that I'd look after you. Samarra made me promise you wouldn't come to a bad end. Nick, are you in trouble with the law?"

He threw his hands up in the air. "Oh, for God's sake, no! But I'd sleep a lot easier if I knew you had a little money set aside for emergencies just in case things don't pan out with me some time."

"Now, Nick, don't lose your temper. You're so like your dear mother. You just set back and think how much better things'll be after you marry that nice Gaynor girl."

It was no use. She was impossible. He was about to try to explain when Rheba Moon's voice interrupted.

"Supper's dished out. You-all coming?"

Nick, indulgent though exasperated, helped Amabel out of bed, smoothed her wrinkled lawn dress and told her if she just combed her hair she'd be his own fair colleen. She obeyed him happily, her headache fading under the new interests of supper and faintly reawakened vanity.

Timby Corrigan was already at the head of the table in a jolly mood, his powerful legs stretched out and his big arms reaching along the table for the fresh-baked loaf of Irish soda bread Rheba had made especially for him. Nick started to seat Amabel at the foot of the table as mistress of the house, but she muttered, "No, not here, on the side. It's —it's easier there. I can reach things better."

Nick looked around at the others. Timby had sliced off a chunk of his loaf and was gnawing at it contentedly. Rheba removed her apron, hanging it on a nail behind the stove and gave Nick one of her grins that revolted him.

Rheba was a tall, buxom woman in her late thirties. Some called her handsome ... she carried herself like an empress, her dark head high, but her big toothy smile, which she flashed freely, never seemed to reach her mud-colored, serpentine eyes. They were expressionless, like the eyes of a cottonmouth, Nick thought, as it lay in wait among the reeds of Great Dismal Swamp. Nick knew she was waiting for him to back down like Amabel and he had to accept her challenge, break her hold on the Corrigans. "Amabel honey, this is your chair," he insisted. "You just have to practice a longer reach, that's all."

"No . . . I'd really—"

"Auntie, sit!"

Amabel fell into the old chair with its woven cane seat the worse for wear and lowered her head to avoid Rheba's stare. There was a dull gleam far back in the depths of those eyes, and Nick felt a touch of his aunt's fear. He said evenly, aware of the woman's gaze on his back, "You can't let Rheba do all the work, auntie. She's our guest. Timby's guest. You just look up some of those old receipts of yours for those wonderful dinners you and grandma used to make. You'll soon be back handling things like they used to be."

"But, Nick . . . with my pleurisy . . . last winter I had it real bad. And this migraine . . ."

Nick put his hand over her trembling fingers. "I know, honey. But Timby will tell you I'm right. He doesn't want his friend doing everything the mistress of the house should do, do you, uncle?"

With his mouth full, Timby waved his knife and mumbled something he hoped would satisfy both his ambitious mistress and the young nephew whose money was always welcome.

Nick kept up the pressure. "I'm sure Rheba agrees, don't you?"

She stepped forward, close behind him, and rested one shapely hand on his neck, the fingers just under the roll collar of his sweater. "Whatever you say, Mister Nick. Whatever you say." She went around to the side of the table and Nick pushed in her chair for her. She looked up. "You're mighty kind, Mister Nick. Your manners show." She glanced at Timby from under her heavy-lidded eyes, but if she had intended to arouse his jealousy, she failed.

He said happily, "Real fine soda bread. Ma couldn't have done better. You there, Amabel. Pass me the cabbage and spuds."

Nick sat down, looked at his wristwatch, and wondered if Dinah had understood that he would be waiting for her outside Gaynor House tonight. His pulse quickened at the thought. The idea of Dinah Faire living in this pigsty with him and his relatives still chilled him, but nothing in life seemed to matter except being with her, taking care of her. And he would accomplish great things for her. He would never be responsible for Dinah disintegrating like poor Amabel, who also had started life with such promise. With Dinah's support maybe he could challenge the rich New York gamblers from those Fifth Avenue mansions who traveled all over the South, scattering their losses. He felt capable of real success thinking of Dinah behind him as Mrs. Nick Corrigan. His natural optimism revised, he reminded himself that his luck was surely running high these days. Anything was possible . . .

Captain Sholto was standing by the glass door of the river parlor, his hand on the knob. "You tell Ellen when you write that Bill Sholto sends his best. She and I were good friends when she was a youngster, no older than you."

Other members of the family had entered the long cool river parlor but Dinah ignored them, trying to worm information out of the man who had once loved her mother.

"Please, captain, I'd like to talk to you about those days . . . how mama fell in love with papa. She makes it sound romantic."

As Sholto laughed Dinah thought of the bitterness, the distance she had always felt between her mother Ellen and her grandmother Maggilee, a mother and daughter fighting over the same man, Bill Sholto. And then the mother giving birth to a child princess like Shelley when Ellen herself was twenty years old. It explained a great deal.

Dinah looked at Sholto, wondering how her mother could ever have loved this man, so much older than herself, when Dinah's father, the so much deeper Jem Faire, was waiting for her. . . . Well, at least Bill Sholto could hardly disapprove of Nick . . . As a young man he had been one of the few survivors of the Seventh Cavalry after the battle of Little Big Horn. One of Major Reno's command, he had escaped the massacre and not been mustered out for another ten years. In 1885 as an ex-cavalry officer with a blue uniform hardly welcome in Virginia he had been lucky again when a beautiful thirty-eight-year-old widow named Maggilee Gaynor, married him and he found himself possessor by marriage of a distinguished family, fallow fields that needed only capable overseers and hard workers to produce profits and a dress salon that Maggilee had made the most elegant and expensive in southeastern Virginia. . . .

Marsh Wychfield came in quietly just then behind Captain Sholto, who was looking at Dinah quizzically now with a little smile. "You must remember, I was much younger when your mother and Maggilee met me."

Good Lord! Did he read minds? Dinah refused to be flustered. Instead she played up to his good humor. "And just as charming as you are now, I'm sure."

His smile widened. "What a very perceptive girl! What do you say, Marsh? Think she's wasted on that poor white trash?"

As Dinah began to blaze, Marsh Wychfield's blue-gray eyes crinkled in a rare smile. "I'm sure any man would think Dinah was wasted on another."

This time she *was* embarrassed, probably because Marsh sounded as though he meant it, and with Captain Sholto you never quite knew whether he was teasing or not. However uncomfortable Marsh's compliment made her, she was grateful to him for not joining in these snide remarks about Nick and his family.

She said now, "I don't regard people who happen to be poor as trash. Black *or* white. I've seen rich white trash now and then, though I will say they don't hang around Lariat very long."

Both men laughed uneasily, and as the captain moved toward her Marsh Wychfield surprised both his father-in-law and Dinah by offering his arm. "We seem to have gotten rather far afield from our original purpose, which was to tell you dinner is ready. May I?"

She accepted his arm and walked past Captain Sholto, who looked a bit annoyed over his son-in-law's quick footwork.

Fortunately for Dinah's much-tried temper no one mentioned Nick or the Corrigans during the innumerable courses of the long dinner. Everyone drank iced tea except young Neily and Dinah, who thought the custom too exotic for her tastes. Neily drank milk under protest and Dinah chose plain water, all too rare in arid Lariat.

Neily sat beside her, greatly admiring everything she did, imitating any of her customs which differed from those he had been taught. He was especially big-eyed when she talked right up to the men, unlike Shelley whose soft accent and mannered conversation were in such contrast to Dinah's broad speech and frank opinions.

Marsh Wychfield observed that the war in Europe seemed to be stalemated on the western front and Shelley reported the latest activities of the Belgian relief drive, and the Red Cross in Tudor County. Sholto added, "We'll be needing our own war relief before another year is out. We're sure to be in it."

Dinah was glad to see the meal ending. She would like, she said, to sit out on the east veranda and write to her mother but first she offered to help with the dishes.

Shelley gave her an astonished look. "But honey, we have a girl to do all that."

For a moment Dinah had forgotten where she was supposed to be. Actually she wanted to go out on this warm early fall night and walk around the rolling lawns to the beginning of the woods on the south side. She might then cross the estate road on the east and watch the wide, well-worn path, that wandered through Gaynor and then Corrigan fields to the town. It was still the easiest way for Ooscanoto River residents to reach Gaynorville on foot. Nick had said he would come "later" and he would keep his promise. "Later" meant later tonight, she was certain ...

Nick Corrigan was in her blood ...

Shelley went about the business of closing the shop one evening two days later, wanting to stay here in the quiet silk-and-velvet atmosphere of the salon, where the air was delicately scented with Coty's latest fragrance, rather than face the unpleasantness of Gaynor House and her marital life at home.

It seemed incredible to Shelley that Marsh could share a house, a dining table and a life with her for the last year and a half and keep silent over his knowledge of her adultery. Worse than all the rest was his damned polite reserve. She had tried a dozen times to explain how little the episode with the buyer had meant to either of them. His only reply to this was, "Yes, it meant little to *you*. Do you ever think of anyone but yourself?"

Shelley inspected the gown about to be displayed alone in the window tomorrow. There had been an argument with Dora Johnson, her black assistant, an older woman whose taste while conservative was an accurate barometer of local sales. This layered, two-piece dress was the first selection Gaynor's would display of the new imitation silk that was being talked about in Paris. Dora Johnson insisted that tighter skirts still held sway and it was too soon to bring in this "fuller, loose look." Dora might know Gaynorville but Shelley knew fashion. She always exhibited the latest style in the windows but kept in stock copies of gowns popular in New York last year and in Paris the year before ...

No use putting it off any longer. She had to go home eventually. She considered walking home instead of driving, which meant taking the well-worn path first across

Corrigan and then Gaynor land. There were silly but useful ploys like twisting her ankle while crossing Corrigan ground, losing her purse in the creek or even stopping to talk with Amabel about next week's ironing . . . Her pride came to her rescue and she banished the idea as she went up the stairs, which like the shop's main room were thickly carpeted in maroon to match the luxury of the circular couch in the center of the salon. On the way up she pressed one of the wall switches that darkened the exquisite crystal chandelier and wall sconces. Only the soft pink-shaded night light still glowed over the extra-large sofa near the dressing rooms, where customers waited to be fitted. It was popularly suspected and even towns up the James River bought their clothes at Gaynor's so they could enjoy the luxurious comforts Shelley offered.

On the second floor, where much of the yardage was stored, Shelley retrieved her hat and purse, glancing through the window at quiet Beauford Street, and decided it was too dark to walk home. There had never been any danger in former times but the current boom in war material bound for Europe had attracted unsavory characters from all over the country and it would be just as well to drive her own car home.

As she pinned her new hat on top of her mass of bright hair she noticed a man across the street walking briskly past the darkened little theater that had formerly housed a stock company of players down from Richmond. Rumor had it that high-stake poker games were played there now on occasional evenings. Shelley watched the man, guessing he had emerged from the theater. His dark coat hung from his shoulders—a habit a little too dramatic for local citizens—and told her, if his unusual height had not, that he was Nick Corrigan. She hesitated to add more fuel to her troubles with Marsh—damn that loudmouthed Persis Kent!—but she certainly couldn't live without male friends and male company.

She gave herself a quick inspection at the full-length standing mirror in front of the cubbyholes where the wrapped fabrics were stored. Thank god she had worn one of her latest New York outfits today! Nick Corrigan traveled a lot. He would know fashion when he saw it. She raised the window and looked out. Luckily she didn't have to call his name, alerting her interest to other passersby. The window's wooden frame and cord pulley screeched through the evening air, and Nick turned at the sound. He didn't seem as surprised as she thought he should be; probably he had seen the lights on at Gaynor's and knew she was still here. He might even be lingering in the vicinity hoping to meet her as she left. He wouldn't be the first one . . . She motioned for him to cross the street. He looked around, saw no one else and accepted her invitation, just avoiding one of Hannah Gamble's jitneys, a newly painted black Ford that rattled and clanked its approach.

"Do you always work so late, Miss Shelley?"

"It depends. Nights like this are rather lonely for hard-working folks." She gave him a practiced smile. "You-all probably think I just play here all day. Well, you'd be surprised at how beautiful my shop is. It takes work to keep it up, I assure you."

"And am I about to see it?"

She looked up and down the street, then lowered her voice. "If you want to. But you'd better come around the back entrance. I just hate gossip."

He laughed at that.

"Between the buildings. Gamble's Livery and Garage at the end of the alley—but you've been there often enough. It's on this side. I'll open the door." She waited to be sure he followed her directions and then she closed the window, aware of the aching excitement of her body. It was a long time since she had been aroused this way by any man—the rapid pulse, the telltale desire below, the triumph of making another woman's man one of her devoted "friends." It would cancel out the disastrous fumbling of the Baltimore actor, the brutality of the New York buyer and her own husband's refusal to accept her in bed, or anywhere else. . . .

She was sure she would find Nick waiting eagerly at the alley door, which she herself frequently used because it was handier when she took the field path to and from town. Moving through the main salon toward the narrow back hall, she was pleased with the look of this room she had decorated herself. Knowing men, she had become aware long ago that a woman's beauty could fade early but that success gave her a special aura, an added glamor. It was still a shocking view, particularly in her own South, but she was honest with herself about such matters however she behaved to others. Yes, the shop has never looked better, Maggilee, she thought, as if speaking to her mother's ghost, which seemed to linger here, "I know now why you cared so much for it. Like mother, like daughter. And I know why you left it to me and not to Ellen. She may have been your older daughter, and maybe she ought to have inherited it, but she would never have understood the first thing about our feelings for Gaynor's. To you it came before any man, even father."

Captain Bill Sholto had been a dashing attractive fellow, arriving in Gaynorville in 1885 at just the point in Maggilee's life when the age of forty loomed up two years ahead on the horizon. Shelley knew her mother had loved this romantic second husband, but she also understood instinctively that Gaynor's Salon always held first place in Maggilee's affections . . . "Like me," Shelley told herself, running her hand over a satin kimono on a wax figure as she passed. Just the feel of the material under her hand was sensual. Good! I'm in exactly the right mood. I can enjoy Nick's company, his kisses and those exciting hands of his if we get that far, maybe without even going to bed with him. He'll be too impressed by his surroundings. He'll do exactly what I want, let me enjoy him the way I want, just short of . . . From time to time she had been accused of being a tease, and to this she always answered directly with her enchanting smile and the full force of her lovely hazel eyes . . . "But if that's so, I tease myself too. I'm punished as much as you are. And, honey, you never would respect me again, would you . . . ?"

Her mother, Maggilee, had overheard one of these scenes when Shelley was thirteen and warned her that she would break her own heart—if she had one. But Shelley only remarked with surprise, "Mama, it's common gossip that you didn't live like a nun all those twenty years between Ellen's father and mine. Aren't you proud to think that I, at least, don't go all the way with them?"

Her slender, redhaired mother had been about to slap her, changed her mind and only complained to Captain Sholto at dinner. "There soon will be no living with that child of yours. I reckon she got to the root of the tree long ago, just like I warned you."

Shelley always became "that child of yours" when she misbehaved. "The truth is," she thought honestly, "I'm the natural product of two not very moral people. What do they expect? . . . But tonight the first hitch in her plan of limited satisfaction came when she opened the alley door, and didn't find Nick waiting, eager to enter. She looked all around into the dark alley which the moonlight reached only fitfully, casting pools and pointed shadows.

How maddening that man was! He'd stopped to peer over the fence into the old Confederate cemetery at the far end of the street. What a thing to do at a time like this . . . Finally he looked around at Shelley, raised his hand in greeting and walked toward the alley door of Gaynor's.

"It isn't everybody who gets a conducted tour of Gaynor's," Shelley told him pertly.

He nodded. "I deeply appreciate that."

"Well, you needn't be so solemn."

He eyed the luxury. "It certainly isn't Grant's Tomb," he said as he stepped into the main salon, then saw Shelley's face, begged her pardon and corrected himself quickly. "Should I have said Lee's Tomb? Or Stuart's Tomb?"

She ignored that. "This is where we exhibit all the latest fashions for the ladies while we serve punch, or cornbread and coffee or pecan pie, depending on the hour. Feel that round couch in the center. So soft, couldn't you just drown in it?"

He pressed three fingers into the thick plush. "There must be better uses for a couch. But I agree, if you were doughnut-shaped, you could drown in it."

"It's awfully good for business. Ladies get so attached to it they keep ordering more things rather than struggle to dig themselves out of all that plush."

She didn't know whether he was impressed or not. He glanced around, then looked her over so slowly until she felt that if she were younger she would blush. She put her hand on his sleeve with gentle persistence. "Would you like to see the rest of my—?" His arm felt tense under her hand but she didn't let that stop her. She saw the way he glanced at the big couch across the room. He couldn't very well miss it . . . the only electric light she had left on in the salon was the wall sconce above the couch and for the first time in her memory she was almost ashamed of her own conniving. She pressed the switch for the elegant chandelier, whose golden lusters suddenly gleamed with dazzling lights. He looked up, saw the curious, not too pleasant smile that seemed to read her mind.

"That wasn't necessary. There was light enough."

She shrugged, came across the room to him. To save face she pretended he was interested in the fitting rooms behind the big couch. She reached for the fitting room door but he stopped her, drawing her down to her knees on the couch.

She protested, all shock and indignation. "Stop this, what are you doing? I only meant—"

She felt Nick's fingers caressing her bared throat and then her breasts, one, the other, and the deep cleavage between. She had never been too proud of her breasts . . . they were, after all, unfashionably large, though they surely intrigued most men. Whether they intrigued this man she did not know, but the desire of her own body at his persistent touch betrayed her. She moaned, whispered, "I mustn't, I never meant to . . ."

Then she saw his face, the clearly amused smile of a man who was teasing *her*, leading *her* on. He had no more interest in her than in a rag doll . . . he'd deliberately lead her on, only to let her go as he did now, pretending obedience to her words he knew she didn't mean. She sat up, pulling her clothes together into some semblance of order.

"I'm sorry, Miss Shelley. Now, don't cry. You don't want to redden those pretty hazel eyes, do you?"

"Why did you really come to my salon tonight?"

"I thought I might pick out a dress for Dinah," he said, "but maybe she'd rather choose her own."

And then he was leaving, and she watched as he stopped in the hallway, touched the satin kimono on the mannequin, felt it slither under his hand. His fingers tightened, pleating the cream-colored fabric. "Aunt Amabel would love this."

She heard the alley door open and close behind him and never moved until a sound in the main salon startled her. "Who is it?"

Her father's voice called to her from the front foyer. There was a sardonic note to it. "I was coming to rescue you but it doesn't seem to be necessary."

She ran toward him, craving the approval he'd always given his only child. Now he strolled through his daughter's shop with what to outsiders was the jaunty air of a proprietor. Only Shelley and her assistant knew how much he had always hated the Gaynor salon and how he resented the fact that there were times, especially during the depressions of 1893 and 1907 when only the earnings from the salon had saved the Gaynor fields from foreclosure by the banks. . . . He put his arm around her and patted her head in a paternal manner but he didn't seem quite as consoling as she had expected.

"Oh pa, he tried to—"

"Honey, never mind what that young fella did. What he didn't do upset you more than what he did do. Isn't that true?"

"Father!" She shook his arm off and went to slam shut a partially opened braid-and-trim drawer. "That girl is going to get into serious trouble, marrying a man like that."

Sholto took off his old cavalry hat, ran his fingers through his still plentiful ruddy hair. "Shelley honey, hadn't you better mend things between you and Marsh before you start straightening out Dinah's problems?"

Shelley turned with a bolt of crêpe de chine in her hand, snapping it angrily. "Damn him, *damn* him . . ."

He caught her hands, shook her. "I'm right willing to damn him if I know just who."

His reasonable, humorous manner soothed her, and her arms went around him. "Pa, you're still the best-looking, sexiest man in Virginia."

"Are you just discovering that?"

Chapter Nine

HAVING salved his conscience over his treatment of Shelley Wychfield—a little of her own medicine was how he thought of it—Nick Corrigan was stepping high on clouds for the next few days. At first he hadn't been able to comprehend the fact that Dinah was actually willing to live with him. With a preacher's blessing, naturally, but the way she understood him was miraculous.

His resentment of the Gaynors had been born during childhood when he discovered that in the world's eyes he was the inferior of these men and women with their clean, faintly flower-scented house, their gentle manners and their easy command of any room they graced. On his rare visits to Gaynor House he had studied these Virginia aristocrats, their habits, manners, and whenever luck was running his way he began to dress with an elegance that he hoped would outdo them. He tried to do the same with his manners. Occasionally he caught someone making fun of him, and although seething inwardly, he turned even this to his advantage, appearing to be the *nouveau riche* young scion of some prosperous family sufficiently distant from his poker game so that his vaguely sketched background couldn't be checked. . . .

Now he appeared to be accepted by the Gaynors. Unheard of even in his most vengeful dreams. He managed to make a fool of that arrogant tease, Shelley Wychfield, and for a day or two he expected to make trouble between him and Dinah. He was prepared to tell Dinah the whole truth . . . if he knew his Dinah, he suspected she would find it pretty funny. When Shelley made no reference to the interlude, he felt a little ashamed, but at least it went some way to cancel out all those childhood humiliations . . .

One of these days he meant to bring Aunt Amabel to Gaynor House dressed in her best, of course, and let her too feel the Corrigans were accepted. And all because of Dinah, his lovely woman. Sometimes he went cold thinking he might have refused Amabel's suggestion to bring Dinah Faire back to Virginia. Nick alone knew why at first he'd jumped at the chance to escort her . . . because it put the Gaynors in his debt, made *them* inferior for once. Then he had seen that rangy, windblown beauty on the trackside and she hadn't been the slightest bit arrogant or coy or devious. She had been his Dinah practically overnight and the whole world had changed for him. . . .

His biggest problem, aside from the eternal one of money, was to get the Corrigan property cleaned up. He spent two days painting the white fence and trying to get the big cross-bar gate back on its hinges while Amabel made an effort to dust the parlor and mend the worn petit-point cover of the footstool she used when her ankles swelled.

Nahum Coates, who had been Jonathan Gaynor's black partner at Gaynor Ferry and now owned the Ferry, came by with some fresh corn and melons for the Corrigans and stayed to give Nick some much needed help, Nick having dropped the gate and gotten the old rawhide locking strip stuck against the newly painted fence.

"You fixing to grow that gate onto the fence?" Nahum asked mildly, not quite smiling.

"No, damn it! But the hinges rusted off years ago." Nick saw Nahum's eyebrows rise and guessing his thoughts, grinned in apology. "I know, why didn't I do this before? Just bone-lazy, I reckon."

Nahum's tone was easy but Nick didn't miss the steel in it. "Kind of more Timby's work than yours, ain't it? He don't go around winnin' poker hands to keep you alive. How's it you're stuck doing his job *and* your own?"

"Timby's out in the pasture. He thinks he's set up some irrigation channels to take care of the feed for his mare."

"No, he's not. He's over in the Gaynor woods shooting up the place. Said he was hunting rabbits for stew."

Nick started to say something but gave it up. What was there to say about Timby that hadn't been said long ago?

Nahum, however, understood that family loyalty came first in the South and said no more. Instead he went to Amabel with his lavish gift and together they took the basket inside. Nick watched Nahum's sturdy figure in overalls and mud-stained boots and thought of his own so-called talents . . . he looked at his hands with the long fingers scarred by cuts, rips and bloody little gashes, all injuries incurred because he was clumsy and stupid about the simplest most basic things in life. Nahum Coates worked at the hardest labor and still managed to be a capitalist. He could buy and sell me and the whole Corrigan tribe, Nick thought. . . .

He hated this damned fence-and-gate business and knew he was never going to be any good at it. He looked off toward Gaynorville, still a sleepy, static town, and on to Ashby, the county seat. Salesmen came down from the North on the noon express and various free and easy young spenders came up from the bayou country on the three o'clock train, congregating at the Ashby Arms Hotel and "Parlor," a euphemism for the high-class saloon. Nick looked at his hands again. They'd be a hell of a lot more useful at the Ashby Arms than here, but he would have despised himself as much as he did his uncle Timby if he walked out on this job now. He managed to present a fairly confident front along with humorous self-deprecation when Nahum came back out and strode toward the gate.

"You still fooling with that gate, Mr. Nick? You really don't have the gift."

"I surely don't." Nick had at least worked the rawhide off the freshly painted fence and stood the long gate in place. He was sweating profusely.

Nahum broke into a smile that softened his serious face. "You know, I wouldn't tackle all this in one day. You sure you know what you're doing?"

"No. And I never did. But I'm getting the hinges back on this damned thing before the sun goes down and it's going to work."

"Well, I must say, I like a man of decision. Yes, sir! Suppose I just get a hold of it at this end and you start hammering. That's a good hinge you're working on, ain't it?"

"Well, it's new. I just got it this morning from Gamble's." Gamble's Hay, Grain, Feed and Livery Store was the hardware store which had grown out of the old horse-and-buggy days and even in these modern days remained the headquarters of all the local males who wanted to get away from pressures at home.

It proved a clumsy business, but between them they got the gate back on its hinges so that the Corrigan property looked impressive enough to anyone passing along Ooscanoto Plantations Road. The long line of fencing even aroused the praise of Timby Corrigan, who came by just after the job was finished and Nahum had gone his way.

"Right pretty sight, nephew." Timby, who carried a string of two catfish, rubbed his grizzled chin and stood back across the road, his boots planted in the muddy runoff from the previous day's shower. "Puts me in mind of how things looked when pa and ma was alive."

Nick nodded. He could see the improvement himself. Even the house looked better for it, set off at a slight distance from the road and its white frame of fence. The next and bigger job to tackle would be the barns, which lay closer to the creek and on the same low level as the house. Nick groaned at the thought of the work that would mean but it would certainly impress the Gaynors.

Timby slapped him on the back. "I just got some idea! How about you working on them pasture fences down by the creek? You doing such a good job here and all."

Nick stared at his uncle. *"Timby..."* Then he saw the older man's twinkle and gave up. In high spirits, an arm around each other's shoulders, they went into the house, where the job of dividing two catfish among five people was carefully worked out. Luckily as Amabel said there was still some cabbage stew left from last week. It was kept on the back of the stove each day and hadn't gone sour.

It was then that Nick, who was sore in every muscle and could hardly move, remembered business in Ashby Junction and excused himself... "I might as well have supper there, give me something to do while I'm waiting."

No one asked what he would be waiting for. They knew....

Amabel reminded him anxiously, "Aren't you going to see Dinah this evening?"

"They're all over at Wychfield Hall for dinner. I don't want to be up late, honey, so I should be home early. Dinah's mother's arriving on the New Orleans train tomorrow and I want to be on my good behavior with her. We still don't know what she thinks of our plans."

Amabel sighed and then reminisced with pride, "Ellen Gaynor and I went to Miss Pettigrew's Girls' School. Ellen was never popular. You-all wouldn't believe how few beaux she had at Bertha-Winn Wychfield's coming-out dance. My dance card was full and Ellen had just your father, Sean, on hers. He was only seventeen. And that Jem

Faire. Of course," she admitted, "all the girls made eyes at Jem."

"He was a good friend to pa and Timby. Pa always said so."

She kissed him. "Be a good boy."

"Be a lucky boy, you mean. But I'm not going yet. I've got to bathe and get into my best."

"Honestly, Nick, I do wonder at all your baths." She lowered her voice. *"That woman* is out back. She meant Rheba. "So you can't bathe in the tub."

Nick grimaced but didn't give up the bath. That and clean, new, expensive linen were all part of his gambler superstitions. Sure enough Rheba was out in the backyard drying curtains on long stretchers so Nick avoided the tub. It wasn't that he was embarrassed to be watched so avidly by Timby's woman, he told himself. But secretly he was always a little shaken by what he thought of as her evil eye. So not for the first time he went down to the creek, which acted as east boundary of the Corrigan land. He found his own dark, willow-hung pool, stripped and dove in. The cold water made all his bruises sting and didn't ease his tired muscles but at least he emerged with a little more energy, and after toweling himself a trifle less vigorously than usual, he reached for his stacked clean underwear. Rheba had made her way to the east end of the curtain stretcher and stood grinning over at him. He raised his eyebrows and shrugged, getting dressed slowly, refusing to give her the satisfaction of thinking she had put him at a disadvantage. Finally he got on his trousers and walked silently by her to the house, where his shirt, tie and coat and clean socks were laid out on his bed. Somehow he couldn't shake the feeling that the Cottonmouth, as he secretly thought of Rheba, was putting a curse on his plans for the evening.

He dressed carefully, remembering to polish his shoes. They were of excellent quality but cracked with wear, which a good thick polishing usually concealed.

He took the paved estate road into Gaynorville to avoid collecting dust on his shoes and well-cut coat. He looked back once and decided the long fence and gate were a good omen. They looked even better in the distance.

As he passed the Confederate Cemetery on the edge of town Nick was offered a ride by Captain Sholto in his new Ford Model T. Nick hesitated. He shared the family bitterness toward "the author of all their woes," as Amabel called Shelley Wychfield's father. On the other hand, a ride was a ride.

Sholto remarked, "You can't be dressed like that for Gaynorville. I'm off to Ashby and I'll bet you are too. I'm damned if I like talking to myself all the way."

This was a lot better than riding to the county seat with whatever driver obliged him on Gaynorville's main street. Nick had often gotten lifts from the girls who worked in the rooms above the Ashby hotel's parlor but he would just as soon not meet any of them tonight or any other night; if he did he had the news of his engagement all ready for them. . . .

"Funny. I was always leery of marriage, but now I don't mind telling the whole world," he remarked as he and Sholto chugged along Beauford Street past the elegant Gaynor Salon with its careful display of one opera glove, a beaded, layered evening gown and a pair of opera glasses.

Sholto said wryly, "That's not always the best of news to the whole world. And who are you telling in this whole world of yours, if I may ask?"

"I was thinking about the girls at the Parlor."

"Good god!" Sholto almost ran into a horse trough. "You haven't been talking to Dinah about Lily-Jo and her girls!"

"I had to. Your beloved daughter told Dinah first. And Dinah understands. There's a rare woman."

Sholto nodded.

Nick went on, "Lily-Jo's girls helped me more than once when I was in a bad spot. In business, that is. And they were always talking about what a great institution marriage was so I want to let them know that I've found the perfect woman for me." He saw Sholto's expression and laughed. "That may not be too smart, telling it quite that way."

Sholto agreed. "Not by a long shot."

He turned out to be a genial companion and it wasn't until they were almost within sight of Ashby's new six-story bank that Nick got around to the subject of his future with Dinah. "Matter of fact, I'm already beginning to feel like a family man," he said, watching for a reaction from Sholto, who gazed back at him.

"Just as well. You and Dinah look like you'd produce good stock. I reckon you're set on boys. Carry on the name."

Nick shrugged. "No matter to me. Long as they're healthy. Even if they're not, which God forbid."

"Well, I've never been sorry Shelley was a daughter. One of the main reasons I married Shelley's mother, matter of fact." Sholto seemed indifferent that he had told a comparative stranger a family secret. "I *almost* married your future mother-in-law. Ellen was about Dinah's age back in '85."

Nick looked at him. Sholto inhaled deeply, slapped the wheel and said, "Maggilee and me, we were two of a kind. It was better the way it worked out, but I'm going to be right there at the station tomorrow when Ellen comes in. In fact before I visit the Kents at the old Ironwood place tonight I thought I'd get the latest schedule for the northbound train. Make doubly sure I'm there at the right time tomorrow."

"You won't be alone."

"No. But frankly I don't think even Dinah is more anxious to see Ellen Gaynor than I am."

"Ellen Gaynor Faire," Nick reminded him, beginning to

think he wasn't the only man who was aching for his woman tonight.

"Not any more, my friend. Not any more. She's Ellen Gaynor again. Just as I've been a widower for these fifteen years. It's sort of fate bringing us together, he and Ellen, and she's not much changed, judging by the picture Dinah carries around of her."

"A picture of her and her late husband," Nick said. "Jem Faire was a good friend to my father and my uncle."

Sholto looked at him, said quietly and without emphasis, "He's dead and Ellen is alive. This isn't India, where the bereaved throw themselves on the funeral pyre."

It looked as though Ellen Gaynor Faire's visit was going to have more complications than Nick had suspected. . . .

He got off at the Ashby Hotel with many thanks and went in to survey any prospects who might wander from the hotel's dim, heavily furnished lobby to the adjoining dining room with its impressive luster chandelier and bracket lights. Here it was possible to eat a good southern-cooked dinner in complete innocence and then return to your hotel room—unless you climbed the red, plush-covered staircase at the back of the dining room which led to Lily-Jo Biedemeier's Parlor. The rest might be history, as far as various itinerant traveling men were concerned.

Mrs. Lily-Jo Beidemeier greeted Nick discreetly as he passed through the rather depressing Victorian lobby. Lily-Jo was a plump grandmotherly little woman. She kept her wispy hair a pale blonde, the only "advertising" she used for her trade since most decent ladies now found hair dye a mark of Mrs. Beidemeier's profession. Lily-Jo had once reminded Nick that in her grandmother's day half the respectable women dyed their hair, a trick as old as nature. All the same, as Lily knew quite well, nobody her age had natural hair that bright color. . . .

"Well I declare, if it isn't Mr. Corrigan!" she said now in

her twittery small voice. "It's been months, surely. Who's my rival, you naughty boy?"

He smiled at Lily-Jo. "You never had one—until recently. What live possibilities have you noticed for my game tonight?"

"Here and there, Nick. What did you mean—until recently?"

He put his hands on her shoulders and looked down at her. "*I'm* going to be married, which is why I'm here tonight."

"You gypsy devil! Do you mean what I think you mean? Bachelor's last night, and all? Tibby'll be happy. Nice, clean, healthy little creature, like all my girls. Always talking about you."

"No, darlin'. I mean I want Dinah to have a special engagement ring. Just as fine as anything she'd get if she married a Wychfield or a Vanderbilt. All I need are a few poker hands to make it . . ."

She stuck her round elbow into his ribs. "There's a pair of boys from down Bayou-way throwing their shinplasters around, asking for a poker game. I heard they stopped off to visit kinfolk and now they're headed north. Now, one of them's carrying a pistol. Not very reliable. Looks like a one-shot derringer."

"Where does he think he is? The Wild West?"

"No. Bound for Canada, I hear tell. I think they want to get into the war. So I reckon the derringer's to be used against the Kaiser." They both laughed. "They're never on the mark, those little palm guns. I used to have one but I got rid of it. Damn thing wouldn't hit a barn door if I aimed at it."

"Thanks. I'll avoid the derringer. Any other tips?"

"A stocking salesman looks good for a few hands. Sold some of his ware to my ladies. Good quality lisle, too . . . Only one thing to remember, those two Loo'siana boys'll be leaving when the northbound train gets in, so don't let yourself get caught with a good hand when the train arrives because they'll leave you cold. Lucky for you, the train's running four hours late, or so the station agent says."

"Thank you, Lily. Give my love to your good ladies."

He sauntered into the dining room, casually seeking out the Bayou boys and guessing at once which one carried the old-fashioned derringer. They were small good-looking Creoles, probably brothers, making their way through a bottle of powerful hill-country whiskey bought from some local boy. They looked quick-tempered and mean but they had all the signs of money and the elder was shuffling cards among the dishes at the dinnertable.

Clearly they had been chosen by a higher power to provide the price of Dinah's ring.

Chapter Ten

ELLEN Faire watched the familiar landmarks rush past into the darkness as the northbound train approached Ashby. A lucky delay of four hours had allowed her to make an earlier Lynchburg connection. Perhaps she should have spent the night in Lynchburg. Now she would have to stay over in Ashby but at least it was closer to home. In the morning she would make a phone call to Gaynor House.

But tonight after a late supper at the Ashby Hotel she would have a chance to walk through the streets, maybe even as far as the river bank. In the moonlight—although it loomed dark overhead right now—she would watch the sluggish Ooscanoto waters moving onward a few miles south past the closed and shuttered plantation house at Fairevale. There long ago she had lived very briefly as the wife of the old colonel, who had tried to salve her deep wounds when Bill Sholto jilted her. There too she had fallen in love with Colonel Faire's nephew, Jem, who had become her husband, and Dinah's father ... The river then flowed past Wychfield Hall and its neighbor to the south, Gaynor House, but Jem was everywhere, the memory of his face, the feel of him. She rubbed her palms together, pressed them to her eyes. In the warm darkness she recalled her husband's touch, his passionate, sometimes violent nature, his silent spells when only she could entice him into a good humor. And above all his tenderness. . . . "It's one of the attractions I sensed in Dinah's Nick," she thought. That and his vulnerability. Jem was never vulnerable in quite that way. I wonder, though, if Nick Corrigan can really be sincere in this affair. I never trusted Timby Corrigan, and as for Amabel . . . Jealousy tinged her girlhood memory of eighteen-year-old Amabel Corrigan with her tossing golden curls and her way with all the males. Well, poor Amabel had paid for her youthful triumphs. It was hard to know what would have become of the Corrigans after their hardworking parents' death if Shelley and her family hadn't donated hand-me-downs and employed Amabel to iron the Wychfield and Sholto linens. With Timby a drunk, his brother Sean dead in Cuba in '98 and Sean's son Nick an incurable gambler, they were considered a disgrace to the county. Still, there was guilt on the Gaynor House side. The Gaynors were responsible for the loss of the Corrigan farmlands. But talk of a wedding? . . . Did the Corrigans think Dinah had money?

Ellen looked out the train window, thought she could make out the rooftops of desolate Fairevale far to the south. No one has lived in the huge old house since the death of the old colonel's daughter, Eliza Faire Warrender. All it meant to Ellen tonight was one more memory of Jem, once Fairevale's overseer, her literal savior . . .

Two sailors came lurching through the car just then, knocked from seat to seat as the train rounded a curve. Their laughing, easy camaraderie reminded her suddenly of Bill Sholto. How strange that she had thought so little about the man who was once her great love! Was it *possible* she had actually considered suicide when she discovered the affair between her fiancé, and her mother? How could I have loved—heavens!—adored that man? Nothing but a cheap charmer . . . I hope Nick Corrigan isn't that sort, though he does have charm. Even I could see that. Did Bill Sholto really have anything or was he just a hollow man? . . . As the years passed, much of that first wild, desperate passion had blurred in her memory. During her ghastly visit back home four years ago after Jem's death all she could remember was that Sholto lived and Jem was dead—the rotten unfairness of it! Sholto at least had had the good grace to absent himself from the doings at Gaynor House and the neighboring estates. He had been pleasant when they'd met but fortunately never tried to bring up the past or remind her of what he had once been to her. She supposed she could thank him for that. . . .

She saw faint lights in the sky now, and was impressed. Since her last visit with Dinah, Ashby had built its first skyscraper—six stories piercing the beautiful night sky of Virginia. It was past nine o'clock and most southern towns were asleep by such an hour. It would be annoying if the hotel restaurant were closed. She should have had a lunch made up in Lynchburg while waiting for the eastern Virginia tidewater connection. Too late now.

By the time the train pulled into the Ashby station there were several passengers waiting—anything over four was impressive. The station agent came out to talk with the conductor while Ellen was helped down from her car by the porter.

"You're going to have two empty berths. Couple of young bucks from Baton Rouge got into a hot poker game. They're staying over. Taking tomorrow's run," the agent said.

The conductor shrugged, and almost before Ellen's old-fashioned valise with its petit-point cover was set beside her, someone swung a lantern back and forth at the rear of the train, the engine started chugging and she was nearly asphyxiated by a cloud of steam.

A small black boy of about ten had been sitting on his

haunches watching the excitement of arrival and departure. Now he jumped up and ran to Ellen, who was about to pick up her valise and start walking. "You goin' to hotel, ma'am? You don't want to get lost now. You got a nickel? I'll tote your bag."

Ellen would as soon have carried it herself. A nickel was five pennies, after all. But the boy's eagerness won her over and she agreed. As they made their way around behind the station and five blocks east through darkened quiet streets of warehouses and the tree-lined colored quarter, the boy looked at her suspiciously. "You been here before."

"I was born downriver near here." She smiled for the first time. It was the unexpectedness of her smile that usually made people aware of her particular beauty. Her usual expression was austere... she'd inherited a good deal of her grandmother Varina's quality—head held high and back straight, a perennial reminder that the Gaynors and the Dunmores were first families of Virginia.

The boy looked at her. "You born near Ashby, ma'am?"

"Gaynor House. Straight down that river behind us there."

"You one of them, ma'am? Ever'body knows them. Them and the Wychfields."

She looked back over her shoulder into the dark. If she and the boy were silent they could hear the water running smoothly at this season where East Creek and a branch of the Ooscanoto met to cascade over the stony bottoms around the big rocks in its path. Thirty years since she had really heard the Ooscanoto's pleasant autumn splash and hum. Or its spring roar as it poured along to flood the swamp area around Gaynor Ferry....

Good Lord, was it possible she was homesick? She smelled the late roses from a bush nearby, got a faint whiff of wild berries growing along the riverbank and just beginning to die. Thirty years ago, she recalled, I rode to Ashby one fall day on Cousin Jonathan's wagon seat between him and Bill Sholto. It was the first time Bill touched me . . . in that way, lifting me out of the wagon and then afterwards when we had that tussle on the riverbank . . . how scared I was that he'd see someone better-looking than me, like Amabel or Persis . . . or mama. And quickly lose interest in me! She could still feel the awful ache of wanting that man of the West who rode into town on his own cavalry horse just like someone in a southern romance. She'd been afraid from the very first that he would fall in love with her mother at first sight. Men always did, especially those who began by expressing an interest in her. But the secretiveness of that affair between Bill and Maggilee had been so awful . . . How could I feel anything at all for Bill Sholto, even at this minute? It's only a memory, the setting. Nothing else—

"You walk fast," the boy said.

"I do. I come from country where people have so far to go it's necessary to walk fast."

"Where? Where you come from?"

"Indian country. New Mexico."

"Gully!" Much impressed, he kept giving her little side glances, no doubt hoping she might shout out a war-whoop at any minute. "Ma'am?"

"Yes?"

"Why'd you make fists while you're walking?"

She hadn't been aware of it and hurriedly unclenched her fingers. That was what came of dwelling in the past. No more of that or she would wish she'd never returned home to set right her wildly romantic daughter . . .

The Ashby Hotel faced the main square of the town opposite the new skyscraper and the white brick colonial courthouse with its pillars. There was more of a bustle here than Ellen recalled in the past—more people on the street and surprisingly many parked automobiles. Her old familiar county seat had clearly entered the twentieth century with a vengeance. She walked up the stone steps, crossed the veranda under the interested gaze of several cigar-smoking men and entered the lobby, wondering why on earth no one thought to cheer up the depressing gloom of this darkly furnished Victorian relic.

The desk clerk, seeing a middle-aged woman in a worn skirt and jacket with a travel-tired look about her blue-gray eyes, put on a correct but reproving air. "Madam, we have no vacancies. You might try the Ashby Junction Commercial House. It's three blocks back toward the river—that is —the station. You must have passed it. You, boy!" He looked down at Ellen's young friend. "You take the lady to the Commercial House."

He was just turning away from the desk in dismissal when those still lovely blue-gray eyes of hers flashed at him and an icy voice reinforced their look. "I think you may find you have room for me somewhere. Be so kind as to give me a pen and I will register. Ellen Dunmore Gaynor Faire."

He dropped the pen in his haste to offer it to her, almost giving her the pointed end, all the time aware of the boy's giggle. It was annoying to reflect that his eagle eye had failed him for once. Why hadn't he noticed her neat, dove-gray gloves and hat, the excellent quality of the traveling suit and above all the imperious carriage of that tall figure which was still excellent and very much in the new slender mode?

"Of course, Miss—Mrs. Faire. Ashby'd be a mighty poor sight if it didn't have room for a relation of the late Miss Varina Gaynor."

"Her granddaughter."

"Just so, just so. And related to the Faires as well. Sad, isn't it, ma'am? That wonderful old Fairevale empty for years. The last of the Faires gone. Unless you, ma'am . . ." he ended delicately.

"I have no son."

"Sad."

"I don't find it so. I'm very fond of my daughter. Do you have another inkwell? This one is dry." She held the pen up delicately in one gloved hand.

He swung around, signaled to an ancient porter leaning with folded arms against a wooden pillar. The porter didn't move quickly enough, and the desk clerk snapped his fingers. "An inkwell for Mrs. Faire. Mrs. Gaynor Faire. Now, ma'am, it so happens we have a right nice little parlor and bedroom that we hold for our special patrons. It has a fine view of our new skyscraper, a branch of the Richmond and Dominion Bank—"

"That won't be necessary. I'm only staying the night. In the morning I will telephone to Gaynor House. You do have telephone service?"

"Certainly, ma'am. What—ah—accommodations would you prefer?"

"A small quiet single room will be sufficient."

"Right away. That is, we've had three guests check out. They just left on the northbound. We'll have your room ready in—say—half an hour? Meanwhile . . ." He didn't know what this surprising woman was going to demand next.

"Very well. I'll have my dinner. I notice your dining room is still open." And noisy. Loud voices, good humor, the clatter of silver, china and glassware.

The clerk seemed uncomfortable. "Matter of fact a few gentlemen waiting for the train—the—ah—Tidewater and Northern—have gotten up a friendly poker game. Perfectly harmless. Several other patrons are just finishing their supper. And the kitchen is staying open to oblige our poker friends."

"They must be waiting for *tomorrow*'s northbound." She smiled. "I've no objection. Where I come from I've played a little poker myself. You may serve me at an adjoining table."

He looked flabbergasted at the idea that this lady played

poker but quickly agreed. Meanwhile she paid the little boy his nickel in carefully counted pennies, then was shown to the clerk's own toilet and washroom and allowed the freedom of the little cubbyhole.

When she emerged refreshed with her waist changed to a lace-collared, feminine silk blouse, her hat off and her whitening hair worn softly in a bun with tendrils waving over her austere temples, she surprised the clerk again by looking almost beautiful. He ordered the bellman to signal him if any other patrons arrived and escorted Ellen to the dining room. She gratified him by remarking on the gleaming lights. "This is more like it."

"The—er—old days. Yes . . . not of course that you would remember them at your age, ma'am."

Her side look showed no offense, only amusement. "My dear sir, I was born in the last months of the Civil War. This is quite another world."

"And not nearly so fine from all I hear."

"You hear wrong. We almost starved to death. I'll take that table."

The table for four was at the far end of the room immediately below a red-carpeted staircase and just within hearing of the five men at the poker table. The desk clerk hesitated, suggested she would be more comfortable at the front of the long room where a few scattered diners, mostly men alone, were still at coffee and cigars. One pair, honeymooners or less legitimate lovers, left the room just as Ellen, insisting on her choice of a table, was seated with a flourish by the desk clerk.

As the only woman at this end of the room, Ellen felt no embarrassment at all. Many a time in Lariat or even in Santa Fe where she was also well known Ellen had eaten in the company of far tougher men than these. And she had never known any such fear here in Virginia. No . . . her terrors in those early days had always been of a different sort, roused by jealousy of a mother who succeeded in winning away every young man she admired. Fortunately in the end she had found that the fierce, singleminded passion of Jem Faire was what she had really wanted all the time. . . .

"This will do very nicely, thank you," she told the clerk. "Will you send a waiter with a menu?" She had peeled off her kid gloves and now blew into them as she had been taught by grandmother Varina, then smoothed them out on the white tablecloth while studying the menu that had been presented to her with a flamboyant sweep of the desk clerk's arm. "Oyster stew, soft-shell crabs—if they are tidewater. Stewed corn and strawberries. And coffee. Strong. Serve it now."

"Strong, ma'am?"

She smiled patiently. "No milk. No cream. Strong."

He went away in a slight daze. Ladies drank half coffee, half milk. Or cocoa or tea. And occasionally on holidays a julep or other fruity liquor. The world was surely changing.

While Ellen ate her oyster stew, probably reheated at this hour, and drank her coffee, she also tried to overhear the game going on at the table next to hers, entertaining herself by judging which player would win the hand.

An old, majestic-looking man with beetling brows and mustache of woolly white hair was nearest her. All that hair recalled her babyhood when every gentleman was hairy, in the face at any rate. She had never liked it, remembering Jem's Indian-hard shaved face, strong and sensual. Bill Sholto, she recalled wore a neat mustache . . . she should have been guided by her dislike of mustaches.

There were two small dark men at the table, almost pretty. Both of them were angry-looking. Though they looked foreign and even raised or called loudly with a slight accent, she suspected they were Americans from New Orleans. They appeared to talk a good deal, perhaps a system of theirs, a trick to upset their opponents. If so, it didn't seem very successful to Ellen, although she saw that the taller of the two had accumulated a neat little stack of chips. The fourth hand, a fat, drunken salesman, kept offering free lisle hose to his opponents if they'd "deal me a hand I can stand on." The fifth and last player had been hidden by the majestic old man who was dealing. Now a young man leaned forward carelessly knocking over his small stack of chips. Or was he careless? She wondered. She had seen the trick before, that deceptive indifference that threw others off guard. She watched his unusually long fingers, which were badly scratched and cut up. What had *he* been up to recently? Most gamblers were very cautious with their hands . . . Interested in this man she felt the others would do well to take more seriously, she studied his face, the profile with the prominent nose and mouth, and with a start recognized Nick Corrigan, the upstart who wanted to marry her daughter. Was he a professional or an amateur gambler? It seemed to matter very much at this moment. A decent, hardworking gentleman might gamble for recreation. She had grown up in the South with this notion. But a professional gambler was on a par with a hopeless drunkard. . . . She turned her chair slightly for a clearer view of the players, the pot being built up and especially Nick Corrigan, to whom she had taken a sudden dislike. She watched his eyes, which looked ingenuous and trustworthy when he opened them wide, and she could see why her daughter had become infatuated with him. No denying his attraction. Which was going to make it all the harder to dissuade Dinah, who had her father's iron will and might insist on going through with this marriage out of sheer stubborn loyalty. . . . Watching the way Nick gathered his chips in a sloppy little pile, Ellen frowned. A schemer and an actor, of course. It was all pretense, including the way he rubbed a finger thoughtfully over his clean-shaven lip and cheek.

A few minutes later after her observation had been interrupted by the arrival of the next course she discovered an odd fact about the other players. They didn't seem to be taking Nick Corrigan seriously. They exchanged knowing little glances, especially when Nick reached often for what appeared to be a whiskey glass. Was he a drinker as well as a gambler? She noticed that the young Louisianans emptied their glasses at a good rate but like most drinkers fondly imagined everyone else drank more. Nick's careless pile of chips diminished slowly. He seldom opened but usually stayed when the stakes were worth it. Ellen had no way of knowing whether he was winning or losing, since she didn't know how he had entered the game, but the longer she watched him the more convinced she became that he knew very well what he was doing. The garrulous fat salesman won big and lost big. The old patriarch was losing steadily and to Ellen's surprise began to exhibit signs indicating a quiet drunk. Nick repeatedly ordered fresh rounds for all and appeared to be drinking steadily.

Abruptly she heard a woman's voice on the red-carpeted staircase above her. The woman spoke so softly that Ellen had to look up to understand her, seeing a comfortably stout little female with dyed blonde hair. "You seem like you know the game, ma'am."

Ellen nodded, and combining the dyed hair with the red staircase guessed the woman's profession. No wonder the desk clerk had tried to keep her away from this end of the room at this hour. . . .

The woman caught her smile and ventured, "Nice boys, all of them. Just a little game in fun. You a lady drummer, I mean a traveling saleslady? We don't get too many of them down here."

"No. I'm visiting friends downriver." This woman seemed to know the players well. Ellen decided she might learn something about Nick Corrigan without revealing her real interest. She looked up, motioning the woman to a vacant chair at her table. "I hate eating alone. Would you care to have dessert with me, Mrs.—Mrs.—"

"Biedemeier, ma'am. Well, I . . ." She shrugged and laughed. "Why not? It would pleasure me, ma'am, if it's all the same to you."

She seated herself daintily after a quick look at the far end of the room to make sure none of the hotel employees were watching. Probably very highly thought of in her profession . . .

Ellen said, "I see you know the players. Are they professionals?"

"Oh, my land, no! Not most of them. The handsome young one there, he might be considered a professional. But I've never seen him pull a cheat."

A squabble seemed to have built up between the two Louisianans and the present dealer, the stocking salesman.

Ellen gestured toward the pair. "Are they brothers?"

Mrs. Biedemeier rolled her eyes. "No, no, ma'am. You took me wrong. The gentleman I'm talking about, he's on that side of the table. Nicholas Corrigan, the one with all the black hair that needs combing. The two you're talking about are from Baton Rouge. I'm keeping an eye on them, you may be sure."

So that was how Nick Corrigan won! "You mean you're signaling this Corrigan?"

Mrs. Biedemeier waved away her accusation. "I told you, Mr. Corrigan don't—doesn't cheat. But those Baton Rouge boys, they've got itchy tempers and this nice town's not for them. They've been making trouble all evening, but Mr. Corrigan and the rest of the gentlemen have kept things calm so far. You lean forward just a little. See the older brother? It's a little tiny gun that makes his chest stick out on this side."

"A derringer?" Ellen wanted to laugh. She hadn't seen such a weapon since her childhood in Virginia. "I should have stayed in Lariat. Even back there derringers at poker tables sound old-fashioned."

But Mrs. Biedemeier kept her vigil. Obviously she had a deep interest in Nick Corrigan, which was also not very reassuring to Ellen. She pursued the matter. "You and Mr. Corrigan . . . are old friends?"

"In a manner of speaking. I'm old enough to be his mother and he kind of thinks of me like that."

Ellen found this interesting . . . after all, it wasn't every young man who boasted of having the madam of a brothel for a second mother. On the other hand, very likely Nick Corrigan didn't brag too widely about his acquaintance with Mrs. Biedemeier.

Voices at the poker table suddenly became clearer to the two women. Apparently Nick Corrigan had won the pot. The elder of the two Louisianans set his whiskey glass down noisily and reached out across the table. "You walking off with my chips there, m'sieu."

"Am I?" Nick's voice was quiet. "How many are yours?" He took two of the chips and tossed them across the table.

The other two players protested the Louisianan's complaint. The old patriarch began, "Now, see here—" The fat salesman took it up as the two brothers rose, recognizing Corrigan's insult.

"Wait, boys. Some of that was the last raise. You boys threw in but I called with them very chips," the salesman said anxiously.

The elder of the Louisianans stiffened. He was standing straight now, with his brother beside him, less steady on his feet. Though Nick remained seated, he managed to dominate the two hot-tempered men.

"Thank you, Mr. Avery. And you, Randy." Nick nodded to his defenders, then settled back, studying the two seething brothers. "What will make you happy and send you on your way, gentlemen?"

"You don't laugh at me, *putain!*"

Ellen couldn't believe this was happening, certainly not in the town of Ashby. Mrs. Biedemeier got up, tipping over the chair, and called loudly, "Gentlemen!" but no one paid any attention to her.

"We surely don't laugh at you," Corrigan said. "Why don't you run along before we do?" He waited. Ellen sensed that he knew what he was doing even though she thought he was a bit crazy. While the brothers worked themselves into a rage he kept a self-possession that Ellen found impressive in a man who looked as though he himself had a quick temper.

The other players put in loudly, urging the brothers to forget it, but they had gone too far to back down now. While Ellen wondered if this was all a nightmare, the older brother said furiously, "We leave when we have our money from this card cheat."

"Wait, wait, sir, you're really not William S. Hart," the desk clerk said, and punctutated it with anxious laughter as he hurried the length of the room, dodging empty tables.

The younger brother was whispering, "Calm, Raoul, be calm—"

But Raoul already had a hand inside the breast of his coat and under his armpit. Such an end to the game had sobered the other players. Both the patriarch and the fat man tried to make peace.

"Nobody cheated, mister. We was in it. We saw."

"You wa'nt cheated, Frenchie—"

"Raoul de Corfe, if you please. And I am American."

"Right, Mr. Rawl. We seen that last play. Weren't nothing wrong. Hell, I dealt. And them chips Mr. Corrigan give you was thrown in by me." Meanwhile, the desk clerk had reached the brothers and slipped behind the armed one for a stranglehold.

All of this was probably more excitement than Ashby Junction had seen since the Civil War, but Ellen found herself suddenly and unexpectedly anxious about Nick's safety. She despised his profession but she admired his nerve and his apparent skill at reading his opponents. It wouldn't surprise her to discover that he had led these hot-tempered brothers to this point, where they would be evicted after he had won a large pot fairly. But it was dangerous and she suspected he knew it.

The desk clerk was now struggling with the armed man while various noises from the other players, including the younger brother, provided a chorus for the scene.

Nick pushed the pile of chips across the table, waving them toward the younger brother. "You two really must be desperate. Adam will cash these in for you. Call it our local charity."

Everyone who heard this looked impressed by Nick's grandiose gesture. After all, he had won fairly and squarely. But it was obvious that Nick enjoyed his own theatrics as much as the winning.

Ellen stood up, and her abrupt movement distracted Nick, who looked away from the fight between the angry Raoul de Corfe and the hard-breathing desk clerk, reinforced now by the waiter.

De Corfe's hand was being wrenched from his armpit just as Nick recognized Ellen Faire. He started up in surprise, and some chagrin, and at the same instant the derringer across the table went off and scored a near-miss through Nick's coat sleeve.

In seconds the two brothers were hustled out of the dining room, the younger pocketing the chips, and Nick was surrounded by shocked spectators. He got up, waving away his fellow poker players and Mrs. Biedemeier, trying to reach through the crowd to take Ellen Faire's hand. It was Ellen who first noticed the fine trickle of blood crawling inexorably into her palm from his. Nick shared her surprise, also directing a look at her that she couldn't fail to understand . . . he didn't want any more fuss and embarrassment in front of all these people.

Ellen said quickly, "Come with me, Mr. Corrigan," before Mrs. Biedemeier or the fat salesman could offer their help.

As everyone stared at their backs, they went out hand-in-hand, which surprised everyone, and none more than Mrs. Biedemeier.

Outside the dining room Nick said, "I'm all right, Mrs. Faire. It can't be very serious and I'm leaving anyway—"

"Don't tell me you intend to drive home tonight with that hand bleeding the way it is!"

He smiled. "No. I've a friend who's picking me up. Matter of fact, he's your friend too. Shall I get your things and we'll wait for him in the lobby?"

"Who is it?"

But Nick wouldn't say. It made Ellen uncomfortable and while she was washing the open cut on his wrist where the bullet had grazed the flesh, she kept trying to imagine which friend of Nick's she could possibly know so well.

Chapter Eleven

ELLEN sensed that Nick Corrigan was in considerable discomfort from the furrow carved through the fleshy part of his arm above the wrist. It had taken several minutes to stop the persistent bleeding, but he still refused to have a doctor called in. She suspected he was trying to put on a brave front for his future mother-in-law and certainly didn't like him the less for that. At least all this excitement had lessened tension at her unexpected arrival a day early. . . .

"You may as well call me Ellen," she suggested when his wrist had been wrapped and he was thanking her. He sat down abruptly on the edge of the chair that the desk clerk pushed forward, then apologized and started to get up. But even his swarthy complexion looked a little green, and she said quickly, "Please don't be silly. Rest. I don't want you collapsing on my hands."

Which made him so indignant that nothing less than a cannonade would have seated him in her presence after that. Gallantly he offered her his good left arm and suggested they go outside to wait for their ride to Gaynor House.

"Who is this obliging chauffeur—my brother-in-law,

Marsh Wychfield, I suppose? I hope that means he's feeling much better," she said as she accepted his good arm and then they strolled to the front doors, which were opened for them by the porter rushing forward. Minutes later he set Ellen's valise beside them on the veranda. Upon Ellen's inquiry about the cost of the room she hadn't used, the desk clerk, arriving late, refused to accept anything except the price of her dinner, adding, "We're always right pleased to oblige your family, ma'am."

After he had left them Nick remarked lightly, "Your name has more magic than mine, it seems." Then, perhaps because he had, after all, had a difficult evening . . . he'd even given away his winnings . . . he added, "I hope Dinah doesn't feel she's making a bad trade—a Corrigan for a Gaynor."

"*Faire.*"

Like Bill Sholto he had almost forgotten. "I beg pardon. I meant Faire, of course."

He sensed this hadn't gone far enough as an apology and she half expected him to begin to use all his charm to win her over. Had he really believed she would welcome such a man as her daughter's husband, the father of her children? A professional gambler? As if that wasn't bad enough, he was an improvident gambler who contemptuously threw away what looked like several hundred dollars for effect. The least he might have done, since he had won fairly, was to keep that last pot. Ellen, a practical woman, felt it difficult to admire such nonsense. She waited for him not to focus his engaging manner on her. From Ellen's experience with the tin horn gamblers who had traveled through Lariat for the past twenty-five years and more, Nick Corrigan should be making excuses. Attempting to borrow money from her might take him a little longer.

Oddly enough he made no effort to win her over after her rebuff about her name, and she found it uncomfortable waiting beside him in silence. He looked distant. Maybe he was truly suffering from the echo of his injury. She began to regret snapping at him when he forgot her married name. She didn't know whether she was more annoyed or impressed by his unexpected pride. She had to keep reminding herself that he was only an itinerant gambler and would, of course, be a disastrous husband for Dinah. Of course . . .

He looked off toward the dimly lighted street that ran along the far side of the skyscraper. "There he is now."

She saw car lights and made out the stiff, upright silhouette of a Ford. It was going to be uncomfortable riding for the three of them—Nick Corrigan, herself and the driver. He must be one of the Wychfield neighbors . . . unless, unless he was Bill Sholto . . .

Her heart began to pound in the most ridiculous way as she made out the well-remembered features of the man driving toward the hotel steps. *Damn* him. She had stopped loving Bill Sholto thirty years ago, and had almost stopped hating him by the time she married Jem. Never at any moment during the years of her marriage to Jem had she wanted to be in Bill Sholto's arms. But now the awful pain of Jem's loss had numbed, and with her arrival in Virginia she found time had turned backward to those wildly uncertain days of her girlhood when she thought Captain William Sholto was just about everything she wanted in life. She could look back from the present and laugh over that romantic girl. Except she remembered those long-ago feelings too clearly. . . .

"Don't tell me that's Bill Sholto," she muttered to Nick, who now seemed to be in a better humor. Apparently he thought she would be pleased at the idea of meeting Sholto.

"He says he used to be your beau, as he calls it."

"In a manner of speaking. To tell you the truth I found he was pretty much everybody's beau."

He laughed, and the sound of that laugh reminded her, by a reverse logic, that the Corrigans had once blamed

Sholto for all their misfortunes. It was partly true, but still they had managed to remain friendly with the Gaynor House family, even if partly to save face. In spite of Nick's apparent friendship with Sholto, Ellen thought some of that resentment must remain. . . .

She had her feelings under control by this time and was able to walk down the steps to the street holding Nick's good arm with a serene expression and an easy, slightly aloof smile. She could see that Nick thoroughly enjoyed her unexpected meeting with Bill Sholto, though she didn't know exactly why. She had met Sholto again briefly four years ago when she'd come East with Dinah after Jem's funeral. At that time the sight of him had turned her stomach, seeing him alive while her beloved Jem was dead. She had made her feelings plain without saying anything—maybe *because* she said nothing to him. The next day Sholto had gone off to Norfolk and Portsmouth "on business."

But something had clearly changed over these past years . . . When Sholto saw her he killed the motor in his excitement and gave out a shout that aroused several near-comatose folks on the veranda. "By the eternal, it's the snow maiden . . . Honey, we get you one day sooner than we expected. How's that for good luck, Nick?"

He reached for Ellen and though she protested he lifted her up onto the seat of the car, then jumped in behind the wheel. "Nick, you crank her up and we'll get started. Not like the old days in those rickety wagons of Jonathan's, is it, Ellen?"

She resented his reminding her of that first ride with him, particularly as she was thinking of it herself. She was quick to say, "Don't let Mr. Corrigan crank the car. He had a slight accident and his right arm is giving him some trouble."

Nick wasn't pleased that she had called attention to his injury—the result of bad company and his profession—but his pride didn't reach the point of stupidity. He made no protest, got into the car on Ellen's other side and Bill Sholto leaped out in high spirits to crank up.

By the time they chugged out of Ashby Junction, avoiding a hay wagon stopped in the middle of the highway with the tenant farmer asleep or drunk on the seat, Sholto asked about Nick's "accident." Nick hesitated and Ellen realized he didn't want the truth revealed if he could help it. She explained that "there was someone in the hotel—a drunk, I suppose—shooting up the place. Mr. Corrigan—" She caught Nick's grateful look and amended—"Nick accidentally got in the way. He was grazed. It was quite exciting for a while."

Sholto asked a few more questions, then changed the subject and got into trouble again by assuming Ellen was in Virginia to witness her daughter's wedding to Nick Corrigan. Ellen felt the tension in Nick as she evaded the issue, none too subtly when Sholto asked what date they had fixed.

"I haven't discussed it with Dinah. As a matter of fact I haven't discussed anything with her."

Sholto subsided and made a great pretense of studying the dark road ahead. "This county gets more backward every day. Are we ever going to have decent lights on this road?"

Ellen was angry . . . she was allowing herself to feel guilty over Nick Corrigan. A bond had been forged between them tonight and if she wanted to be melodramatic she could say it had been forged in Nick's blood. And here she was, fully planning to persuade Dinah that romantic young men might be delightful but that they didn't wear too well. What made it even worse was that she liked him . . . But a gambler, reckless to the point of idiocy, burdened with a drunken uncle Timby and a hopeless aunt Amabel —*no,* she was right. Marriage to Nick Corrigan would be a disaster. . . .

Ellen was not eager to be left alone with Bill Sholto,

but she could foresee problems if Nick came on to Gaynor House with them. Dinah would assume at once that her mother had given her blessing to Nick Corrigan's proposal. The car was nearing the newly painted Corrigan fences which looked handsome and impressive even on this overcast night and Ellen said in her most motherly voice, "I suggest you get a good night's sleep, Nick. If you have any trouble with that arm, you call Dr. Nickols."

Sholto shook his head at Ellen's ignorance about her home country. "Nickols? Honey, poor old Doc Nickols has been under the sod for ten years at least."

Nick understood what she was trying to tell him and said, "You may be right, Mrs. Faire. I'll get out here." He swung down, started to the big white gate but turned and said clearly to Ellen, "You'll give my love to Dinah . . ."

She caught the flash of his white teeth but wasn't naive enough to suppose his smile was a friendly one. She said quietly, "I will, Nick."

"*Thank* you, Mrs. Faire."

There was no mistaking the sarcasm in it, and she was relieved when Sholto drove on. He finally broke the nervous silence between them by reaching out one hand to hers. "Well, sweetheart?"

She moved her gloved fingers away. "Well, captain?"

"Shall I tell you what you're thinking? Along this road on a night like this?"

"Shall I tell you how wrong you are? I wasn't reliving the night I almost made the mistake of letting you seduce me. And yes I remember those kisses and all that went with them. It was right along there where the clump of dogwood used to be. Or was it a few yards farther?"

After a long look at her, he settled over the wheel with one of those crooked grins she had once adored . . . It was not unattractive even today . . . "Ellen, people always used to say you took after that eagle-eyed old harridan, Varina

Gaynor," he was saying. "You know, I'm beginning to believe it."

"You always got on well with grandma, she'd be pleased to know you think I'm like her."

"Even her sarcasm. I'm sorry, Ellen, I couldn't help being glad you were here." He looked ready to stop the car right here on the Ooscanoto Estate Road to repeat the old, painful moments between them. She pointed at the wheel. He didn't stop the car but kept religiously to fifteen miles an hour. "I was in love with you then, Ellen, though I don't expect you ever believed it afterwards. The truth is, Maggilee was my own kind . . . You were better off the way things turned out—"

And he pulled her to him with one arm when she thought he had given up and kissed her hard on the mouth. Taken by surprise she stiffened and then just as she felt her own lips respond, he let her go. She said with a false calm, "Actually, I was thinking about that young man. If looks could kill I'd be dead now. Nick Corrigan certainly hates me."

"Can't say I blame him." Sholto surprised her by his sympathy for one of the family he had injured all those years ago. "Nick Corrigan tries hard. Has a big responsibility with that worthless family. The father and mother and Sean were good people. But that's all."

By this time they were swinging around the pebble drive in front of the white colonial house that had been her birthplace.

Edward Hone, who had been butler and majordomo for almost as long as Ellen could remember, heard the car and came out onto the east porch. A man who seldom showed his emotions, he broke old habits when he saw Ellen, and before Sholto could get out and come around to lift Ellen down as in the old days, he was there offering Ellen his gloved hand exactly as he had when she was coming home from the Young Ladies' School or from a local ball at

Wychfield or Fairevale. His regal manner had always given her more confidence in herself, even after a disastrous evening as a wallflower. . . .

"Home again, Miss Ellen?" Hone asked as she walked with him to the east porch. "This time for good. At least that's what we're all hoping."

She was grateful but reminded him, "It's no longer my house, you know. Maggilee—I mean mother—left it to Miss Shelley."

"That's because Miss Maggilee knew Miss Shelley would need it. Not you." Ellen should have remembered that Edward Hone would never allow a criticism of her mother. She didn't mind, she respected his loyalty to Maggilee, who had kept her mother-in-law Varina, her child Ellen and her dead husband's cousin Jonathan from starving during the dark years after the War Between the States. The Gaynor Dress Salon had begun with a few clever gowns made for the wives who came down from the North with the Freedman's Bureau. Her mother's moral lapses, which had caused Ellen such agony could not cancel out the debt of life itself which so many owed to Maggilee Gaynor.

Ellen walked now into the main hall, which crossed the house to the river parlor, passing the curving white staircase leading to the bedrooms, including the one in which she had been born. She could almost feel her mother's vivid presence everywhere within these walls—the small, fragile-looking woman with a mop of auburn hair and a deceptive strength. . . . She was briefly startled to see a woman of about thirty moving gracefully down the stairs. The dim hall light dulled the glow of her hair but even before this apparition stepped into the light of the river parlor Ellen wondered how she could ever have confused her half sister Shelley with her mother Maggilee. Undoubtedly Shelley was as beautiful, her bright hair a fiery gold, her complexion flawless, her manners perfect, but she was fully conscious of all these. Maggilee had never been aware of her beauty except as a tool to use when in need of a bank loan or in a similar crisis. This very indifference to her assets was one of the qualities that had won Maggilee lovers and admirers.

Shelley was pleased to see her much older half sister a day early. Relieved too, if Ellen was any judge. Shelley must be frantic about her niece marrying one of the Corrigan family, whom Shelley mostly regarded as a source of servants for Gaynor House.

"Well, forevermore! If it isn't Sister Ellen! Come right here." They hugged, Shelley waving to the captain over Ellen's shoulder. "Papa, how did you guess she was coming tonight?" To his daughter Bill Sholto looked more excited than she'd seen him in all the years since Maggilee's death. Even Ellen was aware of the captain's reaction and told herself she was pleased only out of a sense of revenge ... except was it revenge that had made her enjoy that kiss moments ago out in his Ford car? ... She kept thinking what it would have meant to her if he had actually cared this deeply for her thirty years ago. It was useless speculation ... if she had married Bill Sholto she couldn't have married Jem, and for all she knew she might be in her grave as Maggilee was now. But deep within her that old attraction pulled her toward him even now....

She was looking around anxiously for Dinah when a tall girl slipped up behind her and caught her in a bear hug. "Mom, you're a day early! What a darling you are ... now we'll have longer to talk about Nick before you meet him."

"Hello, dear. You're looking well. Having a good time?" Ellen was the self-contained, unruffled woman Dinah had always admired but her embrace was just as unrestrained as her daughter's. The two women understood each other very well. Reared by her grandmother Varina in that strict and careful school of manners, Ellen's love was undemonstrative but her passion was there and Dinah recognized it just as her father Jem had.

Dinah hugged her again. "It will be a good time. When you've met him, I mean *really* met him, you'll adore each other. Tonight's the first night in a week that I haven't seen him. Daisy Wychfield wanted us for dinner but he wouldn't come. Daisy is going to give a ball for our engagement. Mother? You've got that sphinx look . . . all inscrutable. What's wrong?"

They were all looking at Ellen. Even Marsh Wychfield, who had come in with Dinah and was now kissing Ellen's cheek. Tired as Ellen was after the long journey she knew her day hadn't ended yet. She would have to spoil that bright excitement in Dinah's face and the worst of it was that these people all had guessed exactly why Ellen had come, except the person she loved best in the world.

"Dinah," she began, "I know the folks will excuse us if you come up and help me change these dusty clothes."

"Of course, do," Shelley urged quickly with a glance at her husband and then at her father, who hadn't taken his eyes off Ellen.

Dinah went up the stairs ahead of her mother, describing on the way many of the fascinations of her own journey with Nick but omitting a few vital details.

Ellen, almost hating herself, had never seen her look happier.

Chapter Twelve

FOR Nick Corrigan the day had been a disaster. Only his anger against that Gaynor woman kept him from being overwhelmed by depression as he looked at the white fences and the handsomely reset white gate. All that physical labor, never his strong point, had gone for nothing. It certainly hadn't impressed that Gaynor witch... to her the Corrigan property was still trash, a scar on the landscape. Nothing, it seemed, would change those arrogant snobs at Gaynor House.

Except, he hoped, Dinah. No question... she wanted him. He couldn't be wrong about the physical part of their love. He'd known plenty of other women and he knew when a woman was pretending and when she really cared. He couldn't even remember the others now... for him there was just this girl, and only her... He had to allow himself at least a flash of hope that Dinah might ignore all that motherly advice he knew she would be getting... probably at this very moment.

He stopped, looked at the porch. Even in the dark he could imagine the dust, the blown leaves and the porch rail where the recent showers had soaked through an entire season's dust and formed a hundred dirty rivulets. Someone had left an old overstuffed chair on the porch with its insides leaking out and strewn over the porch underfoot. Nick shuddered . . . they made him think of the viscera of some dead animal.

Amabel's voice came to him through the darkness. "Bad run of luck, Nick?"

He smiled and ruffled her hair. "You might call it that."

"Hmm. No engagement ring tonight." She gave this a few seconds' thought, then said, "I don't reckon you know Dinah at all."

"No, you're probably right—"

"Oh, Nick! That's not what I meant. Dinah loves *you*. Why, honey, her whole life is all wrapped up with you."

He took a big breath of the cool night air that smelled of the woods and fields and the flowing creek nearby. "Amabel, darlin', if you're right . . . well, we'll see." He started into the house, then stopped. "How did I ever think I could bring Dinah into this pigsty—?"

"This is silly talk when you know perfectly well you're going to bring her here. We could do some cleaning . . . don't worry. And Timby will be glad to help out. If we had those snap beans sold and the berries down by the creek we'd have the money to hire one of the Finch tenants' girls to help too."

"Well, don't worry about that now. I'll get some money, there's a game at Norfolk Tuesday night. I've always been lucky over on the coast, but all this isn't going to do any good if Ellen turns loose all that elegant Gaynor persuasion on Dinah. She's very fond of her mother, you know—"

"She's *more* fond of you. You're a gambler, Nick. Bet you a ten-cent piece I'm right."

Maybe things wouldn't be so depressing once the house was fixed up . . . He might start to work tomorrow morning early, or better yet tonight. Dinah would at least come to tell him her decision tomorrow, maybe early. There was still time. There were two hours until midnight. After that it was another day. Maybe a better one . . .

In the parlor he took his coat off with some difficulty, and Amabel shrieked at sight of him. "Blood! Oh, my God! It's come to this—"

His nerves snapped. "Don't be such a damned idiot, Amabel. It was an accident."

Amabel's outcry brought Timby and Rheba Moon in from the kitchen. Timby saw the dark stains and the ruined shirt and jumped to the same conclusion. " 'Tis that wicked Sholto. I saw you leave together. He steals our land and now he shoots my nephew. Holy saints! I'll go up and settle with that murderin' Bluecoat once and for all. Where's my shotgun, woman?"

He started into the hall in search of a weapon and it took a running leap and a grab by Nick's good arm to stop him. "Timby, it was a *gambler* and he's long gone north to Canada. Forget it."

"A Canadian trying to kill you? You can't trust a living soul these days, not a soul."

Nick smiled, sent Amabel to bed, asked Rheba to go heat a bag of salt for her and watched as Timby went off to his room too with what remained of some home-distilled whiskey from distant connections in the Blue Ridge Mountains.

Nick felt relieved. If they weren't going to help him they were better off in their own rooms, out of his way. It was almost a pleasure at first, wielding a broom wrapped in wet cloth with his good arm so long as he didn't have to solve any more of his family's problems.

He had worked his way around the front half of the parlor when Rheba came to join him in a cotton bathrobe molded tightly to her full body. At this point Nick would have used anyone, but Rheba's suggestive manner was more tiring than provocative after the kind of day he'd had and he promptly set her to work with curt instructions.

The considerable pain he now felt brought back the depression he'd felt earlier . . . he'd been crazy to start this damn housecleaning siege in the first place . . . Dinah wouldn't be coming here anyway, certainly not in the near future . . . But it at least seemed a distraction from his desperate fear of losing Dinah. As he worked he kept telling himself that the Corrigans were as good as her people, they were all descended from Adam and Eve, weren't they? . . . and this house might be shabby but it could be as clean as Gaynor House and . . . By midnight, though, the angry determination had worn off; his arm throbbed until he wanted to groan, though that was the last thing he would do in front of Rheba. Like a drunkard the morning after he couldn't imagine how he could have begun this wild business in the first place . . . And he couldn't help note Rheba's hips move rhythmically as she crossed the room to him and said, "Whyn't you dust over *here*, Mister Nick? I'll finish that, you just hand over the broom . . ."

Which he was glad to do . . . this wasn't man's work anyway. He hadn't any idea what to do now, though. His arm ached too much to let him sleep; he didn't want to lie in bed and think of Dinah and what might have been. . . .

Rheba no sooner got the broom, made two passes across the wooden floor and threadbare carpet, than she stacked it against the broken grandfather's clock and undulated toward Nick. "Timby's asleep. You look like you could use a hot toddy. I'll fix you one of my specials, with herbs my mammy told me about. She got the receipt from her mammy down to St. Pierre."

"Something Mt. Pelée blew off, I suppose," Nick said with a tired attempt at humor.

"*Before* the eruption. Mammy's folks was in N'Orleans in nineteen and two. Now, I'll just hustle you up a toddy. You come sit here in Timby's chair."

The kitchen was still the pleasantest room in the house —light, airy with many windows, and Timby's big chair at the head of the table by far the most comfortable. Nick knew what Rheba was working toward but he was too tired to make a point of it . . . besides, when she was going to all this trouble, it was a little hard to tell her that her touch made his flesh creep.

He eased into the chair and rested his arm on the table. After Rheba set her concoction of whiskey, herbs and water on the stove to heat she came around behind him. Running supple fingers along his neck, under his collar, she used the heels of her hands to massage his shoulder muscles that ached so. No getting around it, she had talent in her hands . . . he didn't dislike her touch quite as much as he remembered.

"Damn it!" he grumbled. "Those fences never looked better but she didn't even see them. Not to mention the gate. When I think of Nahum and me working on that gate—"

"This feel better, honey?"

He overlooked the "honey." It did feel better.

She moved down his spine carefully, not rushing him. He was thinking about telling her to stop as she moved over his flanks, but out of the corner of his eye he caught the quick, alert glance she gave him, hardly part of the mood she was conjuring up. It was a game now . . . he kept his eyes half-closed, waiting, waiting until her touch became light and finally vanished . . .

"Where're you going?" he asked, pretending to be sleepy.

"Just to make things comfortable for you on the couch." She moved quickly and quietly to the parlor.

Just as quietly he got up and went stiffly to the doorway. She was at the sofa in the parlor all right—going through the old but expensive crocodile wallet he carried in an inside pocket of his coat.

"Just what the hell do you think you're doing?"

She dropped the wallet in her surprise, but after one of her serpentlike stares picked it up again and boldly took out several bills.

"I need 'em for the groceries."

"Damn you, I paid you yesterday morning." He took several steps, got her wrist in his good hand, but she clutched the money in an iron grasp. He twisted hard. She kicked at him, he avoided her knee and before she could kick again got her down on the sofa with his own knee in her stomach. He took back his money—what remained after the evening's abortive game. It wasn't her first try. He knew she often got away with silver and gold pieces or a bill she thought wouldn't be missed. "Get on to bed. Timby's your man. Not me."

Her eyes had narrowed, but her toothy smile was still in place, and as she got up he saw that she was naked under the open bathrobe. Her large breasts with their dark aureoles, the curve of her stomach and the knots of black hair below actually repulsed him... she had come directly from Timby's body to his. Lily Biedemeier's girls were preferable... the one he had chosen was always washed, scrubbed and clean when she came to him... not like Rheba, who smelled of some cheap perfume—and of Timby.

Mostly, though, he knew it was the memory of Dinah that ruined other women for him.

"You had your chance, Mister Nick. Don't you forget it when you set to dreaming about that uppity Gaynor girl. Cold as a root cellar she is. You'll see."

"Think so?"

He hadn't intended for her to understand him but she was never stupid. She pulled her robe together and moved past him, pressing her big breasts against him to reinforce her show of what he was missing.

"That's all right. You just bring that lily-skinned little lady to Corrigan House, Mister Nick. Inside a week she'll be no better'n we are. You leave it to Timby and me. We'll make her over so's she'll be glad to look up to you."

He grabbed her arm. "You lay a hand to her and I'll kill you." He pulled her against him, reached into the old china closet drawer behind her with his injured hand and pulled out one of the silver knives that had belonged to his grandmother. "You see this?" He held the blade across her throat. "I don't mind using it. Remember that."

She had straightened up in fear but still managed to hold her smile. "Sure, Mister Nick. You got your gypsy mammy's blood. You and me, we understand each other. I won't touch Miss Dinah. I don't have to. This house will do it."

He threw the knife back toward the drawer. It missed, fell on the floor but he was too angry to care. "Go on to bed. And next time you try anything out you go, Timby or no Timby!"

Timby's big, unshaven face loomed out of the darkness of the hall as he demanded fuzzily, "What's goin' on? A body can't get a wink a sleep through the ruckus. You got a mean temper, lad."

"Then keep that woman in order. Any more of her and I'll throw her out. And the same goes if I catch her stealing from me again."

Timby and Rheba exchanged understanding looks. Timby must have known all about her thefts. His size looked impressive even in his knee-length nightshirt but he tried wheedling. "Now, laddie, we've barely enough to keep body and soul together. Would you have us starve like?"

"I gave Rheba plenty for the table yesterday. God help you both if you ever try shorting Amabel!"

Duly challenged, Timby marched barefoot into the room. "Is it a battle royal you want then, nephew?"

"You're drunk. Go to bed."

Timby advanced with fists at the ready but stepped on the knife, whose cold flat surface shocked him into sobriety. "I'm wounded, damn it! I'm bleeding!"

Nick looked down as Rheba tried to raise Timby's dirty bare foot. Her smile broadened.

"Timby, you stepped on the flat side. There's not a scratch on you."

Relieved, Timby dropped into a chair, raised his huge foot and examined the sole. "Surely felt like it dug right in. Well, that's one on me." And a few minutes later Rheba got him off to bed.

Nick found sleep less easily come by. The throb of his arm kept him awake and the more he thought about tonight's events in the Corrigan household, the more impossible became any hope of marrying the woman he most wanted . . . unless he could somehow provide a home for his wife away from his family. And yet he still had to support the Corrigans. They *were* his family, his obligation . . . damn them.

And try as he would, Nick couldn't think of anything he did well enough to be *paid* for, except the carnival weight-guessing and other distinctly minor tricks dependent on charm. It seemed hopeless.

Well, at least there was one consolation . . . he wouldn't have the pain of refusing to marry Dinah. Her family was sure to arrange all that.

Chapter Thirteen

ELLEN hadn't bitten her nails since she was a girl, and was shocked to see them now, ragged and torn, as she walked along the river path below Gaynor House. She picked up a pebble to skip it across waters that looked opalescent in the autumn haze covering woods and fields, hurling the stone with her other hand shading her eyes. The stone skittered a good distance almost to the river's west bank near the neglected Fairevale acres.

She turned away from the depressing sight of the house and land whose legitimate blood ties had died out with old Eliza Faire Warrender, Jem's cousin. Such memories were painful, especially those of Eliza's father, Colonel Rowdon Faire, who had reared Jem and been almost a father to Ellen. It had seemed so natural and easy to turn to "Rowdy" Faire, even to marry him when Bill Sholto jilted her. The thoughts of that brief marriage ending in tragedy still haunted her at times, but then there had been Jem and her new life in the West which had, she thought, made up for everything.

Well, Jem was gone, but at least there was only Dinah ... stubborn and lovable ... Ellen bit her thumbnail again. What on earth would become of that high-spirited young woman after a few years of marriage to an improvident gambler, however charming, with a houseful of aging relatives to support? She dreaded going up the green lawn to Gaynor House, where at any minute Shelley would be welcoming her guests for the "wedding preparations" talk. Shelley, she felt, was putting the best face on a marriage she thought beneath the Gaynors.

Ellen thought now about Daisy Wychfield and Amabel Corrigan, who belonged to her own generation. Good-natured Daisy had married Gavin McCrae, a young man so unimpressive that Daisy had reverted to her Wychfield name when he died. Even her son Marsh had been reared with his mother's maiden name. In sharp contrast to Daisy there would be the once pretty, once so popular Amabel Corrigan. Aside from going to school with Ellen, the only thing these two women had in common was a male relation who shared their name. Daisy's was Marsh, her legitimate son. Amabel had Nick Corrigan, whose "talents" kept a roof over her head and food in her plump body.

But I'm being cruel, Ellen thought . . . I shouldn't be. After all, I'm back home . . . Except she didn't *feel* at home. Not even when she saw, with admitted excitement, that Bill Sholto was striding down the lawn to meet her. She well remembered that kiss last night, looked around for escape, then took the short cut up to the north side of the house to avoid him. Anything with him would be, she felt, a reflection on Jem and their happy marriage. . . .

She entered the house by the north kitchen door just as she used to do when returning from her walks to Fairevale as a girl. In those lonely days she had found two havens—one with Colonel Faire, who had regaled her with tall tales of gallantry during the War Between the States, the other at the Ferry House in the Gaynor woods to the south. Now, of course, she knew cousin Jonathan's secret and the reason he lived a hermit's life there. Everyone else who had

had a part in that secret was dead—She nearly collided just then with the fair-haired man in the pantry, talking to one of the black girls working in the kitchen who opened the door for her with one hand, leaning on his cane with the other.

"Brother Marsh . . ." She greeted him in the old-fashioned family way from her youth. She was especially glad to see this quiet young gentleman who was treated with such indifference by his wife Shelley, her half sister. "I can't tell you how good it is to see a friend."

He smiled at that and limped along beside her. His first words surprised her. "Ellen, you're a sensible woman. How can you let that enchanting girl marry such trash? Worse than trash. Nick Corrigan has never earned an honest dollar in his life."

His interest in her daughter's happiness struck her as being a bit out of proportion. Indeed, his violent and suddenly vocal dislike of Nick suggested plain male jealousy . . . or was it Shelley's interest in Nick that especially bothered him? Or was it, as she felt more likely, that Marsh was taken with Dinah himself . . . ? Whatever, she found herself countering him by defending the man she'd nearly convinced herself was wholly unsuitable as a son-in-law only moments before . . . "Marsh, I know how Nick makes a living. Dinah will change all that. Besides, as far as I can see the dollars he wins are honest ones."

Marsh understood what she was saying to him . . . in a phrase, that she understood his unspoken feelings for Dinah, and backed off. Still, for Ellen it was an unwelcome complication and she began to think the sooner Dinah was married and out of this house the better. She supposed, hoped, that Marsh would behave like a gentleman but even so, he could inadvertently reveal his feelings to others and people would misunderstand. No matter how innocent Dinah was, the gossip might shadow her whole life. It also suddenly occurred to Ellen that Nick Corrigan could be very unpleasant if he thought he had real grounds for jealousy.

She was relieved to hear footsteps, any interruption was welcome.

"What's this? You two are looking mighty sober." Captain Sholto was eyeing Marsh pointedly, and she found his jealousy... amusing. It was what he deserved for marrying her mother and in the process putting himself considerably beyond Ellen in age. A lot of years to make up, Captain ... serves you right ...

Marsh finally spoke up. "We were discussing the world fifty years from now."

Sholto laughed. "That's something I won't have to worry about. And neither will you, son, unless you intend to live to the ripe old age of eighty."

Marsh remarked tightly, "My mother intends to. Nothing will stop her."

Both Sholto and Ellen thought of the opinionated if likable Daisy Wychfield and they both smiled as they nodded in agreement... They heard her voice now from the river parlor, as penetrating as ever. Sholto told Ellen, "You'd better run along and join them, otherwise Shelley and Daisy will claw poor old Amabel to pieces when she gets here."

It was good advice. Ellen left the two men and hurried off to meet her daughter and Amabel Corrigan....

In the river parlor Dinah escorted the nervous Amabel to a seat on the sofa between her old school friends. The older woman wore a neat, over-ruffled pink lawn dress of a type popular ten years before but Edward Hone's announcement of her name had bolstered her confidence ... it seemed to Ellen that Amabel was almost her old, head-tossing self with that enviable talent for attracting men. Amabel still looked a great deal more attractive than Daisy, and undoubtedly me, Ellen thought.

Dinah started out the river door and while Amabel chattered to Daisy, Ellen stopped her daughter. Instinctively they spoke in low tones. "Aren't you going to stay?"

Dinah grinned. "You settle it, mama. If I had my way I'd run off and marry Nick in Carolina or Baltimore. Not fool around with those old ladies and Aunt Shelley who's itching to make it a great show."

Anxiously Ellen said, "You still want to marry him? For heaven's sake, if you don't, say so." She hesitated but they had always been frank with each other. "It isn't that you . . . feel you have to marry him, is it?"

Dinah laughed, attracting the attention of the other women. "No, mama. I'm not pregnant. Or as they say, 'with child.' Though I wouldn't mind having Nick's child. He's so delicious that I love every piece of him—"

"Dinah!"

"True, honey, all the same."

"Well, don't go around repeating it." Ellen lowered her voice even more. "I don't like bringing this up, but how does he intend to support you and that family of his? He's been something of a drifter. And I'd hardly call gambling a respectable profession."

"Oh, mama, that's nineteenth-century talk. He does very well sometimes, depending on the run of the cards. But I'll get him into something else. You wait and see. 'Bye now."

"Where are you going?"

"Out to Nick. He's waiting for me on the river path. We're going to talk about my engagement ring and where we'll go on our honeymoon." She whispered then with impudent good humor, "Or would you ladies like to plan that too?"

Her brisk departure left Ellen feeling a deep rupture . . . that she had lost, finally, the last person in the world that she loved. Was she being a possessive mother? Maybe, but realizing it didn't change her feelings . . . As she turned to join the other women she saw Bill Sholto in the hall doorway. He had been watching her and his usual easy manner showed a good deal of understanding.

"How about a picnic this afternoon, Ellie? Just for old times' sake." Seeing her hesitate he added, "Friends. No more . . . unless, of course, you insist."

She smiled. "Well, I'll try and restrain my ardor. . . ."

Nick Corrigan had been striding up and down the river path below Gaynor House. He should be waiting nonchalantly, he knew . . . those old biddies would think he was nervous, that poor-white Corrigan hanging around after a Gaynor woman. Damn it, if only Dinah had been anything but a Gaynor . . . yet he was honest enough to admit that in his earliest dreams, when he bitterly hated the Gaynor-Wychfield clan's smug superiority and refused to wear young Marsh's cast-off clothes, he had pictured marching into Gaynor House or Wychfield Hall as an equal with a beautiful blonde girl on his arm. He had *never*, though, imagined the girl would be a Gaynor . . .

Seeing Dinah now run across the lawn and down the slope to him, he held out his arms, and when she came into them he lifted her inches off the ground and kissed her. "On the neck," she whispered excitedly and he bent his head to her. For several moments they were lost in each other and so aroused they could have stretched out together in the reeds by the river to complete this reunion.

"Our infernal in-laws. They're all watching out the window," Nick said.

Sure enough, Daisy, Amabel and Shelley had pushed the scrim curtains aside and were taking in the sight of Nick and Dinah embracing.

"Let's go somewhere else. We have to go in to Ashby Junction, Dinah. This engagement of ours isn't legal until we do."

"Oh, well, in that case we might as well make all those old busybodies happy." She must know he meant to buy her a ring. He only hoped she didn't know it might involve some back-room bargaining on account of his grand gesture of throwing away his winnings the night before. Still, he could always fall back on the diamond stickpin he'd won at 4 A.M. one morning in St. Louis with a mere full house queen high. He tried not to worry. Dinah was, after all, fast proving herself a real woman. "How could I be so lucky?" he asked the hazy, colorless sky as he and Dinah crossed the lawn to the estate road. He hugged her to him just in case she didn't understand the luck he referred to.

"We'll see about that, sir . . . How are we getting to Ashby?"

He had arranged that too. It involved two dollars in silver plus the price of gasoline paid to Hannah Gamble of Gamble's Hay, Grain, Feed and Livery Stables. Hannah now did a good business in automobiles and their repairs and was especially obliging to her good friend Nick Corrigan. As he had hoped, Dinah was duly impressed. The car was a Ford like the one Captain Sholto drove, a Model T, Nick called it. He helped Dinah up to her seat and Hannah, a monumental woman wearing overalls and one of her aged father's shirts, came around to wish them well.

"So you're his intended," she said, actually it was more a bark. "I gotta say it. I envy you, girl. Wouldn't mind standin' 'fore the preacher with him myself."

Nick shook his head. "Sorry, you didn't speak up quick enough, Hannah. How did I know you were available? Besides, what about those four lads in the feed room you've been playing poker with? You wouldn't want to break their hearts and you know it." He took her hand, gallantly kissed her big, raw knuckles before she shooed him out.

"Get on with your pretty bride, 'fore you make me all hot and bothered. Andy, you there! Crank up the bridegroom."

Echoes of her full laugh seemed to stay with them out of the big stables, along the street back of Gaynor's Salon and past the Confederate cemetery which had begun to look weedy and forsaken as the Civil War families died out, one by one.

Nick piloted the car to the newly paved highway and turned left through Gaynorville toward the county seat, wondering why Dinah was so uncharacteristically silent. His mention of the sultry air produced nothing. Nor did a remark about the traffic problem as two cars chugged south, possibly bound for the Carolinas.

After a while she gave him a sidelong look.

"You get along awfully well with women, don't you?"

"I like women."

"Well—"

"Some men don't." He looked at her. "I do."

She thought it over while he wondered with considerable pleasure if she could be jealous. Hard to believe. For a moment of which he was less than proud, he thought, It's that dream come true, a white-trash Corrigan has aroused the jealousy of a high-and-mighty Gaynor . . .

That errant reaction was quickly put in its place when Dinah said after some consideration, "I'm glad. Some men don't like us at all except for you-know-what."

"No. Tell me about you-know-what."

She jabbed him hard in the ribs and they finished the trip to Ashby Junction in excellent spirits. He parked the car near the Colonial Jewelers, and Dinah was impressed by the area facing the Ashby Arms Hotel, where the square around the statue of General Thomas "Stonewall" Jackson was full of automobiles. Tudor County was a farming area and the buckboards, buggies and wagons of the countrymen with their skittish teams were finding it harder and harder to go about their business.

"Don't think I haven't had a wonderful ride," Dinah told Nick, as they looked around, "but I do think mother's girlhood in a buggy pulled by an old mare was pretty romantic too . . ."

He bent his head and kissed her while a dozen passersby

turned their heads to watch. Embarrassed, she whispered, "Not *now*. In a buggy, I said."

There was good-natured applause as they broke apart and walked into the jewelry shop. The stout, elderly salesclerk looked them over with a supercilious air and was about to wave them over to knickknacks and souvenirs when he got a good square look at Dinah and his manner changed perceptibly.

"Excuse me, ma'am. You wouldn't be any kin to Miss Ellen Dunmore Gaynore that was? You kind of favor her."

I might have known, Nick thought with resignation.

"Miss Gaynor that was and is," Dinah said in her friendly way. "She was Mrs. Faire. She's widowed and I'm her daughter. She's staying at Gaynor House right now."

"You don't say. Well, you just ask her if she rec'lects Albert Dimster. Why, I was that smitten with Miss Ellen and her mother, Miss Maggilee, you'd hardly believe. I went away to college and when I came back with a beard your ma was right cool." He stroked his round, smooth chin. "My beard. She didn't like it. Well, sir! I didn't shave it off until the day Mr. McKinley was elected. Him being a Republican, you know, and me losing a bet and all." He patted Dinah's hand. "You tell Miss Ellen there's no beard now."

Dinah was amused and trying not to laugh. "I surely will tell mama. Albert Dimster, you say."

"Oh I was smitten, I tell you. Purely smitten." He sensed Nick's impatience. "Now then, tell me what can I do for you. May I hope Cupid is involved, you two young people being here together, and that?"

Nick was about to say something abrupt when Dinah put in hurriedly, "Yes, I guess you could say Cupid *is* involved. This is my fiancé, Nicholas Corrigan."

"Indeed, sir." Albert Dimster leaned across the counter to shake his hand. "I knew your grandfather well. Samuel Corrigan, wasn't it? Splendid man. Had one of the best vegetable farms in the county. What can I show you? Engagement rings? And wedding rings to match?"

It was hard to keep resenting a man who spoke so warmly of his grandfather. Nick found himself in a much lighter mood and they all moved happily to the more expensive merchandise.

"We thought we'd look over your rings," Nick explained, "and then consult the Old Dominion store down the street. But I imagine we'll end up here."

Albert Dimster looked stricken. "Oh, indeed, Mr. Corrigan! Right nice little store, the Dominion, but not nearly our selection."

Nick was irresistibly drawn to those stones that winked and gleamed the brightest on their velvet bed, although he had learned something about good taste during his gambling years and nowadays seldom made the mistake of thinking the dazzler was the best quality. But he worried for a moment that Dinah would choose the big diamond with the Tiffany setting. Instead she chose a small semicircle of emeralds surrounding a diamond that looked to him hardly more than a chip.

"Miss Dinah has her family's unerring good taste," the clerk said. "That is one of our finest rings."

Nick, when he caught a glimpse of the price tag, was staggered but managed to maintain a politely interested expression and remarked, "It fits you too."

For some reason Nick noted that Dinah had lost interest in it as she held her hand up to the sunshine at the window. "No . . . the emeralds don't do anything, they don't catch the light. Let me see that one in the corner."

With obvious reluctance Mr. Dimster brought out the tiny solitaire, slipping it on Dinah's finger. She flashed it around, gave Nick a glance he didn't miss. He knew she was studying him for his reaction . . . "I wouldn't have it," he said. "It looks like the worst kind of chip to me—"

"Very *wise*, sir." The clerk cheered up. "You have a good

eye for jewels. Yes, I regret to say it is a chip. But such stones serve their purpose among the"—he coughed behind his hand—"the less fortunate, if you take my meaning."

"Well, *I* like it. And I consider myself *very* fortunate," Dinah said. She eased the ring off. "However, if you don't like it, honey, we could go on to that other place and then come back here."

Nick made a sudden decision. Tomorrow, even tonight, he could start earning back a cushion against times when the cards ran against him. He reached into his vest pocket, unfastened the diamond stickpin and brought it out. The jeweler caught his breath, and Dinah whispered, "I never saw anything so lovely."

He felt like a king. This stone must go into Dinah's ring. "I'd like to see it make up into a ring. What do you think?"

"A family heirloom, of course," Albert Dimster said, almost reverently.

Nick smiled. He hadn't forgotten his grandparents' tales of arriving in New York by steerage after the potato famine, having half-starved on the sailing vessel and keeping only a five-dollar locket, their sole possession of value. . . . "You might say that. I'd like to have it made up into whatever pattern my fiancée chooses—"

"*No*, Nick. Please, I'd never feel right about it." She caught the angry glint in his eyes and amended to, "I'd never feel safe."

"I'll be with you."

"Yes, but it's too big."

The clerk was very much Nick's staunch ally. "Oh, I assure you, Miss Dinah, it would look exactly right on your hand, if I may say so."

In the end Nick got his way and they left the shop. Dinah was still protesting but admitted that no one in the family had ever owned such a ring. Which only gave Nick greater pleasure—a Corrigan was giving Dinah what none of her own people had been able to afford. . . .

Whatever Dinah's reservations about the size of the ring, Nick felt that the two of them had never been happier as they walked briskly up the street, arm in arm, and headed toward the Ashby bridge, which spanned the place where the Ooscanoto and East Creek ran together in a southerly direction past the great river homes and then, at Gaynor Ferry, parted once more, the creek wandering eastward and north almost to form a square. Before the creek shallowed off in late fall it was the chief route by which produce grown in the area was shipped north to the cities near the James River.

Dinah mentioned that the river bank below the bridge was very romantic, "or so mama says . . . I guess when father was sparking her that's where they went." . . . A plump, middle-aged little woman sauntered toward them and Nick had a twinge of uneasiness when he recognized Lily-Jo Biedemeier, but Lily was her tactful self, nodding slightly and passing by.

"Who was that?" Dinah asked, looking after her.

"One of the local businesswomen. She's at the Ashby Hotel."

"Mrs. Biedemeier?"

He was startled, but Dinah only gave him a teasing smile and took a tighter hold around his waist.

"Promise me one thing, Nick."

"Not to make love to Mrs. Biedemeier? I promise, sweetheart."

"No! Promise not to make love to her and her girls without telling me, so I can compete with them. Then you won't have to go to them." He laughed at that but she insisted. "Promise me. Please. I don't want you ever going to them for help when you've got me."

He quickly promised. By this time they had reached the bridge and he forgot her curious intensity, her talk of what he supposed was a matter of his fidelity. What he saw on the rocky riverbank below the bridge made him say quickly, "Shall we start back? It's getting cold. Seems as if winter's coming."

But it was too late. Dinah had looked over the edge of the stone abutment to the bank below, that "romantic spot" her mother had mentioned. Currently it was occupied by a man and woman who seemed to be struggling. The woman was her mother. The man was Bill Sholto, and he was laughing. Ellen herself appeared half-annoyed, half-amused. But her expression had a vivacity absent for the past few years.

Dinah gasped sharply and backed away. When Ellen looked up she saw only a man's figure staring down at her, and for one disorganized moment the past overwhelmed the present and it was Jem looking down at her. The name even escaped her lips, and Nick called out to her, identifying himself. She laughed, a bit too loudly, and the youthful flush drained from her face.

Sholto took it on himself to explain, though he looked a bit shaken himself. "Sorry, I was teasing her . . . It just seemed like history repeating itself. Years ago it was Jem Faire that caught me this way teasing Ellen. Stood just about where you are now, Corrigan."

Nick nodded, said he understood, waved to them both and before they could climb up the embankment and join him he was off after Dinah, who looked frozen. He wasn't surprised. She had loved her father very much and clearly resented *any* other man in Ellen's life. Her reaction only proved that his Dinah wasn't *quite* as perfect as he'd thought. Well, a perfect woman would be hard to live with. . . .

Chapter Fourteen

FOR Dinah the time was endless before the engagement party, which Daisy Wychfield, caught in the past, persisted in referring to as a ball. The ladies of the county had spent most of the days since the sinking in May of the *Lusitania* dutifully knitting socks, helmet liners, sweaters and scarves all bound for the Franco-British allies overseas. Now for a brief time they forgot all the relief organizations and settled down happily to make plans for a glamorous dinner and dancing. The fact that Dinah didn't really want it had very little influence.

As Daisy said, "We'll set out those two vases pa and mama brought back from China on their honeymoon and as everyone is announced they'll see the sign—Marsh can letter it—asking for contributions to the Red Cross. That way we'll kill two birds with one stone, so to speak."

"Daisy dear, only you would put it quite that way," Shelley said with a speculative glance at Nick Corrigan, who had just delivered Dinah to Wychfield Hall for the last-minute planning. Catching Shelley's look and Nick's scowl, Dinah found one more cause for annoyance. In spite of Nick's firm reminder that her mother was still an attractive, vital woman, Dinah had been irritated with Ellen ever since that display under the bridge. Anything was liable to set her temper off.... Now she went out on the wide east veranda to say good night to Nick who was off on one of his mysterious journeys, his black winter coat—well worn but still handsome—hanging dashingly from his shoulders.

"Where are you off to tonight, honey, or is it a secret as usual?"

"Norfolk. Just business, sweetheart. Maybe tomorrow the ring will be ready. I've promised to shoot them all if it isn't on your finger tomorrow night for the party."

"You really like this fool party, don't you, Nick?"

"This one—yes." He was trying to get his arms around her but she seemed very prickly. He warned her, "If you don't stand still you aren't going to get kissed."

"What kind of business is it tonight? Oh Nick, every night? I tell you, it's going to change some when we're married—"

"I certainly hope so . . . my luck's bound to change." It wasn't what she had in mind but he finally pressed her against one of the Wychfield pillars and his mouth silenced any further complaints.

He had one of Hannah Gamble's cars again, and as he drove off she wondered how well he had known Big Hannah. She watched until his car was out of sight. . . .

"Nick, you do look like the hero of the play they gave in the Jamestown ruins last year," Amabel said. "You sort of carry yourself that way. I always said you were as good-looking as those Gaynors any day. Oh, I hope I'm not going to have one of my headaches. I wonder if I should take a little bag of hot salt just in case."

Nick had retied his tie and then run his fingers nervously through his thick mop of coal-black hair. He still wasn't satisfied with what his reflection showed him—that shanty-Irish, or was it a gypsy?—look. It took the golden Marsh Wychfields and Bill Sholtos, the Kents and Warrenders to impress this world he'd been born into. But he took his mind off such matters to reassure Amabel that the Hall surely had plenty of seasonings, including salt. His aunt seemed twenty years younger than her normal faded-rose appearance, he thought. His good-luck streak had held through the last two weeks, and Amabel's new layered evening gown of deep pink crêpe de chine trimmed with beads was remarkably becoming with her carefully piled and curled yellow hair. In her hand she carried the egret fan which had belonged to her mother.

"Auntie, you're the prettiest girl in the county!"

She laughed, fluttered the fan to cool her cheeks. "They used to call me that when I was a girl, but you mustn't fib, Nick. The prettiest girl tonight will be your Dinah."

He smiled and turned to offer her his arm. At the door she whispered, "Wait 'til they all see you put Dinah's ring on her finger. Reckon nobody ever had a ring more elegant."

His talisman for entering that monument to first family pride, Wychfield Hall.... For transportation he had rented one of Hannah Gamble's Fords. Bless her . . . the huge woman was like a mother to him, nothing like his own gypsy mother with wide, black eyes and strange copper skin that he had inherited and which made the children at school make fun of him. Hannah had certainly helped when she had given him the tip about the "club" in Norfolk where free spending shipyard and navy workers came across the river to gamble their money away with no plan, no system, no attempt to read their fellow players. And Nick knew from long experience it was this study of other players that made the difference between a consistent winner and a loser....

Amabel settled herself now in Hannah's Ford and carefully wrapped a new flesh-colored georgette veil around her head, tying it lightly under her chin. Then she sat up very straight.

"Don't be scared, auntie," Nick said gently as he cranked up the car and jumped in.

"I'm no more scared than you are," she said, and almost meant it.

They chugged past his white fences and soon came to the manicured Gaynor properties.

Amabel pointed out, "Papa laid down crops all through there. He and Timby and Sean were experimentin' with crops like peanuts after the tobacco worms got to be too much. But there didn't seem much point. Peanuts never was a good money crop. Not compared to tobacco." She sneaked a look at him, trying to judge his mood. "When you marry Dinah maybe we can get some of our fields back . . ."

He laughed shortly. "If there's one thing I want to prove, it's that I don't need the Gaynors. Someday they'll need me. You can put your chips on that."

"Oh Nick, I wish you wouldn't use gamblin' talk. It's so awful vulgar."

"Honey, you want to talk away my only talent? It keeps us alive."

She sighed. "I reckon Dinah's due for a shock, livin' poor after bein' so rich."

"For the hundredth time, she isn't rich. She doesn't have a cent to her name. Nothing! I'm the one who's going to support her. Me . . . a Corrigan. It's exactly how I want it. And damn it, Amabel, *don't cry!*"

She managed to say haughtily, "I wouldn't dream of cryin' when you use such language."

Nick always felt a deep twinge when he hurt his aunt's feelings, but he was relieved tonight that Amabel, in a huff, made it unnecessary for him to talk further. It gave him a chance to order his thoughts . . . He hoped he would present a portrait of calm confidence as he entered the greatest house along the Ooscanoto River, but he also knew the Irish-gypsy boy looked out occasionally from behind that tall, carefully groomed exterior. Perhaps he would be supported by his sense of humor, one of the qualities he shared happily with his Dinah. Meanwhile, he touched the little box in the pocket of his overcoat and pictured Dinah's face as he slipped the engagement ring on her finger. It was enough. He speeded up to twenty-five miles an hour.

Dinah, who had arrived early with the Gaynor House clan to stand beside Daisy in the receiving line, found Marsh Wychfield on her other side, asking the obvious question but with more than his usual gravity. "Are you really enjoying yourself?"

"I soon will be." Her eyes were on the door. Nick was due any minute.

Marsh couldn't take his eyes off her. She was radiant in her harem evening gown of white sashed silk with a neckline that revealed her slim throat and a tantalizing half-view of the cleavage between her smooth, pale breasts. She wore no jewelry, unlike the other young women present who were bedecked with pearls.

Discarding his normal reticence Marsh said in a tight voice, "I've never seen you so lovely."

His intensity startled her. She looked around, wondering if his comment had been meant to pique his wife. But Shelley, Ellen and Persis Kent stood together in a near corner of the ballroom, pointing out changes in the once forested area north of the estate. So Marsh's compliment was meant only for her, and it made her uneasy. . . .

She thanked him briskly, but ignoring the tone, he took encouragement from the words. "Believe me, Dinah," he said, "I genuinely hope you're going to be happy . . . If anyone can handle the Corrigans, I suspect you can . . . with your sympathy and understanding . . ."

She was aware that Marsh looked his best tonight. He had more color, seemed more alive, his blue eyes sparkling, his hair, as burnished as the gold frames on the ancestral portraits. His thin, pale lips, though, made her apprehensive. She sensed something more personal entering her relationship with Marsh, a man she had before both pitied and admired—She heard Daisy draw a sharp breath, and then Shelley came hurrying to join her husband. "My heavens! Did you see that entrance?"

Dinah stared at the great Wychfield doors, feeling her heart begin to race, and was angry with herself for that first stirring of feat that in his desire to please these arrogant people Nick might somehow make himself ridiculous. She couldn't bear to have this proud man hurt by their laughter.

Nick had been ushered in by the butler at the doors, Amabel Corrigan just ahead of him. Daisy went at once to make her especially welcome. In those brief seconds Dinah was intensely aware of Nick . . . of his black and white sartorial splendor that was theatrical enough to cause a ripple of gasps. Unquestionably Marsh Wychfield and some other men present were more conventionally handsome but they lacked the presence Nick had acquired through years of traveling and relying on his wits. It served him well among these men and women who imagined themselves his superiors. The men might be secretly amused but the women, she judged, felt far different emotions . . .

Dinah gave him just enough time to enjoy his effect on this glittering company, then stepped out of the receiving line in front of Daisy. Nick saw her, and before the rapidly gathering circle of guests embraced her, lifted her inches off the floor and kissed her soundly. As she returned his kiss, Marsh, Daisy and the others welcomed the nervous Amabel with gentle courtesy.

A servant reached for Nick's overcoat, which he

shrugged from his shoulders—Dinah delighted in the gesture, so like a cape flung aside—but suddenly Nick had reached into a pocket of the coat and pulled out a black-velvet jeweler's box. Everyone saw him, guessed what was in the box.

Although Daisy had intended to announce the engagement at dinner, they were smothered by well-wishers, Ellen, as she was obliged to do, leading them. Nick had barely stripped off his gloves when she came forward in high-waisted, floor-length ice-blue satin . . . Dinah remembered Bill Sholto calling her the "snow maiden." But Ellen's smile softened the imperious picture she made as she took Nick's two hands and leaned forward to brush his cheek with her lips. He was taken aback and studied her, trying to judge her real feelings. "Welcome, Nick. Be happy," was what she said.

When dinner was announced, Daisy chose Nick as her escort and motioned for her son Marsh to take Dinah, the other guest of honor. Nick touched Dinah's hand, and then they separated, unwillingly. In view of her earlier discovery about Marsh, Dinah was particularly uncomfortable with him as her partner and froze him into silence by speaking past him to his gregarious law partner, Barney Kent.

In the long dining room, where the windows opened onto the pillared south porch, Dinah was seated between Marsh and Bill Sholto. As if this weren't bad enough, Nick was at the far end of the table where on one side Daisy deafened him with her bellow and on the other Shelley Wychfield, in ravishing green taffeta with paradise feathers in her hair, tried her fetching best to bewitch him. To make matters worse, Barney's dark-haired mother, Persis, seemed intensely interested in Bill Sholto, which annoyed Ellen, in spite of herself. Dinah didn't care what Persis Kent did with Sholto but she wanted Ellen to be in good spirits, and never more than tonight.

It wasn't at all the way they had imagined their engagement party. When Daisy Wychfield rose to make the announcement and proposed a toast, Nick and Dinah couldn't even reach across the table to touch. Amid smiles and laughter and a chorus of voices repeating Daisy's trumpeted good wishes, Marsh murmured to Dinah, "It will all be over soon. Then we'll go home, away from this bedlam—"

"We?" She pronounced distinctly with her great-grandmother Varina's hauteur.

He colored. "I meant, of course, those of us from Gaynor House . . . forgive me, I didn't mean to offend you."

Aware that both her mother and Nick had observed but not made out the context of this low-voiced exchange, and looked uneasy, Dinah quickly changed the subject.

Daisy now signaled that the ladies would retire to freshen up for the dancing, and Nick hurried over to Dinah. The calm he showed the others didn't deceive her . . . the excitement was in his eyes, if not his voice.

"When do you want your ring?"

Everyone was watching them. "I wish it could be when we were alone, just the two of us." Too late, she knew she had said the wrong thing and put in quickly, "so I could kiss you properly to show you how I feel."

Which satisfied him for the time being. "I have to give it to you here, sweetheart. You can see how disappointed they'll all be otherwise."

She knew *he* would be disappointed, as of course he had a right to be, so she suggested, "Why not just before we start to dance? We two will be the first so when I put my arm around your neck, just everybody will see it."

He whispered, "Why can't I give you the damned ring now and we both run away and make love?"

"Let's!"

But they were quickly surrounded by friendly jailers. In the crowded ballroom the orchestra was beginning a waltz,

"The Beautiful Blue Danube." Daisy told her guests, "Even if the Austrian Empire is one of the Central Powers, how can we have a dance without Mr. Strauss?"

With all eyes on them, Nick came to Dinah. She held out her arms to him but just as his right arm went around her, his left hand slipped the ring on her finger. She had time only for a gasp of delighted disbelief as he whirled her out on the celebrated Wychfield ballroom floor. Wherever he had learned to dance—and she didn't really want to know—his teachers had been fabulous.

The ohs and ahs and buzzing all around them were all Nick could have wished for but Dinah was even more impressed than the others. Contrary to her secret fears, he hadn't created an extravagant setting in an attempt to dazzle. The stone was beautifully bedded in a circle of tiny pearls. Knowing her mother had never taken any fine jewelry when she went to the Arizona territory with Jem Faire, Dinah hadn't wanted to seem to outshine Ellen, but this ring said so much about Nick's good taste that she kept moving her fingers through the hair at the nape of his neck in order to see it sparkle.

He had never been happier. "You like it? You really do?"

"Nobody in the whole world ever had anything so beautiful . . . or anyone," she added, fighting to restrain herself from taking him up on his earlier offer right then and there.

Other couples had stepped out onto the floor, and Nick drew Dinah closer as they whirled around the turn. All necks craned and eyes focused on her hand.

By the time a late supper was served everyone agreed that it was Daisy's best party. Nick and Dinah went out on the veranda with plates of lobster pate, ices, cakes and punch, but they set them down haphazardly and fell into each other's arms, indifferent to the chilly night, aware only of themselves . . .

Timby Corrigan now crossed the gravel estate road toward them, in his twenty-year-old evening clothes and a new white shirt and new shoes only a little dusty from his walk. His hair was combed and his grizzled, leonine head looked positively distinguished. Everything about him was right . . . until he stepped into the veranda's lantern light and revealed that he hadn't shaved for days. It was the only thing he had forgotten. Still, he had made a splendid effort, and for Timby's own sake as well as to please Nick, Dinah freed herself from Nick's embrace and went down the steps to welcome the latecomer. Behind her, Marsh Wychfield had suddenly appeared and lunged forward in anger, struggling with Nick, saying, "No drunken Corrigan is going to ruin my niece's evening."

Dinah had to move quickly. "Timby, how good of you! You came to our party. You're awfully late but better late than never."

The big man had been stalking along almost too straight-backed. Not drunk, she decided, but he had been drinking, probably to get his courage up. He was thrown a bit off stride by the force of her greeting, and unbent with a near-comic haste. "There's a fine colleen you are. Not too proud for your poor relations, are you now?"

She offered her hand and he almost shook it off. She knew there would be shock, anger and maybe even violence if he walked into Wychfield Hall this way. Worst of all, it would seem to humiliate Nick . . . She said quickly, "If only you had come sooner. We've finished the dancing and supper but I'll get you a plate. Can you wait?" She was relieved when Nick joined her, having subdued Marsh, who still looked on suspiciously at a distance.

Nick was tense in spite of his easy way with his uncle . . . "That's a good idea. Timby, come and sit down. You're looking mighty well." He took Timby's arm but the older man was contrary. Faint strains of music came from the ballroom where the orchestra played tea-concert music to accompany the chatter of guests still lingering over the long tables of food. Nick and Dinah maneuvered Timby up onto the veranda where Marsh Wychfield stood like a brooding presence.

Timby was complaining, "I had it in my heart to share one dance with my new niece-to-be." He began humming. "There's an old tune. Takes me back. Ma used to sing it. Comes from the war." There was only one war. Dinah didn't make the mistake of confusing it with the one being fought now in Europe or the Cuban war in which Timby had lost his brother.

"I'll go and get a plate for you."

Timby caught her hand, and Nick reached for him quickly as Marsh straightened up. Before it all turned into a disaster, Dinah went into Timby's arms and they danced the length of the veranda, dipping and whirling to a song written more than fifty years before about a lost love . . . Over Timby's shoulder Dinah told Nick to "get him some food, for heaven's sake!" Nick hesitated but Dinah looked fully able to cope with Timby, so he went . . . Dinah herself was heady with the excitement of the evening and in spite of the tension she was enjoying herself. Like his nephew, Timby was a good dancer, which was considerably more than could be said for some of the other so-called gentlemen here . . .

Marsh moved slowly from pillar to pillar so that he was never far from the dancers. The slap of Timby's new shoes on the veranda floor began to draw other guests to the doors, which Nick had left open in his abrupt departure, and some interested faces peered out through the east parlor windows . . . Nick finally returned from a loaded tray and was making his way through the crowd in the doorway at the very minute Daisy Wychfield all but shrieked from a parlor window, "Shadwell, Jummo; throw that creature, that disgusting drunk out . . ."

The two Wychfield servants pushed their way past Nick and rushed out toward Dinah. One of the big black men got a lock on Timby's shoulders from the rear. Dinah was flung aside while Timby managed to heave one man over his head only to have the other leap at him.

Nick threw the tray and plates of food across the veranda, barely missing Marsh and a second later reached Dinah, who was already on her feet.

"I'm fine, help Timby."

The first of Daisy's servants was up again to join the attack when Nick's fist caught him across the neck and he went down in a sprawl. Timby, still confused, struck out wildly, missing his assailant and wound up against a pillar with the enemy still coming on. Just as Nick swung again on his own opponent, Bill Sholto jumped in, wrenching Daisy's man from the bleeding Timby.

Dinah kept shouting, "Stop it, stop it, he wasn't doing a thing! Leave him alone!"

It took several minutes to disentangle the affair. The two burly servants were taken to their cottage by Marsh Wychfield to have their bruises attended. Most of the party guests blamed Timby, but Ellen and Shelley joined the trembling Amabel to patch up the Irishman.

Dinah took Nick's handkerchief, made a pad of it and patted the blood off his temple and cheek. Nick winced. "Never mind my head, sweetheart. It's my hand. I make my living with these." The flesh of one hand was badly torn. "It would be this one! I had a little accident with it two weeks ago. Don't look so cross, darling. You were wonderful."

"You were pretty wonderful yourself." She knew he was bitter and furious beneath the teasing manner. "Nick, it was Daisy's fault. Once and for all, she's not going to have anything to do with our wedding."

He put his hand over hers, stopping all her soothing efforts. The anger in his voice almost frightened her. "What about tonight? Getting married, I mean."

She kissed his injured hand, and he *didn't* wince. She said slowly, "We wanted to anyway, didn't we? I'll send back a note to mama." Her voice picked up. "We'll just go!"

He took her face between his hands and studied her features. Apparently he saw what he was looking for. "You know what they'll think."

"That I'm in the family way, of course. You mean we have to wait until I'm *really* in the family way?"

After a startled second or two he laughed and the gentleness returned to his eyes and his voice. "There's a thing they say in my mother's land. And now I know it's true. You are my own heart's darling."

One by one, the family drifted into the comfortable river parlor of Gaynor House to discuss the campaign they all agreed was necessary against Dinah's disastrous engagement. Shelley had silenced her husband's indignation as they walked home by the river path.

"Later, honey. She can hear us. Daisy caused enough damage with her ranting and raving."

Marsh, whose invalid days had been further exacerbated by constant visits from his well-meaning mother, at once stopped complaining. Slowed by his limp, he was at the back of the procession. Dinah, apparently having said her good night to Nick, went first, almost at a run. Behind her came Ellen and Shelley's father, Bill Sholto, talking in low tones. It boggled Shelley's mind to consider the relationship that would come about between her half sister and herself if her father should marry Ellen, his sweetheart of so long ago . . .

Finally there were Marsh and Shelley. While Shelley heard the muttering and easily took in the general opinion of this affair, she herself was having second thoughts. If the engagement should be broken off with all the resulting bitterness, there would be no chance meetings, no contacts with Nick Corrigan at all. Since that night in the salon when he had made a fool of her, she had dreamed often about the steps that should have followed inevitably. She simply hadn't had time to make herself irresistible. No real man of flesh and blood could have aroused her so efficiently without arousing himself, providing she'd been able to turn on the full force of her powers. Then, what a delight there could have been between them!

But how could he know? She had always acted so damn superior, conscious of who she was and who Nick Corrigan was. All *that* would have to change. He had to discover the real her, tender and warm and passionate. And he'd never have the chance if he and Dinah broke their engagement and he never came back to Gaynor House again.

So Shelley was prepared to argue the case for the lovers, though not too vehemently or Marsh would become suspicious. He might even divorce her and claim custody of young Neily and she couldn't bear that. The disgrace would be terrible. Besides, everything she did in the world, every profit from the shop and the land must go to Neily some day. She wanted the boy to feel toward her all the devotion she herself felt for her own father, Bill Sholto . . . Maybe I haven't given Neily enough attention, she admitted to herself. And he's such a good little boy. Everybody says papa spoiled me, and *I* turned out all right. . . .

Half an hour later they straggled into Gaynor's river parlor, all waiting for Dinah to come down from her room, meanwhile exchanging angry or at best anxious opinions.

Ellen looked older, Shelley thought. She must care a great deal. Marsh and Ellen were agreed that Timby Corrigan's behavior had been about the last straw. And as Marsh pointed out, "He's just a symptom of what's happened to that family. I've seen other families go like that, even some of our best families that started down after the War. They never got out of the mud again. Look at the poor Finches."

"Well," Bill Sholto said, "if we're talking about good catches, I guess Corrigan is less than that . . . though I will say he's a likable scamp. I could even wish him well if he was after somebody else's rich daughter—"

"But that's just it," Shelley put in, "he's not marrying a rich girl."

Ellen looked momentarily brighter. "That's true. At least he must love her. Fact is, I'm convinced he does."

Shelley watched Bill Sholto gently lay his hand on Ellen's shoulder. The possessive gesture annoyed Shelley. Things would be mighty unpleasant if she and her half sister had to live under the same roof for very long. They had never been the least bit alike and Ellen would probably put Bill against her. It would be very difficult for her to go on without the total support of her father . . .

Bill was saying, "So we know he's not marrying Dinah for her money, but there's a greater risk. He'll almost surely end in bringing her into the poverty, and worse, of that family's life. God knows how they live in that house, presided over by Timby's mistress. Pardon me, ladies, but that's one vindictive, mean female."

Ellen said almost to herself, "Oh god, I can't let her . . . Dinah's always been so free, so trusting . . ."

Things were clearly going from bad to worse. Shelley had to bring them back to where she wanted them. "I think we should go slow on this. Just tell Dinah we want to know Nick better. See more of him. Invite him to Gaynor House more often—"

"And have his drunken relatives assault the rest of our women?" her husband said unpleasantly.

She ignored this. "Just keep prolonging things until Dinah sees the Corrigans as they really are. Then it will be Dinah who breaks off the engagement for her own legitimate reasons."

"And we all know what our legitimate reasons are, don't we?" Marsh asked, his voice heavy with irony. Shelley, realizing she had gone a bit too far too fast, tried without success to avoid his icy stare.

Dinah checked the list of things to be done. Most important, the note to her mother was written. Her suitcase was packed. Everyone in Gaynor House would soon be gathering in the river parlor to hold a kind of postmortem over the evening's events and expecting her to join them. She could miss that with great pleasure. She would simply leave Ellen's note on the bed. Too bad there wasn't a mantelpiece, she thought with nervous humor. Elopement notes were always left on mantels.

Had she packed everything? Did the note say all she wanted to say, about loving Ellen but belonging to Nick and his family now?

No matter. Nick was waiting for her at the river door back of the pantry. And after what had happened, the way poor Timby had been mistreated and Nick and Amabel humiliated, nothing else was possible. Her father would have done the same. Maybe Ellen would too.

Dinah picked up her suitcase, feeling ridiculous at all this secrecy, this sneaking out down the back stairs. Just before she opened the door, she set the suitcase down and went back to the bed. She took her note to Ellen out of one of Shelley's delicate envelopes, and reread it.

Mother dear,
    You said once that you ran after father down the Gaynor drive and proposed. Nick and I feel the same way. I found tonight I couldn't be both Gaynor and Corrigan. Nick and I are going to make the Corrigan name as proud in Virginia as you and papa made his name in the Southwest.
                          Your loving Dinah.
P.S. I don't care what the others think but I want you to know I'm not in the family way, as you call it. We really *want* to be married. When we come home to Corrigan House from our honeymoon, all our real friends will be welcome. Especially you, dearest mama.

Dinah folded the page again, tried to fit it into the envelope. It stuck and she stuffed it in impatiently. She propped the envelope up on the bed's finely knitted wool blanket, balancing it on top of a ridge in the bedclothes. Then she looked out into the hall. She could hear them all buzzing away in the river parlor, their voices trailing out into the hall and up the graceful white staircase.

In the hall Dinah hesitated, listening, heard the virulent opinions of the Corrigans and moved quickly along to the back staircase. In the old days this staircase had been used solely by slaves and later the Gaynor servants. These days young Neily often raced up and down them; they were handier and he was less likely to be scolded for making a racket.

Dinah thought, "When I walk down these dark stairs, I am no longer a Gaynor." Well, this was the way it had to be after tonight's punishing spectacle at Wychfield. She hurried down, hesitated before passing the open doorway to the kitchen, but the big room appeared to be empty. She was just hurrying by when hands reached out at her from the darkened kitchen. Startled, she caught her breath in panic when she felt Neily Wychfield's thin young arms squeezing her as he chuckled, "Caught you, cousin Dinah."

She released herself, bent to him and saw the bright excitement in his eyes. "Neily, do you know what I'm doing?"

"You're running away. Nick's waiting. I saw him right outside the back door. He said I should see nobody stays in the kitchen. I was to tell them I was sick and they'd run for Bethulia. It was my idea."

"And a very good one . . . this time. Neily, Mr. Corrigan and I love each other and we don't want to have any more trouble like what happened tonight. You understand that, don't you?"

" 'Course I do. It's like being a spy. And you're running away from the Yankee army."

She laughed. "I wouldn't say that to your parents, if I were you. Anyway, wish us luck."

A bit shyly, he kissed her cheek.

"Good-by, Neily dear."

He opened the door for her, watched her go into Nick's arms with the suitcase still in her hand. Then he closed the door, nervous but proud over his role in the elopement.

Nick pulled Dinah out onto the lawn. She dropped her suitcase and returned his embrace. She made a fuss over his raw knuckles, but was glad to see that at least they weren't bleeding any longer. She asked about Timby.

"He's fine. Amabel and Rheba are fussing over him. They've convinced him it was all a mistake. The Wychfields thought he was someone else . . ."

"Good. And what does Rheba Moon have to say to it all?"

"She's surprised. She was sure you'd back away and join the enemy camp." He looked her over in the starlight. "Darling, I've been standing here for the last half hour just wondering. Any minute I was afraid Neily would stick his head out with a nice little note saying you'd changed your mind. But here you are. Neily told me you weren't the kind to back out. Smart boy."

"At least that should teach you not to listen to Rheba Moon."

He picked up her suitcase, then set it down again and took her back forcibly into his arms, as if he had to be sure she was here. This time as they kissed they were interrupted by sounds near the door . . . servants in the pantry arranging tea or coffee for all those family members who waited to lecture Dinah on her choice of a husband. There were no sounds from Neily. He must have sneaked back upstairs before the servants came in.

Dinah whispered, "Quick! Let's go someplace where we can be alone—"

Nick took her arm and her suitcase, and still holding her close to him ran with her across the lawn to a dashing, new but borrowed Buick parked under a willow tree at the corner of the drive.

Nick watched Dinah, and with his gift at reading faces and mannerisms he soon became convinced that Dinah meant what she said. Her instinctive actions on the night of their engagement party *might* have been based on pity and resentment over Timby's treatment, but Nick couldn't be wrong about her happiness during the days and nights that followed.

They would always have the memory of that cold, starlit drive toward the Carolinas on the night of their elopement. "Two against the world," they had proclaimed themselves while Dinah sat close beside him, his free hand locked around hers. They spent the night in a two-story hotel in a little Virginia town neither of them knew existed.

Nick sensed that Dinah had hidden fears about their economic future and tried to assure her that problems would occur only if he ran into a bad-luck streak and so far luck was running his way. She didn't argue about it, thank god. His Dinah had a perfect right to her own idiosyncrasies, like seeing that young fellow in an Atlanta flower shop on their wedding morning and pointing out what a nice steady job he had.

"What? At twelve dollars a week? Honey, that wouldn't even be big enough stakes for a decent opening hand."

"But it would be yours. Earned fair and square."

"Dinah, I've never cheated anybody—never had to—in my life. I *play* fair and square, as you call it."

"I know, dear. I didn't mean it that way. I only meant that it would be more of . . . a sure thing."

"Not as sure as a royal flush," he grinned. She returned it and the brief squall was over. . . .

They always thought of the night they spent in the little Virginia hotel with the peeling wallpaper as their real wedding night. They saw themselves as two adventurers, nearly as romantic in their outlook as young Neily. Nick was delighted to find Dinah just as loving and eager to learn in bed as she had been on their cross-country trip. It aroused him tremendously when she began to experiment with his body, and when he ran his long, expert fingers over the whole length of her he could see her small firm breasts and abdomen and even her flanks respond to his touch. He was sure that he was the luckiest man in the world, and waited carefully for the right moment to join with her so that they shared and prolonged each other's deep pleasure. . . .

They were married in Atlanta before driving on toward New Orleans, where Nick told Dinah he had business.

The marriage ceremony itself was brief but jolly, thanks to the stout little minister they found in a Methodist church, though Nick seemed anxious that the minister should think they were well-to-do. He offered the minister a tip for "giving my girl to me." The tip made her cringe —not one but two twenty-dollar gold pieces. Five dollars would have been ample—forty was enough money to keep them for two months . . . but Nick was so proud she hadn't the heart to discourage him and later, to please him, she asked frequently for money to buy little knickknacks— ribbons for dresses, gloves, feathers for hats and other small things she told him she simply had to have. He loved the thought of Nick Corrigan supporting a Gaynor, giving her everything she asked for, treating her like a queen. He was relieved that he had left over a hundred dollars safe at home so that no one at home would go without while he and Dinah were spending on their honeymoon.

Whenever Dinah wrote to her mother, he took time to send off a postcard to Amabel. His cards usually were more elaborate than Dinah's, covered with glittering dust or picturing a glamorous woman with an elaborate hairdo seated on a crescent moon. Amabel liked these cards very much and often imitated the hairdo, he told Dinah.

"No cards to Rheba Moon?" Dinah asked one day when he was picking out another card for his aunt. Nick had suspected for some time that Dinah was just a bit jealous of Timby's mistress. It was beyond his understanding that she could be uneasy over anyone so repulsive but he wasn't going to bring his Dinah home to unhappiness just to please Timby. He made his decision at that moment.

"No need. I'm writing Timby a letter. We won't be wanting a housekeeper. We'll hire girls to carry out your instructions. The Finch tenants always have a dozen daughters glad of the job. Rheba has got to go. I'll have Amabel pay her something for her trouble—"

"Oh?" She sounded doubtful and Nick tried to reassure her. "The woman will leave if I don't pay her. Stands to reason."

A cloud was lifted with that decision and they could go back to enjoying the honeymoon. Today was all that mattered. . . . They made a game of recalling all the places where they had made love in some particular way or for the longest time. They also counted up the times the car broke down, the horrible, unpaved, backcountry roads, and tried to remember the different wallpaper patterns of a dozen country inns before they reached New Orleans.

Nick was relieved when Dinah said she didn't want to stay at one of the Crescent City's more glamorous hotels, like the St. George. She much preferred "something cozy." Three years ago he and five acquaintances had been ordered out of that hotel for gambling and—in the case of the sixth card player, Harold Vorhees—using the suite for immoral purposes, since the players' drinks and food had been provided by a beautiful, expensive courtesan named Lettice du Vaux. . . .

Nick and Dinah had settled on a secluded old house in the French Quarter, staying in a second-floor suite lent to Nick by a gambling friend now making the rounds of Baltimore and points north. Dinah liked to slip out through the long jalousied windows, squeeze between the jalousies and the grillwork and watch the people in the narrow street below. Sometimes he woke up in the morning to find her out there already fully dressed, peering into everyone's secret life, as she put it.

When he called to her she came inside and made a face at him, insisting her "morning world" was better than his "night world." But that didn't prevent her from unfastening her dress, strewing petticoats over the floor and falling into his waiting arms. Sometimes they made love to start the day. Sometimes, in each other's arms, they talked about the future, about making the Corrigan farm prosper again, about parties they would give and how the yard would look full of parked cars for some glittering occasion.

"Like our tenth wedding anniversary," he suggested, tracing a vagrant strand of her long hair, beginning where it lay across his throat to where it trailed just above her ear.

She blew the strand away and tugged at his hair where it rose above his forehead. He pushed himself up in bed, thoroughly awake now, and bent over her, all plans forgotten as he took her into his arms. . . . Afterward, while he was dressing, he decided to broach a delicate matter. He couldn't, after all, put it off much longer. In the mirror he saw the bed, Dinah half-reclining on the rumpled covers, her eyes catching his in the reflection.

"Sweetheart, you get a passel of fun out of watching that street out there, don't you? In the evenings I've seen you standing there just looking out." Maybe she guessed what was coming. "I mean, there's all the activity, the cafes, the little music hall, the tourists in the streets."

Sitting up straight on the side of the bed, she said flatly, "You have some business tonight."

He nodded.

After an uncomfortable pause she sighed and looked

away. "Well, I took that when I married you. There's only one thing."

He knew she was going to say, "Don't lose our money," and he was ready for that. He could state proudly that he still had over a thousand dollars left. Instead she stared grimly at his reflection. "So long as it doesn't involve another woman. I don't want you coming from her bed to mine. Not ever, Nick Corrigan."

He laughed at that absurdity, crossed the room in two strides and kissed her. Though her body felt stiff at first when he touched her, she softened under his caress and added with a reluctant smile, "*Just* so you understand."

"I swore it before. But I'll do it again, sweetheart. No women. I don't need anyone if I have you. Couldn't handle them anyway . . ."

She smiled, half-assured, and gave him a final, lingering kiss.

By the time Dinah's eight o'clock dinner was delivered that evening, still warm from the little French cafe across the street, she seemed in good spirits, and he was enormously relieved. He walked around the dainty, kidney-shaped desk where the covered plates were being laid out. The crab and other seafoods were still a treat to her even after weeks near coastal Virginia, but her favorite was the dish of creamed sweetbreads in delicate pastry shells. The jambalaya didn't interest her and it was Nick, perched on an arm of her chair, who kept sampling the brightly colored dish until it was half gone.

She caught him glancing surreptitiously at his wristwatch, the first time he had done so, and she ordered him off to his business good-naturedly. "Just leave that chocolate mousse to me and you can stay away all night." She reached for his hand. "No, I didn't mean that, honey. And you know it . . . come home as soon as you can."

He left in good spirits, but her jest reminded him that this would be the first evening they would spend apart since their marriage two weeks before, and he decided that his love for his wife suddenly made his profession something of a chore. Maybe florists' assistants did get more out of life . . . He didn't really like the prospect of leaving her alone and wandering in at some ungodly hour after dawn, drunk on smoke and other men's stinking whiskey fumes and cards dancing before his bleary eyes. . . .

Still, just now there was no alternative . . .

Chapter Fifteen

NICK strolled down the street. No matter how much he thought he wanted Dinah before their marriage, there had always been the nagging thought . . . what will it be like to lose my freedom, to be at a woman's beck and call? No more strolling down some fascinating street alone, looking for adventure, no more close encounters with other gaming souls . . .

Well, here he was, alone on the loose tonight, and still he couldn't get his mind off Dinah. If they were sharing this walk, they would also be sharing a dozen private jokes about what they saw.

Meanwhile, he had a thousand-dollar purse. Too risky. Marriage and the responsibility of supporting a wife had already taught him that. He could chance a few hundred, a small enough loss to make up if he had to some other night when his luck was in.

Delicious odors of Creole food trailed out of a little cafe as he passed. He and Dinah would have laid imaginary bets on the ingredients. Two foreign-looking tourists passed. He and Dinah would have discussed them . . . Europeans, probably, but with their war on what were they doing here? "Spies!" Dinah would have hissed dramatically. . . .

He turned the corner before he reached Canal Street. A young man was parading stiffly up and down in front of an elegant residential-looking building that was actually a private gambling club. The young picketer was evidently an American but as Nick approached he spoke with an accent verging on the French.

"German murderers! Killers! U-boat Huns!"

Nick offered the impassive doorman his card containing three expensively engraved lines:

Nicholas Corrigan
Corrigan House
Virginia

The impudence of it had once amused him but he had used it for so long now that he almost believed the pompous announcement that told the truth so untruthfully.

The young man wore a peajacket and appeared to be a seaman. Two passersby stopped to question him and as the doorman politely pushed open the forbidding grilled door Nick lingered long enough to hear what the boy said.

"My brothers signed on the tanker *Gulflight* out of the Texas Gulf. He drowned after a U-boat attack by the dirty Huns . . ."

Nick couldn't understand what this talk of U-boats had to do with an elegant little New Orleans gaming club and asked the doorman, who shrugged. "One of our guests tonight is German, I believe. But not a U-boat captain," he added and shook his head.

Nick had no love for Germans, or for the English either, so his family did not share the east coast passion to be drawn into the European War. The arrogant Prussian embassy staffs were notoriously unpopular—and hardly flush with funds. But German "businessmen" might be accommodated . . . these men represented big war-boom profits, all ripe to be taken . . .

Surrendering his overcoat to the girl in the foyer, he strolled into the main salon, which rather resembled the east parlor at Gaynor House, all delicate white and gold with green brocaded chairs and a carved mantelpiece with a great mirror above.

His friend, tough, burly Harold Vorhees, owner of a fleet of freighters and other cargo carriers, came over to greet him. His beautiful, raven-haired mistress Lettice du Vaux was beside him. Lettice was the official hostess at the club but Nick knew Vorhees had money invested in Lettice, so in the long run he probably owned a piece of the club. Vorhees hadn't taken lightly to being thrown out of the Hotel St. George.

"Evening, Corrigan. Glad to see a gentleman in here. Last hour I've been pestered by everybody talking business, wanting my freighters to plough right into the war zone. I'm not that crazy."

It was an odd thing to say, and so loudly, to a man with little interest in the shipping business, and Nick decided it was intended for other ears. He looked about. There were several men who looked like rugged Scots or darker Cornishmen who had overheard the remark. The British Navy, blockading many American ports, was nearly as active as the German U-boats.

He left the war talk behind when Lettice took his arm, guiding him to a waiter carrying a tray of champagne before escorting him to the inner room, where the heavy gaming action took place. Her bare shoulders gleamed in the light of the chandeliers as she preceded him to the roulette and faro tables. In one corner a knot of men were watching a blackjack game; the poker table, not usually popular among these international gamblers, was full.

Lettice du Vaux was professionally insistent. "Do not let the eyes wander yet, Nicholas," she said. "You must pay homage to the more elegant games. It is only proper. Here . . . the roulette. Watch the little wheel . . . then you will wish to play. Silver or gold or chips, as you choose."

Once he would have found this lady's bare throat and shoulders something to desire for the evening . . . now he merely wished her perfume were not quite so cloying. He didn't envy Vorhees his public mistress.

Lettice left him with a champagne glass in his healing hand, his other thrust into his pocket, aching with the pain of having to squander perfectly good poker stakes on the turn of a roulette wheel, doubtless rigged in favor of the house. However, he knew he had to pay his admission. He only wondered how small a loss he could get away with before moving to a poker table where something more than luck would come into the play.

He studied the roulette table with its European wheel, slightly different from the ones he was accustomed to in the West. He calculated the number running but found nothing systematic. He bought five-dollar chips and the stack of ten-dollar gold pieces that were his trademark. He would soon use their glitter to good effect . . . this well-dressed crowd seemed to be made of money, thanks to war profits.

Near the croupier he saw a frosty-eyed, bullet-headed man look at him with what he thought was contempt. The man, wearing some sort of cross on the lapel of his evening jacket, threw down a ten-dollar chip on a line-bet split between nineteen and twenty-one. Nick, telling himself he was behaving like an amateur and an idiot, just as contemptuously tossed a gold piece on fifteen . . . he and Dinah had been married for fifteen days. Others placed their bets with impressive stacks of silver, and the wheel spun to come up thirty-five. An elderly woman with money on a three-way split chuckled happily as she raked in her winnings.

Before the next spin the croupier addressed the cold-eyed man. "Count von Hartweig?"

"Well then, one more," the German agreed and pushed forward the last of his ten-dollar chips, five of them on the one. A second later as the crouper started to call, Nick had an idea. He pushed out four gold twenties beside the German's stack. The German opened his mouth, perhaps to protest . . . he looked angry enough. The ball spun around the outer rim, seemed about to fall into the one. Nick caught his breath . . . the ball skipped into the next pocket of the wheel, a twenty.

I should have known, Nick thought, one hundred dollars lighter. Dinah is twenty years old . . . I had a hunch to play twenty . . . He almost believed it. He had thought the German's good will was important enough to the club for the management to let him win on his parting bet. The club proved either too honest, or too greedy.

Having paid his entrance fee, Nick sauntered around, pretending interest in the faro game and taking another glass of champagne, which he set down after one swallow. Poker, he'd always felt, was much too serious a business to mix with liquor . . . he left the champagne for his opponents.

It was an hour before things began to look hopeful at the poker table. He had, though, put his time to good use, wandering around the room, always at an angle to observe the six men playing poker. They seemed serious, one of the more soberly dressed players making angry remarks now and then with a Scot's burr.

At the last minute, with the pot well over two hundred dollars, a dispute arose between the Scot and an aristocratic-looking German, probably from the local consulate. The Scot angrily accused the German of palming a card. The German, equally angry, demanded, "What does he mean, this palming?"

Everyone else tried *not* to explain but it was impossible to silence the Scot, inflamed by too much champagne. The unpleasantness rose; so did the combatants. Nick, who had been watching the play and the quarrel, deliberately got in the way when the German, having checked his gloves in the foyer, tried to slap the Scot with a bare hand. Nick's elbow caught the slap but club employees were already closing down the poker table, politely encouraging participants to try roulette.

A little desperate, Nick looked for Lettice du Vaux in the hope of finding a private game but had no luck. From low-voiced talk, he heard that the poker table would be closed down for the rest of the week while certain "antagonistic parties" were in town. There seemed to be nothing for it but to go home three hundred dollars short. It was the thought of looking into Dinah's eyes and confessing his failure that made him hesitate. He would much rather have met the infuriated German's pistol at twenty paces.

While he debated the least of several evils, Harold Vorhees walked by and asked why he didn't try his luck at roulette. "You don't want to be a Cheap-Jack all your life, boy. Roulette is elegance. You look like an elegant player. Be one." He reached up and slapped Nick between the shoulder blades. In spite of his reach, it was a patronizing slap. "You've got to move with the times, boy."

Nick resented being characterized as a Cheap-Jack and knew he was being maneuvered into a situation that would be beyond his control. But neither could he afford to offend his most influential New Orleans acquaintance. "Good idea. I may develop a knack for it."

When Voorhees disappeared Nick wandered around the tables, took another drink and set it down on the other side of the room. Lettice du Vaux was keeping an eye on him. Strolling to another roulette table, he studied the action and bought a stack of five-dollar chips. No more twenties. He noted a white-haired woman seated and playing while a very smooth younger man stood leaning over her shoulder. The woman won consistently, not large amounts, but Nick was surprised to see how it accumulated. The answer seemed to lie in multiplying each win and hedging bets on three or more numbers. The wheel was running to the last third. The white-haired woman placed her chips on four numbers.

With more hope than confidence Nick put a chip on each of the final four numbers, thirty-three to thirty-six. The white-haired woman won on thirty. All his instincts told him to double next but he refrained. On the fourth turn his thirty-five came up. This time he doubled with his winnings and lost them all. He went back to one chip on each of four. Someone gave him a glass—rum, this time—and, against his rules, he drank it.

Somebody remarked that it was midnight. How much longer will I be here? Nick asked himself. He felt a kind of deathly calm . . . he had seldom been so cold. He bought more chips but had to stop and rub his hands before going on. There was something about a twelve . . . Of course! He had met Dinah on the twelfth. He began his play again but hadn't nerve enough to put everything on twelve. He quartered his bet, including the twelve, and lost three times in a row. How much did he have left of his original thousand-dollar purse? He couldn't remember . . . God! A little less than four hundred.

He bought fifty dollars worth of chips, hating the look he thought he read on the croupier's face, giving the whole transaction his best poker face in return. The wheel spun. The white-haired woman gathered her winnings and left with her smooth friend in tow. Nick smiled deliberately. It was all gone now . . . all but the three hundred and some dollars he hadn't touched yet. It was preposterous, but he made it a point of honor not to spend that. Automatically he drew his hand out of his pocket, holding two of the bright twenty-dollar gold pieces between his fingers . . . he had forgotten all about them. Very precisely he stacked the two coins, one on top of the other, between the eleven and twelve.

The ball rolled around the rim of the bowl, fell into the twelve pocket. A slight warmth returned to his veins. With a semblance of that elegance Vorhees had praised, Nick turned away from the table with his winnings, handsomely tipping the croupier, the waiter and finally the girl who helped him on with his overcoat, her fingers lingering hopefully on his arm.

When he left the club the air was damp with fog. He walked slowly but his pace soon increased while he calculated his wins and losses. He had entered the club with a thousand dollars and change. He now had about one thousand twenty dollars. He had experienced excruciating hours that subtracted years from his life to earn a profit of roughly eighteen dollars.

He wondered again if there wasn't something to be said for shop assistants and their twelve dollars a week. . . .

He came to the little street where Dinah would be waiting. He turned the corner, heard voices singing in the foggy distance, probably at the cafe opposite their apartment. Someone was playing an accordion. "Alexander's Ragtime Band" ended on a rising note. A minute later the cafe's patrons, led by the accordion, began the poignant strains of a new war song from England, "Keep the Home Fires Burning." It was a pleasant, haunting sound. He wondered if it had kept Dinah awake. He himself was exhausted . . . The tension had begun to tell. He wanted only one thing—to scrub off the club's atmosphere and go to bed with Dinah in his arms. He began to hurry. . . .

The cafe doors were open in spite of the fog, but nobody in the cafe seemed cold. They were all sitting at one big table around the accordionist, singing the last strains of the plaintive song. Nick looked away, feeling for his key, then looked back blinking in disbelief.

There in the semicircle around the accordionist was his own Dinah, bundled in the new cloth coat he'd proudly bought her in Atlanta. But though she was wrapped up she was by no means cold. Five other people, including the accordionist, were swaying back and forth in friendly harmony . . . It was very clear she hadn't missed him at all . . . but he could hardly blame her . . . *he* was the one who had left her behind. He pulled himself together and crossed the street, noting that two of the girls in the semicircle stopped singing to watch him with interest. It took Dinah a little longer, but as he reached the doorway and the music stopped she jumped up and tugged at his hand to bring him inside.

"I'm his wife," she dramatically announced, giving him top billing.

He waved to them all, took his wife with one arm and they kissed theatrically. Though the kiss had been partly in fun, the fire built up between them, and she murmured, "Let's go home."

"Right now."

Hearing this, one of the girls sighed and pushed the man beside her.

"No," Dinah insisted. "I mean *really* home, to Corrigan House."

Chapter Sixteen

BOTH Nick and Dinah wrote some careful letters to those at home before they left New Orleans. On the way home they compared notes and decided that they had behaved with positive brilliance in every detail.

By the time they reached their small but charming hotel in Atlanta, a note from Amabel reached them saying that there had been loud words between Timby and Rheba Moon in their room but she had seen Rheba's old carpet bag and it looked as if she were definitely going. At Nick's instructions they gave Rheba a whole hundred dollars, which should last her for months and months, much too large a sum in Amabel's eyes. Meanwhile, Amabel had gone over to the Finch place and hired two girls to help her clean up the house and was going to work real hard herself as soon as her migraine let up. Everything would be spotless when Nick and Dinah returned, she assured them.

"You see?" Dinah said. "I knew it would all turn out fine. Please don't frown so."

She cheered him up as she always did, and for a little while it seemed that they hadn't a thing to worry about beyond Nick's earning power. Then came more good news from Ellen, who wrote to say she loved them both and as soon as they would like her to visit them she would. Otherwise, would they come up to Gaynor House or meet her somewhere else so she and they could really celebrate their happiness?

"I know it is happiness," she added, "because Jem and I married after a great many unpleasant, even tragic things had happened to keep us apart. So forgive a mother's hesitation and please let me give you my 'blessing' face to face. My love to you both. Ellen."

They were not exactly thrilled by the note they received in Atlanta from Gaynor House signed by Shelley, Marsh and Bill Sholto . . . it sounded very much like Shelley's doing and the signatures were certainly all hers. She wanted them both—she made a point of including just the two of them—to come up to Gaynor House, where she knew there would be furnishings and what-not in the attics and unused rooms that just might suit them. "And as for clothes, well, we'll talk about that when you get home."

"I'd rather see you stark naked than wearing her damned handed-down clothes," Nick snapped.

Dinah teased him back, "Well, if you say so. But winter is almost here and—"

He cuffed her playfully under the chin and kissed her and there was no more talk of Shelley's handed-down clothes or furniture. . . .

For some reason, in spite of the generally hopeful news from home, Nick wanted to arrive at the Corrigan house in the evening, which meant driving all day. Dinah was careful not to upset him, since the car itself, for all its splendor, was apt to stop dead at unexpected moments. But unlike some drivers Dinah had seen on the roads, Nick didn't seem to lose his temper at such times. He enjoyed and catered to the car and regarded its temperamental outbursts as a part of its charm. She decided that he thought of it as a woman. She was convinced that he was gracious and kind to almost all women—if she excepted the patronizing women of the river homes—and this odd but nice quirk must have been born out of his long responsibility for those at home who adored him.

As they neared Gaynorville one early winter afternoon, Nick began to look tense, his knuckles tight on the wheel. Dinah guessed what he was anxious about and tried to relieve his worries without his awareness that her efforts were deliberate. "I'm glad we ate that big dinner at noon. We certainly won't need any supper. We can just talk a few minutes with Amabel and maybe Timby. They'll probably want us to tell them a little about the Carolinas and New Orleans and all those fascinating delta places—"

"And full details of our wedding," he said morosely. "Lucky that fellow took our picture. Just to prove it really happened." He put one hand in her lap and she took it tightly in both of hers. His fingers were cold.

"They'll have to believe it," she said. "I pressed and dried the mignonettes and a lily of the valley. I've got them in mama's envelope."

They drove into the south end of Gaynorville where the estate road started west past the Confederate cemetery to the plantation homes on the Ooscanoto River. The first property beyond the outskirts of the town was the Corrigan farm, separated from Gaynorville by the Dunmore East Creek. Dinah sat up stiffly. She had been so sure she wasn't going to be nervous or pessimistic . . . now she needed all her confidence to support Nick's uneasy cheerfulness.

"They've had rain but it looks like beautiful weather. Good for the crops and all . . ."

He looked at her and laughed. "Sweetheart, tell the truth. What do you know about Virginia crops?"

"Well, the rain was good for something, anyway. Oh— I love those fences! They look marvelous. Do they go completely around the property?" She saw that she had struck a bright note. The white fences were important to him for some reason.

He was much too casual. He pressed her fingers before waving airily at the fences ahead. "They were fixed weeks ago. Before we left. You probably didn't notice . . . you being used to decent upkeep of land."

It was partly true. She hadn't paid attention to the neat white-painted fences before their marriage but she laughed now at his idea of how she had always lived.

"If you're talking about back home, I'm used to broken fences, unpainted fences, sometimes barbed wire and most of all no fences. So these beautiful white ones truly are impressive to me."

He was pleased, no question about it. Had he done it all himself? She moved nearer and he responded as always. She hoped he would never change . . . She had never found reason to be cynical about love in her parents' house, but living with Shelley and Marsh had shown her how far apart a husband and wife could grow. There were moments during her stay at Gaynor House when she thought Marsh was trying to hint that he and Shelley might even separate, and then followed the unpleasant feeling that she herself had awakened Marsh to the fact that he no longer loved his beautiful, popular wife. Or was this presumptuous . . . ?

"I'm glad we're not going to be living any closer to Gaynor House," she said aloud. She watched him watching for the white Corrigan gate. "I never liked Aunt Shelley too much. She seems to have led Marsh a merry chase."

"How is that?"

"Flirting and being the belle of the ball all the time. Surely you've seen how she flutters around you, making herself irresistible every chance she gets."

"I hadn't noticed." He didn't smile. "Ah, there's the gate. We ought to hang lanterns on the posts if we're going to travel much at night."

Thinking of the gambling, she asked, "Are we going to travel much at night?"

He pulled up, got out and went to the gate. "Sweetheart, I can't very well conduct all my business by daylight. You know how it is. There are laws in certain towns."

She sighed. "Well, I guess I'll just have to find some more friendly folks who like to sing. That evening was really fun. I often think about it. I mean New Orleans." He turned around quickly and she went on innocently. "Luckily, we know so many people around here. It will make it easier. You mustn't worry about me."

He was still looking at her as he opened the gate and got back into the car, frowning slightly. Well, she had given him something to think about. . . . He rode through the gateway calling, "Amabel darlin'! Home at last! And what a trip! Wait 'til you see what we've brought you. Sweetheart—" this to Dinah—"where did we put the—you know?" He motioned to the rear seat. Dinah nodded. They exchanged conspiratorial smiles and were back again to the camaraderie of their honeymoon.

Nick was staggering with suitcases and valises while Dinah carried boxes of assorted sizes from the barn-garage up to the house, and then Amabel came running out on the porch. She had stopped to tidy her still pretty hair, used rice powder on her pink complexion and changed to her blue serge winter dress with the white frilled collar. Now, with all her wishes fulfilled, she burst into tears of happiness.

Dinah and Nick stumbled to the porch, strewed boxes and suitcases around and all three embraced. After a first warm hug, Dinah stepped back to enjoy Nick's reunion with his aunt. She didn't doubt that in some ways he was spoiled by this loving woman, but Amabel had also taught him devotion and responsibility. Dinah suspected she would be increasingly thankful for that as the years went by. And his long habit of caring for the Corrigans just might help her to fit him into some position a little more steady than the casinos . . . Meanwhile all this so openly expressed devotion was rather new to her. In spite of all the love between her mother and father, they had never been demonstrative in front of others. But then Dinah remembered Nick's public and private devotion to her on their honeymoon and she *never* wanted him to change that. . . .

Nick finally broke away from Amabel to carry in the luggage, leaving the pile of presents in the parlor. To Dinah, he seemed unusually interested in the various rooms, looking into corners, surreptitiously running his hand over all the furniture near at hand and allowing her to sit in certain chairs only after he had tested for cleanliness with his handkerchief. He was acting much too careful, as if she were a guest, not a member of the family. . . .

"Soon as we're through opening the presents," Amabel promised, "we'll go and have a big scrumptious supper. I put it outside in the cooler but we can heat it up in no time."

Dinah and Nick said in unison, "Please, no trouble. Some other time," but it was evident that preparations had been made and they were expected to eat. Nick couldn't stand to disappoint Amabel, and Dinah couldn't disappoint Nick.

While Amabel was unwrapping the paper from a gorgeous pink dressing gown with a feather boa around the collar, Dinah tried to go and hang up her coat, but Nick would have none of that, insisting on putting her coat and hat away while she "just sit comfortable-like," as Amabel put it.

Dinah decided it was too late in the day to create problems, so she sat and looked properly contented while Amabel opened and tried on the rest of her present. But when Amabel brought supper into the warm cozy kitchen from wherever the outside "cooler" was located, Dinah saw Nick's reaction and made up her mind *never* to serve him cabbage. He looked so sick at the overpowering smell that she said hurriedly, "How nice! It's such a shame Nick ate that spoiled cabbage in New Orleans. The doctor absolutely forbade him to eat it again. Nick, why don't we fix you an omelette and then the rest of us will enjoy this delicious cabbage and potatoes."

There was an anxious little flurry from Amabel, who felt that eggs were a bit exotic any time after noon and not nearly substantial enough to stick to a man's ribs. Nick protested to no effect through all this, but when Dinah tucked a towel into the neck of her dress, began to break eggs into a bowl and even borrowed a boiled potato to slice into the pan with some sausage, everyone started talking again. Clearly, this new wife knew what she was doing.

Amabel wanted to know the details of the spoiled cabbage but Nick changed the subject quickly, asking where Timby had gone . . . had he followed Rheba Moon.

"I do trust not," Amabel murmured, still uneasy in her place at the foot of the table. "I do, indeed. They left together. It was sad, though. Poor, dear Timby. I'm right sure that creature turned Timby into a drinkin' man."

Nick shook his head. "Can't quite go that far. Uncle Timby was drinking thirty years ago when the Gaynor shop burned down."

"Dearie"—Amabel lowered her voice and frowned a warning—"we don't talk about that sad business in front of our guests. You-all heard pa say it, time out of mind."

Dinah was listening hard over the sound of the food she was frying. To her relief Nick reminded his aunt, "True, but Dinah is my wife, you know. One of the family, honey . . ."

Amabel fluttered, protesting, "Oh, I never meant—I'm sure—I only—" Nick reached over, patted her hand and she subsided, shifting cabbage, potatoes and boiled pork jowl around on her plate with one of the family's last treasures, a genuine silver fork.

Dinah seated herself at the side of the table nearest the stove and Nick wound up in Timby's place at the head of the table. Just as they were all finishing their unwanted supper Amabel looked up. "Somebody's outside. Timby!" she whispered.

Dinah was annoyed with herself for feeling frightened too. What was the matter with her? She had danced with him, defended him in a fight on the Wychfield veranda—why be scared of her new "uncle" now?

Nick got up and went through the back porch to the screen door, prepared either to greet Timby or throw him out if he became obnoxious. The women watched the porch doorway nervously. They were stunned when the author of the Corrigans' original misfortunes, Captain Bill Sholto, walked in with Nick. Again Dinah noticed the peculiar code among men that she had been aware of in her father. While women held grudges forever, menfolk seemed much readier to ignore past differences.

With the air of a friendly host, Nick presented Sholto, who removed his ancient cavalry hat and bowed over Amabel's hand, looking into her eyes as he said, "The bluest eyes in Tudor County, I do swear."

Nick came around to Dinah, sharing her relief that the ice had been broken between the Corrigans and her Gaynor House relatives. Sholto kissed Dinah's forehead in fatherly style and wished the newlyweds all happiness.

As Amabel rose to get him "a slice—just a mere sliver" —of her peach pie, Sholto explained his unexpected visit. "I promised Ellen we wouldn't bother you until you'd gotten home and organized, but here I am. I know poor Ellen's been thinking about nothing but whether you got back safely so I thought I'd just mosey over and find out for myself . . . say, thanks, Miss Amabel, how'd you know peach pie was my very favorite?"

He had certainly won over Amabel, who now bustled around as she hadn't been seen to move in years, getting him the pie and a threadbare but neatly ironed linen napkin before she washed one of the few silver forks and presented that to him. Nick, his arm around Dinah, whispered, "One enemy bastion's fallen anyway."

"More than that," Sholto informed them. His hearing seemed as acute as it had been when he scouted Chief Crazy Horse's camp for Major Reno out in the Dakotas forty years earlier. "My little girl Shelley wants to give a fancy dinner for the newlyweds and we're all invited."

Dinah put in drily, "We've had enough fancy dinners to last us a while. That Wychfield affair taught me we don't want to mix with Daisy and her hired bullies."

Everyone but Dinah was embarrassed. Nick said, "I wouldn't put it quite that strong, honey. There was a misunderstanding, it's true, but Captain Sholto was on Timby's side. Remember?"

"Besides," Sholto put in, "we're not mixing Daisy Wychfield into this. Just a family dinner at Gaynor House. Miss Amabel and you two. We've persuaded"—he broke off but not before Dinah had picked up on his slip of the tongue.

"I don't think Marsh is too keen to have this dinner, is he?"

Sholto shrugged. "In my opinion, Marsh is acting mighty funny these days. He's cold as the Klondike to my daughter. If I didn't know better, I'd say there was another woman."

Quickly, because she didn't want to arouse doubt or suspicion in Nick's mind, Dinah said, "Marsh was an invalid for so long he probably doesn't like a lot of fuss and talk. Maybe we could make a brief visit some day." She noted that Nick seemed tense now and he removed his arm from around her shoulders. She backtracked. "What do you think, darling? Some nice little afternoon visit to Gaynor House?" Maybe he felt out of place there. "Not for long. Just a few minutes."

His casual words didn't match his stiffened features and

voice. "Sounds all right; Amabel, you and me . . ." Then added after the briefest of pauses, "Afternoon visits last about a quarter of an hour, don't they? I reckon we Corrigans could behave ourselves that long."

"Let's do go. If you're willing I am," Dinah said quickly to Amabel, who began to stammer that she'd be ever so pleased. Dinah caught Sholto's eye and was furious at the odd little gleam of pity she read there. She raised her chin and rubbed her cheek against Nick's sleeve as he stood beside her chair. His hand went out to her hair, stroking it.

"If my womenfolk are willing to go, it's agreeable with me," Nick said. "We'll go up in style." He was in a more decent humor again, and for an instant Dinah even wondered if he wanted to visit Gaynor House "in style" to see Shelley Wychfield again. Dinah was hardly blind to Shelley's interest in Nick. He was an attractive, normal man, while Shelley was still just about the most beautiful woman in Tudor County . . . She decided she had better pay a little more attention to her own looks. . . .

She was glad when Captain Sholto finished the pie and took himself off home, promising to give Ellen the love and affection of the newlyweds. "And now that the newlyweds are here, Ellen will be coming to see you right soon. She had this idea we shouldn't bother you 'til you were settled in, as it were. But I paid no mind to that. 'Night, ladies. Corrigan."

Dinah disliked him more now than before his visit. Every time he mentioned Ellen's opinions, thoughts and desires in that proprietary way, he absolutely set her teeth on edge. . . .

Sholto had hardly left Corrigan property before Nick was embracing Dinah. "Sweetheart, it's been a long day. Forget all this kitchen business and let's get to bed. Right now."

Amabel pattered around, rushing dishes into the big dish

pan. "Dear me! You-all run along and be company. I'll clean up."

There it was, the constant thought of her as someone temporary... *company*. But with Nick's body pressed hard against hers and his arms imprisoning her, she put her mind to more basic matters.

The newlyweds went off to Nick's bedroom. Electricity had been brought into this entire end of Tudor County a few years before, but it all cost money and the Corrigan house still relied on oil lamps. Dinah found it hard to get used to such dim lighting everywhere except in the kitchen. However, she studied the bedroom as she undressed and washed in the basin of water on the stand beneath the window. It was a small room, but the bed had a good mattress and was large enough for both of them.

She raised her arms to slip on her nightgown and had just let it drop over her head when it was lifted off and she felt Nick behind her, his hands closing around her breasts. He drew her back to his cool, naked body, whispering against her hair, "How did I ever win you, Dinah Gaynor Faire? I'm running in luck."

"Dinah Corrigan."

"A stickler for accuracy." His lips touched her shoulder and her arm and then he turned her deftly around. She remembered thinking some weeks ago that he was a man of considerable experience, but as his mouth brushed the hollow between her breasts she murmured dreamily, "I don't care if you are, darling."

Startled, he raised her chin and stared at her. "You don't care if I'm what?"

"A man of too much experience." He still looked as though he didn't quite understand, and she said straight out, "With women, darling. With women."

He began to laugh, so hard she had to remind him, "Think how shocked Amabel would be. I'm sure she believes sex is a very grim matter."

He glanced at the door. "Now where did we leave off?" He lifted her to him again. . . .

They finally sank into sleep, only to be aroused around midnight by an infernal racket on the front porch. Dinah sat up, half asleep. "Lord, it's Pancho Villa on the warpath!"

"Pancho Villa doesn't sing in a Gaelic brogue," Nick told her. He swore and got out of bed, feeling for his bathrobe.

"Oh lord, don't fight Timby tonight, darling. Please. He may be in a better mood in the morning—"

But Nick was at the door. He looked out across the hall to the parlor. Then, while she held her breath, he closed the door and to her amazement turned the key in the lock. "He's in a bad mood right now. And he's alone."

"Thank heaven for that!"

"Looks like he got drunk to ease the pain of Rheba's departure. He seems to be cussing her out right now." He sighed. "If I'm to support this family, looks like I'll have to get one of those things ma used to call a 'legitimate job.'"

Dinah tried not to show her pleasure at hearing such news. "If you do, maybe we can afford our own house in a few months—"

"On twelve dollars a week?"

"You're worth much more. Come back to bed and I'll show you. . . ."

He did. She did. And Timby and his problems were at least temporarily forgotten. . . .

Chapter Seventeen

SHELLEY and Marsh Wychfield arrived early on the little portico of the Community Church in order to beat Daisy Wychfield, who always held court there. Shelley wanted to talk to Olaf Holderson, who was enlarging Gaynorville's branch of Holderson's Ashby Emporium. Holderson, dry-humored and a sinewy combination of Norwegian and Swedish, agreed that help was impossible to find these days, what with everybody hiring out for war work in the Newport News shipyards and the Norfolk navy yards.

"I know young Nick well. Seen him around times out of mind. Makes a right good appearance and he sure would get the ladies into the store. I want him honest, though. None of them poker hands in the back room."

"I'm sure he's honest," Shelley put in while Marsh listened with an aloof contempt that she had tried to ignore.

"He's not talking about that kind of honesty," he said distantly as Holderson nodded agreement. "He means the fellow would be expected to put in an honest day's work."

"Like you, honey?" Shelley asked, dripping sweet venom.

His features froze, and he walked away to meet and talk shop with Barney Kent and to greet Barney's mother, Persis. Holderson continued to complain about the high price of yard goods, asking how Shelley got things in from France with the war raging, the British sealing up American ports and the Germans playing havoc at sea. Normally Shelley was happy to discuss the business so close to her heart, but right now something was much closer to her deepest interests... She broke into his unhappy discourse.

"Why, there's your new floor manager! He's with my niece and sister Ellen. Don't tell me he won't sell expensive French yardage for you."

"Hmm... but everybody knows he gambles." Holderson then asked her shrewdly, "Why don't you hire him for *your* shop?"

"Salon, Olaf. The difference between your prices and mine." She considered the man and three women approaching while absently brushing at Neily's jacket. Her smile was slow in coming and a bit wistful. "Nick Corrigan at Gaynor's? Afraid even I couldn't get away with that." She flirted with Holderson in the way she added, "He's only just married. Unfortunately."

Holderson pretended not to understand. "I see Marsh is going over to say hello to them. Maybe I'd better too, seeing Corrigan's married into your family."

Shelley stayed behind for a few minutes watching the enthusiasm that lighted her husband's austere face as he shook hands with Dinah, and then less enthusiastically with Nick. She was both pleased, and shocked. Pleased because Marsh could hardly point a finger at her now. He certainly showed all the signs of silly puppy love over her niece. An annoying, stupid little love that had nothing physical in it.... just more bookish, dreamy love thoughts, so typical of Marsh.

Except, to be fair, there had been a time when she had adored this handsome, aloof man. In her school days she would daydream to herself about Marsh Wychfield sweeping her up in his arms and telling her he couldn't live without her ... Strange now after all this time to feel even a little pinch of envy when she saw the sudden life in her husband's eyes as he looked at another woman, a girl ten years younger at that. ...

Nick brought forward his aunt Amabel and Marsh took her hand in the kindly way he had when he chose to.

The nerve of them! They were all going into the church without even waiting for her. Shelley looked around. "I'd rather die than go in alone," she thought. People would be sure to think she didn't approve of the marriage, which, of course, was nonsense. There was nothing she wanted more than to keep Nick Corrigan as a member of the family. She was just wondering if she would have to walk into church with her mother-in-law, Daisy Wychfield, who hove in sight. But Daisy was quickly surrounded by the Kents and elderly Reverend Sheering.

Luckily, Shelley's father came along, and she went up to him. Bill Sholto gave her a resounding kiss just under the brim of her new wide-brimmed velvet hat. "Prettiest girl in town," he said, and offering her his arm, they went in together.

Men—they'd come and go, Shelley thought, but when you got right down to it, there'd never been one to match the love and understanding she got from ... and felt for ... her father Bill Sholto ... Inside the church, however, he deserted her when she sat down in the pew always used by the Gaynors. He went right past Neily and Shelley and Marsh, begged a few pardons and sat on one side of Ellen Faire ... If only dear Ellen would go back to Lariat where she belonged! But still, while Ellen remained at Gaynor House occupying the small neat bedroom she'd been born in, the newlywed—*Nick*—was much more likely to come visiting. ...

Shelley leaned over Marsh now and said to Ellen, "Olaf Holderson has a truly grand job for Nick, running his whole store. Please tell Dinah what a great thing it would be . . . keep him from running off to all parts of the world all the time. And it will keep the dears close to us."

Both Marsh and Ellen looked pleased, for different reasons. . . .

"You must admit, Nick, everybody thinks it's a marvelous idea, you have all the qualities for it—"

Nick studied what he saw in the mirror, grimaced at his reflection and said too patiently for the hundredth time, "Anything else in the world, sweetheart . . . but not this . . . not spending all day in a damned country store surrounded by junk that I'm expected to sell to unfortunate people who don't know any better or can't afford any more." He gave up on the comb and ran his fingers through his coarse hair.

To change the pace she said, "I think you look thrilling."

Which broke his mood and made him laugh. Then, sparked by a sudden memory, "Do you know what they called me in school?"

"*Devastating* with the ladies, I'll bet."

"The kid with green skin." Even saying it now brought back the memory, and he felt more than a little queasy thinking about it.

She came up behind him, put her arms around his waist and held him tight. He smelled the light, airy perfume she wore, which made him think of the grassy outdoors on a bright wind-swept day. He saw her wonderful fair skin and marveled that she seemed to love him as much as he loved her. It was sometimes hard to know what she saw in him. He was not a modest man. He knew the full worth of the creature he had invented, the care with which he had learned how to delight women, analyze men. But all these things were on the surface. Underneath was the real Irish gypsy with wide black eyes and green skin. Bronze or sallow or whatever they called it when you were grown up, beneath it all he saw in that mirror a taller than average, sinewy boy who was the only Irish gypsy in Tudor County. And very likely on his way to making trouble with his knife if that reliance on sharp gypsy blades hadn't been beaten out of him by the fists of his father and his uncle. . . .

As if she guessed his painful thoughts, Dinah pressed her head against his shoulders. "You're only going to see this man to please me. I know that, darling. And I love you for it—"

"For going to see Holderson?"

"No, silly. For being you. I'm very lucky."

He didn't answer that. He knew he was the lucky one, but was afraid to say so out loud . . . it might break his luck, make him lose her . . . gambler's superstition . . . instead he took a strand of her fine hair and trailed it across his upper lip. "Like me better with a mustache?"

"No, darling . . . seriously. You'd be wonderful, they'd all adore you in this job . . .

He appeared to give up . . . "Well, if that's what you want . . . and it is true your aunt Shelley promises to keep me fed. In fact she thinks I might like to eat lunch every day in her place. I can go through the back door, Holderson's direct to Gaynor's—"

"You'd better not or I'll come down and pull all her hair out."

He loved the idea of her pique, used it to kiss away a frown, and then a few minutes later she was helping him on with his coat, smoothing the shoulders, giving him a pat of approval and reminding him, "Timby has turned over a whole pasture, he wanted to do it early in case the ground froze. I think he has some idea of experimenting with peanuts in place of that tobacco with those worms that crawl in and hide in the leaves, or whatever they do. Of course he says the land needs to rest for a season. He wants to see you this afternoon . . . I think he needs money for the spring planting." (In the week since Timby had come home he hadn't touched a drop of liquor . . . maybe he could still pull his weight, Nick thought.) "I know he misses Rheba, but he's trying awfully hard to make up for what he's cost you in the past. I don't think he'll forgive himself for throwing away so much on a woman who deserted him for a hundred dollars."

"It's money," Nick said, his thoughts on their own situation . . . After his obligatory interview with Olaf Holderson this morning he would look for a game, probably at the Winchester Coffee House on the outskirts of Gaynorville. It had once been the finest inn and tavern in south Tudor County, but after the turn of the century a lively crowd had begun to take it over and it was outside the limits of little Gaynorville. After all, everyone knew gambling and prostitution went on there, but the trade was salesmen and people passing through in this new age of the automobile.

He kissed her nose and lingered longer on her mouth.

Twenty dollars a week . . . trying to live off the farm just like the poor-white that he'd always been . . . God, but sooner or later he knew he would strike it big. The percentages were there. Meanwhile, to help Dinah get the Corrigan house into some kind of livable condition he spent the last two weeks doing kinds of jobs he hated . . . because she'd asked him and the rewards of her love afterward were worth it. But all the time he knew what he was good at and common sense told him that one night of poker was worth more than months of any other work around the house . . . and it was still the surest source of income he knew. Sooner or later Dinah would understand that. . . .

"Good luck," she called as he left.

He went into town, past Gaynor's to the Holderson Emporium, where someone was arranging a display in a front window of Gaynor's. He didn't look around. He was wondering whether his luck was in or out. . . .

Shelley Wychfield draped the long opera glove over three little black-velvet steps and then moved around the display window on her knees, trying to get the scene in perspective. She called to Dora Johnson, who was carrying away the green taffeta evening cape that had been the previous single display.

"Bring me the pearl necklace."

"Land, Miss Shelley! Real pearls?"

"Certainly. They're my own. I can do what I like with them." She draped the double strand along the steps just above the glove and then, as a shadow crossed the window in front of her, she looked out.

He had already passed but she stared after Nick Corrigan, aware that at the sight of him she had grown quite warm. "Just the sight of him gives me a flush," she thought, and watched him until he disappeared into Holderson's new store . . .

Dora Johnson asked from inside the salon, "You want something else, Miss Shelley?"

"I want *him*, all right. How I want him!" she was tearing the pearls and gloves off the display step and starting again. "More than that stupid girl, what does she know about love, that silly, arrogant child—?"

"What's that, Miss Shelley?"

"Never mind, I'm through." She hadn't realized she was muttering loud enough to be heard . . . well, I'm not through, she thought. I haven't even begun. I could make him forget all about her. She hugged herself as her imagination took over. Papa says Nick's known many women. There's a man who could teach even me a few things. She sat down on the top velvet step and relived, as she had so often, those minutes in the salon when she had nearly let herself be seduced by him . . .

Her imagination frequently ran wild with images of what could have followed between them if she hadn't somehow . . . she still didn't understand it . . . put him off. He was too passionate to stop the way he had . . . she knew men. She had been too close to him to be fooled . . . unless, of course, he had been thinking of someone else at the time. That was one of papa's theories. Almost as bad, he claimed that Nick had deliberately led her on, teased her. . . .

The idea made her sick, so she banished it as she did all painful thoughts, and got to her feet. "Give me your hand, Dora. I'm coming in."

But Dora was busy greeting the young third wife of the aged Richmond banker, Harleigh Duckworth, and Shelley climbed out of the window into the salon to meet the vulgar, pretty woman. While she was demonstrating new net and silk fabrics for Darlee Duckworth's spring social whirl, Shelley was remembering those girlhood years when she and her young friends attended classes with Nick at the small Gaynorville grammar school. He was always at a distance, even if he was seated in their midst . . . admitted on sufferance. Though she had been attracted to him, she had also despised him without quite knowing why, except that her friends did. He was a member of a family whose conduct shocked the county . . . and he looked different. . . .

Then, ever since he had made love to her that night two years ago, Shelley saw him in a new way. She berated herself for the stupidity of those girlhood years, suspecting that the old memories were what turned him away from her now. Well, she just had to let him know how she had changed, how wrong and cruel she knew she and the others had been. . . .

As soon as Darlee Duckworth was taken care of, two other customers appeared but this time Shelley forgot corporate profits. Her thoughts were next door with the man in Holderson's branch emporium. She explained to the clients that Olaf Holderson had asked her to inspect his new "department store." She was careful to ignore Dora Johnson's indignant look. Too often Dora acted as Shelley's conscience, all because she had once played the same role as Maggilee's assistant.

Shelley went into the emporium through the front doors where she saw three salesladies, all respectable local women in white shirtwaists and navy-blue serge skirts, gathered in a tight knot just inside the entrance. They were talking with great animation but stopped abruptly as Shelley passed, returning her nod with what she was sure were applied smiles. Shelley didn't trust any woman . . . Long ago, like her half-sister, Ellen, she had discovered that her most dangerous rival with men was her mother, Maggilee, which gave her a distinct distaste for all other women. . . .

Now she heard Nick Corrigan's name spoken, and while she pretended to examine the long counters, the shelves and the cubbyholes behind them, she gathered that Miss Finch, Miss Abercromie and Mrs. Hopkins thought dashing Nick would be a real asset to Holderson's. They were, of course, right.

"Such a romantic air he has, don't you think? I declare, you'd never know he was kin to that dreadful Timby Corrigan . . ."

Romantic air, was it? Shelley smiled. It wasn't Nick Corrigan's put-on aura of aristocracy and romance that Shelley gave a damn about . . . She had the real thing in those departments at home and much good it did her. Nick was distinctly something else . . . Now he and Olaf Holderson were at the back of the long barnlike room, walking together up the few steps to a narrow balcony with a ceiling so low Nick had to duck his head as the two men strolled over to Holderson's big rolltop desk.

Shelley lingered, trying to look like a customer. Young Mr. Phipps, a friendly little man who handled gentlemen's accessories, was waiting on two ladies choosing Christmas presents for their menfolk, but he scurried over to Shelley.

"Dear Miss Shelley, could you wait just a smidgeon? I'll be right with you."

Nothing easier. She gave him her best moist-lipped smile and strolled along the rear counter immediately under the low balcony rail, then went around behind the counter, examining the gentlemen's linen shirts and the loud vests. A foolish buy, she thought, fingering the vests. They and the equally vulgar watches and fobs set out in trays cheapened the merchandise. But why help the competition? Let Olaf find out for himself.... Meanwhile she overheard Holderson explaining the job to Nick. It seemed as if the less interest Nick showed, the more desirable he became as a prospective employee. Shelley was getting impatient, tapped her fingernails on the counter and wished Nick would hurry up and give in. Time was passing. She wanted Nick over in the Gaynor salon for lunch, the only time during the day when she could be alone with him, and the minutes were slipping away....

Little Mr. Phipps had come up behind her, had spoken twice before she was aware of him. She was desperately straining to hear Nick's answer to Olaf's offer. Finally Nick was saying, "Frankly I don't think I'm suited to it, my experience has all been confined to—other fields."

Mr. Phipps repeated, "Exceptional quality, ma'am. The shirts are imported direct from the North. New York, I mean."

Shelley said vaguely, "Yes, for my husband, you know. Marshall Wychfield." She stepped back so that she could be seen by the two men on the balcony. "No offense, but Mr. Wychfield is a tall man ... perhaps if we could measure one of those shirts on Mr.—who is it up there? Oh, yes. Mr. Corrigan would just do. A trifle thinner than my husband but I think we might persuade him just to stand here while we measure the length of the sleeve."

"Quite, Miss Shelley." Phipps raised his voice. "Mr.—er —Corrigan! Sorry, Mr. Holderson, but Miss Shelley would like Mr. Corrigan to measure a shirt for her husband."

Shelley studied Nick's expression when he saw her. She

was intelligent enough not to believe the wide stare that pretended to admire her. The fact that she felt his contempt both annoyed, and enticed her.

The two men descended the steps. While Nick obligingly took up the most expensive shirt, measuring the sleeve against his own, Holderson muttered in Shelley's ear, "I'll be expecting considerable of your business after this."

"He's worth it already, wouldn't you say?" she asked with a sassy, innocent wink.

They were very pleased with each other. Shelley glanced at the three salesladies at the front of the long center aisle. Two customers, both female, had come in and were herded to various counters. The extra saleslady, Mrs. Hopkins, her chunky shape laced into a tubular form, came tip-tilting on her high heels to join Nick and Mr. Phipps.

"Do let me show you some of our better quality gentlemen's garments. Mr. Corrigan, would you be so good as to help me? This way."

And of course, Shelley thought resignedly, he would be charming to fat old ladies . . . a great deal more charming than he's ever been to me. I wonder if he's afraid of me. He doesn't appear to be but you never know. Why else would he break his neck to be nice to old hags? The irony of him doing what she'd set up for him to do escaped her . . .

Meanwhile Holderson's enthusiasm and that of the female employees seemed to have stirred Nick to action. While Shelley watched, Nick reached up and brought down the box of shirts for Mrs. Hopkins, presented them to her with a smile and she and Mr. Phipps sold them to Shelley, who concealed her complete indifference to the sale.

Another pair of customers strolled into the shop. Nick was called on for his advice to a prospective bride and groom about their "going-away" clothes. . . . After two hours of this it was easier than Shelley had anticipated to get Nick over to the Gaynor shop. He refused at first, as she had expected, but she had a sudden inspiration . . . "I think you're afraid of competition. I knew it. You, the best poker player in the county. And me with a game for you."

Sure enough, he was caught and turned away momentarily from long-faced Miss Abercromie who had asked his opinion of her high-necked batiste shirtwaist . . . did it make her look too thin?

Nick forced himself to return to the subject at hand, and while Shelley waited, his long, skilled fingers folded down Miss Abercromie's collar so that the scalloped edges lent her face a new and softer look. Or maybe the softness was the result of Nick's attention to her.

"Well?" he said shortly as he joined Shelley, "where are these competitors, these great poker players?"

"Come along." She took his arm and they went around by the back doors to the comforts of the Gaynor salon. Holderson looked after them, made a comment to Mrs. Hopkins, who, literally, sniffed and said out loud, "I must say, I always thought she was a bit fast. Like her mother . . . you do rec'lect Miss Maggilee?"

Shelley pretended not to hear but seeing Nick's frown she realized the woman's malice was to her advantage, likely as it was to make him sympathetic to her. He opened the door and they went out to the little street that was scarcely more than an alley. He waved to Hannah Gamble, out cranking up a Ford in front of the livery stable. At the last minute, just outside the Gaynor back foyer, Nick hesitated. "Who are these poker players?"

"You'll see." It was late in the lunch hour. They had already wasted fifteen precious minutes and she would quickly have to set up something. She told him to wait. In the little kitchen off the rear foyer she got out the tray of sandwiches and iced tea from the cooler. As she started across the main salon he took the tray and set it on a marble sidetable.

He smiled, but there wasn't much warmth in it. "Well,

aunt Shelley? Are we the game? You and I?"

She looked at him carefully, decided to ignore his sarcasm and try to play her part lightly. "I do believe you're afraid of me. If you're not, prove it. Isaac is an awfully good poker player. He's the handyman. He'll be back any minute." Thank God for Darlee Duckworth's visit. It gave her another name at random. "Mr. Duckworth from the Richmond and Dominion Bank is coming by to pay his wife's accounts. He'll love to have a game." At least Nick was reacting to that news . . .

He shrugged, reached over, took a tall glass of iced tea and began to sip it. "I can wait a few minutes. But I do have some business out at the Winchester."

She fussed around, offering him a sandwich and when he refused it, she began to eat it herself out of more nervousness than she thought herself capable of.

"You were always my favorite person at school, did you know that?"

"No, I didn't."

"But it's true. You were stronger than Marsh and better-looking than Barney—"

"You forget I was there."

"But it's *true*, Nick. I used to watch you a lot. I—I wished you'd ask me to walk home with you sometime and—"

He swirled the tea around in his glass. "Walk home to the Corrigan farm with me? I don't think so. Trouble is, Shelley, I remember how it really was. And among other things how the little Princess Shelley-Ann Sholto despised me, and my family."

She dropped the sandwich on the tray. "No, Nick . . . anyway, people can change. *I've* changed." She looked at him, her eyes actually rimmed with tears. "Nick, aren't you ever going to forgive me?"

He set the glass down. She had annoyed him, which was hardly her intention.

"What difference does it make?"

Well, she decided, it was now or never. Stop the fencing about. She stretched a little, held onto his shoulders for leverage and kissed him, her mouth clinging to his until he removed each of her hands, after several satisfactory moments and set her away from him.

He had enjoyed that kiss, she was sure . . . she had felt his body harden against her . . .

Her prospects, she decided, were definitely looking up.

Chapter Eighteen

BEFORE going down to breakfast that day Ellen went through her small unimpressive wardrobe, wondering what she would need for the next week or so. Then she could pack the rest and be ready to leave any day, as soon as she felt Dinah was reasonably settled into her marriage. Ellen was certain the greatest problem in that marriage would be money . . . and Nick's sense of obligation to his family. Like most good southerners, he was born with an almost religious conviction that the remaining members of his family were his responsibility. A blessing and a curse, it was also reinforced by the fierce clan loyalty in his Irish and gypsy blood.

Ellen was still thinking on this when she met Bill Sholto with a sweat-stained stetson perched on the back of his curly graying hair, his thumbs in his pants pockets. It was a sight to evoke her western home, in combination with the easy romantic air of the South that Sholto had adopted.

"I've been flirting with Amabel. There's a beauty when she wants to be. Mighty taking ways."

Ellen noted his mocking tone. "I suppose I'm to be flattered, if you're trying to make me jealous . . . but let me tell you, Amabel was always the prettiest girl in the county when we were twenty—"

"And still could be if she wasn't so beat down by that family . . . Well, you're *not* beat down, and are a most fortunate woman that I've come to rescue and take off to town for breakfast, and other wild adventures."

She laughed and took the arm he offered. "Adventure in Gaynorville? Lead on, sir . . ." He could still get to her . . .

Sholto drove the Model-T because, as he explained it, his beautiful lady could be closer to him. They were both feeling the excitement of their renewed—if still uneasy—relationship, and when they saw the ice-cream parlor in town opening for the day next door to the abandoned legitimate theater he suggested "strawberry ice cream for breakfast."

Ellen cooperated by saying she thought he was crazy. As the first customers of the day, they took wire-backed chairs at the small round table by the window, and while Bill consumed a plate of three ice cream flavors topped by strawberry jam, peanuts and apricot preserves, Ellen ate flaky biscuits, drank tea and watched the Gaynor salon across the street.

Sholto tried to get her attention. She was sure he guessed her thoughts and wanted very much to prevent her from thinking about his daughter. If this were so, then he had to know how much trouble his precious Shelley had stirred up . . . "Ellen, I can see that street is more exciting than my conversation."

"No, it's just that Shelley has changed her windows—"

"Clothes? I've never known you to be interested in dresses and frills. You're too sensible." When she wrinkled her nose he reached across the little table and caught her hand in his powerful grip. She hadn't the strength, or will to pull away, remembering . . . feeling . . . how once she would have given her soul to know he really loved her. She told herself it was to wipe out the past that she sat here enjoying what seemed to be another declaration of his feelings . . . but she wasn't too convincing, especially to herself—

A movement across the street distracted him. Following his glance Ellen saw Shelley come out of the salon. On the newly paved sidewalk she stopped to study her display windows, a figure of fashion herself in the latest full-skirted blue-green taffeta gown with a belted tunic and a little draped turban to match.

Ellen, watching Bill Sholto, saw his devotion and pride as he observed his daughter, her appearance, the successful shop which was now all hers. Then he turned back to Ellen, whose face was set in the stony look she had worn the night she had sent him off to marry the pregnant Maggilee, her own mother . . . It shocked him. "Ellen, please. I know she flirts a little but it doesn't mean a damn thing. I flirt, her mother flirted. I guess it runs in the family."

She took a long breath. "*I* think she's trying to break up my daughter's marriage. Just what mama did to me." Before Bill could protest, she put her hand over his. "Bill, if you ever loved me, just please help me now. Somehow she's got to keep her hands off Nick Corrigan."

"Why not ask Marsh? It's his job." But he avoided her eyes.

She laughed at that. "Why? It's my opinion he has a crush on my daughter. He'd probably enjoy seeing Nick and Dinah's marriage collapse almost before it's begun."

Their hands were tightly clasped now. They both looked down at them. Under the influence of that warm contact Bill Sholto promised, "I'll do what I can, it's possible, I reckon. He's the kind women do seem to be attracted to . . ." He added, "Unless this isn't Corrigan's doing in the first place . . . the more I think of it, the more likely it seems to me that it is."

She took this with a grain of salt. "Do you suppose that's why Shelley is headed into Holderson's Emporium right now? Look there. If Nick's responsible, he must have enticed her by long distance."

Forced to admitting what he saw, Sholto paid the check and said briskly, "Come along. I don't want my daughter carrying on with Nick Corrigan any more than you do."

By the time they entered Holderson's Emporium they were following in the wake of half a dozen customers. Sholto's eyes searched for his daughter's unmistakable figure, while Ellen looked around for Nick. She wasn't happy to discover them both at the same counter—ladies' bathing suits. Bill moved up the center aisle. Ellen moved around to the rear of the bathing-suit section, hoping against hope that she would interrupt nothing more significant than Nick's advice on a choice of a suit.

Shelley was saying, "But I'm not afraid of the newest styles. I never have been. Nick dear, can't you just see me in the one-piece suit at Virginia Beach on Saturday?"

"Well, I'm not likely to, Mrs. Wychfield. I'm a working man now. My family and I won't be able to go to Virginia Beach or any other beach on Saturdays. But I can certainly imagine you in that suit. Black against your bright hair."

Ellen was briefly relieved. Nick was certainly behaving at his best and with an eye to business. The bathing suit he was showing was the most expensive in the shop and the saleswoman, Miss Abercromie, who had called him over at Shelley's order, seemed perfectly content.

Sholto too had heard them and, apparently satisfied, moved into the next aisle to shake hands with Olaf Holderson, who would normally be off administering his big store in the county seat. Ellen felt she owed a little trust to Nick and went around unseen behind him past the gloves and accessories counter to join Sholto and the shopowner. Holderson was assuring Sholto, "We've had right good business this morning. I lay a part of it, from the ladies at least, to your son-in-law, Miss Ellen. He does know how to sell. And he's got an uncanny eye for the most expensive item in every category. Good taste, that boy." He jogged

Sholto in the ribs with his elbow as he warned Ellen with a smile, "Better tell your daughter to keep him on a tight rein . . . what the devil—beg pardon, ma'am—what the devil does that Miss Shelley want with him now?"

Sholto put his arm around Ellen. "Honey," he told her, "don't you fret about Shelley's foolery. She's just a born tease." (And then some, Ellen, as a woman, thought to herself.)

What Shelley wanted, and after an argument backed up by Nick's new boss got, was to have Nick come over to her salon and give her an opinion while she tried on one of the bathing suits with the long stockings. The customer, Holderson told Nick, was, after all, always right, and just now Shelley was the customer.

Nick looked about to explode. Whereas Shelley, Ellen saw, seemed so nervous her hands were trembling. In anticipation . . . ?

On their way out, Shelley managed to take Nick's arm . . . "To help me around those muddy holes in the alley," she said brightly.

Ellen looked pointedly at Sholto, who shrugged. "I haven't seen her look this happy in a long time. Tell you what, we'll go over and play chaperone if it will make you feel better."

At the rear door Nick saw them for the first time. He was uneasy at sight of Ellen and seemed to resent her interference while Shelley was urging her father plaintively: "Daddy! Must you?"

Nick informed Ellen with a trace of irony, "I promise you not to seduce her so she won't need her father's protection. Or yours."

She surprised and pleased him by grinning mischievously. "Quite the reverse."

That made him laugh. He must have begun to see that their presence would save him from trouble at home.

It would, she said, but knew Nick would surely resent it,

not to mention Shelley. Nonetheless she did like Nick Corrigan and with the firm support of Bill Sholto she went into Shelley's salon, leaving the explanations to Sholto.

The place had been modernized since Ellen had worked there for her mother thirty years ago, and of course this was a newer building—the original had burned down all those years ago, thanks to Timby Corrigan's ridiculous boyish "prank" of shooting at a candle on a salon table. But even with Shelley managing the place it still had unpleasant connotations for Ellen. Everywhere she looked she felt the presence of her late mother, Maggilee—her gifts for creating clothes and decor, the staircase, the exquisite drape of a sash here and a scarf or a hat there. And the sensual quality of it . . . There was little subtlety since Shelley had taken over the salon and made it pay. Under Maggilee's direction the shop was forever mortgaged, but Shelley was more of a businesswoman in spite of her busy social life. And she never put quality before profits, as Maggilee had always done.

Sholto was speaking to Ellen now in a low voice. "What is it about this place . . . ? Lily Beidemeier's has nothing on it."

"And you'd know all about that, wouldn't you?"

"I respect professionals, if that's what you mean."

And compared to a rank amateur like me, Ellen thought, mama was every inch a professional at getting all she wanted . . . especially at the expense of her darling daughter, who in her younger days didn't dare to bring a beau home to Gaynor House for fear he would fall hopelessly in love with her mother. . . .

After charmingly arranging her father and Ellen on the sofa at the far end of the salon, Shelley asked Nick to sit on the deep-piled crimson sofa in the center of the room. He didn't, only putting one knee on the sofa as he waited with irritation for Shelley to model the suit. Ellen paid as much attention to Nick's reaction as to Shelley's dramatic preparations. And then Shelley made her grand entrance. She was clever enough not to come out prancing like a showgirl, she walked slowly, giving them—especially Nick—a deceptive length of limb from her hip to her toes, aided in this illusion by pumps with French heels.

Her father almost audibly caught his breath. He would, Ellen was sure, have appreciated it on most anyone else, but for his own daughter to exhibit herself in a skin-tight black suit that revealed so much of her ample breasts and rounded stomach and the rest . . . well, this plain shocked him.

Nick knew exactly what Shelley was trying to do to. He got up, walking around her, not speaking, for so long that Shelley's hands tensed. "Well?"

Nick looked her up and down. "You're very . . . small, aren't you?"

She smiled, accepting this as a compliment.

He went on. "Somehow I'd pictured you as taller. I'm afraid it's more for someone with long legs . . . like my wife . . ." It took its effect quickly as she glared at him, then shrugged and hurried back to the fitting room.

While Ellen and Sholto stared at him, he nodded, smiled and said, "Honesty, they say, is the best policy, especially with a customer." Then, looking at his wristwatch and glancing toward the fitting room, he said to Ellen, "I'm expecting Dinah any minute and don't want to miss her, I'm going back to the store. I'm sure Holderson will be happy to send over another bathing suit for aunt Shelley. You tell her that will you . . . ?"

Ellen smiled and said she'd be glad to. Sholto decided something had to be done to turn his little girl away from temptation, and the hurt that could go with it. . . .

Chapter Nineteen

NICK hated that moment of parting a little more each morning when he kissed Dinah good-bye at the back door and went off by the field path to what he regarded as a kind of servitude in Holderson's Emporium, and at night it took *all* of even Dinah's by now considerable skills to partly take his mind off his hated work, to half restore even a part of his old self-respect . . . There were a few pleasant moments . . . he liked the other employees and was amused, yes, flattered by Shelley Wychfield's calculated visits to Emporium. But on the night he had brought home his first week's pay and dropped the twenty-dollar gold piece into Dinah's hands, he had also thought how damnable a payment *this* was for a week's humiliation. Dinah, of course, had been pleased, but he couldn't help remembering that by raising with a single gold piece at the crucial moment he had often won a pot worth ten times as much, the gold piece serving to intimidate the other players . . . they seldom called when he threw out one of those gleaming little coins. Now, though, it represented quite the opposite, he felt . . .

On this particular autumn day the Emporium was filled with customers all morning but business slackened off after lunch when the misty air grew thicker. Nick had gone home at noon in the hope of spending half an hour with Dinah but she was up at Gaynor House with Amabel. Only Timby was on the farm, turning long furrows in the north field and complaining to Nick that "they do say that bitch Rheba Moon's taken up with a cousin in the Shenandoah Valley. Wouldn't you know?"

Feeling guilty over the vanished Rheba's effect on Timby, Nick went back to the Emporium, and almost before he'd taken off his big rain hat and boots was told that Shelley had been in, asking for him, that Marsh Wychfield had come by, "looking for cuff links," and also asking if Bill Sholto had come in yet.

Quite a parade, Nick thought, feeling not the least flattered by this Gaynor family attention. Before he could speculate too hard about possible motives, he saw Bill Sholto come in with two men he didn't recognize. He kept walking to his rarely-used desk on the balcony where he took up a sheaf of sketches from New York that he pretended to study. When he looked up it was to see Bill Sholto signaling to him. He got up and started down the stairs as elderly Miss Finch called up from gentlemen's wear, beneath the balcony rail, "Oh Mr. Corrigan, these gentlemen would like you to help them personally."

For the next fifteen minutes the three visitors seemed to be mildly interested in the store itself, asking why certain items were carried in certain places, where the best quality goods were obtained, and all the time Nick wondered why they were really here. After some minutes the subject of poker began to creep in.

"Gentlemen, take my word for it," Sholto said. "There's no one in Tudor County with my nephew's skill at reading poker faces. I reckon that's our relationship, isn't it, Nick? Technically, my grand-nephew-in-law, except that makes me feel so damned ancient."

Everyone laughed at the idea of Bill Sholto getting old.

The rugged old cowpuncher they called "Slim" hit Sholto's arm.

"You'll never get there, Billy boy. After they bury you, boots and all, Old Scratch will take one look at you and throw you back. 'Too young for my batch of sinners,' he'll say. You always was, Billy boy."

In an odd sort of way it was probably true, Nick thought, which only backed up Nick's own ambivalent feelings about the man who had in his fashion ruined the Corrigan family . . . he at least preferred Sholto to the so damned upright and sinned-against Marsh Wychfield.

Sholto's other western friend, Tevins, a stocky, square-jawed man with white hair, pursued the remark about poker. "Think you can read my face, Mr. Corrigan?"

Nick had never made any such claim and could only assume Sholto was guessing, but if he denied it they would at once figure he was trying to fake it. Unlike his usual careful self, he said with a weak grin, "It's my system. Great system. I worked it out myself."

The most easily defeated players were those who bragged about their foolproof systems. He wanted to plant that idea in their minds, and as he had expected they exchanged tolerant smiles. One thing was very evident. Sholto and his friends were working up to a poker game. But why bring it up in the Emporium? He decided to find out. "Gentlemen, are you game?" A bad pun, he'd always thought.

They jumped at the invitation so quickly he had no doubt it was all planned. Why?

"The very thing," Sholto agreed, rubbing his hands. "The next question is where."

"Are either of you gentlemen staying at the Winchester House? Or would you rather make it some room in Mr. Sholto's home? I'm sorry I can't invite you to Corrigan House, but my uncle has a broken foot and as Bill will tell you, he's fond of whiskey so he'd be in the way—"

Sholto waved away any further discussion of the Corrigan farm. "Can't do it tonight anyway. Slim and Tevins have to get the afternoon train. They're on their way North to meet the owners of a spread out in Wyoming. Want to buy them out."

Slim put in, "But we've got a little loose change burning holes in our pockets. What say we test that system of yours, Mr. Corrigan? Right away."

Nick waved a hand expansively. "I'd admire to try my system on you gentlemen. But I'm afraid I'm needed here. Now if you could just stay over one more night, maybe we could have a real game."

He knew Sholto was watching him, eyes narrowed, as if he didn't quite believe Nick's impersonation of an overconfident gambler. Sholto shifted his boots, moved slowly along the aisle toward the stockroom door. The others watched him, they seemed to know where Sholto was heading. Nick felt uneasily that he was being set up but somehow didn't really care. When he thought of the endless weeks ahead, the one lonely gold piece or worse, the stained and torn paper dollars, the prospect of a lifetime in this place . . .

"What's going on behind that door there?" Sholto asked Nick.

"A storeroom." Nick was sure Sholto knew all about the room.

"Any lights? Windows?" Sholto opened the door. "And an old chopping block. All we have to do is clear the block of all that junk."

Sholto's two friends shuffled along after him. Tevins looked back as if suddenly recalling Nick. "Sounds right as rain. And speaking of rain, it's coming down so heavy you're not going to be swamped with customers the next hour. Let's have a look at this chopping block. Anybody got a deck?"

Slim pulled out an unbroken pack. "Never travel without 'em."

Nick was well aware of Olaf Holderson's strictures about gambling, but also hated to let Sholto know how his job hemmed him in. He said nothing. Meanwhile Sholto's friends kept discussing a game, peering into the stockroom. When Snubby Gamble, the stock boy, returned from his late lunch and Nick put him to work removing the new merchandise from the stockroom, they considered they'd won the battle for a poker game, although Nick had been intending to move the merchandise out on to the counters even before the arrival of Sholto and his friends.

Nick looked around the stockroom, where a single window illuminated the heavy, scarred butcher table. He had made damn near heroic efforts to fight his craving for a game . . . enough was enough . . .

In no time Sholto and his friends were crowding into the stockroom, ostensibly to examine some old-fashioned walking sticks racked in a corner of the stockroom. Nick followed them, describing the canes for the benefit of the other employees. The stockroom door remained ajar while the relative merits of the canes were argued loudly enough for the other clerks to overhear. Gradually the door closed. . . .

The four men now sat on one chair and three boxes of various heights. "Jacks or better," for openers, Sholto said. Luckily, Nick still had fifteen dollars from the previous Saturday's pay as well as a lucky fifty in paper which he kept for a crisis . . . like this one. He wasn't the least surprised when the white-haired Tevins produced enough paper money to make change for the gold carried by Sholto and Slim.

To Nick's way of thinking, four men only were pretty small potatoes for a worthwhile game but prospects improved when all agreed to make openers progress from jacks to kings, and a sizeable pot was anted up.

Remembering the role he had assigned himself, Nick worked his so-called system religiously during the first few hands, "reading everyone's face" with calamitous results until he felt he had convinced them that they had nothing to fear from him except pure luck. Sholto was playing rather badly, which surprised Nick. Once he drew one card, betrayed two in his hand when he sneezed: "So much dust in here," and Nick could have sworn he was drawing to an inside straight. Even more amazing was Sholto's expression when he appeared to have drawn the eight he needed; yet, after raising twice, he dropped out and threw in his hand. It occurred to Nick, who won the pot on ace triplets, that for some reason Sholto had let him win. Since Nick considered himself a better player he resented this and began to apply himself to beat Tevins and Slim with no tricks.

The next deal produced a situation Nick hadn't seen in so long he found it necessary to resort to some difficult playacting to make the most of it. Before the draw he found himself with a diamond straight flush, queen high. He began by separating the nine and eight from the face cards, hoping to make it appear that he only held a full house. He couldn't get away with a stronger bluff. He couldn't discard. He could only hope someone else held a hand higher than a full house and would therefore raise him.

After the draw Tevins dropped out, but Sholto and Slim kept the pot boiling. Nick hardly dared look down at that tempting pot. When Sholto threw in, Slim and Nick raised, then Slim again. It was all or nothing, Nick thought as he threw in his winnings. Slim called. He held four aces.

Nick turned up his straight flush.

Sholto and Tevins let out a loud warwhoop and while Nick scooped in his winnings, trying not to let his fingers shake, Slim examined Nick's cards with a sigh. No one heard the stockroom door open but something about Sholto's suddenly alert expression made Nick look up.

Marsh Wychfield stood there in the doorway, with Olaf Holderson beside him. While the store owner frowned, Marsh looked amazed, then said with forced calm, "Now where did you say the carpet samples were to be found?"

Holderson fumbled for the heavy sample squares on the shelf and handed them to Wychfield without looking at Nick or the other players. "Excuse me, Mr. Wychfield. We're not too well organized today, what with our manager, Mr. Corrigan, resigning and all . . . gentlemen, can we have the stockroom vacated so it's easier to get at the merchandise?"

"Right, sir," Sholto said affably. "Gents, are you coming?"

His friends went silently, but Slim was grinning. Nick pocketed his winnings, two hundred ninety dollars. Less the sixty-five he had started with, this gave him a profit of two hundred twenty-five dollars. He had made more money in an hour than he could in ten weeks of proper misery.

He held out his hand to Holderson, who was too surprised to refuse it.

"Thank you, sir," Nick said, and meant it. "You have done me a great favor. I appreciate it more than I can express."

Chapter Twenty

HE had to go home sooner or later. On the whole he preferred later.

He had walked to the edge of town with his usual nonchalance in case anyone was watching but he couldn't recall any detail of the walk. He still had several hours before he was expected home. At the Confederate cemetery he considered whether to head for Corrigan House along the Ooscanoto estate road and start explaining or to give himself a little more time.

He didn't want to quarrel with Dinah, but more importantly he wasn't going to have her pitying or berating him for being fired. If their marriage ever reached the place where *she* looked on him with pity, as the older Gaynors had when he was a kid, they would be all over.

There was no use asking himself why the devil he had gotten into the poker game in the first place. He knew it had been bound to happen.... Dinah probably hadn't left Gaynor House yet. He might walk up and meet her ... and the sight of him, calm and unconcerned, would probably annoy Marsh, who had been looking mighty superior when he walked into the stockroom with Holderson....

The long white Corrigan fences loomed ahead of him in

the post-sunset glow and he was relieved to see that the lamps had been lit. He wanted to tell Dinah the news before trouble-making biddies got to her.

The curtains were drawn but he could see slits of light where the shades were cracked or torn. He was surprised at how chilled he had been and how welcome the fire in the newly cleaned fireplace would be when he walked in and took Dinah in his arms. Her willingness to make love with him was going to be very important tonight . . .

He squared his shoulders, concentrated on the two hundred ninety-five dollars in his pocket and walked up onto the front porch, carefully scuffing the mud off his shoes on the ancient mat.

Though warm and cozy the empty parlor seemed unusually silent without the chatter of the women. Hearing the rattle of dishes in the kitchen, he closed the front door firmly, went to the kitchen doorway, saw Timby at the foot of the table with his stocking feet propped up on a chair and Dinah lifting a pan of biscuits out of the oven with two cloths wrapped around her hands.

She looked beautiful to him, her fine hair tied back at the nape of her lovely neck . . . Seeing him suddenly as he stood in the doorway she almost dropped the biscuit pan. "You startled me! You usually come in through the back porch."

He came forward, swung her away from the stove and began to kiss her playfully on the lips and the throat and around the back of her neck. After a little hesitation she laughed, shivering pleasurably in his close embrace and reminding him between gasps, "You want to shock Timby? He's waiting for his supper—"

"I can wait," Timby spoke up, spitting snuff into the corner. "I was young once meself, so I was."

"Hungry?" Dinah asked, freeing herself as Nick looked over at his uncle.

"Hungry for the cook, sweetheart. Do you have a minute? I want to show you something."

She moved the kettles and frying pan off the direct heat and stood watching him expectantly. To brace himself— her, too—for the story of the day he pulled coins and bills from various pockets in a dramatic gesture. He hoped she would be dazzled by the line of twenty-dollar gold pieces he trailed along the tablecloth in a glistening border. Each could have represented a whole week's work at Holderson's . . . he hoped she would think about that.

"Where did you get it?" Dinah asked slowly.

Might as well get it over with. "I left Holderson's."

"You left—"

"Quit. Gave in my notice and quit on the spot. I had to, sweetheart. It was hell working there, ordered around: 'Corrigan, do this, Corrigan do that.' Who did Holderson think he was talking to? Nobody knows better than you, sweetheart, that I couldn't take that kind of treatment—"

For a long moment Dinah just stared at him. Finally she said without expression, "So you quit of your own free will and then found a game and got into it and won all this?"

"Exactly!" Thank God she understood, though she still had that unnerving blue-eyed stare, as if she could read into his soul.

Behind them Timby coughed, cleared his throat and reached out to examine the collection of gold. "Right nice pieces too. Look how they shine."

Dinah, ignoring Timby, took Nick's face in her hands. "I said I'd forgive anything but a lie. You're relieved to be free of that job, aren't you?"

He had no hesitation in confessing to that. "Relieved? Darling, you will never know how relieved—"

"And what are you going to do now? We can hardly live the rest of our lives on this, even if it seems like a fortune now."

Timby broke in, "What the hell? Nick will go back on the road like he's always done."

She looked at Nick. "Is that what you had in mind when

you deliberately quit your job, as you said?"

Nick, seeing that he was getting tangled in his own proud lie, tried to get around it with some truth. He hoped she could take it. "Sweetheart, a long time ago I planned to try my luck at the big Panama-Pacific Exposition out in San Francisco, it'll be closing soon, there's lots of money in a place like that . . . let's us go together—"

"When, Nick?"

"Tomorrow?"

"Why not?"

"Tomorrow . . . wonderful . . . then we can take a steamer from Frisco down to Los Angeles, and by Christmas it's be home to celebrate our winnings with the folks . . ." For a finish she swept all the coins across the table. "It all sounds *perfect*—for somebody Neily's age. *When* are you going to grow up, Nick . . . ?"

He flinched as if he'd been slapped. His face felt hot. "You knew it was my profession. I've never lied about it or pretended anything else."

"You lied when you said you quit your job. Couldn't you trust your own wife with the truth?"

Marsh, he now realized, must have run all the way home to give Dinah the worst version of what happened. "All right, I was *fired* for doing what I do . . . I hated the job, you always knew that. No one forced me to play the game, but that's real money there on the table . . . more than I'd make in weeks of damn floorwalking—" He took a deep breath. "Come on, sweetheart, come with me to the Exposition. Think of the times we can have crossing the *whole* country together. I've always done well in Denver . . . then there's Reno and by the time we get to Frisco we may have a year's profits saved up . . ."

Dinah said nothing at first, then finally, "I don't think you understood me too well, Nick . . . Well, by all means, go to San Francisco. But please don't expect me to be your dutiful guardian, saving your money, holding your hand when you lose. And you will lose . . . no, just go . . . but don't try to fool me, or yourself, about what you're doing."

He nodded, face tight. "I wouldn't think of trying to fool a sweet fine lady like you, my dear . . . I'll be on my way tomorrow."

Timby looked around anxiously. "You be home for Christmas like you said, though, boy."

"Naturally. My home is here."

Or was it . . . ?

Chapter Twenty-One

ELLEN, feeling she was very much in Shelley's way at Gaynor House, had her portmanteau and suitcase packed. She wanted only to know that Dinah was all right before leaving as soon as possible. There was the matter of Bill Sholto too, but she tried not to think of him. She couldn't deny, though, that it was rather satisfying to have him pursue her, and the notion of him as a companion, helping to fill the awful loneliness she felt, first after losing Jem, and now Dinah, wasn't altogether unattractive . . .

And then she learned that Nick had lost his job at Holderson's. The whole of Gaynor House seemed to be gossiping about it that morning when she was called down to breakfast and came in interrupting an argument between Shelley and her husband.

Marsh was saying, "The fellow only got what he deserved, he was caught breaking the rules of the store—"

"Rules! Just something Olaf thought up because he's probably a terrible card player. Well, I'll certainly take my trade elsewhere. He'll see quick enough he can't make a fool out of a Gaynor—"

Everyone stared at Shelley, and Ellen asked. "What is it? Has someone shaken the family tree?"

"Olaf fired Nick for playing a little old game of poker in the back room yesterday evening before quitting time." Shelley's anger was rather obviously all out of proportion to the alleged cause.

Bill Sholto turned to his daughter. "Nobody's been trampling on sacred Gaynor rights. Not only is Nick Corrigan far from being a Gaynor, but strictly speaking, so are you."

Marsh laughed. "If you want to be technical, my dear, the only purebred Gaynor in this house is sister Ellen."

Before Shelley could flare up at this Ellen asked quickly, "What's Nick going to do? Did he say?"

Nobody knew, but not unexpectedly Marsh was cool about it. "His kind always fall on their feet. He's bound to return to his first love . . . gambling."

Ellen felt caught between a desire to console Dinah and Nick and the worry that she might only be interfering. Shelley was less reluctant. When she came home from the salon that night she was thoroughly bad-tempered, near-obsessed by the "fate" of Nick Corrigan.

"He's gone already," she snapped as she came into the river parlor, where the family had gathered in its traditional way before going in to dinner.

"Who has gone where, my dear?" her husband asked sardonically."

"You know who. I happened to be dressing the windows today when Dinah went by on her way to the butcher's. She said he'd gone to San Francisco, of all places."

It was even worse than Ellen had expected. "You mean, he went alone?"

"Alone. A fine wife Dinah is, I must say, to allow him to go away alone, and so soon after their honeymoon. Of course, they quarreled. It was clear enough to me. She had that tight, stiff look. No feelings. I just don't understand that girl."

You wouldn't, Marsh thought. Then aloud, "Dinah must be lonely now, with her dashing bridegroom off to the wild West to seek his fortune. Again."

Neily, who had been playing with his train and its new parts, looked up. "I'd like to do that." He ran his train onto a siding. "I'd like to go to the wild West. Like grandpa did."

Ellen looked at Bill Sholto, told Neily, "I'm afraid things aren't quite so wild nowadays. Still, you never know where you'll find adventure . . ."

Ellen thought there was something rather smug, satisfied about Sholto's tone . . . not that she was altogether surprised. Naturally he would be glad that his daughter's temptation had been removed. Still, the tone did puzzle her some . . .

"Anyway," Marsh put in, "it was no doubt all for the best, although this leaves the poor child alone among strangers—"

"Alone? She's got that tribe of Corrigans swarming over her," Shelley pointed out.

Marsh got up, holding his hand out to Neily. "What do you say we go for a walk, my boy? Now that Corrigan has to make a living over the poker tables, Dinah would be better off right here at home with people who love her . . ." And warming to his sense of mission he added cheerfully, as if on the spur of the moment, "In fact, if she stayed here at Gaynor House for a few days she would have her real family around her to ease things. Ellen is here, and the rest of us . . ."

Ellen held her breath.

"Maybe not this soon," Sholto suggested, noting that Shelley was near-apoplectic at the idea of Dinah moving in.

"It occurs to *me,*" Shelley said, trying to control herself, "that I can help Nick. After all, he's the one who's been hurt by all this, we owe him something . . . I happen to know one of the San Francisco officials, Police Commissioner Peretti. He was in New York at a convention last summer. He might be helpful . . . She glanced at her husband with a sly smile. "In fact, I intend to make a little trip out West myself with a sheaf of my designs before the Exposition closes. Who knows . . . I just might see him out there."

Her husband turned sharply, and as Ellen quickly noted he seemed more enthused than annoyed by her brazen hints. "I agree, I see no reason why you shouldn't make the trip this fall . . . you've never even seen the Golden Gate. Might be right interesting for you . . ."

The more Ellen saw of this devious pair the less she liked them. Sholto was a relief compared to his daughter and son-in-law, and she was glad to let him escort her to dinner. Afterward she only wanted to be alone to think over what had happened and perhaps think of something that might help to mend things for her daughter . . . Hugging her arms against the first chill of autumn she walked out of the dining room, sensing Bill Sholto close behind her.

"I know you're worried, Ellen, but they'll be the better for it. This just was no place for young Corrigan. Adventure. The world outside . . . that's what he wants. I know . . . I was the same at his age."

"I'm sure you were." All her faint suspicions of the day coalesced now. "How did you manage it?"

He knew what she meant and didn't hesitate. "Well, honey, we agreed that things between Shelley and Corrigan had to be broken up, you remember."

"There was no 'thing' on Nick's part."

"You know what I mean. He was a constant temptation to my poor girl."

"Your poor girl? Poor, defenseless little Shelley! About as defenseless as my mother was. But do go on. I can see you were mighty clever about it—"

"I wouldn't say that." He was sensing dangerous shoals ahead. "I brought some friends into the store. It didn't take much to tempt the boy." He added, "He won too. Made quite a haul. And when Marsh came in with Holderson—that was all it amounted to." He looked into her face . . .

saw the rigid, icy shadow of Varina Gaynor. "But, honey, it was what everyone wanted. You too . . . I thought you'd be relieved."

At the foot of the stairs she stopped and stared at him. Suddenly she was just very tired. "Bill, even if what you thought was true, did it ever occur to you that what you did, the underhanded way you did it said something about you . . . ?"

"Me! I'm not the gambler. I only put a little temptation in his way and he took it. Grabbed it . . ."

She nodded, realizing it would do no good to try to carry this on any further, and started up the stairs without looking back. "Excuse me now. I've got to finish packing."

"Ellie . . ." He reached for her but she shrugged off his hands. "I always hated that nickname."

"I'm sorry . . . but, honey, you can't just go off like this. Not now . . . it's been so good between us, now that we've found each other again . . ."

She smiled. A chilly smile. He rushed on, "If I hurt your daughter I didn't mean it, I thought you'd thank me and be relieved . . . Ellen—"

"If I'm to make the westbound connection at Ashby tomorrow night I'll really have to be getting my things ready—"

He took the stairs after her two at a time. "Don't do this, Ellen. I'm not going to lose you a second time."

In front of the door to her room her fingers tightened on the knob. She glanced back at him. "Bill, I don't think you ever had me the first time. I just didn't know then how lucky I was."

The door opened and closed.

Amabel's timid, plaintive voice annoyed Dinah more than shouting would have . . . "You're working so hard, dear, I hope it's not to forget that silly little fuss with Nick, don't you worry, he'll be back soon . . ." And every time she thought about the postcard that had arrived for "The Corrigans" that morning, well, she wanted to kick someone . . . On the front was a fat, vulgar woman sprawled out on a sybaritic couch, wearing nothing beneath a curtain of dusky hair full of sparkles that came off on Dinah's hands. The message on the back was even worse:

"Miss you all. Love, Nick."

The card was postmarked Chicago. Was that the best he could do from the city where he and Dinah had first made love?

"Nick's always been so romantic," Amabel had remarked with her customary insight.

Romantic? Dinah had made an elaborate performance out of slapping her hands together to brush off the damned sparkles, which accentuated the curves of the postcard lady.

Where he would go after Chicago she had no idea. Nor did she care, as she told Timby who got out a map he had used countless times before to trace the travels of his wandering nephew. Now he took the only writing instrument in the house, a carpenter's flat, wide, yellow pencil, and worked out Nick's likely route. "I'd say he'd head for Denver and then Cheyenne, maybe Reno, and after that on to the Bay. You could send a message to him in any one of them places. That's what Amabel did the time the creek overran our lower pastures. Caught him smack in the middle of a game of stud poker at the Railroad Hotel. He cashed in and came right home. Left Cheyenne like it was poison."

"Lucky Cheyenne!" Nick would come straight home because a stupid pasture on the edge of a creek flooded, but he wouldn't come home to the wife who loved him. And, yes, she still did . . . very much, though she wasn't advertising it . . .

On the third morning after Nick's departure, while Dinah polished the windows of the parlor and Amabel's bedroom, all of which faced on the porch, Amabel called out suddenly, "I declare, if it isn't Ellen Gaynor coming to call! Kind of like old times when we were girls. 'Course, I was a belle in those days and poor Ellen was—well, poor Ellen . . . my dear Miss Ellen, this is right neighborly of you. I'll go set the kettle on. I make real good Irish Tea, you may rec'lect."

Ellen walked across the front yard from the Ooscanoto estate road, dressed for travel in her well-fitted blue-serge suit with an equally plain blue shirtwaist. The only frill about her was the tiny yellow rosebud pinned on her lapel, which Dinah suspected came from Captain Sholto. If Dinah had ever been tempted to like him before, that feeling was destroyed by his role in the loss of Nick's job. Actually, she had always disliked him. He was after her mother, who so far as Dinah was concerned, still belonged to her father. Maybe it was foolish, but she couldn't help it. That was the way she felt. Besides, her mother was far too lovely, too good, for the likes of an opportunist like *Captain* Bill Sholto . . . Today even the felt hat pinned jauntily on her pale hair couldn't divert from her worried look. She still carried herself, though, in that elegant, graceful way she had, which Sholto's daughter could never hope to achieve in spite of all her fancy clothes. . . .

Dinah dropped the cleaning rag, wiped her hands on her apron and went down the steps to hug her mother. Unfortunately the first thing Ellen asked was, "Have you heard from Nick?"

"No, mama. Why are you all dressed up? Going visiting? I hope you're not looking so grand just to come here." Dinah tried to lighten her edgy remark by a laugh as Ellen and Amabel were shaking hands. "You know you needn't bother, hell, look at me, I'm a sight, I swear."

"We'll go into my dress-up clothes later, dear. First I was just curious about your husband's trip. Is he doing well?"

"You mean is he winning or losing? I can't imagine. I'm

not too interested in poker." There was a curious tension about her mother, not like her at all. Whatever its cause, it annoyed Dinah, enforcing as it did her own edgy feeling . . . "Mama, I know you mean well, but if you've come to talk for Nick I think I should tell you don't bother. He's got to come home because *he* wants to."

Ellen looked at her, wide-eyed—also uncharacteristic . . . "Why no, dear, why should I do that?"

"I thought you liked him."

"Oh, well . . . I'll admit he's talented, in a certain fashion, but the way he's acted, letting the likes of Bill Sholto outsmart him, losing a good position, rushing off . . ." She sighed rather too elaborately, glanced at the lapel watch that fastened the yellow rosebud. "Captain Sholto will be along to drive me to Ashby any minute now."

Dinah began furiously scrubbing another pane of glass. "You know what Bill Sholto did to Nick and you still let him fuss over you . . ."

"Well, it's only as far as the Southern Railway Station at Ashby. I'm leaving for home tonight. Which explains what you call my dress-up clothes."

Dinah was shaken. It had been annoying enough to hear her mother speak so about Nick. . . . She could criticize him but nobody else, thank you . . . and now she was abruptly leaving her . . .

"I must say," her mother was saying, "you apparently were right when you made fun of Nick the first time you saw him—"

"I did not! I'd never laugh at him—"

"I'm sorry, dear, but you did say he was ridiculous, didn't you?" She had to suppress a smile when she said it . . . her psychology seemed to be working . . .

Dinah was furious. "How could you, it isn't true, I never . . ." But she wasn't so sure of her ground, recalling that she had said some such thing to cover her own instant attraction to Nick. It had only been a defense against his startling appeal, but she wasn't going into that now, and changed the subject . . . "But mother, I thought you would stay here until things were . . . more settled." It panicked her to realize that with both Ellen and Nick gone she would be left here among virtual strangers. Her cool defenses distinctly began to crack. "Mama, I wish you'd wait. Just a little while. Until Christmas maybe?"

Amabel put in, "You'll have us, honey. And when Nick gets back for Christmas . . ."

If Nick comes back, she thought miserably . . .

Her mother was kissing her on the forehead now, studying her flushed perspiring face. She hoped she hadn't laid it on too thick, been too casual . . . in any case, now was the time to reverse her field, switch to the positive from the negative to make her point . . . "Dear," she said softly, "think about *happiness* . . . think about your father and me. It wasn't perfect, nothing ever is . . . but that was real happiness all the same . . ." Dinah was silent. Staring back at her, Ellen caressed her cheek with a forefinger. "Dinah, ask yourself when you were happiest in all your life. And when you find it again, keep it this time." Dinah nodded slowly, almost smiling, and, encouraged, her mother said forcefully, "You *can*, you know, if you keep one thing in mind . . . It can't be all perfect and no problems, but if it feels right to you down deep inside, well then, you will have found something few people ever know. Good-by, dear."

"Please don't go—"

"But I have my house and the newspaper to run. Maybe I'll just run off to Europe and report on the war for Lariat readers. Who knows what I might do? I'm not dead yet, you know."

"I'll go with you to Ashby . . . mother, I need you—"

Ellen smiled. "You have your husband—when you decide you need him. You don't really need me at all."

Chapter Twenty-Two

SHOLTO decided he had never seen Ellen Gaynor looking so full of life and hated to think that it might be due less to his presence than to the fact that she was leaving him, returning to that desert patch where she claimed to have been so happy with that half-breed Jem Faire.

Marsh Wychfield's car had stopped among the wagon ruts in the Corrigan front yard, and anxious to get to Ellen, Sholto had the door open before the motor was dead. Even so, he couldn't beat Marsh. It didn't take him long to guess the reason Marsh got out from behind the wheel and limped so rapidly over the grass to the Corrigan porch. Ellen's daughter, of course . . . damn it . . . he'd apparently ruined his own chances with Ellen in order to solve Shelley's problems, and here was Shelley's *husband* making his calf's eyes at another woman . . . Sholto followed Marsh at a more seemly pace, not wanting to imitate this other middle-aged adolescent, panting over a woman who didn't belong to him. It annoyed him even more to see how well his son-in-law seemed to be handling the situation. . . . Marsh made no reference to Nick's absence nor did he ask whether Dinah had heard from him and how Nick's luck was running on his journey across America. Instead, he said, "Isaah Kincaid hasn't anything to do these days, with the crops all shipped and nobody riding fence any more, he'd surely appreciate doing that washing and scrubbing for you. We keep him on a kind of retainer, as we lawyers say, and I'd like to have him busy for at least a few hours a day."

Not a bad move, not bad at all, Sholto thought, reflecting that this was the first time in years that Marsh Wychfield had expressed the slightest interest in the working of the Gaynor farmlands. Strictly speaking, this was Sholto's job, as it had been since he first married Maggilee Gaynor. The devil of it was, Sholto couldn't refuse to back up Marsh's generosity without looking like a skinflint.

Marsh glanced around at him now. "We can certainly spare Isaah, can't we, Captain?"

Sholto grinned and pushed his old calvary hat back with his thumb. "Why, sure, pardner. Sure, we don't need him right now . . . Ellen, honey, can I help you?"

Ellen said quickly, "You have my bags. Well, that's all . . . Dinah, I really must go now."

Dinah's face, Sholto observed, showed clearly her strain and her unhappiness. He felt she'd been a fool, should have jumped to go along with Nick, which was better to think of than that he'd been the architect of her troubles . . . His conscience seldom bothered him . . . most of the time he hardly knew he had one . . . but Dinah's misery reminded him painfully of the way Ellen had looked one night over thirty years ago when she learned of her mother's pregnancy by one Bill Sholto, *her* presumed lover . . . He wondered if Ellen ever thought of that night any more, and wished he could somehow please her by setting things right for her daughter, but at the moment there seemed no way to do it . . .

Dinah was still coaxing. "Mama, can't you please change your mind? If you could just stay over for another week or so . . ."

Ellen kissed her in a brisk, almost businesslike way. "You don't need me, Dinah, you have your own married life now . . . just try to remember what I told you. 'Bye, dear." She took Sholto's arm. "Shall we be on our way? Are you coming, brother Marsh?"

Sholto wondered if she had deliberately interrupted Marsh just as he was basking in Dinah's thanks for the offer of Issah. Dinah had put her right hand in Marsh's and then covered their fingers with her left hand, a gesture in which Marsh chose to read a good deal more than gratitude. "I'll be over with Isaah tomorrow around midday," Marsh was saying.

"Shall I drive?" Sholto asked loudly.

Which finally broke up the group except for the last embraces of the women. When they were in the car Marsh insisted on driving. They rattled and bumped over the Corrigan front yard to the estate road and on to the Ashby Junction highway. Ellen sitting silent between the two men.

"You mustn't worry about your little girl," Marsh told her. "We'll see that she throws off that Corrigan bunch . . . only a drunk and a feeble-minded old woman for company . . . what a time for that Nick to desert her! And how predictable . . . well, he played his last card when he forced his way into this family . . ." He smiled in appreciation of what he considered his clever turn of phrase . . . "I've no doubt in the world that's why he married a sweet pure young woman like Dinah—"

Ellen said drily, "Do you really think so?"

Sholto, for a change, understood and caught the sarcasm in her voice, but Marsh was too absorbed in his own fantasies to notice.

Sholto moved in with, "Now I'm of a different opinion. Wouldn't surprise me to see them behaving like regular lovebirds again if they get back on the road together. That's where they belong."

Marsh tried to deny this, but subsided when Ellen forcefully agreed. "You are right, captain. Dinah always loved travel. And she and Nick were mighty happy on their honeymoon . . . until they came home—"

"People are usually happy on their honeymoon," Marsh said quickly. "Shelley and I were—no matter, that was a long time ago . . . the truth is, we all knew this was a misalliance from the beginning—"

"Misalliance?" Sholto pretended to shudder. "That's a notion I just don't hold with . . . maybe because a passel of people thought Maggilee committed a what-you-call-it when she married me."

Marsh said predictably, "That was different. Maggilee wasn't one of the first families. She herself came into the family when she married sister Ellen's father during the War."

Ellen laughed. "How silly all this would sound out where I live! You sound as if we were still in the nineteenth century—"

"Thank you . . . I think," Sholto told her with a smile, adding, "I wonder where young Corrigan is right now."

Ellen became alert, he could feel her slim body stiffen beside him. "Timby Corrigan might know. Amabel says he follows all of Nick's travels by map."

"When he isn't drunk," Marsh said.

Sholto dismissed this with, "Old Timby and I have had our differences, but we can still hold a conversation over a whiskey bottle."

The car spurted forward, and though Marsh apologized it was Sholto who held Ellen back, saving her from a nasty jolt. Ellen glanced at Sholto, and he told himself her look definitely said he was on the right track with her in trying to make amends for her daughter's unhappiness.

As usual he was about half right.

In Denver Nick walked away from the U.S. mailbox with a renewed confidence. He was feeling a return of the pride he couldn't exist without for long. It would take several days for the one hundred fifty dollars in paper money to reach rural Virginia but at least the family—no, make that Dinah—would know he was thinking of them. He had left one hundred dollars with Dinah to take care of family expenses. In the ordinary way that much money would last the household for several months, but Nick wanted to be sure there was enough to meet any emergencies.

By the time he'd lost seventy dollars in Cheyenne and come out even in Laramie he was able to tell himself, honestly, "Don't fool yourself. You also keep sending money home because you want to show Dinah you can make it and be as easily generous as the fancy folks at Gaynor House."

At any rate, Dinah was sure to be convinced, finally, that he truly had a natural gift for his profession after losing in Cheyenne, breaking even in Laramie and making a killing of two hundred dollars in Rawlins and sending another sum home. He thought that Dinah would now come out to meet him . . . after all, they'd never been so happy as they were wandering the country together. . . .

When the Union Pacific locomotive came puffing past the little Rawlins station and Nick found his way to his lower berth, he was working out the quickest way he could get Dinah to the West Coast. Any way he figured it, she couldn't make it in less than a week. He should have swallowed his damn pride and anger that night he lost his job, told her the plain truth right off, then coaxed, persuaded, charmed or whatever it took to get her to go off with him. Well, it still wasn't too late. Timby would know where he usually stayed. . . . But now, as the train rumbled through the red-rock canyons of Utah, skirting Salt Lake City where men of his profession were never welcome, he felt far from confident.

In Ogden, on the Utah-Nevada border, he tried to telephone long distance to Hannah Gamble's office in Gaynorville. He had made a call two days before and gotten no answer at Gamble's Livery and Garage, forgetting it was one A.M. Eastern Time in Gaynorville. This time he made the call early in the evening, and had better luck. Hannah herself came on the line, flattered to receive a call from so far away. "Well, I never! Why, they only invented this long distance thing this year. To 'Frisco it was. You sure you're really out West, Corrigan?"

"It's the real West, all right. I can practically reach out and touch it. My train will be crossing into the Nevada desert just an hour after they change engines. Hannah, I wonder if you'd—"

"Tell you what, Nick boy, I'll be right happy to give a message to your family. They're doing fine, case you're worried."

"Dinah hasn't left yet?"

"Where would she go? She don't even know where you are, does she?"

"Not exactly, but I thought she might—no matter . . . Timby hasn't been giving her any trouble, has he? No going off on drunks or anything like that? He's supposed to be running the farm."

"I wouldn't worry if I was you, Nick. Timby's only been drunk once that I know of. He means well, that boy. But your Dinah don't need him, the way they lent her Isaah off the Gaynor land to handle the fall housecleaning and all."

He asked her to repeat this. "I don't understand, you say she's been getting help from Gaynor House? They've never lifted a hand to save our crops, much less to housecleaning."

Hannah chuckled. "Well, Mister Marsh's turned a lot nicer'n you'd believe. He works like a dog over on your farm. Gets there at sunup and don't get through 'til after dark. Real help to your family, I'd say. Now, my sakes, boy, don't you go spoilin' it!"

It hit him then . . . "And I suppose Dinah's properly grateful to dear old uncle Marsh."

"Well, I'm sure I hope so. See here, Nick, you're not fetchin' up to be jealous, are you? Because Cap'n Sholto was over there couple of days ago on his way to Ashby, and you know he wouldn't let nothin' go on—"

"Don't be silly . . ."

"I'll tell Dinah you called. If you wasn't on long distance I'd say just hold while I send to Corrigans to fetch your bride—"

He was too proud and angry to let himself do what he wanted to do. "No, she's busy, and besides, my train's leaving. Thanks, Hannah. Good-by." He hung up and just made the Southern Pacific train on the run.

The heavy iron cars set out steaming and smoking across the northern reaches of the Great Salt Lake. He had intended to find a game among the Pullman passengers but he was too depressed by his phone call to try. Instead he went to bed early, only to spend the hours obsessed by memories of other nights he had spent in a sleeper . . . with Dinah. . . .

Along about six in the morning he was awakened by a jolt and a series of screeches as the emergency brakes operated, steam poured from the train and the cars came to a standstill. Nick raised the shade with difficulty and looked out to see what appeared to be the desert wilds, all autumn gold and brown with a scattering of trees but an abundance of low desert scrub growth. A conductor and two porters set off to walk to the front of the long train, and Nick was relieved to see the narrow pass ahead which meant that the railroad town of Sparks, adjoining lively Reno, was just around the corner. At least this wasn't too far from civilization. Although gambling was against the law in Reno, the town was the mecca of Nevada cattle and sheep men, and those hard men didn't come to Reno to drink the waters of the nearby hot springs. Ordinance or no ordinance, there was plenty of action in Reno if you knew where to find it. . . .

Eventually the train moved on, passing the cause of the delay—a derailed freight car on its side against a bank of sagebrush. However, the train had developed a hot box after the emergency stop and the passengers, most of them bound for the wonders of the San Francisco Exposition, were put off at Sparks.

This posed no problem for Nick. He hopped onto a street car with his suitcase and rode the three miles into the heart of Reno. Luckily the McKenzie Hotel still stood facing the railroad tracks several blocks beyond the S.P. station. Nick knew from past experience that the McKenzie, a four-story skyscraper with a fifth-floor beer garden, was good for any number of games in spite of the ordinance against gambling. He got off the interurban street car and checked in at the McKenzie. Here his name was known and appreciated, the reason why he preferred this hotel over the elegant brick Riverside on the Truckee River amid its golden-brown border of elms and cottonwoods. From his hotel window Nick could see the waters of the river two blocks south rolling down from the High Sierras. These towering walls separated California and the Pacific from the little green oasis of Reno and the deserts to the East. He had always been lucky here. Considering the view, the good food served at the hotel and the excellent mattress on the big bed in the corner, he thought about Dinah and how she could have been happy here.

And if she never came to join him? If their marriage was over almost before it began, thanks to those *gentlemen* in Gaynor House? He tried to put it out of his mind . . . He was almost amused when a young woman working for the local madam accosted him as he crossed the hall to the elevator, an innovation still new in some western towns. The woman wasn't as young as she might be and brunette at that . . . Nick, dark himself, had always been more attracted to blondes. Not that he was interested in what this woman had to offer, he told himself hurriedly, but it was still a good feeling to have a pretty woman making a fuss over you . . . just because I'm married doesn't mean I'm dead, he thought. Telling himself that at this very minute Marsh Wychfield was hanging around Dinah, trying to make himself and his money irresistible to her, Nick spoke to the dark-haired girl with his usual good manners as she rode down in the elevator with him.

"Just call me Flo. I do favor gentlemen from the South," she murmured seductively. "My mama was born in Gold Hill, on that mountain near Virginia City."

"You don't say?"

"You can just bet your ace on that. We was—that is, mama was real partial to the Confed'racy. She used to say all her—all the real gents come from the South."

They emerged into a lobby swarming with newcomers from the stalled train trying to check in. Nick gave Flo his best smile along with the accent that went with his portrayal of the scion of rich plantation folk in "Lou-siana." "Seems like I'm running in luck, Miss Flo, meeting somebody like you. Almost homefolks, you might say."

She fluttered, fastening plump but not unattractive fingers on his sleeve.

"Would you consider being my guest at breakfast?"

"Oh, I don't know if—well, I reckon I shouldn't. But why not?"

"Good. And what with me being in luck and all, you might know where there's a game going on. Draw poker?"

"Oh. You're one of them." She was disappointed but she didn't let go. They were out on the street, the raised ties of the railroad tracks before them, and now she looked somewhat older than in the pleasant dim lights of the hotel. But she wasn't badly dressed and she had nice hazel eyes. "Yeah, I know a place or two . . .

reckon you aren't even from the South, are you?"

"We like to call ourselves the upper South. I'm from Virginia, is that southern enough for you?"

"No kidding? My daddy was from Virginia. Place called McLean, where the war started."

"And where it ended. So your father was a Virginian?"

"So mama said. I never knew him myself. He . . . died before I had time to know him. He was a professional gambler. You ain't one of them, I hope."

He answered, not untruthfully, "I'm usually considered an amateur when I sit down to play."

"Well, I hope so." She looked around but no one was near enough to hear them as he boosted her over each of the four steel rails and they crossed the wide street. "My daddy was shot 'cause of a poker hand."

"I'm sorry." He was sorrier than she knew. A bad luck omen like this discussion might jinx his next game. But he was sorry for Flo too . . . she looked like she deserved a better hand than she'd been dealt so far.

They enjoyed a hearty meal on Second Street in a cafe whose heavy silverware, white napery and sparkling water glasses put Nick in mind of the happy times with Dinah in New Orleans.

"Thinking about your home, ain't—aren't you, Mr. Nick?" she said, having put away a tidy breakfast of eggs, biscuits, ham, fried potatoes, half a pork chop and a preserved peach.

"Not of home," he said quickly, and changed the subject. "Now then, are there any games at this hour?"

"Sure. There's always something . . . Mr. Nick, do you have any friends in town?"

He was surprised at the curious change in her tone, the sudden vigilance, and he looked around. "Not that I know of. Why?"

"Nothing. He's gone now. But it's the same fellow I saw half an hour ago. He sat over there, first table by the door, and now he's left. He sure was watching you. I could've sworn—anyway, he's gone."

Some gambler, Nick decided. Somebody I've won from. "Can you describe him, did he look like trouble?"

"I wouldn't say trouble . . . and as for looks, he wasn't young, but he's sort of nice-looking. Kind of reddish-grayish hair and skin like somebody been out of doors a lot. Nice but tough, you know?"

It didn't sound like any player Nick had ever taken. Gamblers of Nick's acquaintance didn't have a "nice but tough" look. They were usually just tough. . . . He shook off his misgivings and paid the check.

Shortly after, Flo took him to a stately wooden house on the long bluff above the river. The dark parlor, the double doors separating it from the dining room and the big kitchen beyond were like a thousand others throughout the country, but upstairs the front parlor was a cozy game room with tables set up for poker, blackjack and the old mining camp favorite—faro.

A handsome jowly man of sixty with exquisite manners seemed to be in charge. Flo introduced Nick to him as "Mr. Sackett, he's from New Jersey originally." Mr. Sackett reviewed a number of Nick's acquaintances until they hit on Harold Vorhees and Lettice Du Vaux of New Orleans, who provided the open sesame, and Nick was allowed to risk his money.

Nick preferred rugged miners, thrill-seeking rich young travelers or salesmen looking for a way to kill time, but when Mr. Sackett, late of New Jersey, ushered him in to make a sixth at draw poker, Nick began to wonder if he had gotten in over his head. There was another New Jersey gentleman, Louie Apperson, who looked mighty formidable, and two tough silent men who looked to be bodyguards for either Sackett or Apperson.

Nick began by winning on a ten high straight, hardly the greatest hand in the world, but he soon saw that they were playing him the way he played suckers. They let him win for openers, but afterward things tightened up and he found his luck incredibly bad. He saw Flo once, having coffee with a fargo dealer. She gave him a big smile but looked worried. The sixth player at the draw-poker table changed several times and each new player appeared to be a longtime friend of Mr. Sackett.

I knew it when I woke up this morning, Nick decided with a sinking feeling. The wreck and then Flo talking about her father getting shot. The omens were all rotten ... I should have studied them like the Chinese study the bones they throw.

In no time he had lost over one hundred ten dollars and the position of the sun in the clear blue Sierra sky told him the morning was only half over. He applied himself seriously to the problem. Neither Mr. Sackett nor Mr. Apperson troubled to outbluff him, but they had him boxed in and they were signaling each other somehow. Belatedly he realized he had been giving himself away, unconsciously twisting his wedding ring every time he saw himself in trouble, thinking of what his losses would mean to Dinah. A stupid habit he had often marked in other players ... All right, since his opponents had spotted it, he decided to use the nervous twist of his wedding ring for his own signals, and to his advantage. When he drew a fourth king he managed not to look surprised. He had hoped merely for a pair to compliment his king triplets. Instead he began to twist his ring. Ever so slightly, Apperson signaled Sackett by scraping a tooth with his fingernail. Sackett raised and the bodyguards stayed. Nick, twisted his ring round and raised again, presenting a perfect picture of a bluffer trying to keep up his front against all odds.

Finally Sackett called with three aces and a pair of queens. Nick's four kings took the pot, a sweet win of almost seven hundred dollars.

Nick knew better than to walk out now but was relieved when Sackett suggested time out for coffee. One of the bodyguards went off to the toilet and Nick followed him, leaving his overcoat across the back of his chair to show that he'd be returning . . . actually he was giving a lot of thought to a quick exit. He'd heard about too many gamblers who'd made the mistake of winning too much and winding up on the riverbank below Reno, very dead. . . .

Nothing doing in the toilet. The room had a high window about two feet long and even this was barred. As if that weren't enough, the bodyguard eyed him obviously before going back into the game room. Nick followed, deliberately tripped over a shoelace and knelt to tie it, getting a good look around. In the entrance to a room that smelled strongly of boiling coffee, he saw a familiar figure lounging against the door, idly drinking a mug of coffee.

Captain Bill Sholto . . . ? And looking exactly the way Flo had described the man she said had been following him . . . graying tawny hair, a ruddy outdoorsman's complexion, eyes that might be "nice" to a woman but were certainly tough. He was still wearing his sweat-stained calvalry hat and boots, and he tilted his hat back now with his bent thumb, motioning quickly to Nick.

What the hell was Sholto doing in Reno? For once Nick decided not to look a gift horse in the mouth and followed Sholto's signal. Figuring he was being watched, he also called out to anyone who might be in the kitchen, "I'll have a mug of that, no sugar, no milk. I'm on a winning streak, don't want to fog up my brain . . ."

Sholto stepped aside easily, still playing the stranger, and Nick found only Flo in the impoverished kitchen that had once been a back bedroom complete with flowered wallpaper. She poured him the coffee, her hand shaking. As she put the mug into Nick's fingers she whispered, "Says he's your friend. Don't do nothing 'til I get out in the game room. Don't want 'em blaming me."

He didn't waste time answering but closed his hand over hers, and she smiled a faint acknowledgment. For a moment after she had gone Nick looked around, puzzled. Except for a side door which was locked as he expected, there seemed no way out. Sholto, flipping two silver dollars like an inveterate gambler, finished his coffee, still not revealing any connection with Nick, and stepped into the kitchen to drop the mug into a bucket of soapy water. He was close to the side door now, and while Nick watched him he produced a key, unlocked the door and motioned with his hand. Nick didn't need any urging. He ran down the dark stairs, heard Sholto lock the door from the outside and quickly follow him.

Out on the residential street elm leaves rustled in an autumn breeze and crunched under the rushing feet of the two men. By the time Nick and Sholto reached the river at the foot of the street and were padding across the bridge, Sholto got out between short breaths, "Don't know much about criminal types, do you, son? But I'd say those are mighty dangerous characters to play with."

"Never mind that . . . what's the fastest way out of here?"

"Train you came in on, son. Hooked on two new engines for the climb over the Sierras. She'll be steaming out of here in ten minutes. We cut it kind of close, we'll have to sprint to the station and pray that gang don't miss us yet, or worse, that they figure we're making it for Frisco."

"But my suitcase, my clothes at the hotel . . ."

"If you don't leg it along you aren't going to have a body to hang those clothes on. There's plenty more in Frisco. Now—sprint!"

They did.

Chapter Twenty-Three

"DAMN, but this bay air is freezing!" Nick hugged his arms in their thin black jacket. "If only I hadn't left my overcoat in that sinkhole!" Then he reverted to the subject Bill Sholto had begun to be heartily sick of. "You say you saw Dinah when you passed the farm the last time. How was she? How did she look to you?"

"Again?" Sholto asked. "All right. Again. She misses you. But my son-in-law seems set on taking care of that little problem." He looked closely at Nick as he said it.

They stepped out from the dark Oakland Mole onto the deck of the Southern Pacific ferryboat that would carry them on the last leg of the cross-country train trip to San Francisco.

The glistening bay waters were crowded with ferryboats and naval craft. Off over the Golden Gate an aviator in a frail biplane was stunt-flying to thrill the crowds at the Exposition grounds on the Marina. The double wings and propeller all looked dangerously flimsy, and the crowd on the ferryboat's upper deck began to buzz over the recent death of the renowned aviator Lincoln Beachey during just such a stunt to advertise the Panama-Pacific Exposition.

"You call gambling dangerous," Nick said to Sholto,

pointing to the stunt flyer. "Now that's what I call dangerous. I'd a whole lot rather be playing out a poker hand."

Sholto shrugged and pointed. "You see those bay waters boiling up against Yerba Buena Island? Good graveyard for enemies of those fancy lads in Reno. The one called Sackett used to be active up and down the Potomac and Chesapeake. I've seen him on steamers that travel from Washington to Old Point Comfort near home. I hear he wants to set up business in a gaming ship along the Texas coast or off Santa Catalina Island near Los Angeles."

"Scattering bodies all the way?"

"One of them might have been yours, son, if you'd been stubborn about losing back to them."

Nick confessed readily. "I'll lose to them gladly. I'm no hero. With me it's a matter of business. No more." He almost believed it when he said it.

"Glad to hear it. You don't plan on finding some classy card parties in the city, I hope."

Nick hedged. "Not exactly. In San Francisco I thought I'd—why not?"

"Because that's where they'll be looking for you. Can you do anything else for a living?"

Nick thought of Holderson's Emporium and inwardly shuddered. "I've made extra cash now and then in the amusement zones. You show me a plump female with a respectable taste for a man's touch and I'll show you a highly successful weight guesser. Of course that was before I got married."

"Too bad that pretty wife of yours can't be persuaded you need her. She'd make a nice cover-up. Your friends wouldn't be looking for a married man."

Nick hit the white-painted deck rail with the flat of his hand. "I don't *want* Dinah here as a cover-up. I need her because I—damn it, because I need her." In a hurry to get Sholto on another track he asked, "How the devil did you know I'd be coming to Reno?"

"A gambler like you would be bound to stop off in Reno sooner or later. And you did. Though I almost missed you until you came into the Grand National Cafe. Pure luck, that part. However, I was sure to find you up at that house Apperson owns. Sackett put some money into it but he does the traveling, smelling out prospects and locations, near as I can figure. Anyway, I could see you were in trouble with that big win of yours."

"And don't think I don't appreciate your help," Nick admitted with controlled enthusiasm. "Of course, if it hadn't been for you in the first—oh, never mind, I'd have done it anyway . . ."

After the boat bumped its way into the slip under the sheltering south wing of the ferry building, Nick headed toward a fashionable men's shop for the wardrobe which was his stock-in-trade. Sholto had ideas along the line of a pair of rooms at the Palace Hotel . . . "I've always stayed there, and Shelley writes to me there—" he caught himself, glanced sideways at Nick—"on the other hand that's maybe not such a good idea—"

"Why not?" Nick grumbled. "At least *she* might want to see me." He noted with some satisfaction how this upset Sholto. "Maybe Shelley needs someone who's glad to see her. That impotent fop she's married to sure can't take care of her."

Skillfully eluding the four car tracks that circled in front of the ferry building, Sholto pushed Nick toward a taxicab. "Make the Palace your headquarters today until that precious wardrobe of yours is shipshape, then you can move where you have a mind to. Meanwhile I wouldn't believe every little tale my girl spreads about Marsh's impotence. I could tell you a few things about old Marsh and the ladies."

Nick couldn't help reacting in spite of himself . . . So the arrogant Marsh is capable of seducing my wife—and he spends most of his time at the farm with her . . . he felt a kind of panic set in . . . "I'm not concerned with Wychfield, impotent or otherwise," he lied. "But Dinah was always happiest traveling with me . . . I've a notion to send for her—"

"And will she come when you ask her?" Sholto was pushing for his goal now . . .

Nick reddened. "Why shouldn't she come?"

Sholto grinned. "Why not? And just to be on the safe side, I'll call Shelley, tell her not to come, that you've left for . . . L.A.?"

Nick scotched that idea in a hurry. "Not if Dinah's coming. No point in having the two meeting out here and L.A. is my next stop."

Sholto laughed out loud. "All right. I'll tell Shelley Seattle. Can I help it if you lied to me?"

When they reached the Palace Hotel Sholto made his call to Gaynor House, where there was a newly installed telephone. Unfortunately, according to Edward Hone, "Miss Shelley left two days ago. For San Francisco, I believe, sir. Mr. Marsh was mighty upset about it."

"That's good news, at any rate. He must miss her."

Hone coughed delicately. "Well, sir, you see, Mrs. Corrigan is gone too. So in a manner of speaking, Mr. Marsh finds himself rather alone. As I said, he's quite upset. Shall I ask him to call you?"

"Lord, no! I've enough trouble coming up at this end. Just give my grandson my love and tell him I'll bring him something special from the Exposition."

By the time they transferred at Chicago, Shelley had had enough of the hovering presence of her young niece. Aside from a certain tension around her eyes and mouth, Dinah had never looked more vital, and if there was one thing thirty-year-old Shelley didn't need as a traveling companion it was a more attractive female ten years younger.

Yet here was the younger Dinah—hanging onto Shelley like glue. Her excuse for this sudden trip to California, in the company of a woman who clearly resented her, was that "since we both have some business in San Francisco, I just thought I'd go along."

"What a way to talk about one's husband!"

"Business, indeed . . . my heavens, Dinah, you act like he belongs to you."

"He does belong to me. And I belong to him. That's how we see our marriage" . . . her mother's parting words had sunk in . . . "Nothing is perfect, but Nick and I feel we're down deep closer to each other than *most* couples I know . . ." Shelley didn't miss the reference to her own failed marriage. . . .

Still and all, the two women were united by blood ties and ancestral memories, and as they moved West, encountering an assortment of travelers bound for the San Francisco Exposition, they inevitably turned to each other for reassuring companionship. As two attractive women traveling alone, they were just as inevitably the targets of male interest, and privately began to compare notes on such as the Cincinnati piano salesman who couldn't make up his mind which of them he preferred to sit beside in the diner, and the tough, flirtatious cattleman from Cheyenne, who rode to Reno in their car . . . "Puts me in mind of pa," Shelley whispered. "He must have been quite a scallywag when he was young . . . By the way, I wonder where he is now . . ."

Captain Sholto was a subject of little interest to Dinah. She still couldn't understand how he had made both their mothers, and at the same time if you please, and each different generations, fall in love with him. His charm eluded Dinah. She sat back in the stiff daytime seat of the Pullman watching the bleak brown desert change to the autumn gilt of western Nevada. But she was thinking hard again about the wisdom of her mother's parting words . . . "nothing is ever perfect, ask yourself when you were happiest and when you find it again keep it this time . . ."

She glanced at Shelley who was smiling good-by to the cattleman across the aisle, and decided, "Aunt Shelley is *not* going to get my Nick—not by a long shot. She's not even going to be alone with him . . . I'll see to it . . . her and her precious 'business' deals out West!" . . . She remembered the jolt she'd felt when she heard the news from Amabel that Shelley was leaving to sell her "designs"—in more ways than one—in San Francisco, her own husband Marsh seeming to think it was a perfectly proper idea. Dinah unfurled her family banners, she packed and set off in half an hour, barely getting to the Cincinnati connection at Ashby in time to attach herself to "dear auntie," as she persisted in calling Shelley . . . She half-smiled to herself now, flexing her fingers, as if to examine the claws. Meanwhile the train had moved out of Sparks and was pulling along past the Reno station. Their flirtatious cattleman got off and Shelley leaned over Dinah's shoulder to wave to him and blow a kiss. It didn't take her long to find a replacement, as she nudged Dinah and said, "Look what's getting on, terribly distinguished . . . that man with the silvery hair and prosperous look . . . a gentleman, as anybody can see, and he's coming into our car . . . isn't it lucky we still have lunch ahead of us, it gives us time—"

"For what?"

Shelley waved her hands airily. "To enjoy the Sierra scenery, of course."

"Of course." Good, Dinah thought . . . let her get as interested as she likes in that silvery fellow . . . he must be sixty if he's a day and on the verge of being fat . . . aloud she said, "He's nice-looking for an old man, I guess most men his age go stout like that."

Shelley considered. "Maybe . . . but in a sort of first-class sort of way . . . President Taft was fat, and President Roosevelt was, well, heavyset. I kind of like it . . . in a moneyed man, that is . . . it fits, somehow, and I always—quiet, here he comes . . ."

The gentleman in question came in and took the seat vacated by the cattleman. Shelley was impressed that the gentleman's baggage, his valises, were carried by two lean, powerfully built men with blank faces who followed him, left the valises under his seat and still without a word walked to the end of the car where they shared a seat.

"Servants," Shelley whispered. "His personal servants. Wouldn't you say a valet and a private secretary? He must be a really important man."

Dinah smiled. "In cattle and sheep no doubt."

"Maybe. But he has a back-east look. Men like him always have connections with the stock market. I wonder . . . I could use investors, ever since old Duckworth got sick and drew his money out of Gaynor's—"

"He may be from back east, but if those men are stock-market investors I'll eat my hat. They look like—I don't know what, but I for one don't like their looks."

"You don't know the first thing about men of their caliber."

Dinah subsided. Any time Shelley became interested in a man who wasn't Nick Corrigan, she should be encouraged, not derided, she reminded herself.

It didn't take Shelley long. Her lower legs were visible below the hem of her pleated blue harem skirt, and now she crossed her ankles in a brisk movement that the distinguished gentlemen across the aisle couldn't miss. It took him a little time . . . he started off by closing his eyes in an attempt to sleep during the dramatic climb over the Sierra Nevada mountains to Donner Summit. The progress over the incredible mountains, canyons and lost little pockets of gold-mining settlements held the passengers hushed until they came out on the fertile Sacramento plain and everyone breathed a sigh of relief as the riches of California were spread out before them. Then the waiter came through the cars announcing, "First call for lunch . . . first call," over the clatter and rattle of the wheels. Shelley said sweetly to Dinah, "Shall we?" And then in the act of decorously smoothing her skirts appeared to notice the silver-haired newcomer for the first time, blushed and turned her head away but not before she had given him a little smile.

As they went off to lunch Dinah was aware that the silver-haired gentleman was right behind them. It was too early for the diner to be crowded but when the headwaiter ushered the women to a table for two, Shelley just wasn't happy with her seat . . . too near the far door, she would prefer one of the tables in the center of the car . . . This, of course, was easily arranged . . . Shelley and the headwaiter had long since discovered they were both "home folks," born within two neighboring counties in Virginia.

Dinah was not a bit surprised when the silver-haired gentleman with the soft jowls hesitated in the narrow aisle, inquiring in what Dinah recognized as a New York voice, "Is anything available in a more central location? I'm afraid my digestion seems to require it. . . . If these ladies have no objection, sir." . . .

Shelley said, holding out a hand, "I think we might trust this gentleman. It's difficult, lord knows, when ladies are forced to travel alone, but in this case, surely . . ." Her sweet southern voice trailed off and the gentleman touched her fingers lightly before being seated opposite them.

He introduced himself as Arthur Sackett of New Jersey, out West for his health. After a hesitation beat that Dinah regarded as distinctly coy, Shelley introduced herself and her "kinswoman." No "niece" here, with its implication of youth . . .

Dinah was distinctly put off by Arthur Sackett's mouth . . . much too highly colored for an old man like that. The fleshy red lips tightened and he blinked as he acknowledged "Mrs. Nicholas Corrigan," but when he saw her watching him his lips quickly spread into a smile. Dinah preferred him without that smile . . .

"I declare!" Shelley was rattling on. "It's so good to meet one's own kind out here in the wilds, so to speak. Reckon you must just hate being separated from those wonderful white lights of Broadway, and all."

Mr. Sackett agreed, adding, "The West has its own charms, and it has been beneficial to my health." This time he addressed Dinah. "Beneficial to the pockets of some shrewd card players too. Not that I object. The air is remarkably salubrious in Reno. I'm afraid I'm addicted to poker . . . stud or draw, no matter how much I lose I seem to go back for more. A hopeless case, it would seem."

Shelley said quickly, "But that's a remarkable coincidence. My . . . Mrs. Corrigan's husband loves to play cards. As a pastime, that is."

"Naturally."

"We must get you-all together in San Francisco, Mr. Sackett. What a lovely coincidence, isn't it, Dinah honey?"

Dinah nodded uneasily. Arthur Sackett was just too much the portrait of the distinguished gentleman, except for his mouth, which made her queasy . . . Maybe he was an easy mark for a good card player like Nick, but if he really was how had he become so successful?

Shelley and Sackett were talking about her Gaynor creations and Dinah was startled by Sackett's voice as he talked to her directly. "So you're journeying all the way to San Francisco to be with your handsome young husband . . . I envy him . . . By the way, I'd like to have a game with him. You must give me his address . . . your hotel—?"

"The Palace," Shelley put in.

He seemed remarkably glad to hear this. "And you—Mrs.—may I call you Miss Shelley since you are my first friend on this train? . . . where will you be showing your delightful fashions? I've always thought there would be a real profit from investments of that sort."

"It isn't perhaps for me to say, but there have been investments in Gaynor's before, and I think I can say, without immodesty, that they were all profitable . . ."

Things proceeded very pleasantly from there, and when Shelley and Dinah were washing up in the women's restroom after lunch Shelley was delighted at her own brilliant conniving. "Not only is he likely to put some of his spare cash into Gaynor's but I've got him positively making an engagement to play cards with Nick. Heaven knows, that should help. This Sackett talks like he's used to losing his money."

Dinah was less enthusiastic with so little to go on. "It doesn't seem *natural*, somehow. And just maybe Nick won't much want to play cards so fast after I get there—"

"He will. He always did."

Dinah ignored this omniscient remark. "I wonder how he knew Nick was young and handsome . . ."

Shelley laughed. "Don't be so modest, honey . . . how else could he imagine a young man two such good-looking females know so intimately . . . ?"

Chapter Twenty-Four

FOR once in her life Dinah was grateful to the ubiquitous Captain Sholto. He embraced his daughter, who while peeling off her squirrel-trimmed hat and coat and throwing them across the Louis XV brocade couch in his hotel suite asked, "And where is poor Nick? We treated him so rudely, I wonder he'll ever want to see us again. We've got to put things to rights. Why isn't he here?"

"Because he's out earning a living," Sholto said evenly.

Shelley clapped her hands. "How providential! We met a gentleman on the train who is simply aching to lose money. He'd love to play cards with Nick. Wouldn't he, Dinah?"

Dinah had started to pull out her long hat pin but she stuck it back in now, repeating Shelley's question, "Where is he, captain?"

"Out at the Exposition grounds. He wanted to make as much money as possible before you and he leave for Los Angeles." He looked hard at Dinah. "The boy spent most of his money on clothes for you and him. He had a mishap and lost his suitcase, but he thinks about you until it's downright monotonous, let me tell you. You aren't going to disappoint him, I hope."

Well aware of Shelley's tense eagerness, Dinah had never been more firm. "Oh, no. We talked about a boat trip. I'll be with him. Whereabouts on the grounds can I find him? And how do I get there?"

Shelley put in quickly, "I'll show you, dear. I know exactly where all that marina area is." She began to struggle into her coat.

Sholto, thinking more of Dinah's mother's good graces than Dinah, reached for his daughter and held her there, squirming half in and half out of her coat. "Now, now, Shelley... Dinah is a big girl. We oldsters should leave the newlyweds to enjoy their privacy—"

"*Oldsters,*" Shelley said—gasped was more like it—"and privacy at an exposition?"

Sholto tilted his head toward the door. "Go along, Dinah. Take the Hyde Street cable car and walk over at the end of the line. Or better yet, a taxicab or a jitney will get you there."

Dinah was already at the door before it fully occurred to her how extensive the Exposition grounds were... Nick could be anywhere. "But where on the grounds is he?"

"The Zone, it's called. All kinds of games, rides, a safety racer, a scenic railway, an educated horse—well, you know the sort of thing. Look for the big South Pole exhibit, it shows the way Captain Scott and his men died. Nick's weighing machine is just beyond."

Shelley turned to plead with her father, but he hadn't lost his touch... "Honey, you've hardly given me a pleasant smile. Come along, act decent or I'll send for that husband of yours to make you behave."

That did it, and, considerably relieved, Dinah rushed out for the elevator ride down from the fourth floor. Passing through the wide foyer on the main floor, she saw the humorless, blank-eyed pair of men who were in Mr. Sackett's employ. She didn't like the way their eyes seemed to follow her. They reacted uncertainly to her passing, glancing around to see where her attractive companion had gone. Why she and Shelley should attract them so was a mystery to Dinah. They certainly hadn't shown any romantic interest. . . .

Out on Market Street, the widest thoroughfare Dinah had ever seen, she got up enough courage to ask a taxicab driver if he knew the way to the Exposition grounds. He pulled his cap further down over one eye, said in a bored voice, "Only make a hundred trips a day. Hop in. Want the main entrance, Tower of Jewels? Don't s'pose you want the Zone. Van Ness near Fillmore."

"The Zone, please."

He looked surprised but cranked up and drove off, turning abruptly across the four streetcar tracks while Dinah held her breath. He avoided two automobiles by the skin of his teeth but worse was to come when he took her over the highest, steepest hills she had ever dreamed existed this side of the Alps. Miraculously they arrived intact at the festive, flag-draped Zone entrance of the Exposition. Dinah counted out the fare and added a nickel tip. Two overdressed women with henna-colored hair grabbed the taxi door and took her place in the cab. "Ferry building . . . and don't spare the horses."

He didn't.

Smiling with relief, Dinah paid her admission and found herself on a huge street crowded with strollers—women in fashionable suits and wide-brimmed "French-style" chapeaux, men equally elaborate in bowlers or felt hats and velvet-collared overcoats, and a few jumping, yelling children. It surprised Dinah not to see more than two or three military uniforms, the usual navy blues one would expect to find in any port city.

At a distance the exhibits looked as exotic as the Far East, but close up some of them were rather garish, either vulgarly suggestive or freakish, like a cheap carnival back home, and the sideshows defined themselves, attracting men who all seemed to wear caps and striped suits. Overhead the light poles on either side of the street were joined by garlands or brightly colored, exotic designs that reminded her of the pictures she'd seen of Chinatown. In the distance she could make out the gleaming Tower of Jewels, like something out of the ancient past she had seen pictured in her history books . . .

But what about Nick? Was this his world, this area called the "Zone?" She hated to think of him having to live in this dingy atmosphere. Everywhere she looked there were papers and half-eaten candy and cones and discarded food. None of which fitted her Nick . . . In the distance she could see the top of the South Pole exhibit the tribute to the late explorer, Captain Robert Scott, constructed of imitation snow and ice with a sailing vessel that seemed to be floundering. Below the ship was a huge, gaping entrance dripping with icicles. Nick would probably be stationed nearby, operating some kind of weighing machine . . . A huge Mexican village loomed up, beautifully executed, and she felt suddenly homesick for her friends back in Lariat. The village and other equally artful exhibits increased her confidence in what she would find when she located Nick's concession—

She came on it unexpectedly, just past the Scott exhibit. At one side of the street, tucked between two large exhibits, a small line had formed, obscuring a weighing machine with a swing-seat for customers and a huge clock face announcing weights for the audience to read in unison with the weighing expert. Most of the shuffling, snickering customers in the line were female and under twenty. Three wore the dark uniform of a local Catholic high school, doubtless playing hooky to visit the Exposition.

Dinah could hardly see Nick beyond the line-up, but she would have known that blue-black cockscomb of hair anywhere. Her heartbeat increased and she felt her pulse pounding as she thought of all those barren, empty nights without Nick, and of the times ahead for them together. His nearness seemed to tear down all the mental barriers she had thrown up against him when they separated. . . .

Now that he was so near she could afford to wait just a minute or two longer and watch how he handled those pretty young high school girls. But he must never find out . . . he'd certainly consider it underhanded, spying. . . .

To get a clearer view of Nick as he handled his customers, she moved around the edges of the crowds waiting to enter the South Pole exhibit. Much of his success was due to his professional charm, the never obtrusive way he had of running his long, slender fingers lightly over the body of the patron and his cleverness at estimating correct weights. A fat man with a wife and two small children had just presented himself, urged on by his teasing family. Nick entered into the fun, announcing once more that he allowed himself a three-pound leeway and guessing a wildly inadequate "hundred and fifty," which struck everyone as hilarious. Then, as if suddenly discovering his error, he decided the man had to weigh two hundred fifty-five. Reconsidering, he added four pounds. The fat man sat down in the weighing machine, whose dial bounced up to two hundred sixty-one.

Amidst the gasps of his admiring audience, Nick pocketed the twenty-five cent payment for having guessed the weight within three pounds and ushered the next customer up to the machine. This was one of the uniformed highschool girls. Nick's hands moved expertly over the nervous, excited girl—never, of course, touching her breasts or stomach—with a touch that was feather-light before he took the flesh of her wrist between thumb and forefinger and announced, "Unlike their small brothers, our young ladies like to use soap and water. So naturally that reduces the weight by a pound or two." The girls considered this hilarious. The older ladies in the line smiled appreciatively. Nick guessed the girl's weight at eighty-seven pounds. She was delighted, and when the scale proved he had erred on the light side by ten pounds, Nick bowed, ushered her back to her friends and refused to accept her money. "I was more than three pounds off." He looked her up and down with a perplexed expression, black eyebrows raised. "I'd never have thought it. The young lady surely looks like eighty-seven pounds." Immediately several heavy-set women who had been watching crowded into line.

Dinah couldn't help appreciating Nick's skill at reading the people rather than their weight. It also went far to explain why he won more than he lost at poker. Finally she stepped into his view, and saw his face light up brighter than any exhibit lights. She waited, not wanting to interfere but he rushed through it, guessed another weight correctly and pocketed a surprising collection of quarters before he reached the end of the line.

Now he promptly took Dinah in his arms under the wide-eyed stare of several girls who dragged their feet in departure. Dinah protested weakly that people were watching but Nick paid no attention. When he kissed her, holding her tightly, she felt the excitement in him, knew their craving was mutual.

"Sweetheart, let's go somewhere. *Right now.*"

She couldn't have agreed more . . . "But where? The hotel? Captain Sholto and aunt Shelley are there."

"Oh, lord, why did you bring her?"

"I didn't, darling. In a manner of speaking, she brought me."

"Never mind." He still had her pressed against him . . . and his manifest desire made her feel as eager as he was . . . "We'll keep going until we find some place. We'll go out to the beach. It's windy today, too cold for crowds."

She couldn't imagine making love on a public beach with crowds everywhere, but she was beyond making objections. She waited while he went around to the back of the South Pole exhibit, found his relief man sleeping off a drunk and got him on his feet. "Time to stand in for me, Paddy."

The fellow stuck his cap on and stumbled out to take over from Nick. He walked Dinah to a side exit of the huge fairgrounds, where he found a taxicab. In the back seat he took her hands, imprisoning them between his body and hers as he leaned over her. He began to explore the old familiar joys of their kisses while his fingers worked their way over her back and hips.

Trying to get her breath, she managed to whisper, "The driver will see us, he'll know—"

"He's probably seen everything," Nick told her, and silenced her again. In spite of her inhibitions in public, it was impossible not to respond.

By the time they reached Sutro Heights and the Cliff House, the weather hadn't warmed up but the sun was still out in splendor and the long beach below was dotted with waders and a few hardy swimmers. A number of immobile sunbathers lay stretched out on the sand hoping for a tan to be absorbed through knee-length bathing suits and, in the case of the women, black hip-high stockings.

Holding hands, Nick and Dinah ran along the beach close to the waterline. A chill salt wind beat against them and Dinah's good suede shoes were ruined by the wet sand, but they were oblivious to all but each other. They found a cove far down the beach, sheltered from sight of casual passersby, and settled down to make love.... The danger of discovery only added new excitement to their lovemaking.

Later, having made themselves presentable, they returned their thoughts to the world. Dinah asked Nick why he had abandoned his beloved poker and reverted to the weighing act. She saw his face muscles suddenly tighten.

"... I just didn't want to get involved with gamblers here in Frisco, that's all. They begin to size you up for trouble if you become too well known."

She considered this, not sure whether to be concerned or relieved. And then came the inevitable question. "Did you miss me?"

He turned over in the cool sand, studied her face. "Do you know, there's something about your eyes that I've never seen in any other face. Like somebody polished the sky . . . a spring sky, I'd say." She liked *that* well enough. "There's no one like you, sweetheart. *No one.*"

She reached up and drew him down to her, holding him with her arms clasped behind his back. "I don't see how I ever could have let you go, even for a few days. I guess I'm just not very bright . . . well, at least I'm lucky . . . we're together again, we've got another chance. Nick, I love you more now than the night we ran away from Gaynor House."

"*I'm* the lucky one."

They argued this one to a mutually satisfactory conclusion and then agreed, reluctantly, that they really had to get back to the Palace.

"Shelley will be so *pleased* for us," Dinah said with a straight face, brushing off sand. "I'm sure she came clear out to San Francisco like a good auntie just to reunite us."

"*Meow,*" Nick said, laughed—and then straightened up, staring toward the end of the streetcar line.

"What is it?"

Intently, he watched the passengers climbing into the car and then seemed to relax. "Just thought I saw a . . . business friend I met on the road. But he always travels in a pair. This one's alone . . ."

"He can't be much of a 'friend,' to judge by your expression."

His look softened. "Sweetheart, let's go and announce our glad tidings and listen to the rejoicing of the Gaynor clan."

"Sholto. Not Gaynor."

"All the same to me. So long as they run Gaynor House.

You know, Dinah girl, you look delicious, good enough to eat."

But happy as he seemed, Dinah couldn't help thinking his mood had darkened since he had caught sight of that stranger in the distance. . . .

Chapter Twenty-Five

AT the last minute Nick and Dinah decided to eat dinner alone at an Italian restaurant on their way into town. Both had unspoken reasons for putting off the confrontation with Shelley, which would be polite on the surface but alive with innuendo underneath. It would prove to be a costly delay, since neither Shelley nor Sholto would be able to find them when the urgent need arose. . . .

At her father's suggestion Shelley wrote a warm note to Neily describing the wonders of the trip West, but the inevitable moment came when the letter-writing was finished and the view of busy Market Street from the front windows palled.

"What can they possibly have to say to each other that takes up five hours?" she said, knowing—and not liking—the answer to her own question.

"Four hours," Bill Sholto corrected her. "And, my dear, when two lovers meet after a parting they don't usually spend all their time in conversation—"

"Oh, please . . ." She pulled the curtains aside to peer out again. "Their taxi ought to be arriving any minute, though I suppose Dinah has chosen a streetcar. It's so like her."

"What do you mean, 'Oh, *please?*' I'm surprised to hear

you, my darling daughter, dismiss it so cavalierly."

"Don't be sarcastic. You always did take up for Dinah. Just because she's the daughter of your precious Ellen. But I notice you chose mama instead of Ellen."

"No," he said, suddenly quiet, "Ellen chose to give me up. She sent me to Maggilee . . . to make an honest woman of your mother. And I must say it's lucky for you, young lady, that I did . . . otherwise you'd be among Tudor County's more attractive illeg—"

"Never *mind.*"

Her father had been watching her more closely than she liked. Now he strolled across the room, reached for her nervous fingers, which were about to drum on the window. She felt—as she had more than once before—that he seemed almost ashamed of her . . . as if *she* could help being what he had made her . . . She was aware of the sinewy strength in that hand, which she knew had killed men in his youth. She had never been foolish enough to pit her will against his at such moments as these, when she felt his full power . . .

"Why do you really want this two-bit gambler, honey? And don't lie, because I've had a whole lot more experience at it and I can top any whopper you give me."

Because she didn't exactly know the answer, she partly evaded it. "Reckon the same reason you wanted mama. A hunger . . ." And that was no lie.

He shook her hand, a bit too hard. "Not quite the same reason, my girl. My lord, girl! Do you really think I had to work as hard getting her into bed as you've worked on young Corrigan? He *was* a loose one maybe, loose as me . . . Lily Biedemeier's girls could tell you a thing or two. But he wanted Ellen's girl because to him she was something special, not one of the common run like you and me . . . *and* him. Is that how you'd like to get him?"

She tried to say yes but her mouth was too dry. Her beloved father was still a stranger, telling her brutal things she didn't want to hear. . . .

"All right, then. You don't want to settle down with him. Or marry him. Not any of that. You never did. You just want Nick Corrigan because you can't have him."

"He's a wonderful lover . . ." She eyed him, saw his eyes blaze. "It was several years ago. Just once—"

"You do that again while he's married to Ellen's daughter and I'm through with you. I mean it. *Do you understand me, girl?*"

She did, at this moment as well as he understood her . . . maybe better . . . "This is all very silly, pa, such a fuss over a stupid flirtation . . . I'd never do anything to make you—"

"Good, then we understand each other."

He smiled, but she knew there was no fooling him. It was one of the things about her father . . . he understood her so well, and yet he loved her in spite of everything. She was sure of it— "Actually I'm being so unselfish you'd hardly know me, pa. I made up to a rich east coast stockbroker on the train—and so did your noble Dinah—just so he'd play poker and lose money to Nick. He even said he liked losing."

"Then I wouldn't trust that fellow as far as I could throw him. Nobody loses money unless he expects to get something in return. And you can bet on that, my dear."

Shelley had such pleasant memories of the silver-haired gentleman with the soft jowls. It hardly seemed possible that a man connected with the stock market in New York could be after anything but the obvious from two good-looking females. Unless, of course, he had a secret reason for striking up the acquaintance. It was hardly the first time in Shelley's life that a man had built up an impressive picture of himself to win her favor . . . She dismissed suspicion to ask, "Why on earth should Nick be back working for some carnival-weighing concession? It doesn't look good when I'm busy trying to get up a big poker game for him."

"There are times when it pays better dividends to avoid gamblers . . . especially people like Louie Apperson and friend Sackett—"

"Apperton and *who?*"

"Apperson. A crook from your beloved New York . . . or New Jersey. Somewhere around there. The senior partner is an unsavory lad named Artie—"

"Arthur Sackett? *But that's our stockbroker* . . . the one on the train . . ."

Sholto looked at her. Seconds ticked by, and then he asked, "Did you tell him your name, and who Dinah was?"

Beginning to appreciate the full danger, she nodded.

"And where would you be staying?"

"Worse. I told him Nick would be staying here too. You see, I hoped to set up a game for Nick so he could win a little money—"

"I'm afraid that's already happened," Sholto said grimly. "If we could trust these hoodlums not to beat Nick up—or worse—he could simply lose back to them. But I'm afraid men like those two enjoy taking their pound of flesh along with their profits. It teaches others not to run away winners."

"What on earth can we do?"

"Keep Nick from coming back here, first of all."

He went out into the foyer to the telephone and spoke to the operator. Shelley had no idea how her father could contact a single carnival exhibit on the huge Exposition grounds. She listened nervously as he tried—and failed—to get a message to Nick at the weighing machine. He hung up the receiver and looked across the little mahogany credenza to Shelley. "We'll just have to let them come back here and hope for the best. It won't be the first time I've figured out a quick exit to get someone off my neck. And I'll lay you odds it won't be the first time for Nick Corrigan either."

"But they might kill him—why can't he just give back the money he won?"

"I'm not sure he's still got it. We left Reno in a hurry, and he had to get a new outfit here in Frisco. Then he bought some doodads for Dinah—I'd say he isn't exactly flush."

She groaned and went back to the window to watch for the Corrigans' arrival at the hotel's Third and Market taxi entrance. It was already dark, which at least might, she thought, help Nick. On the other hand, Sackett's men must be watching from a closer vantage point.

Her father, who had been silent, considering various possibilities, now said, "Don't worry, maybe a little scare is just what Corrigan needs. Shake him up, toughen him so everything doesn't bother so much . . . calluses on the soul, that's what he needs. It's downright tiring just being with him . . . his pride, mostly, I'd say . . . !"

"Yes, he cares . . . when I married Marsh he cared about me like that—"

"Well, daughter, you aren't blaming Marsh for getting calluses on his soul, I hope."

"No, of course not. Incidentally I wrote a note to Marsh, told him about being with you so he wouldn't think—well, you know . . ."

Her father knew. "So now you surrender young Corrigan and substitute good old neglected Marsh. Don't know but what I'm beginning to be a mite sorry for that poor soul. You lay him off and put him back on like a hair-shirt."

"He's all I've got for sure— Pa! That's one of Mr. Sackett's men leaning against the lamppost. He's sure to see Nick and Dinah when they drive up."

Sholto looked down over her shoulder, and make up his mind about the ploy he would use . . . "Sackett had only two men when he boarded the train?"

"They were the only ones who got on with him."

"Just two . . . but that's enough. See here, I'm going down

to lead them on a little chase. Then, after you have dinner downstairs or here in the suite, you're going to have to figure out something you can do this evening."

"Alone?"

"You're a fine big girl now, Shelley-Ann. You can eat alone. Afterwards there's that big vaudeville house, the Orpheum. Catch the first acts and leave at the end of the first half if you get bored."

She began to understand his plan. "So they'll have three parties to handle . . . Nick and Dinah, then you and then me. We'll keep them busy. Pa, you're so smart!" She hugged him.

"A lifetime of practice, my dear," and then he reminded her, "what I've got to do, and you too if you can manage it, is to be seen going out several times. It will be easier for me than for you, but the more times we do it the less they'll know who to follow."

"Whatever you say, and I still think you're the cleverest man I ever knew."

"Naturally. I only wish I could get Ellen Gaynor to agree."

Her arms dropped away from him. She had almost convinced herself he was doing this for her . . .

Nick and Dinah, it turned out, were to spend the evening at the Exposition. Nick wanted to show her the city from Twin Peaks at night, the rough, windy thrill of crossing the Golden Gate on the Sausalito Ferry and countless other wonders, but she was determined to see the Exposition's Tower of Jewels by night with every bit of colored glass giving off a different glow under the gleaming searchlights.

He also wanted to give her everything, anything she expressed the slightest interest in, which was a bit disturbing . . . she didn't need dozens of little trinkets and the more expensive gifts he promised were waiting for her at the

Palace Hotel. If he were only a little more practical he wouldn't have to work at so many jobs that were beneath him—but then she became conscious of his arm close around her, heard his voice, and remembering how empty life had been without him she returned his embrace and accepted with enthusiasm an armful of kewpie dolls, stuffed teddy bears and a souvenir sofa pillow in bright green felt on fire-engine red. She couldn't resist Nick, or Nick's nearness. And there was no good reason to try, she lectured herself . . .

It was getting on toward nine o'clock now and the wind had died down as they strolled past the dimly illuminated lagoon that the round-domed Palace of Fine Arts floated in. Nick was pointing out Dinah's reflection, but before he could go on she saw a reflection beyond Nick's head and abruptly turned around. Surely that dead, emotionless face reflected in the calm lagoon waters belonged to one of the "secretaries" who had dutifully followed Mr. Sackett onto the train. She nudged Nick, whispering, "Let's move back into the bright lights. I don't like it here . . ."

Before Nick could react to her sudden change of heart the man she'd spotted spoke up. "Our friend would like to see you tonight, Mr. Corrigan."

Nick ignored him, said coolly to Dinah, "Well, if you've seen enough, sweetheart . . ."

"Yes. By all means." She felt his tension, admired his act. He took her arm and started to walk off with her.

The blank-faced man reached out, caught Nick's shoulder. "Tonight, I said. Better come along with me . . . our friend gets impatient—"

Nick turned to face the man, dislodging a hand that had been put on his shoulder. Nick's own hand was in his coat pocket as he said quietly, "I don't think so. Not tonight, perhaps some other time . . ." Just then half a dozen drunken merrymakers—they'd been working on it all day

—poured along the path and in the semidarkness almost bumped into the tense group by the lagoon. Nick, seizing the moment, grabbed Dinah's arm and pulled her away at the run . . .

Back in the bright lights of the main concourse, Nick knew from the way Dinah clung to him that she understood how dangerous their shadowy pursuer could be. "Sweetheart," he said, "you had a peculiar look on your face when you saw that man . . . how did you know what he was up to?"

"Because we met him and his employer on the train this morning. They got on at Reno very early with another man. Shelley and I thought this one was just a secretary, or something."

"Do you think they followed you off the train? But how would they know you were my wife?"

She looked miserable. "Worse, darling. Shelley . . . that is, she and I . . . introduced ourselves. Now that I think of it, Mr. Sackett was interested in a game of poker with you. It was Shelley's idea that he would like to lose to you, something idiotic like that—"

"I'm afraid Sackett has already lost a lot to me. Which is why Sholto and I had to get out fast. I met Sholto at Sackett's and Apperson's place in Reno. That's why I didn't dare to get into a poker game here. They were sure to track me down."

"But honey, if you won a lot why take this job—?"

Getting edgy, he told her with forced patience, "Because I had to leave my suitcase and clothes behind. When we got to San Francisco I had to buy a whole new outfit. This overcoat, for instance. And a few things for you. Darling, wait 'til you see your beaded bag and the blouse, it's a kind of blue-green color, wonderful with your hair . . . and the little lavaliere—"

"Nick"—her mind was on more urgent matters—"isn't it possible to play a few games with this Arthur Sackett? He can win it all back, and there won't be any threats or problems with him—"

"I can't do that. They don't play that way. I mean—they expect more than just to win back their own money. It's sort of a way to keep players from doing the same thing again. And besides, I couldn't . . . anyway, it can't be done."

"Then the thing for us is to get out of San Francisco without your friends knowing—or maybe I should say our friends, since it's Shelley's and my fault they found you."

He looked at her, then pulled her to him and kissed her, oblivious to the onlookers on the concourse.

"Sweetheart, there is *no one* like you in the whole world. We'll get our things out of the hotel and take tomorrow's sailing to Los Angeles . . . they're sure to think we'd be going by train if we got away at all . . ."

"Perfect," she agreed with a kind of desperate gaiety. . . .

Chapter Twenty-Six

THE first time Shelley left the Palace Hotel that night, dressed to the teeth, she took a taxi to the St. Francis on Union Square a mile or so away. The elegant six-course dinner she ordered was much too heavy and precious little fun alone, but it had seemed a clever idea to hail the taxi in full view and hearing of Sackett's man and enjoy herself in the famous St. Francis dining room. Later, back at the Palace once more, she went up to her father's suite, powdered her nose and returned to the lobby, where she noted Sackett's man hustling out of the elegant dining room with the corner of his napkin still tucked into his vest. It might have seemed comical if she hadn't known just how dangerous this game was . . .

Half an hour later she was in a box seat at the theater pretending to watch three jugglers in the opening vaudeville act. She had seen no one remotely like Mr. Sackett's bodyguard and was just settling down to breathe more easily when there was a slight disturbance behind her. The usherette showed in a gentleman whose pleasant, unctuous voice she remembered all too well . . . "My dear Mrs. Wychfield. What a pleasant coincidence. Permit me?"

Terrified, she still had the presence of mind to invoke her

much practiced Southern Charm. "How nice to see you, Mr. Sackett! I'm afraid I was just feeling sorry for myself, sitting here all by my lonesome. Most improperly, I declare. I could never do this down home."

He settled himself near her . . . but not too near. Everything about him was so very gentlemanly . . . knowing what she did now, she wondered if his aura of danger would have attracted her in other circumstances . . . well, never mind, it was *this* circumstance that concerned her . . . Arthur Sackett had threatened Nick, the one man who'd gotten away from her. Maybe, just maybe if she saved him from a beating or whatever gamblers did when they had it in for you, he would come to his senses and realize that Shelley Wychfield was preferable to his precious Dinah . . . far more so, she told herself . . . after all, I'm risking my life to be in the company of this awful man . . . She looked up into his face, murmuring as if they shared a secret, "It's not a very good show so far, is it?"

"I'm loathe to contradict you but I must say any show that finds me in the company of so beautiful a lady is well worth any admission."

"Chamingly put, sir. Really, one would think we were at the Governor's Ball down in Richmond, I swear."

"Ah, the South. I've fond memories of Atlanta. And New Orleans. Business friends there. Unfortunately I've never had the good luck to visit Richmond but I have pleasured myself playing poker in Washington, which isn't too far from there. Lost almost a thousand but it was worth it. We played for eighteen hours steady . . ." He sighed. "Pity I can't seem to get up a game here in Fris—San Francisco."

"We're getting to it," she decided, and played to his performance. "I call that a real shame. I'm right sorry my niece's husband didn't stay here long enough. Heavens! Poor Dinah no sooner arrived than they went off in the rudest way, leaving pa and me."

"Does this young man drive?"

She had heard her father mention Nick's plan to sail for Los Angeles by the coast steamer so she confided with bland innocence, "No, but he adores to ride the train. Reckon he and Dinah are on their way back East now by the Overland Limited."

He considered this. "Then I presume it was someone else my secretary saw on the Exposition grounds tonight." He was looking at her closely, and she felt it.

"Must have been." She hoped he believed her . . . men usually did when she exerted herself. She decided she'd better work even harder on her innocence. "I saw Nick buying tickets at the Ferry Building for the Southern Pacific ferryboat and the Overland Limited."

Thanks be, he seemed to take her word for it. He smiled, patted her hand and motioned toward the stage, where a young British singer began to rend hearts with the new hit: *"Keep the Home Fires Burning,"* followed by *"Pack up your Troubles in your Old Kit Bag",* in which the audience joined with a rousing, *"and smile, smile, smile."*

While Shelley wiped away sentimental tears for the dead of Flanders Field and the whole Western Front, Mr. Sackett observed more or less to himself, "A lot of money being made in this Europe war . . ."

Though it was doubtless true, Shelley felt her first distinct revulsion toward Mr. Sackett. She found it difficult to sit out the full show, afraid she might betray Nick in some way, but she decided she had to stay until the end because it would be keeping Sackett with her during these hours, which in turn might help Nick.

At the end of the first half Sackett asked if she would like to leave now and perhaps have—he hesitated—"an ice-cream parfait or something before heading home?"

"No, if you don't mind. They do say the dancer who is the main attraction is tremendously entertainin'."

He wanted to leave but it was evident that he was also happy to stay in Shelley's company . . . Well, at least I haven't lost my appeal, she told herself with some satisfaction... He was a talkative man and she was smart enough to wonder once or twice if he wasn't trying to get some information out of her, but mostly he gave her tales of Paris and Berlin and St. Petersburg before the war, and it seemed pretty evident to her that his real interest was in her... which most men sooner or later were.

After the theater Sackett found a taxi for her, which was a great relief. She loathed doing such unfeminine things for herself... that was what gentlemen were for, after all. The taxi driver took them the long way back to the Palace, and Sackett obligingly pointed out the distant lights of Oakland and Berkeley across the Bay. "And over there you can just make out the funnels of some steamers... that one sails for Hawaii on Saturday. Pretty exciting, don't you think? And that one at the next dock, the steamer H.F. *Allison* of the Coastal Line, sails for Los Angeles tomorrow. Ah, Hawaii ... what memories!"

She sat forward, trying to make out the dim silhouette through the izinglass of the car window.

He went on casually, "I myself am one of those who prefer land travel. Get seasick, you know. Not like your niece's husband."

"What... ? Oh, I see the funnels now."

"I mean boats being young Corrigan's favorite mode of travel."

Which startled her. "How do you know?"

He smiled, said offhandedly, "Mrs. Corrigan told me. You remember, in the diner."

She couldn't remember but it was very likely. Dinah was stupid enough to betray such a face and just when it could matter so desperately to Nick. Shelley tried to erase the damage. "That may be, but poor Dinah simply can't stand water travel. She even gets seasick crossing the James River on the ferry back home."

"I see."

All the same she didn't like the way he was studying her, and it was almost a relief when he reached for her gloved hand. "What lovely, graceful fingers . . . excuse me, I had no right—"

She looked down modestly, then, "Well, here we are, the hotel . . ."

Very proud of herself, she allowed him escort her into the lobby.

Nick got out of the cab a block up Market Street from the hotel, saying to the driver as he paid the fare, "The lady's husband . . . you understand . . ."

The cab driver did, flipped a finger to his cap and drove off toward the Palace Hotel, where Dinah got out, nervous but feeling triumphant under the bright lights at the entrance. She strolled into the lobby without turning her head, though she took in her surroundings and noted that neither Sackett nor his men were anywhere to be seen.

But she was shocked when she stepped into the elevator, and was joined by the fellow who had accosted Nick at the Exposition grounds. In spite of the presence of the operator, she prepared for the worst, her muscles tense, ready to scream if Sackett's bodyguard got off the elevator with her. An elaborately dressed man and woman returning from the opera entered the elevator just as the door was closing, and proceeded to debate the merits of *Faust* until they reached the fourth floor, where they followed Dinah off.

Sackett's man, of course, was looking for Nick, not his wife, and so didn't even follow Dinah out of the elevator. She was hardly relieved, though . . . realizing as she did that he would go back downstairs to wait for Nick's arrival. . . .

She was trying the door to Captain Sholto's suite when it opened abruptly, throwing her into his arms. He was looking uncharacteristically anxious and she assumed it was on account of Nick . . . "Is he all right?"

"I've no doubt! His kind lives forever." Sholto peered along the empty hall. When he closed the door he blurted out, "It's my Shelley has me bothered, she should have been back before this. She said she would leave the theater after the first three acts."

Since it was clear Dinah didn't seem appropriately concerned, he added with an edge, "She wanted to distract one of Sackett's men, for Nick . . . You know about the danger there?"

"I know now. One of Sackett's men threatened Nick at the Fair tonight. Captain, how are we going to get away from them? Can't we pay them somehow?"

"I'm afraid they want more than money. They want Corrigan to be an object to discourage other winners who run off—"

"I don't know why he did run off, frankly."

Sholto had gone to the front windows to look out, and now said over his shoulder, "When anybody wins that fast in a game stacked by the dealer, it's generally figured he was cheating. Corrigan wasn't, but they don't know that, can't believe it."

Before he could go on they heard a familiar laugh in the hall. Sholto threw open the door, and Shelley scurried in with Nick right behind her.

Neither Dinah nor Sholto much liked the combination.

"It was such a *darlin'* coincidence . . . I saw him come up the stairs when I got off the elevator, he'd—"

"I got in through the delivery entrance downstairs, never saw a soul until the elevator stopped on this floor, and there was Shelley with Sackett himself. Fortunately he didn't get off—"

Shelley put in proudly, "No accident, Nick . . . I told him pa would go gossiping to my husband if he saw me with an attractive man. He swallowed it all, thank the dear lord . . ."

Nick had taken Dinah's head and framed it between his long, narrow hands. When he kissed her, beginning tenderly, progressing to an intensity that took possession of him, she clung to him, thinking of nothing, of nobody except this man she now was sure she could not live without . . . never mind *what* she did . . .

Seeing the depressing effect this display had on his daughter, Sholto took her arm and led her off to the door of the bedroom Nick had used before the arrival of the women. "Honey, it's late, you've had a mighty exhausting day and I suspect tomorrow's going to be worse. Why don't you just take a bath and go off to bed."

By the time Nick and Dinah were ready to leave for their new bedroom down the hall Shelley had reluctantly given in to her father's advice . . . to Dinah's considerable relief.

But Sholto had some orders of battle for the next day. . . . "Corrigan, you'll take the H.F. *Allison* at four P.M. tomorrow. Is that your plan?"

Nick agreed. "With Dinah, if it's safe. I'll call in the morning. They'll give me a double cabin, they know me from other trips."

"Good. I'll go down to the ferry building and get you two tickets for Chicago on the Southern Pacific. I'll be properly secretive about it . . . enough, I hope for your sake, to convince Mr. Sackett. . . .

Chapter Twenty-Seven

IT was decided that while Sholto, Shelley and Dinah should go out on wild-goose chases, Nick would remain in his hotel room until the very last minute and then leave by the delivery entrance.

Nick had different notions. He felt almost euphoric after his night with Dinah . . . the heady effect of danger apparently providing a special impetus for Dinah in her lovemaking. She couldn't help feeling a bit embarrassed next morning when Nick made reference to it, but also was secretly pleased.

Nick sat now on the arm of Dinah's chair, toying with her pleated collar. "They'll expect to see me. I'll go and get the decoy tickets."

Sholto shook his head. "They won't go for that. And if they decide to quietly pick you up it would take some doing to get you away from them . . . By that time we might not recognize you."

Which clearly upset Dinah and Shelley, and though Nick waved it off he agreed to listen to reason. It was only when Sholto and Shelley had gone off in their different directions to follow the captain's plan that Dinah knew Nick shared at least some of her tension. Meanwhile she was turning an idea over in her mind.

"Nick, Captain Sholto says they'll know you wouldn't go out in broad daylight and buy tickets for your real destination—so let's do just that."

He looked at her a moment, then threw his arms around her in delight. They went out together, exaggerating an air of secrecy. Once inside the building that housed the Coastal Line Company offices on Lower Market near the Embarcadero, they purchased tickets for a double cabin, returned to the hotel by way of Mission Street, then took a Valencia streetcar and while they were at it rode out to Daly City on the outskirts of town and then back again, even though the weather looked threatening.

"That ought to keep them guessing," Nick said. "Nothing much beyond Daly City but the cemeteries."

"Nick—"

He tried to warm her chilled hands. "Think about pleasant things, our ocean honeymoon . . ."

The first autumn rain of the season had begun to sprinkle the streetcar windows, and Dinah was reminded of something Shelley had said. "Suppose I *do* get seasick, the way Shelley says she told Sackett I always do . . . it was to give him the idea we'd never take a ship, but I hope it wasn't prophetic . . ."

"We'll figure something out," he told her solemnly, and then they both allowed themselves a small laugh. Life or death, it might be, but the tension had to be relieved occasionally to make it bearable.

Back at the hotel they matched notes with Shelley and the captain, and all had one report which puzzled them. Shelley voiced it. "I swear, not a soul followed me. Or if they did, they were right careful. I'm pretty sure I would have known . . ."

Sholto said he hadn't seemed to rouse any interest either.

Nick took the optimistic view. "He must have believed Shelley when she told him we were taking the train . . ."

Trying to be as hopeful Dinah added, "After all, he seemed convinced when Shelley left him last night . . . why wouldn't he believe her?"

Sholto was less impressed but tried to play down his skepticism.

In the end they agreed with Nick that they were probably all exaggerating the danger. Nick pointed out that Sackett wouldn't want a lot of bad publicity, "and if anything happened to me Bill here would let the story out, which couldn't help Sackett in his—business."

"Anyway," Sholto said, "there's nothing else we can do, except see that you two get onto the H.F. *Allison* without Sackett's men knowing it."

"Agreed," Nick said. "This should be the crucial time."

In the end it was decided that Shelley would go down to the Ferry Building with Sholto half an hour before the boat pulled out, to catch the Overland Limited leaving Oakland for Chicago and points East. "You lend me that grosgrain redingote of yours, Dinah. We can shorten it in ten minutes . . . and I'll wear my highest heels and your big-brimmed fuzzy fedora hat. Then you and Nick can slip out by the back way and get onto the steamer."

When it came to saying good-by Captain Sholto embraced Dinah—though no real affection on either side—and Nick gave Shelley a hug and kiss along with genuine thanks.

"Let us know how you make out at the card tables in Los Angeles," Sholto reminded Nick, adding, "by the way, Dinah, I intend to visit your mother in New Mexico once I've gotten this girl of mine home again. Wish me luck."

Feeling distinctly two-faced, Dinah wished him "all the luck you deserve, captain . . . you've certainly been a great help to us . . ."

Shelley, disguised as the tall, rangy Dinah, added behind her father's back, "Don't worry, Dinah." She wrinkled her nose. "Sister Ellen has such bad taste she's bound to refuse pa. Good luck, Nickie dear. You *will* let us know how things turn out, won't you, honey?" And she was gone.

In spite of Shelley's enormous help during the last few hours, Dinah couldn't help mimicking her . . . "Good luck, Nickie dear. . . . Let us *know*, honey . . ."

Nick decided no comment was the better part for him, and only said, "It's our turn now, hon, let's go."

They slipped out through the alley, Nick carrying their two valises, got onto a Mission Street car, transferred and finally arrived finally at the Coastal Line dock in the North Beach area instead of Market Street. They were early enough to pick out every face on the long dock as they boarded. There was none associated with Arthur Sackett. There were several uniformed army officers, half a dozen sailors and two stern-faced nurses in white headdresses with the distinctive red cross to remind the passengers that war might not be far away. But it seemed that Sackett had been deceived by all their elaborate charades.

Nick and Dinah walked now up the impressive main staircase, following Nick's steward friend Mac Pettibone, a good-natured, lanky fellow of about thirty-five who promised Nick, "I'll get you up a game soon as we're out past the Farallon Islands."

"Not this time, Mac, we're on our honeymoon."

"Sure thing, can't say I blame you." He gave Dinah an appreciative smile, though she suspected he'd have preferred Nick alone, a potential player and big tipper . . .

They passed the lounge, a spacious public room in the center of the ship full of wicker furniture that made it look like a transplant from some South-Sea idyll. Two navy men and a marine were already ensconced in the little smoking room next door, almost lost among the deep leather chairs.

"Waiting for drinks," Mac observed, adding cheerfully, "looks like we'll all be wearing the old uniforms and ploughing through that Flanders mud pretty soon, the way the boys in Washington are building us up for it. One thing . . . there's always gay Paree. I could really make myself at home there."

Mac showed them their cabin, which looked out onto the open Promenade Deck, pointing out upper and lower bunks, a mirror over the porcelain washbasin with running water and a "thunder jug" in case they didn't want to leave their cabin during the night. The tiny room was whitewashed and more immaculate than most of the second-rate hotels travelers had to put up with.

"Dinner served from seven on," Mac added. "What with this rain and the rough waters along the coast here, you won't have any trouble getting a table. And if you do get up a game, lots of luck."

As soon as he was gone Dinah said, "We shouldn't even mention gambling tonight, honey. If Sackett should happen to have anyone on board, that would have to attract him . . ."

Nick shrugged as she began to unpack. "Maybe . . . but it sure would help to win at least a little stake, what with the expense of these tickets and the money we'll need in Los Angeles to get the train back East . . ." He noted that familiar Gaynor frown, added hurriedly, "However, like I said, you're probably right."

She took out her white cotton nightgown with the blue satin ribbons at the neck and wrists, was about to lay it across the bunk when he put his arms around her waist, pulled her against him and began to kiss her, first on the neck and then, unbuttoning her shirtwaist, as far down as she would let his warm lips linger on the pale flesh of her throat and breasts. At that minute she wanted him fully as much as he wanted her, but her body was also vulnerable to the tensions of their trip to the dock, the anxiety to escape Sackett's men and a vague, elusive fear that one day soon she might lose him to the faraway European war . . . She protested weakly, but gave in, her body finally proving more than capable of overcoming all her restraints to respond to his lovemaking.

Although the predicted rough coastal waters made the steamer pitch and toss, the unpleasantness had no effect on Nick and Dinah, and by the time they went down to dinner, singularly refreshed and invigorated, even Dinah felt that the danger was gone. She took Nick's hand, aware that she shared some of his gambler's optimism. As they made their way down the grand staircase with its huge mirror on the landing, Nick admired her reflection, wearing the new georgette blouse he had bought her in San Francisco, and for her part Dinah thought she had never seen any man more desirable than Nick in his stark black and white . . . though Nick in any colors would have been the same for her.

Their pleasure in each other was abruptly shattered by a raucous voice, as a thick-necked man in a plaid suit clattered down the stairs behind them, dripping wet, pushing other passengers aside.

"Hot damn! That's what I call *weather* out there . . . and talk about seasick! The landlubbers are giving it up all over the place."

Dinah hoped the plaid man was talking to someone else, but he caught Nick's reflection in the mirror on the landing below them and pointed a fleshy thumb at him. "Don't I know you from someplace?"

Dinah looked at Nick. It was clear he recognized the plaid man but couldn't place him . . . until he saw the huge diamond on the stubby little finger. The stone reflected light like the glass it was made of, which triggered Nick's memory.

"A Chicago hotel room . . . you were one of the three salesmen who got up a poker game." Nick's manner changed in front of Dinah's eyes . . . Now he was the innocent scion of a great house, ready for the plucking. "You were in ladies' hose and silkwear—"

"Rayonwear, it's newer. Good quality, though. I'm Dinty Harmor and you're . . . Nick . . . Nicholas Corey."

His belligerent thumb turned into a fleshy hand, which Nick shook. It was plain to Dinah that Nick didn't want to introduce the salesman . . . he simply told her offhandedly, "Darling, Mr. Harmor and I played a few hands in Chicago this summer. He sells—"

"Yes. I heard. How do you do, Mr. Harmor? You must be soaking wet. You should get into something dry or you'll catch your death of cold."

"Sure thing, ma'am. I'll do just that. Well, Corey, after dinner I'm going to see if I can find me a poker game. You owe me one, you know."

"How is that, sir . . . ?"

"Well, you got to admit you had a good run of luck last time."

"Beginner's luck, I'm afraid. I haven't done so well since then. I reckon I just can't figure the fine points of the game, somehow."

"Sure you will," Harmor promised. "You'll learn a lot from my salesmen friends."

Nick gave Dinah a side-glance, said, "I'm sorry, not this time . . . my wife being with me and all."

Dinty Harmor was cheerfully persistent. "I'd take it right unkindly if you didn't give me a chance to even things up. What say to nine o'clock? There's a little card lounge upstairs . . . We usually get together on these voyages, ma'am, just to kill time, you know?" He was ingenuously proper to her.

Dinah saw that Nick was familiar with the room in question, and also that it was awkward for him to refuse the invitation.

"See you after dinner then," Dinty Harmor said, taking Nick's silence for agreement. "They got good food on these here steamers. Got to, I guess, to try to take your mind off the rough spots. I'll come and locate you in the dining room if you ain't finished by nine. Can't start too late, they say we dock at nine tomorrow morning." He climbed back up the stairs, two steps at a time.

Nick seemed out of sorts, but Dinah suspected it was partly show, that he probably didn't want her to know just how much he really wanted to get into that poker game. "Damn, I should never have won from him in Chicago. They always want their revenge. Goes on forever, it seems . . ."

Dinah didn't allude to the trouble Nick was in with Arthur Sackett over just this same point. Instead she took his arm and they went down to the lavish dining salon, where the headwaiter came to them between almost deserted tables and inquired where they preferred to sit, with a group or otherwise.

"Alone, just us two," Nick told him, pressing Dinah's hand. As they were led to their table at the side of the room Dinah tried to play the understanding wife she had vowed to become.

"Honey, if you have to play, you have to. I know it's not your fault. If that Harmor man hadn't showed up you wouldn't be playing tonight."

"Believe me, I *wouldn't* . . . and I still don't like the feel of it. Why did Harmor come rushing down the stairs like that, just when we were going down? Then, after he ruins our evening, he turns right around and runs back up again."

"Well, darling, he was soaking wet, and he had to go and change—"

"Why didn't he change in the first place? I don't like it—"

"Then don't play at all, for heaven's sake. There's no law says you *have* to."

But there was. She could see it in his face. . . .

They ate fresh San Francisco cracked crab, mushroom soup followed by delicious lemon salmon, and finished off with cheese for Nick and rice pudding for Dinah. They didn't get back to their cabin until close to nine. Dinah was still in her optimistic mood, which made it all the more difficult for Nick to leave her. And to it the black Irish depression he couldn't shake ever since that damned Dinty Harmor had showed up . . . I'm going to lose tonight, that's about it, he told himself. He took Dinah by the shoulders, looked into her eyes and saw what he felt he needed most —assurance that she loved him no matter what . . . "Sweetheart, did I ever tell you how much I need you?"

"You'd *better* need me . . ." She kissed his nose, then tenderly, his mouth. Still in his arms, she said softly, "you really do worry about that poker game, don't you, darling? I can feel it in you."

It bothered him that she noticed. "Lord, no! I won't stay more than an hour or so. And I promise not to lose over—"

She silenced him with her forefinger. "No promises. It might be bad luck, and in your business that's not good. Go on, darling. Come back as soon as you can. If you don't, I promise you, I'll come after you." . . .

Even after he left the cabin, pulling his coat collar up against the rain slanting in across the rail, he had a notion to forget the game and go back to her. Nothing to it, he told himself. Dinty Harmor wasn't dangerous, he was just a silk —no—a rayon salesman. Hardly a man like Sackett or Apperson. Just another gambling fool like so many of the others . . . *not like me, of course . . . oh no, of course not* . . .

Face it, face yourself . . . nothing left for it but to go through with this hated game . . . He stepped over the sill into the passage, smoothed his coat collar, ran his fingers through his hair.

Mac Pettibone came lurching now toward the open deck, shook his head as he and his unfortunate charge passed Nick. "I'll be doing this the rest of the night," he complained. "Nobody wants to use the basin in their cabin. And dammit, my last victim lost his upper plate overboard!"

Nick grinned, then concentrated on the night ahead. By the time he reached the card room he felt a surge of confidence, a little of the old spirit and excitement. A short game or two and then back to Dinah, he promised himself. . . .

The card-room door usually stood open. It was closed tonight. A really private game must be in progress. He opened the door and stepped inside to comfortable leathery furnishings under warm, subdued lighting, all in support of a poker table in the exact center of the room. He hardly noticed the luxury. He was fighting to compose himself so as to exhibit as much *sang froid* as possible at sight of the men around the table.

Because the men were Arthur Sackett, the two blank-faced bodyguards, Dinty Harmor, and behind Nick, quietly closing the door, a third bodyguard he didn't know, as expressionless as a zombie.

Sackett beckoned to him, smiling pleasantly. "Ah, Mr. Corrigan! A true player. I knew we could count on you."

Chapter Twenty-Eight

NICK nodded formally, came forward, holding out a hand to Sackett. "You really are a determined man, Sackett. Well, here I am, ready to give you your chance to win back your seven hundred . . . Well, gentlemen, shall we begin? Nick loosened his tie and reached for one of the vacant chairs.

The bodyguards exchanged looks, shrugged and waited for a signal from Sackett, who nodded and a new unbroken deck was produced by Dinty Harmor. As for Nick, now that the confrontation he and Dinah and the Sholtos dreaded was taking place, he felt a calm settle in, a sense of relief that the battle was finally on and there was no more wondering, waiting, anticipating . . . Of course, he could always avoid unpleasantness by losing gracefully enough to make Sackett happy. Or could he . . . ?

Without seeming to, he studied the two bodyguards. One definitely carried a gun, making no effort to hide the bulge around his chest.

Sackett said, "Plain draw poker, throw out the jokers. So we can feel each other out?"

Nick had two hundred fifty dollars left from the seven hundred he had won in Reno. If they expected him to lose a full seven hundred . . . well, they were in for disappointment . . .

He was relieved to win the first hand, which put him over three hundred. If he could manage to win enough, he could then lose most of it and maybe that would satisfy them. He lost the second hand but went down less than fifty and came back to take the third hand, bringing him well over four hundred.

Studying the faces around the table, he decided he had better start losing, fast. He was, he decided, in trouble . . . deep trouble. He'd been prepared for cheating, palming, anything that would give him an excuse to announce that the game was too steep for a country boy and back out when he lost five hundred or so.

Dinty Harmor passed around a whiskey bottle and shot glasses, then returned to deal. The third bodyguard, the man new to Nick, downed the whiskey in one gulp. Sackett sipped. The others didn't touch their glasses, and Nick only pretended to drink. Setting his glass down, he examined his cards before playing a high bluff and letting himself be called. He might satisfy them now with a big loss if he managed it right. But he had been dealt king triplets and a queen. He drew another queen. His hands shook slightly. He just couldn't bring himself to throw in such a hand, not even to save his life . . . Next time, he promised himself . . .

Sackett seemed to find Dinty Harmor interesting, then returned to his hand. After Nick took the pot and Sackett raised the ante to multiples of ten, Nick won again on a nine-high straight. He had been sure of losing this one when Sackett called. He felt hot under his elegant collar, very much aware of the looks of the bodyguards, along with Sackett's puzzled frown.

It broke his heart to drop out two hands later when he had drawn another ace to the two he held. He was having a calamitous run of good luck, and in the other players' experience this sort of thing didn't happen accidentally.

Sackett managed to recoup on a big pot, mostly from the silent bodyguards, but Nick saw by the twist of his mouth and the flexing of his fingers that between Nick and Dinty Harmor, Sackett was trying to decide which was the villain of the piece. Dinty had done well, not as well as Nick but he had to be over a hundred fifty ahead by now. Nick wondered if Harmor was somehow managing the game. Nick seemed to do particularly well when Harmor dealt. And it certainly wasn't out of fondness for Nick . . .

A setup . . . Harmor was setting him up as the card cheat. Each time he won a pot so large it was sure to stir up Sackett's interest, Harmor won a neat little pile. Nick was to be the lightning rod while Dinty enjoyed his much more modest profit. Cleverly thought out, friend Harmor, and it could cost me a sight more than money if I don't do something in a big damn hurry . . .

He began to drop out of each hand early. He still couldn't bring himself to pour back into the pot the larger share of his winnings, but he made a show of losing and after several runs of "bad hands" he talked about "cutting his losses" and "going to bed."

"One more hand, Corrigan," Sackett said in even, low tones that left no room for argument. "You going to horde your winnings there?"

"No, indeed, gentlemen. Out they go first time something shows here."

The "something" turned out to be a king, ten and nine of hearts. Then he drew a queen and jack of hearts. Such luck hadn't ridden with him in months, but with inner pangs he started to throw in his hand when the play reached him. Dinty Harmor, who had dropped out, caught his wrist.

"Hold it, man. That's a straight flush you're tossing in."

Nick could have killed him.

Luckily the lounge steward opened the door of the card

parlor, put his head in and asked, "How are things going, gentlemen? I've got another private party that would like to take over any time you're through."

Sackett said grimly, "We're through now . . . need an escort to your cabin, Mr. Corrigan?"

"I'll manage. I feel real bad winning all this from you gentlemen." (Sackett must know just how bad!) "Would anyone like to play another hand? How about it? One more hand, gentlemen . . . ?"

"No, thanks." Sackett laughed without showing his teeth. "Not with your luck. Or someone's luck. Take good care of yourself, young man. It's not always safe these days, carrying over a thousand dollars."

"Are you sure you won't play another?" Nick laughed hollowly. "One more hand and it might all be yours—"

"In this business it may be mine next time we meet, Corrigan."

Nick read the threat in this, but there was nothing for him to do except leave. He started toward his cabin, then veered away, worried about Sackett's men dropping in on Dinah. Better at least lead them a chase around the decks. Whatever was going to happen, he'd give them his winnings and take what was coming, but he cringed at the image of Dinah finding him beaten up . . . Damn that Dinty Harmor . . . in the end it was all his doing . . .

He saw Mac Pettibone in the distance, helping a heavy-set, middle-aged woman into the passage from the open deck outside. Mac . . . maybe his last hope . . . Nick walked briskly toward him.

Mac said, "You look pretty hot. A bit of that wind out there ought to cool you off."

"Thanks, Mac . . . by the way, I seem to have won from the wrong party."

"I know the feeling. Want to borrow my cabin 'til we dock? It's just a hole and practically at sea bottom but I can send your wife to you for company."

It was a reprieve. "You may be saving my life," Nick told him, and meant it.

"Wait. I'll get the lady back to her spouse over there in the lounge. A little under the weather himself. Now stay right here by this door. It opens onto the deck and there's a ladder—staircase to you, landlubber—down to my deck. Don't go away."

Mac moved along the passage and across to the lounge, half leading, half lifting the heavy woman, who looked green and had her handkerchief pressed to her mouth.

Nick waited. He was sweating again. He could cope with enemies one at a time but when he thought of them crowding up against him there was an echo of the fierce hatred and fear he'd felt as a boy when his battles with one enemy at a time became mass attacks . . . and he'd *had* to run. Nothing else for it . . . Still, he hated it. Sackett's gun-toting bodyguard was stalking past Mac and his burden. As he reached the side passage he didn't seem to see Nick but turned and looked back, watching Pettibone's struggle with the seasick passenger. Nick opened the door behind him and ducked out onto the open deck. The wind lashed across his face in fits and gusts. The running lights plunged the deck into alternate pools of brightness and deep shadow. He was still watching the door, wondering if Mac would know enough to look for him out here, when a voice in the darkness behind him sliced through the windy gusts.

"Corrigan—"

One of the bodyguards. Nick started. There was no help for it. He'd been completely taken by surprise. He felt sick. He thought of that choppy black water out there, the fathomless depths, being eaten away by whatever lurked there in the cold below . . .

Somehow, in spite of the horrific fantasies, he managed to pull himself together . . . "Good evening again. I don't recall that I ever heard your name."

The bodyguard was tall, about Nick's height, but his jaw

and neck looked flabby. He also wasn't the one carrying the gun. He didn't answer Nick directly. "Anything the boss takes to unkindly," he said with grim emphasis, "it's a card cheat."

Nick snapped, "Better look to your friend Harmor. I think he set me up. And won a couple of hundred himself in the process."

The bodyguard's eyes widened, but he didn't back off. "Just hand it over and don't get smart. Up North here we get kind of mad when you Rebs figure to take us for suckers."

"Sure." Nick began to pour coins into the fellow's open hands. He stopped. The bodyguard said, "No more smart plays. You're going to get yours, you know. This don't stop nothing." But his movements were sluggish and his big fist telegraphed its intention.

It was the pitching of the ship that gave Nick his chance. He promptly dropped several gold pieces, and as the bodyguard, distracted by the rolling coins, looked away, Nick chopped powerfully across the back of the fellow's fat neck, sending him sprawling full length. But before Nick could get away the other bodyguard ran out the open door and pressed the icy weight of steel hard against Nick's throat.

Nick Corrigan had never felt so close to death. His flesh seemed to lose all sense of feeling. He closed his eyes, a thought of Dinah's lovely face, most of all of their unlived years. . . .

Dinah had found it impossible to go to bed. She stared now at the walls of the tiny white cabin, feeling stifled. She picked up magazines and put them down impatiently, all the time wondering how Nick was. When her watch read eleven-thirty she bundled up in her coat, wound a scarf around her hair and went out onto the windy deck, passing an unsavory blank-faced man who looked vaguely familiar.

Buffeted by the gale, she had stepped inside on her way to the lounge when she realized that the unpleasant loner out on deck had the same expressionless features as the man who had come at them on the Exposition grounds.

The card-parlor door was open. Eight men were filing in, most of them chewing the ends of cigars. Nick wasn't among them . . . but his lanky friend Pettibone was just coming out of the lounge. He shook his head, remarking to Dinah, "Now if she can just keep her mind over matter and stop thinking about that supper she ate she may make it 'til morning, poor soul."

"It is always this rough?" Dinah asked as she fell against him and he carefully restored her balance.

"On this run, ma'am. That's because we're not far off-shore. But you seem to be as good a sailor as your husband."

"Yes . . . well, he isn't in the card parlor, do you know what happened?"

"Sure thing, Mrs. Corrigan. His party broke up a few minutes ago. I was going to meet him and—" that is, he seemed to think his friends might not like his winning so much. Old Sackett's pretty much a—"

"Sackett? My God! You've *got* to help us . . ." She shook his sleeve, knowing she was behaving like a crazy woman but she was desperate. "I saw one of Sackett's men, I'm sure it was, out on deck. He may be waiting for Nick now."

"Can't be, ma'am. Nick's waiting for me inside that passage up yonder." With remarkable skill he kept his balance without once clutching the wall as he took long strides to the place where he was to meet Nick. Dinah followed him, staggering and holding the wall, until she reached Pettibone and the door opening onto the deck.

Nick was gone.

"I told him to wait," Mac said, shaking his head.

She pushed past him, trying to open the door. Her hands felt stiff and froze to the latch. When she forced them off they had no feeling. She turned back. "There are some men out out there . . . I think one of them is Nick—" Mac was nudging her . . .

"Ma'am, you're seasick. Bad. Let's go . . ."

She'd barely gotten her wits together before he put one hand under her arm and pressed his big white handkerchief to her face, then pushed her out onto the deck into the gusting wind, all the while talking with a loud enthusiasm . . . "Easy does it, ma'am. Try and take a breath of this nice clean air, here we are . . . one big breath . . ."

She saw men in a huddle just inside the shadow of the lifeboats . . . and one of them without any doubt was Nick . . . she couldn't for a minute mistake his tall figure in black-and-white . . . and their silence struck her as more ominous than the noise of a fight . . . Mac nudged her hard now, and she did her best to playact as directed, groaning dramatically as he leaned over the rail. Far below in the darkness she could see the foaming wake of the ship. The terror of her thoughts momentarily paralyzed her . . . would they really dare to throw Nick over the side . . . ? Not a sound behind her under the hanging lifeboat. Were they only waiting for her to leave the deck?

The passageway door opened. A silver-haired man with a square face and too well-remembered jowls strolled out —no question, it was Sackett, coming, no doubt, to supervise his enforcers . . . She did her best to camouflage herself by pulling her scarf around to cover her face, hoping, without much confidence, to conceal her identity from Sackett . . . "A little trouble with this storm?" Sackett said to Mac.

"Well," Mac said, "some folks seem to get riled by the pitching," and then turned solicitously to Dinah . . . "Feeling better, ma'am?" and shifted her along the rail, moving her in the same motion away from the group under the lifeboat. She responded with louder groans, which were interrupted by Sackett's dry, flat, "Very impressive, Mrs. Corrigan . . . well, look here, somebody seems to have dropped a bit of change . . . belong to you, Mr. Corrigan . . . ?"

Interrupted by more witnesses than even he could afford, it appeared that Sackett had decided to change his tack, put a new face on the ugly business he intended. Nick quickly took advantage . . . "Not mine, Mr. Sackett, must belong to your friends there . . ."

One of his "friends" was still trying to get his breath, eyeing Nick and obviously waiting only for a go-ahead word from Sackett to even the score. Instead he heard, "Pick it up . . . well, Mr. Corrigan, Mrs. Corrigan, it seems there's been a bit of a misunderstanding . . . Mr. Harmor has just told me what really happened, or so he says, and I'm inclined to believe him" . . . at least, Nick thought, as long as it's convenient . . . "So no hard feelings, Mr. Corrigan. Wilkens, I'd say you'd better pick up that money there before it's all pitched overboard for the fish."

While the bodyguards crawled over the deck collecting gold and silver coins, Nick decided to seize the moment and buy what he hoped would be a little gambler's insurance . . . He took out a roll of bills, the ends fluttering in the strong wind, said, "If your friend Harmor had anything to do with our game this must belong to you."

Sackett eyed him, took the bills, tucked them into a vest pocket and signaled to his men, who followed him through the passageway door. Only then did Nick take an easy breath, and with it also took Dinah in his arms. "Good Lord, sweetheart, you scared me to death"—he was, he reflected silently, already nearly there in any case—"showing up like that . . . you too, Mac . . . I thought we were all about to be fishbait for sure—"

Mac shrugged, shook his head. "Could have worked out that way, I grant you, but even guys like Sackett think twice before killing people on a public boat." He didn't add that regardless of what Sackett had implied about believing Nick, he might well have just been saving face for the moment, that he was buying time, just as Nick for his purposes was. He didn't have to say anything to Nick . . . the looks they exchanged said it all . . . "Well, better get inside before we all freeze to death," and they started across the slippery deck, Dinah giving her own private thanks for Nick's safety, for his arm warm and tight around her.

He chose the moment to make a confession . . . "We're almost dead broke, honey—"

"I know, and I don't care. It's surely better than having that man mad enough to kill her."

Nick said nothing, why spoil the moment . . .

"Well, don't look at me," Mac said. "I lose my poke regular at the track."

"No matter, I'll just hock my cufflinks," Nick said. "That should at least get us out of Los Angeles . . . they have diamond chips . . . the links, I mean."

"What we should do, darling," Dinah put in, "is pawn my engagement ring"—she felt his body stiffen and added quickly—"for a few days, just to see us through this . . ."

He considered, then hugged her even closer. "But *only* for a couple of days, just long enough for me to win a stake . . ."

She thought of how she had felt scarcely ten minutes ago when she believed Nick was about to die. The ring turned on her wet finger. It had always been a bit too large anyway . . .

"I'll never miss it," she told herself firmly, and tightened her arm around her husband's waist, as though never to let him go. . . .